Beth's eyes were fixed on the stretcher where a figure lay exposed, scantily covered in green. She stared harder. Her eyes teared. The body's skin. It wasn't human. Instead of soft pliable tissue, the body was covered with hard, brown, animal skin.

Gasping, Beth drew back as the creature's eyes opened wide. Frightened pinpoints of yellow light darted around behind dull, tightly wrapped gauze.

Suddenly, as though an alarm had gone off, the creature's body shot forward and began to curl together into a ball, cowering like a frightened animal.

ICE ORCHIDS

ELENA YATES EULO

BERKLEY BOOKS, NEW YORK

ICE ORCHIDS

A Berkley Book / published by arrangement with
the author

PRINTING HISTORY
Berkley edition / April 1984

For information address: The Berkley Publishing Group,
200 Madison Avenue, New York, New York 10016.

ISBN: 0-425-06322-4

A BERKLEY BOOK ® TM 757,375

PRINTED IN THE UNITED STATES OF AMERICA

FOR KEN . . .

who persists in dreaming
these impossible dreams

"I don't want to go among mad people," Alice remarked.

"Oh, you can't help that," said the Cat, "we're all mad here. I'm mad. You're mad."

"How do you know I'm mad?" said Alice.

"You must be," said the Cat, "or you wouldn't have come here."

—Lewis Carroll, *Alice in Wonderland*

ICE ORCHIDS

PROLOGUE

She was alone. Breathless, she paused on the brightly lit campus walk. In the silence, there was only the sound of wind which brought the chill factor below zero and sucked the oxygen from her lungs.

An aching center of cold had settled high in her chest. She made a fist of her right hand and pressed against the pain. To no avail. If anything, the pain hardened; became a tangible lump of indigestion. Quite suddenly, she thought she was going to be sick. Not surprising. All indications were she had a whopping case of the flu. Despite the chill, she knew her temperature had risen and, under the heavy wool of her collar, her throat had begun to itch like all hell. She felt terrible. Worse, she was afraid.

Illness scared her. It always had. According to her first shrink, she bordered on hypochondria, but she cared nothing for his opinion. For one thing, he was free. Hard to have respect for anyone free, especially in light of why he didn't charge. He was enamored of her genius I.Q. To put it unkindly, he was a mind voyeur—a sort of psychological peeping Tom. Which must have meant that he had a lower I.Q. than hers. This made it nearly impossible for her not to look down on him. But primarily she hated the shrink because he was fat and had no chin. For this, she denied him what he most wanted . . . "the psychology" of her mind. Unbelievable. A figure like hers, a face like hers and that marshmallow Buddha-bodied Freud wanted her mind. She became much more silent. A game developed between them, a sort of staring contest. His eyes were bullets, hers blanks. She was on tilt, as it were. She won and because there had to be a loser, he lost. Her mind still retained its cherry.

A hypochondriac, she remembered now doubtfully, but she felt a little steadier. Probably she was making too much of a flu bug, or whatever it was. Her speculation ceased as in the distance hurried bootheels clicked on concrete accompanied by the whining gaiety of schoolgirl soprano voices.

"Jesus," she said softly and shrank from the light. On no account did she want to come face to face with the curiosity of her fellow gifted students. Not tonight. Not, in the name of God, tonight. Everyone should have been safely entombed in "the dome" by this time. She had counted on that. Tonight was Forum night, Part I, welcoming the Young Republican Club of Hartford, Connecticut, and buses lined the circular drive in front of the dome, that rounded glass-walled center of student activity.

The bootheels hurried closer.

Irresolutely, she lingered for an instant and then quickly swung from the lit path. Her heels made crisp virginal imprints in the frosted earth as she half-ran down the steep incline that led to the campus lake. She felt giddy from adventure or possibly from fever, but she no longer cared.

She was approaching a once-in-a-lifetime moment in her life. She hoped she could make it pay off big. Humming slightly, she got her bearings. The lake lay before her, shimmering in a new coat of ice. To her left were the modest instructor cottages, to her right through a brief patch of woods was the white low-slung infirmary and research center. Adjoining the research center were the plusher accommodations of researchers and V.I.P. guests to the Triesius campus. She laughed softly. Tonight Mr. V.I.P. himself was waiting for her.

An answering chuckle resounded in the air around her.

She whirled around, squinting to see through the strangely glittering darkness. It was as though diamonds fell from the clouds to earth. Frost blowing from the trees or snow, possibly.

"Who is it?" she asked hoarsely and then smiled as she recognized the man who strode toward her. She smiled until the moonlight glinted against steel and then her mouth fell open.

"What is it?" she breathed and glanced over her shoulder. "What's the matter?"

She gasped; could not move as the knife in his hand plunged downward. Scant inches from her chest, the blade hesitated.

She screamed.

At once, his left hand smothered her mouth and nose. The knife's tip engraved a dot into her temple.

"I won't hurt you," he whispered. His breath, rich from whiskey, struck her warmly in the face. "I want you. I just want you."

She stopped screaming. Tears welled in her eyes and froze instantly to her lashes. Shuddering, she felt the blade trace a line from temple to jugular vein. She didn't speak, didn't give a sign of recognition, didn't—oh, Christ—didn't give him any reason at all to press deeper, any reason to . . .

Desperately, she hoped she looked all right. There was the flickering thought that perhaps her life might depend on it. Pathetically, she wet her lips and let her head fall back on her neck in a way she judged to be provocative.

"Yes," she whispered. "Tell me what to do. Only don't—don't hurt me."

His hands opened her coat now, briefly cupped her breasts as though weighing them, then moved downward.

She shrieked as cold-hot pain filled her belly. Only then, staring down at the wet stain that snaked navel-high across her snug-fitted dress, was she aware that he still held the knife . . . yes, there it was tucked into the indention between his right thumb and hand . . . and that he had, carelessly or deliberately, sliced a wound into her stomach.

She moaned and pressed both hands against the spreading stain. Weak little gagging moans. Tearful, fascinated, she listened to the sounds she made. She was sorry . . . terribly sorry for herself. Jesus God, the blood . . . why couldn't he share the pity of it . . . the fear . . . oh, the blood seemed to flow faster as she moaned.

"Be quiet," he murmured thickly. "That's not the right way of handling this. Tell me. Tell me how you like me. Don't look at me. Just tell me . . . you like it. What I'm doing to you."

His hands pressed deeper. As though untouched by the cold, his fingers seemed to burn through her clothes.

"I like it," she whispered, choking on the words. She said it louder then, to be sure he heard her. "I like it." She tried to smile and, imagining that he smiled back, she found the courage to lift her own skirt, to win another point toward the saving of her life.

Her mind skittered as he forced her to the ground. A confusing cacophony of images and then she settled onto chess, of all things. She had a habit of replaying memorized chess games, just as something to concentrate on when she was upset. Chess was more than a hobby, it was second nature. Especially the Sicilian opening. She knew the Sicilian backwards and forwards, could recall at will any Bobby Fischer tournament game in which he used this strategy.

She gasped . . . felt the silk of her bikini underwear give. Her attacker struggled to undo the belt to his pants . . .

White pawn to King 4. Black pawn to Queen's Bishop 4.

Cold . . . so cold . . . hard steel against her throat.

King's knight . . . King's knight to . . .

He penetrated her almost immediately, taking time only to stroke himself several times into mammoth hardness.

She gasped, keeping her eyes focused over his shoulder onto the frozen lake. Mechanically, she continued to recite the elementary moves. King's knight to Bishop 3. Black pawn to Queen 3. White pawn to Queen 4. Black pawn takes pawn. Now she was managing to get down only every fourth or fifth breath.

He lunged again, harder this time, his body riding hers as a stallion gone berserk.

She moaned and he laughed, thinking the moan was of pleasure rather than pain. Panic.

She felt his body tense as he began to pulsate inside her. His mouth fell open and saliva drooled onto her lips.

There. It was over. Now he would kill her. She understood.

For just an instant, he was off-guard as he rolled off of her. Grunting, he fumbled at his zipper. He was finished with her now. Done.

With both hands on her gut, she struggled to her knees, then managed to rise. She forced herself to endure the pain that stabbed her as she began to run.

His hand grabbed hold of her leg. Pulled. She kicked out blindly, hoping to hurt him. Then she was running again. But not faster than the fear that tailed her footsteps, chasing after her, making her crazy that she wasn't going to make it.

She knew that any moment she would feel a hand on her shoulder, cold steel at her throat. She had to go faster-faster-much faster. Oh, I hurt. I hurt so bad, so bad. She pumped harder, strained from the gut, forced her legs to push forward, to fly, to try harder, just a little harder to go faster-faster . . .

Too late, she saw the iced lake in front of her, felt her feet fly from under her and then she was sliding forward on her stomach. The roughness of the lake's frozen surface cut brutal gashes into her knees, blistered the palms of her hands. She could hear herself screaming.

"That won't do," said the mild voice behind her.

Tears coursed down her face as she craned her neck to stare back at him. Unconsciously, she let her head fall back in the old model's pose. Her hair hung around her shoulders in a wave. Her throat shimmered white under the moon.

The only conscious thought in her mind now was that she wished she had never come to Triesius in the first place. But she'd had her pride. Sometimes she had wondered about the motives of the other girls, but that was one of the things they never discussed. One of the few things . . . she tried to look away from the knife. From the very beginning, it had all been so strange at Triesius. Just moments left to make sense of it. But even at the beginning when there was plenty of time, none of them had been able to solve the riddle. God knew, they had tried often enough. Not that anyone would have believed them, even if—

"I think you deserve to know this much," he whispered as he slid the steel blade against her throat. "Although science will benefit from this, it is not done without love."

A quick thrust of the knife and she gurgled; choked on her own blood.

She closed her eyes. Saw the color red. Deluxe red. Explode in back of her eyes.

PART I

The Beginning

ONE

MEMO

Highly Confidential

TO: All Participating Researchers

FROM: Alan Randelar, M.D., Ph.D.
Project Leader, Triesius
Rosemont, New York

RE: Subject Selections for Triesius College

The category has been narrowed to twenty-five young women. Of these twenty-five, at least five will be dispensable.

All subject I.Q.'s are between 170–200 on the Modified Stanford-Binet. Thematic Apperception and vocational preference tests reveal that all have highly challenge-seeking personalities. Neutralization should be possible due to the youth of the donor colony. Ages vary from fifteen to nineteen, with the norm being eighteen.

We look forward to commencing this exciting research and extend our warmest welcome and appreciation for your dedication and belief in the Triesius project.

Cordially,
Alan Randelar

Two

In the center of the longest greenest lawn of the college of Triesius there was a plaque. The plaque was dwarfed by the turreted sprawling castle that had been converted to Administration, Video Room, and Library. But there was a flagpole nearby and a walkway and flowers before the first frost killed them and even a white iron bench facing the plaque where one could sit and study—which could mean that someone took seriously the slogan on the plaque: Genius is an orchid. Delicate in hue and fragile of outer leaf. Stained brilliant at the heart where to see is to kill.

Beth Allen sat alone on the white iron bench and absently plucked grapes from their stems. She consumed them two or three at a time and spat seeds upon the ground in staccato rhythm. It was a thoughtless way to treat grapes that had been specially flown in from the Tropics, grapes that cost upward of a quarter apiece, but her mind was occupied. When she thought, she thought viciously, as her father was fond of saying. If she were to think of black then not a sliver of white would filter through; if of white, then not a speck of black. It was late afternoon on the twenty-fourth of September, the end of her first week at Triesius, a college for young women handpicked for their 170-plus I.Q.'s. Beth was rated at 180 and it was like a bank balance of a billion—too much capital to ever see, just paper money, paper brains. They told her she had all those brains, but she only knew she had a quick ear for Russian, Italian, Greek, Chinese, Spanish, French, language ad infinitum. A leaning toward the mathematics. World politics. Economics. Etcetera, etcetera. But something had happened at Triesius that she could make no sense of, none at all, so maybe all along they'd had her rated wrong.

She was thinking of the three-day admission physical that she had just completed, painful and puzzlingly intense. When they had scraped under her fingernails carefully, one nail at a time, it hadn't made sense. Nor had it made sense that on the third and last day of tests, each girl had been put to sleep for part of the examination. When Beth had woken up, she'd been sore on the inside.

"Hey, Doctor, you did know my brains are not up there, didn't you?"

Dr. Hamilton had not been amused and then later, after he'd left the room, she had found that a patch of skin had been removed from her inner thigh. Odd. Or rather way beyond odd, past all reason.

Beth spat the last grape seeds with deadly accuracy at the plaque. The spittle struck the letter "i" of the word genius. The remnants of pulp that bound seeds together adhered to the sign for an instant, then as though the dot over the "i" had loosened, it began to slide downwards, leaving behind a light purple smear.

Genius is an orchid, she repeated walking through the dishwater twilight. Shane would like that. The thought of Shane made her smile. She had a weakness for Shane, who was famous and rich and a singer and an actor and a playboy. For Shane who was her father. In one of those rare instants of perfect understanding, she understood that who Shane was was no accident. The force of his personality and his talent had made superstardom inevitable. She also understood how lucky she was that she had the genius thing. It helped create a mysterious symmetry between them. It felt comfortable, made sense, that they were father and daughter.

But off on her own, she sometimes regretted the differences between other girls and herself. It made things awkward. For one thing, she knew most of her friends lusted after her father. She had especially begun to notice it last year at Radcliffe.

Of course, the girls all pretended it wasn't so. They would go out of their way not to bring up his name. But somehow they just couldn't seem to help themselves, and invariably she would find herself with a bevy of girls hovering at her elbow, all hoping to meet *the* Shane Allen. All wanting a famous lay, not the specific man.

In any event, their desires made friendship—true friendship—as obsolete as the mythical Golden Fleece.

She was occasionally so aware of her own isolation in a crowd of other young girls as to feel the very flesh on her bones as a boundary line. Here Beth Allen ends and the real world begins. Forever separate, but not from Shane. That helped.

Beth tried to be very objective about her father. She thought he was very nice-looking but not a gorgeous hunk; that he looked younger than fifty-eight, which she believed to be his true age, but older than forty-five, which he tried to hint that he was; that he kept himself in good athletic shape by running five miles every other day and lifting weights in his private gymnasium.

She knew things about him that no one else knew. That he wore a toupe to fill in the front of his hair a little. That he had a different shape nose than he had in secret younger pictures. That he had never really loved another woman since her mother had run out on them twelve years ago. She thought it was a little embarrassing and a little sad that he loved being famous so much. It was also rather sad that he drank so much and that he tried so darned hard to be Shane Allen the star. Shane. She'd never called him anything else because she knew how much he loved the sound of that word. Shane. Much better, much much better than Dad or even Harvey, the name he was born with. Beth loved Harvey. Would have loved saying Harvey even more than Dad. Harvey was a man nobody else knew except for Grandmother Allen and her. When she was ten, she'd told Grandmother Allen that if she ever had a baby and if that baby was a boy, she wanted to call him Harvey. But she was afraid it might make Shane mad. Her grandmother had looked very thoughtful and very teary-eyed and said she thought it would be all right, that there were far too few Harveys in the world these days.

Maybe it was because of Harvey who lived in that vulnerable spot way back in Shane's eye that Beth had agreed to come to Triesius when she hadn't really wanted to come.

"I like it at Radcliffe, Shane."

"Why, because of that cockamamie boy I like?"

"You do like him or you don't?"

"I do like that cockamamie boy who isn't worthy of the lace on my baby's shoe, yes."

She laughed. "It hasn't anything to do with Kent."

"Thank God. Then—"

"No. I won't go to that—that experimental nuthouse for geniuses."

"It's important to me, baby. It's a big honor to be chosen. I have the inside scoop it's a big honor. I want that for you." Shane paused, then added significantly, "If Triesius wasn't the goods, you know I wouldn't—"

"No. I won't do it, Shane. Don't ask me."

"It's important to me," Shane said once again and far back in his eyes was the plea, that look she couldn't resist.

Not then, but three days later, she said, "Okay, Shane. I'll go to Triesius. I just decided."

It had been a tense three days. There was the matter of Shane's nervousness that bothered her. His nervousness always alarmed her. It was one of the signs an alcoholic's daughter looks for. The first two nights she stayed up with him, rambled on endlessly about nothing in particular, and kept a zealous watch over the amount of vodka he consumed. The third night he disappeared after dinner and was out until four in the morning. He came home—miracles did happen—sober but in his eyes there stood Harvey warning her: "Careful, Beth, he can't hold out much longer." After that, it was an easy decision. Triesius would make Shane happy. She was going to Triesius.

A small warning bell went off now in her mind and she instinctively began to hurry past Administration to the newly built four-storied Frazier Hall, where the majority of classes unrelated to medicine or biology were held. As yet she hadn't glanced at her wristwatch; she had a sixth sense for time, was almost never off more than three to five minutes.

Inside Frazier Hall, she ran quickly up the steps, not waiting for the elevator, and swept into L-210 with two other late-arriving students. Panting slightly, now she did check the time by the wall clock and saw that the long minute hand had just clicked in flush with the twelve, making it seven o'clock on the button.

Jesus, what a way to spend a night. Mental synergetics with Professor E. Vandevere; E for God only knew what—Elizabeth?—Eunice?—and some of the girls joked that despite mounds of formless breasts, the E stood for Edward.

Vandevere now stood and began the first oral equation. No

preliminaries; just a slightly simpler beginning as a warmup. She subjected herself to the same rules as the students. Equations were to be done orally without visual aid. The mind was all. If a problem arose, the blackboard was not to be used to resolve it. No pencils or papers or books. And no volunteering, so that, in effect, the pressure was doubled as no one had the slightest idea of when she would be called.

Even so, Beth found her attention wandering. Vandevere's voice was so God Almighty monotonal. She focused on the girl wonder who sat at the next desk, Vala Hayes.

Vala sat slumped in her seat, feet nervously crossed. Thin straight hair, no makeup, no energy of expression.

She was no beauty, Beth acknowledged. But now and again, Vala's eyes had a way of reaching out and grabbing hold of you. Red-veined eyes under puffy lids—proof that what everyone said about Vala was true. That she cried all night every night and at inappropriate times during the day.

Vandevere drew an audible breath and spieled off her first real challenge of the day; a toughie on space-filling polyhedra. She hesitated and then looked directly at Vala Hayes, showing the sort of hostility toward the girl that one homely woman reserves for another.

Vala's already dull complexion greyed. The vagueness behind her eyes plainly told that she had been caught day-dreaming and missed something vital to the solution.

Four tetrahedra and two octahedra, urged Beth mentally, and wished she didn't have a mother complex for the helpless creatures of the world. Come on, Vala, for Chrissakes. Come *on*. Show her you're the Vala Hayes everyone says is the new Einstein.

Vala had tears in her eyes. They spilled over.

"I take it," Vandevere said, "that you don't know the answer, Miss Hayes."

Vala knuckle-dried her cheeks and said, "eight tetrahedra and four octahedra," with a hopelessness that said she knew she had given the wrong solution.

Vandevere's lips became a thin straight line neatly tucked up at the outer extremes of both corners. "Wrong, Miss Hayes. The answer is four tetrahedra and two octahedra."

A slight murmur went through the class which Vandevere quickly cut off by a severe jerk of her head.

Vala tensed, struggling for the right words. "You forgot the portion of the cube on the reader's side of the plane," she said into her hand that partly covered her mouth. "It also contains four tetrahedra and two octahedra, and so the supercube would contain eight tetrahedra and four octahedra. And, of course, the truncated superoctahedra contains thirty-two tetrahedra and sixteen octahedra. And the condition for space filling is therefore . . ." Her voice died off as she seemed to hear the furious silence of thinking that had suddenly gripped the room.

No, Beth thought. No, that's all wrong, and yet . . . She began again. Bisected her supercube as before. Beth shook her head. No, Vala was wrong. Had to be wrong. And then suddenly Beth got the point at the same moment Vandevere got it. Three cubes beyond the plane, three on the reader's side of the plane and therefore . . .

In the next instant an audible murmur of admiration filled the room, which put Vala lengths ahead at the finishing line, Beth and Vandevere in a dead heat for second place and the field close behind.

Vandevere's broad face burned tomato red. She was finished for the day. She was on automatic. Mental synergetics sagged. Vandevere herself sagged, her fat hanging heavy around stomach and jowls. She had lost—what?—something vital.

"I saw you today," Vala said to Beth after class. "In front of Administration. You were sitting there for a long time."

"I didn't see you."

"Oh."

"If I had seen you, I would have said something. Come on, let's walk back to the dorm together."

"No, it's okay," Vala said with some alarm. "I just wanted to ask you something."

"Come on and walk. I'm listening."

The walk was a mistake. Vala stumbled; she burst into sudden speech; she stopped talking; she walked with her arms clenched over her chest as though in pain. Beth clapped her hand briefly over Vala's shoulder and felt her recoil from the contact. In the dusk, Vala's face looked oily, slick with sweat. At Beth's door, Vala's chewed-down nails dug into the door frame.

"Come on in," Beth insisted and dared to take Vala by the

arm and pull her forward. "Have a glass of something. You want a Coke? White wine? It's all cold. See, I have a small fridge. It's very small. Tiny, really."

Vala's tension increased. "I don't need anything."

"But—"

Vala paused just inside the doorway. "I'm not very good at taking anything," she said thoughtfully. "Even a glass of Coke. I'm better at giving. I believe that's because I know people don't find me easy to be around. So I guess I try to pay them off."

Beth stared at her. "Good God," she said after due consideration. And then, "Sit down, Vala. Sit down, for goodness sake." With straight brows drawn tightly together, Beth knew what she was trying to decide. If she too paid people off. By a Coke or white wine, cold from the fridge. By an introduction to Shane and lunch at the Brown Derby. She glanced up to where Vala sat stiffly in the chair beside the bed. "By the way, you should know I don't find you difficult to be around."

Vala said quickly, "I know. I could tell you tolerate me easier than the others. I can always tell. That's the primary reason—"

"The word," Beth said, "is not tolerate. That's a terrible thing to say."

"It's true," Vala said.

Without asking her, Beth walked to the refrigerator and poured two glasses of white wine. "Here. If you feel guilty drinking it, you can slip a dollar under my door. I think a dollar is fair. It's very good wine. Do you really mean people feel that uptight about your I.Q.?" she went on thoughtfully and sipped.

"Oh, no. I don't think it's that. I think it's because I'm a social misfit. It's because I'm emotionally sick and I can't seem to hide it. I'm like a glass jug. Everyone can see right through me. If only I was more attractive, maybe it wouldn't matter so much, but . . ."

"Vala—"

A light tapping sounded on the door. Beth called, "Come on in," and then regretted it when she saw Vala flinch. By that time it was too late. Georgia Urie stood languidly in the doorway wrapped in a long white terrycloth bathrobe that had seen better days. Damp hair in a towel turban, no makeup, no pretensions; she was ravishing. Even like this, she was the most uncommonly lovely girl Beth had ever encountered, including all of Shane's Hollywood set.

Beth heard Vala stir uneasily, but was incapable of turning to look at her. Unfair. The comparison between Vala and Georgia was unfair.

Long and lean with firm full breasts, Georgia had translucent skin over exquisite bones that gave her high cheeks and set off her enormous green eyes. Her mouth was cupid-bowed, pink without lipstick, and full without being fleshy. Usually her hair was twisted up; sometimes she let it fall straight past her shoulders. Lively spun champagne-blond hair, colored by nature. In back of this lushness of beauty sat Georgia herself, unmoved by her own image, a cool scrim of indifference over her gaze. Sometimes Beth would be a little startled at a stray sympathetic gleam in Georgia's thickly lashed wide eyes. At the moment, she was merely inscrutable.

"Could—could I help you?" Beth stammered, thinking that, damn it, she at least shouldn't feel so inferior next to a beautiful girl. Actually, she didn't, she was merely like everyone else—unable to keep from staring.

Georgia's deep green eyes wandered over to meet hers.

"I have a letter for you," Georgia said, taking an envelope from her robe pocket. It had been folded twice. She allowed a slight smile to soften her lips. "You see, a strange thing happened in the mailroom today. Someone's hand was in your slot. That someone saw me staring and then nervously dropped this letter—" she held it up for emphasis, "on the mailroom floor. In my own Sherlockian way, I made an assumption. I assumed that your father's name was probably on it. That led me to the further assumption that someone, especially this particular someone, had all intentions of lifting a souvenir, so . . . I grabbed it up." Wryly she shook her head. "It's not like me to do such a thing. I don't know what came over me. Apologies and all."

Beth took the offered envelope. "No, it's—I appreciate it. I'll make sure Shane doesn't put his name on the envelope anymore. Thanks, Georgia."

"No problem." Georgia threw a careless smile in her direction, a smile that also drew in Vala Hayes, and turned to go.

"By the way," Beth said with carefully low-keyed curiosity, "who had her eye on Shane's letter?"

"Oh, just your average collegiate cupcake." Georgia lifted

languid shoulders and let them settle back into place. "I'll put it to you like this. The culprit will be the one who comes to you and tells you she saw me steal your letter. At least, I think she will. She's a genius, but not very bright." Georgia gave a small chuckle that was subtly warm around the edges. "I believe I heard you're enthusiastic about Russian."

"I am."

"I speak Russian too. It's my preferred language."

"Really? I'd enjoy speaking it with you every once in a while."

"That'll be fine. I'm more sociable in Russian than I am in English. More charming. Although," she said dryly, "I'm sure you find that hard to believe. That I could be more charming than I am already. The truth is I'm not a song bird in either language. Goodnight." She threw the word over her shoulder with an exhausted indifference. Greta Garbo couldn't have done it better.

When she had disappeared, Beth said with marked irony, "Vala, I believe that's the only person I ever met who has a lower opinion of herself than you do."

Vala gasped. "She's—she's magnificent."

"So are you if you only knew it. Have some of your wine. You're not drinking it."

"Oh, God, I forgot. What I was going to ask you—"

"Yes?" Beth said helpfully as Vala paused to put her hand to her scalp.

"What I wanted to ask you," Vala went on hurriedly, "was whether they took the hair follicles from you."

"Hair follicles?"

"I heard some of the girls talking about the physicals. But they didn't mention anything about hair follicles, so I was wondering—"

At a loss, Beth said, "Vala, is this related to health, evolution, biology, in other words, what in the world are you saying? Hair follicles . . ."

"Is there a sore place on your scalp?"

Beth took another sip from her glass and set it down. "Yes, as a matter of fact, there is. I noticed it when I was washing my hair last night." She felt for the spot. It was toward the crown of her head, not even half the circumference of her fingertip. "Are you sure? They took follicles?"

"I leaned over and looked at the spot in the mirror. My

hair's so fine, I could see it really easily. Here. Look at my scalp and you can see." Vala bent over and parted her hair.

Beth stared disbelievingly and saw several small incisions similar to something she had once seen on the scalp of an actor friend of Shane's. He had had hair follicles taken from the thicker part of his hair and transplanted to the balding area. The missing follicles had left small round empty wells caked in dried blood, which had later been concealed as the hair grew around them. The empty wells had been exactly like the punctures in Vala's scalp.

Vala raised her head. "Well?"

"Yes. Check mine." She pulled her hair away from the spot.

"Yes," Vala said, drawing away as though uneasy at the close physical relationship of their two bodies within the room. "I . . . what do you think it means?"

Beth glanced up to see her standing at the door. "I don't know. Maybe it's something we'll be doing. Transplanting it into a rat or something and check the chemical change."

"Maybe. Well—" Vala's hand edged toward the doorknob.

"Vala, before you go. You told me the negatives about you . . ."

"Only some of them," Vala corrected smiling. "It's just that I don't find myself as interesting as they say I should."

"Tell me one thing," Beth insisted, "just one thing you find interesting about yourself."

Vala paused to think. "I didn't talk until I was almost four," she said with an unfamiliar chuckle and closed the door behind her as though she had dared too much.

Beth shook her head at the closed door and then once again raised her hand to her scalp. Her fingers explored the incision area. Before she had paid little attention to the burning itch. Now that she was aware of the spot, it was annoying as hell.

Craziness, that's all, she decided crossly. All things, when examined too closely, gain a disproportionate measure of importance.

Don't they?

The question lingered in her mind, then was abruptly wrenched away. She turned, startled. There were loud voices in the hallway, followed by a commotion. It sounded as though two of the girls were arguing.

"Stop!" someone cried. "Stop it!"

Beth moved quickly to open her door.

Jennie Dobbin turned to stare at Beth as she stepped into the hallway. "It's all right, she—"

"It's not all right," Doris Encoda screamed angrily. "What business is it of yours what I choose to do—"

"Doris—"

"WHAT I CHOOSE TO DO!" Doris repeated, her temper out of control. Then she began to convulse. She stopped shouting and stared down at her body as though it were something quite apart from herself. "I can't help it," she muttered thickly. "You don't know what it is . . . I'd do anything . . ."

Still she stared down at herself as doors began to open and girls moved into the hallway. Murmurs began to spread: "What is it? What's wrong?"

Saliva now showed on Doris's lips. She tried to speak, but failed as she seemed to lose her bearings. Her eyes were dilated, unfocused, and she had begun to pant. "I really don't feel well," she said drunkenly.

"What's the matter with her?" Vala Hayes hissed into Beth's ear.

"God, I don't know."

"Take a look at her eyes," Georgia Urie said from behind them. "Oh, Christ, she's going under."

Talking stopped in the hallway as Doris swayed on her feet. One hand went to her throat; her nails appeared to form claws; she dug them under her black turtleneck sweater and then stopped.

Feeling like she was moving in slow motion, Beth sprang toward her. Georgia, faster, moved past Beth and almost managed to get her hands on Doris. Too late. Doris took one uncertain step backward, her body arched, then in a graceful swan dive fell forward.

Some of the girls cried out and then silence reigned as Georgia turned Doris slightly, felt for the pulse in her throat.

"Is she—" began a voice.

"She's fainted," Beth said decisively. "Get Fazio. Quick."

In a hush, the girls formed a semicircle about the two girls who knelt over Doris and then fanned outward to admit the housemother who came quickly, took one look and ran to call infirmary emergency.

The stretcher arrived within five minutes. Doris Encoda was

lifted carefully and placed on it, still unconscious, her black hair pulled back to accommodate a cold wet cloth. A pitying murmur went around the hallway. Doris's bangs and thick hanging hair had concealed a deformed forehead.

"She doesn't even have a forehead," one of the girls shuddered. "It's . . . it's just that deep purple line . . ."

"Be still," said Vala unexpectedly. "Don't you know she may be able to hear you?"

"All right, girls," snapped Mrs. Fazio. "Back to your rooms. She's going to be all right. She's just fainted. Nothing to worry about . . ."

Almost before the words were spoken, Doris Encoda was swept from view, Mrs. Fazio having disappeared almost as quickly. The hallway was suddenly still.

"Well, goodnight," Vala said and moved away, almost reluctantly.

"Goodnight," Beth said and turned, the hallway suddenly a slow backward shuffle of feet. A kind of distasteful memory seemed to linger as Beth joined the others and closed her door.

An hour later Beth rolled onto her back and stared at the ceiling, now starkly shadowed with moonlight. She still couldn't get Doris Encoda off her mind.

It wasn't the fact that she had fainted; it was her deformity. Not the deformity itself, but Doris's need to hide it. That was somehow the saddest thing. The last thing Beth saw before falling asleep was Doris's squashed together face, with the long drooping bangs carefully hiding her secret. Poor Doris.

Far back in her mind she had started to piece together an odd puzzle, but she wasn't aware of it yet. Not yet.

THREE

From a yacht somewhere in the Pacific where the air smelled of salt, suntan lotion and expensive perfumes and aftershave; where the rich could mingle with the rich; where in the evening sable coats were worn over bikinis as their owners danced on deck under a full moon; where in the daytime a blazing sun soaked stale alcohol from the pores of sunbathers who sipped fresh alcohol from frosted glasses; from there Shane Allen finally reached Beth at Triesius Campus where it was raining for the third consecutive day.

"Hmmm . . ." she said ominously.

It was cold, he said in haste and he wasn't having a particularly good time and half of the yachting party was Oriental and spoke primarily in Japanese.

"And they don't even know I'm a goddamn star, so I get no respect. I get a lot of privacy, but no respect. They serve buffet and I have to get in line. You know I hate buffet," he said and Beth could feel him grinning into the phone, feel him pulling the laugh out of her.

She laughed softly, not with mirth but with affection.

"How are you, baby?" he asked.

"Oh—"

"What's the matter? Is something wrong, because if it is, I can be there right away. You know that, don't you? That I can be there—"

"I'm okay, Shane. Just a cold. I'm getting ready for a hot bath and bed."

"Not a sore throat or anything?"

"Just a cold," she repeated firmly. "A product of over-civilization. Here in the west we all suffer from colds. Also headaches and an overall low pain threshold. Too much sugar and salt in the diet and not enough of the vitamin B's or C."

"Are you taking plenty of C? And don't forget your fluids. You sound a little hoarse to me . . ."

"Shane, I've been trying to reach you for days. You're not doing your usual trick?"

"What trick is that?"

"Your trick of disappearing off the face of the earth."

"I do that?"

"You do that," Beth said grimly.

"Well, this cruise came up all of a sudden and I just realized I'd been pushing it too hard, baby. Just too hard, every day, every day, every day. Christ, I had to get off the treadmill . . . it's crazy. You know me when I work—"

"Are you guilty about something, Shane?"

"Guilty? Why would I be guilty?"

"Who am I to say," she demurred, "but you did run away from home, didn't you? You're usually guilty about something when you run away from home."

A long silence and then he laughed grudgingly. "I had to have a smart-ass daughter."

She chuckled. "I miss you, Shane."

"Miss you too, sweet."

"Did you call Sara? She's called me four times."

"Oh, Jesus. Everything's a mess out here. I haven't had a minute to myself. Portland's here—"

"God. Is she drunk?" Beth had an image of Shane's frequent co-star, Portland Lee, still beautiful well on the wrong side of forty but more pathetic every year.

"She's doing one of her numbers on the Captain of the ship," Shane hissed. "And the Captain's doing one of his numbers on the first mate who's a darling boy of about nineteen. So you can imagine—"

"Just don't let her get to you, Shane. She'll have you drunk every night."

"No, baby. Honest to God."

"Don't get God into this, Shane. Not while you're in the middle of the ocean. And don't forget to call Sara."

"I will. I'll call her now. She and I . . ."

Beth suddenly caught a glimpse of Yvonne LeSabre, the

headmistress of Triesius, coming from a nearby doorway, her slender hand on the bony shoulder of Mrs. Fazio. LeSabre stopped talking now and glanced in Beth's direction, a studied smile in place. As usual, the headmistress's blond image was well put together; no telltale black roots for her. Nevertheless, Beth was convinced that the bleach bottle had been carefully tipped over not only hair but eyebrows and even delicate facial hair. LeSabre's eyes were keen, her features delicate. Perhaps she'd had a nose job, but enough nose was left over to allay suspicions. She was forty, perhaps, or even older, but her skin was still tautly stretched over a rather average bone structure. The total image could be considered glamorous to an observer or only neat, as if saggy skin and a crooked nose would be so much sloppiness, not to be tolerated.

"Beth, are you there?" asked Shane.

"Yes. You were saying . . ."

Yvonne LeSabre continued to stare in Beth's direction. The looks were what the headmistress did the best, Beth thought. LeSabre would have made a damn good psychiatrist. She had a way of appearing so totally relaxed while she said nothing. It was unnerving.

Yvonne LeSabre turned suddenly and whispered something to Mrs. Fazio. Then glancing at her own image in the hall mirror, she moved away down the hall. Fazio shuffled away at a funereal pace in the opposite direction.

Perhaps it was the sudden appearance of the headmistress that had caused Beth's thoughts to skip. Or perhaps it was her free hand which had wandered to the small side by side punctures in the crown of her head.

She started to speak and then stopped. It was crazy. There was Shane on the high seas; here was she about to complain about a couple of strands of missing hair. Permanently missing, she reminded herself. And there was the matter of the small scar on her inner thigh where they had taken the skin patch. She didn't like it. She didn't like it at all.

She said it. "Something nuts happened."

He laughed when he heard the details. "Jesus, what a physical. That's worse than the Army's. Although probably by this time the Army has all that too. Only worse. Anything civilians have, the Army takes and adds their own brand of sadism to it. The Army probably takes their hair follicles from the nose."

"Shane, did anybody ever tell you you're a—"

"They did. They do. I am," chuckled Shane. "But that's a damned interesting story. Sounds like Triesius has got the best of everything. How do you like that? My baby's getting tested for diseases I never even heard of. My last physical, they had all they could do drawing blood out of my arm."

She hesitated. "And you don't think anything could be . . . well, wrong?"

"Wrong?"

A twinge of anger colored her voice. "I don't remember signing anything that said they could put me to sleep. Did you sign anything? Because the way it looked to me at the time, they slipped me a needle and that was it. Did you sign something?" she repeated.

A short silence went across the wire and then Shane said somewhat testily, "I probably did, yes. I'm sure I did. Listen, Beth, what I think is we shouldn't make a big thing out of this. It's over and you're okay, right? But just to play it safe, in the future we'll steer clear of their space-age infirmary. There must be an old-fashioned G.P. in Rosemont if we need one."

He sounded to her knowing ear a little uptight and so she let it go with only a murmured, "I just thought I should mention it, that's all. You know me, Shane. I overstate things. That's from being your daughter."

"Sure," he said sounding relieved that, after all, she wasn't going into adolescent paranoia. "Listen, baby. I'll call you from California next week. Take care of that cold."

"I will. Hadn't you better hurry? The buffet line must be forming."

"Who cares? You've seen one melon ball, you've seen them all. Well . . ." A slight pause and Shane added, "Tell your friends I said hi, right?"

"Right," she echoed.

"Love you."

"Love you." She waited until the line went dead before she dropped the receiver into its holder. Without glancing up, she knew Carmel Ritchie had sidled up behind her. A musky animal scent, recently applied, said that Carmel had been out to seduce the phone. Beth tensed, the musky perfume cloying her nostrils. On the opening day of Triesius, Carmel, who was blond and worked hard on sex appeal, had exchanged a meaningful glance with Shane. Beth had seen that certain look in

Shane's eye and she knew what that look meant. It worried her.

"Would you happen to have a cigarette?" Carmel murmured, her robe tied loosely to show ample breasts unencumbered by bra.

"I don't smoke," Beth said and had the pleasant thought that if Carmel continued braless, she'd need a breast lift by the time she was thirty.

"Oh, that's right." Carmel licked her lips. "The next time you talk to your father—would you tell him I said hello?"

"I'll do that," Beth agreed, using body language to signal: You're blocking my door, Carmel. Wiggle your ass stage left.

"By the way," Carmel said, her left hip supported against Beth's doorframe. "There's something I should have told you. I don't know why I didn't mention it. I should have. I really should—"

"What?" Beth asked bluntly. *Aspirin*, she thought. *I really need aspirin to deal with you, Carmel.*

"A few days ago in the mailroom, I saw . . ."

Beth's head came up. Her mouth dropped open. "What?"

"I saw Georgia Urie take something of yours. A letter. She took it out of your mailbox." Carmel paused uncertainly as Beth's gaze iced over. "Well, I just thought you should know." She stepped aside. "Like I said, tell Shane—tell your father I said hi."

"Right," Beth said over her shoulder and thought: *Like hell I will.* The door closed behind her with a muffled thud. She grinned. At the moment all she was thinking was that Shane was out in the Pacific Ocean and, thank God, Carmel Ritchie was stranded here at Triesius. For a girl like Carmel, it was a punishment similar to being covered with honey and buried in an anthill.

Four

Southwest of and overlooking the Triesius campus lake was a small grey cabin. Damp and cold, heated only by a wood-burning stove in the kitchen, it was a flimsy, cheaply built structure, meant to be used by summer fishermen. On the walls were shelves filled with men's belongings—decks of cards, poker chips, old reels and fishing lures, a glass jar of hooks and a grey and torn fishing hat with a limp red feather straggling up from the plaid hatband. There were also tools and a miscellaneous assortment of useless and necessary items, impartially mixed together. A can opener lay close beside a bent nail. A red cup that bore the name Ted was filled with dry kidney beans. Scattered on the floor were buckets and trout lines, cane poles, piles of canvas, rubber boots, a lantern, an anchor.

Karl Immer had brought no trace of his own personality to the cabin. If he were to have been asked why he had not, he would have done a double take and looked around as if he had just discovered the space. In truth, Karl took little notice of his surroundings. He was busy examining his own thoughts.

Early in September, he had told his father, Jack Immer, that he needed a year away from college. He was "fucked up on the inside," he said in a father and son heart-to-heart talk and Jack Immer had been too wise to mention what bullshit that was or to permit the amused smile that was tickling at his lips. "I know of a cabin in upstate New York," Karl said. "I'd thought I'd stay there for a month or two." "Good—good," Jack Immer told his overly dramatic son. "And meditate. Very good."

He paused to cough into his hand, thereby successfully disguising the slight chuckle which he could no longer restrain. "You'll find yourself. You know, like Thoreau at Walden's Pond." ("He'll find his ass frozen is what he'll find," he told his wife Molly. "That's not funny, Jack," Molly had said and frowned, putting down her novel. "The kid needs toughening up, Molly. You'll see how much attention he'll give his soul when he's chopping his own wood in zero-degree weather. He'll be glad enough to get back to Columbia next semester." Jack pulled his shirt over his head and went into the small bathroom past Molly's makeup table. A few moments later, she heard him chuckling to himself and then the shower went on. "Find himself," murmured her husband's voice as he stepped into the shower stall.)

On September tenth, Karl packed his Volkswagen and left for the cabin. It was a chilly fall. Jack had a side wager with his brother that Karl would return within the month. "I know my kid," Jack said. "He can't stay away from McDonald's hamburgers longer than that."

Arriving in the town of Rosemont in upper New York, however, Karl was not thinking of hamburgers or the comforts of living. He felt that he had reached a spot somewhere outside his old self. A runaway spot where living could be resumed safely. If there was such a thing as safety, when all life ended in termination.

The sky was pearl grey, empty, full of space. Karl gripped the wheel. He was on a backstreet in the town. Cold wet sheets flapped on a line. He knew they were cold. Cold ghosts strung up to dry.

He drove faster.

What had happened at Columbia had never seemed real to him. It was more like a story, a short story, that he'd read to while away his time. It occurred to him now in a cynically honest way that he hadn't given a damn about Joyce and now that it was over, he still didn't give a damn.

And yet there was the aching, the crying out, so far within himself that it was out of reach. No, he could not reach it, not yet, to grab it and shake it by the throat, to kill it, to rid himself of it. Not yet.

"Let go of it, go on, let it out of your mind," he said in an endless monotone, his lips stiff and dry, forming a stream of words he was hardly aware he was saying.

The speedometer continued to climb until finally the last shabby breadbox house was behind him.

He found the cabin dark and cheerless. He was forced to sleep on a cot beside the kitchen stove for warmth. The electricity had been turned off for the winter and a kerosene lantern had to be utilized for light.

Days passed into nights, nights that turned brittle under the sudden bleakness of autumn. Karl spent countless hours staring from the cabin window, or at the large hunting knife in its sheath that was slung over a chair.

Too often, too long, he stared at the knife.

One day he went outside and selected several pieces of good wood which he attempted to whittle with the knife. The knife was too large for whittling and it was unsettling working with his hands. Stupid hands. Awkward. The knife slipped and he cut a large gash in his left palm. He stared at the red flow of his own blood and wondered if he would bleed to death. The strange thought occurred to him that if he died, the world would cease to exist, that he had imagined the world and was keeping it alive in his mind. The thought panicked him and he ran to the lake to plunge his hand into the cold water.

He read until his eyes ached. Plato and Socrates, Sartre, Camus and DeSade. Herman Hesse stupefied him. He couldn't help comparing Joyce to Agnes in *Narcissus and Goldmund* and himself to Goldmund. Agnes had wanted to die and Goldmund had wanted to live. Karl wondered if it were insensitive of Goldmund to want to live or just stupid of Agnes to want to die.

The month came and went. Karl began to keep a journal in which he recorded his thoughts. He was quite certain that no one, including his father, would have understood a word he wrote. He didn't particularly care.

He cooked for himself, mainly food from cans which he heated, and spaghetti and fish from the lake. He began to get horny for women. He found a stack of *Penthouse* magazines in a corner of the bedroom and sometimes he masturbated while looking at the pictures but it wasn't the same thing as actually being with a girl. He wondered if the men who had bought the magazines were married. If so, it was like being unfaithful to their respective wives. At least it was if they got off on the pictures.

At twilight at the beginning of October, Karl was sitting on a cracked step of the grey porch picking out a song on his guitar. It was no song that he'd ever heard, but he was not trying to compose. He made no effort to remember it or to write it down so that he might play it again.

A tall pretty girl stepped unexpectedly from the trees that separated the lake from the cottage. "That's a sad song," she said.

He continued playing the melody, listening to decide if she was right.

"It's the minor chords," offered the girl, laying her head to one side. "That's what makes it sad."

"It's a peaceful song," Karl said after a moment's thought. "At least, it is to me. Actually, that's exactly what it is—peaceful. A song of silence."

"My father was in a picture once called *The Silent Song*," she said. "It's about a man who has a lot of intelligence and ability but because he has to take care of his family, he never gets educated or amounts to anything. Except that he turns out to be a wonderful man. And his life, you know, is the song."

"Jesus, that's beautiful," Karl said and kept picking out chords.

"I like your song," she said. "Or maybe what I mean is—"

"What's that?"

"Your song says . . ." She hesitated, then finished the thought with an approving nod, ". . . something rather nice about you, I think."

"It says something nice about you that you say so."

She smiled and he caught his breath. She had a bewitching smile that made her suddenly not merely pretty but beautiful in the way a child is beautiful. All eagerness and softness and vulnerability. "I like you," he said. "Really."

The girl—Beth—had sat on the step beside him and listened while he played. When they got around to talking, he found out that she was a genius and a student at the experimental school for geniuses close by and that her father was a film star.

"Is it going to cause any problems?" she asked directly. "I mean with us being friends."

He took a moment to think about it and then said, "Not about your father. I don't feel any barriers about that. Maybe about the genius thing though. Maybe that could be too much to deal with. I mean, I've got a jeep brain and you're driving a Dusenberg. The question is," he said, the corner of his mouth quirking up in a smile, "can those two cars travel down the same road? After all, jeeps are for bumpy roads and cutting through back cow pastures. Dusenbergs are for tooling down the main drag."

"I like jeeps."

"I like Dusenbergs."

Two weeks later, they made love on the cot next to the kitchen stove and when they finished, Beth was crying. When Karl asked her why, she said, "Because you make love like the song," as well as she could for sobbing. It would have been fun to say, "I love you," but almost self-consciously they avoided the words as though to name the spell they were under might break it.

They talked about everything else: where they had been, what they had seen, what foods they liked, what kind of music, hobbies—hers, ice-skating; his, music and philosophy. ("I only named one," she said, "so you can only name one." "Okay. Musical philosophy. I philosophize to minor chords.")

She told him about vacations in Spain and the south of France. He told her about going clear to the Grand Canyon on a motorbike his senior year in high school.

"What happened to the motorbike?"

"I wrecked it not half a block from my house that same summer. It was okay. I was ready to quit riding it anyhow. I mean, I'd *done* it with the bike, if you know what I mean."

She was the first girl he'd told that story to who actually took five minutes to imagine him out there on the bike pulling up to the Grand Canyon. Then she drew a deep breath and said, "I know what you mean." And he had the odd feeling that she was the first person who really did know.

After that evening, Beth came back twice a week, not more often, because Karl explained he had come to the cabin for isolation. Still she wished she could go more often; by the end of October thoughts of Karl had seeped through into the days when she did not see him; there came a night she could say it actually bothered her to have such limited access to the cabin. It was during that night when it occurred to her that perhaps it was in her own mind Karl wouldn't want her. True, he had set the rule, but that was during the initial days of their relationship, before he knew what they would be to each other.

She talked the matter over with herself.

"It's not like he has any other company."

Musingly, she shook her head.

"He's probably over there right now, bored to death."

She nodded.

"He never has any good food. What if I surprised him with that ten pounds of chocolate nuts Shane sent?"

"Um," she said to herself appreciably.

A half hour later, chocolate box under her arm, she came upon the cabin. Tonight, it appeared to tilt precariously, threatening to drop on the first passerby. The facing boards were rotted and broken; the whole structure seemed to give up, asking only to be left to fall.

Strange. Beth had never seen it quite in that way before. She hesitated. A pale light flickered from the front window, danced on the upper portion of the dilapidated roof that covered the sagging porch.

She looked up. Concentrated on the puffs of smoke that told her Karl had made a crackling fire in the stove. Just a few steps and she would be inside watching Karl eat his chocolate-covered almonds.

She hesitated. Why did she suddenly feel she had never walked up that particular path to that particular porch and knocked on that particular door?

Darkness swirled around her and nudged her forward.

What if he's angry? What if he closes the door right in my face?

She picked her way steadily up the path. Karl was probably sitting by the fire, she thought. Yet something felt odd. A wind had started up and moved the branches of the trees together like crickets' legs. A brittle sound. Beth glanced around nervously, then hesitantly she knocked on the door.

"Karl?"

No answer and she was paranoid enough to think: He knows it's me and he won't let me in. She knocked again. There was a silence; but a more intense kind, palpable.

"Karl?"

Her hand closed around the doorknob. It turned and the door swung open easily. Her nervousness increased as she stepped into the darkened cabin, lit only by the embers of a dwindling fire.

She stopped abruptly, an odd stench catching in her nostrils. It came wafting from the stove, a fetor that had no name. Burning things, she thought at first, charred, food gone to corruption. Yet it lacked permanence, it was a more subtle odor, willing to go unnoticed.

"Karl? Are you here?"

In the bedroom to the right of the kitchen there was no light, not a glimmer. She moved to the archway and peered in. The light from the stove behind her burst forth as the wind fanned the room. Simultaneously, the front door slammed shut.

Beth turned with a start. "Karl?"

Abruptly it occurred to her: all of Karl's books and papers—magazines—were scattered and torn and thrown across his bed. As if someone had ransacked the cabin. *Penthouse* mingled with Herman Hesse. She looked closer. Two of the *Penthouse* magazines lay open at the foot of the bed, the naked portraits of women slashed, their legs and arms severed from their bodies.

Now the light faded again, leaving the bedroom in total darkness.

She reached for the matches that Karl always left on the kitchen table. Quickly she lit the oil lamp.

Holding the meager light in her hand, she gazed confusedly around. Nothing in the kitchen seemed amiss—the casual order of the room was seemingly undisturbed.

Using the lamp as a beacon, she moved slowly into the bedroom. The loose floorboards creaked beneath her feet. She worked her way into the center of the room, the thin flickering light from her lamp casting grotesque shadows over the bed, ceiling and walls. A half-open drawer of the dresser caught her eye. She moved closer, holding the lamp ahead of her, and then came abruptly to a halt.

Beth's eyes opened wide. She was taken aback for a moment, but she quickly recovered her composure. There in the drawer was money. Stacks of bills still wrapped in the bank's white bands. She took a step closer trying to determine the denominations of the bills.

At the same moment, something moved behind her.

"Karl!" she cried.

Karl stepped from the shadows. He did not say anything for a moment. He just went on looking at her, not staring—just looking at her with mild interest.

"My God," she breathed. "You nearly scared me to death."

He stood motionless.

She said, "I didn't hear you come in."

"I'm as surprised as you are," he said. He was smiling now, but there was a curious lack of warmth to his voice. "I saw you come up the path, only I wasn't sure it was you."

"Who else would it be?" she said and thought: God, now he thinks I'm prying. She quickly added, "I didn't see you."

"I was out back getting wood."

There was an uncomfortable pause. The oil lamp flickered, dimmed. The light between them grew darker now and Karl Immer appeared distant, standing alone in the archway, his lean body stiff and unyielding and clad only in denim trousers and plaid shirt. The light burst full again and picked up his facial features. It was an image of all bone, meager of flesh.

He hesitated an instant longer, then began to speak in a low, almost inarticulate voice. "I didn't think it was you, because —I mean, we agreed. Twice a week, right?" He rubbed the back of his hand slowly across his forehead. "Maybe you didn't understand. My privacy is very . . ." He broke off, his eyes boring into hers. "Have you been here before when I wasn't here?"

"No," Beth said nervously. "I swear it."

He nodded slightly weighing her words.

"Are you angry with me?" she asked.

There was the least pause and then he said, "No—no, not at all. Look, let's just forget it, okay? Act like it never happened." She was certain his eyes went to the dresser drawer. "Why don't we do that—just forget it," he said.

"All right," she murmured.

For the first time he came closer to her, his gaze keener for a moment and then softer as he appeared to let go of some last remaining anxiety. He was smiling again; an easy smile, soft and lenitive. "Come on," he said, "let me take your coat."

"I feel a little embarrassed." She allowed him to help her out of her fur jacket. Together they moved into the kitchen. She sat nervously at the table.

"Look," he said as he hung her jacket on the wooden peg. "I'm a little uptight, that's all." He turned back to stare at her. "I suppose you've noticed the mess in the bedroom?"

"Sort of."

"Someone broke in. Can you imagine that? I live in a place like this and someone still thought I had something worth stealing."

"Anything missing?"

"A good pair of my shoes, damn it. Wouldn't you know the thief had my size feet? Shit." He regarded himself in the small mirror over the sink.

Beth shrugged. "It could have been worse."

"How's that?"

"Well, they could have taken the money."

He was silent for a moment and then shrugged. "To tell you the truth, I'd rather have the shoes. The money doesn't mean a damn thing. You should understand about that. How parents send money when they haven't got any extra love to send."

Beth shook her head. "Shane isn't like that. He's generous, but that's a part of his love. Not a replacement for it."

"I guess you're right," he said, then laughed softly. "Today it's the thing to have a generation gap, so I guess I just automatically fell into that trap. Easy enough, isn't it?" He shook his head, smiling. "Good for you for making me feel ashamed of myself."

He turned, his eyes twinkling under his thin, well-shaped brows. "Now, what say you we just get all cozy and settle in. I'll get the fire started again, and—how about some hot buttered rum?"

"Sounds great."

Quietly he approached her and put his hand on her shoulder, a firm grasp on a soft shoulder, and held it there unmoving; she felt the full power of his fingers knot around bone, pulsing with fire from beneath his palm, surging, buoying. She straightened a little, smiled; looked back into his calm eyes.

Then he turned and went out into the darkness.

Beth's gaze moved unwillingly to the bedroom, to the torn magazines strewn about the bed. Drawing a deep steadying breath, she wondered why Karl hadn't straightened up. She looked down at her hands. They were trembling slightly.

Karl was snorting vehemently, in irritation, puffing his lips out as he came back into the cabin with an armload of wood. "Damn it! damn it, damn it!"

"What's the matter?"

"I just remembered I'm out of rum!" He opened the stove grate and flung more wood on the fire. "Terribly sorry; really I am."

"No, Karl—I'm sorry," she murmured and lowered her eyes. "I know it was a crazy thing to do . . ."

"What was?"

"Coming here tonight. You didn't expect me, I shouldn't have—"

In two swift strides he was beside her. "Hey, relax." He kissed her. "I'm glad you came, okay? So relax. Everything is all right now. Really. I'm glad you're here."

She pressed her cheek against the back of his hand. "I miss you, Karl. When I'm not with you. I miss you."

He stared at her. Close up, he just missed being handsome. His features were strong, but not chiseled; well placed, but not symmetrical. His eyes were slightly too close together. But the planes of his face were powerful, all muscle and bone. His skin was good.

"I miss you too," he said and moved closer until she felt his warm intimate breath on her face, her throat. It seemed to her she had been feeling it all her life.

Without speaking then, they sat on the cot in front of the stove cradling cups of coffee. She didn't know when it happened, but sometime before midnight she was in his arms, dressed first, and then naked.

She lay back and stared at his sweating face over hers. For a moment, her mind burned a warning thought. This boy was unlike all the others she had ever known; his passions ran deeper. Perhaps she shouldn't get further involved.

Yet, she knew it was too late.

She stirred slightly, pulling his body closer to hers, closer. She heard his breath quicken as her hands moved on him, guiding him, moving him into a more penetrating position.

"How do you feel?" he asked. His voice was husky in his throat.

"Good," she whispered. She pressed herself closer, locking him within her embrace. His shoulders moved over her, wide for such a lean body and bulging with unexpected muscles. Muscles that twisted and pressed still closer. Her breasts flattened under his chest.

"Hold me tighter," she breathed.

He gazed down at her, swallowed hard.

And then, hardly aware anymore of what she was doing, driven by an urgency that could no longer be damned or halted, she gave herself to him fully and completely, made love to him until she was totally spent.

Lying still now, he told her he was lonely and afraid.

She loved him for the confession.

Finally he fell asleep while she held him, with the moonlight slanting in from the narrow box-pane window and falling across his face. He looked so peaceful now, so absolutely relaxed and unafraid. She kissed him lightly on the forehead, then relaxed beside him. After a moment she fell into a deep, dreamless sleep.

Only once during sleep did she imagine she heard someone cry out. Or had someone screamed?

Five

He was no more than a pair of eyes glinting in the darkness. When the girl came out of the library, he focused on her long blond hair, her firm figure, her long striding legs that pushed free of her black raincoat.

It was nine p.m. by the tower clock.

He watched as she fastened her coat against the gusting wind and, slinging her bag over her shoulder, began to head for the dorm.

He stepped onto the lighted path and followed after her.

Halfway up the walk she whirled as if she were suddenly uneasy. But she saw only rows of trees, an empty flagstone walkway, a slight mist that had begun to settle over the campus. She turned and went on walking.

He stepped from the shadows and strode after her. In the distance she hollered to a group of girls who had just bounded from the dorm. They stopped to talk for a moment, then each went her separate way.

He checked his watch: still nine o'clock. He adjusted the lapels of his coat, fighting back a smile of excitement. That was the one thing he never allowed himself to do—to smile when he was alone.

His eyes roamed freely over the vast front lawn of Triesius and its small hills and well-manicured shrubbery. He checked off all the familiar sights: the Administration building, the infirmary, the dorm. There his gaze rested.

He thought: *Without the mind of man, without imagination and courage, what pleasure would exist in the universe?*

Now the area was deserted and bleak. Here and there a light

would suddenly flash on in one of the dorm windows. From where he stood, he imagined he could hear the buzzing of voices, girls' voices, their conversations regimented and predictable.

He began to stroll the sidewalk. He was in no hurry. He ran his fingers lightly along the shrubs . . . sometimes allowing a finger to grab hold, tugging at a branch playfully . . . yes, he was absolutely in no hurry. He had all the time in the world.

Was anyone watching him? No, he did not think so. At the edge of the pathway he began to walk faster. He headed around the side of the building. All familiar to him, like a secret language that only he understood.

He stopped. He needed only to stand there, his feet solidly planted on the ground, balanced, his mind concentrating on the task before him—giving slow accurate directions to his body—he could do anything, he could restructure entire lives. He could perform magic, his magic . . . when there were fools who thought he was a puppet . . . performing *their* magic. All sleight of hand. Just part of the act.

And then—just this once, he allowed himself to smile.

SIX

"So why did he scream?" Vala Hayes asked with rather bland curiosity. Most of her attention was riveted on the fudge brownie she nibbled crumb at a time to make it last.

"I didn't say Karl screamed," Beth objected, taking scissors from her dresser. "I said *someone* screamed. Maybe it was me."

"Why would you scream?"

"Oh, for God's sakes. I probably dreamed the whole thing. Listen—by the way, you didn't mention Karl to anyone, did you?"

"What and die six times?" Vala quipped. "That's how many times you made me swear on my life I wouldn't tell."

"I just have this feeling that Karl—" Beth broke off as she tucked a towel inside of Vala's collar and dipped a comb into water. "He's a very private person, that's all," she added, and reluctantly half-admitted to herself there was a side to Karl she hardly knew. Images conflicted in her mind. *Penthouse* models, slashed and mutilated—Karl's eyes boring into hers—"Have you been here before when I wasn't here?"—Karl's mouth, tender and warm against her throat—money. A drawer full of money. Why so much of it? All in cash.

A certain sense of being observed made her glance down now to meet an intent gaze. She smiled reassuringly and began to comb water through Vala's thin strands of hair, noting that when dampened, her hair seemed to disappear, creating an illusion of baldness, blending Vala's face into scalp, scalp into face, space-age style.

"Why do I seem different from the others?" Vala suddenly asked, changing topics in her usual blunt fashion. "I know, I *know* I am, Beth. I say something and people stop talking and look at each other. That look that's embarrassed for me. What do I do that's strange?"

"Small talk, Vala. You have to learn the art of small talk. You're too tense. I've got to teach you to stop walking up to people and spilling your guts."

"When did I . . . ?"

"Every day, Vala," Beth said patiently. "People don't talk about their parents and cry. People don't tell sad awful stories about religious conflicts. Not over wine and popcorn. Got it?"

"What *do* you say then? Over wine and popcorn?"

"First of all, have some of the wine. It'll relax you. Secondly, don't use those eyes of yours like claws. They tend to dig into people. You have clinging eyes, Vala. Very clinging eyes."

"Then what?" prompted Vala, chin tucked downward into the bony hollow of her throat.

"What?"

"What do I do then? Over the wine and popcorn. After I've drunk the wine and tried not to look very hard at anybody."

"Oh. Then start counting. Every seven exchanges, think of one sentence to say. Just one lightweight sentence," Beth mumbled, her mouth full of clips. She began to divide Vala's hair into sections, clipping each section as she went. "And whatever you say, just throw it out, you know—don't care whether anybody hears you or not. Nothing intense, nothing profound. Got it? Something like: 'This sure is good popcorn.' Something simple. Then let another seven exchanges go by and say one more sentence. No more than one at a time." She laid her comb aside and picked up the scissors. "Your problem is you let two hours go by without saying anything and then feel like you're supposed to give a fifteen-minute monologue."

"Oh, I see." Vala giggled, the high-pitched squeal of someone unaccustomed to laughter. "All right. I'll try it. But what if somebody says something to me before the seven exchanges are up?"

"Act like your mouth is full of popcorn," Beth gasped laughing.

Vala laughed too, clasping her stomach as though it would split, her mouth stretched wide in delight. Only her eyes were solemn as they continued observing; always observing. Now they had glued themselves to the reflection of Beth's face in the glass.

Beth smiled. By this time, she was used to being the object of Vala's observation: the face cream she used, the expensive perfume she dabbed on from a gold-sealed bottle, the way she bent over to brush the underside of her hair. She didn't mind. She wanted to do things for Vala. To help her socially, to coordinate her clothes, to encourage her to wear a touch of makeup. To have endless conversations about the art of conversation.

Sometimes she discussed Karl with Vala, who listened with as much curiosity as a would-be traveler examining a travel brochure. Except on certain evenings lately, when Vala's energy level would suddenly plummet, leaving her drained, too tired to walk to the dome for a hamburger; too tired to even pretend to be otherwise than exhausted.

"You look like you always feel so good," Vala said somewhat enviously. She had finished the last of the brownie. Now she licked her fingers.

"Why not? On the subject of feeling good . . ." Beth paused to observe that Vala's hair seemed to have gained no new life from the cutting. It was going to be another one of those sessions of combing, curling and teasing hair that wouldn't, couldn't, show a trace of life; hair that dropped from her fingers flat against Vala's scalp. "Maybe a headband," she muttered in disgust.

"Maybe," Vala agreed hopefully.

"Vala, what I was going to say. You seem like you feel better tonight."

"Oh, I'm fine. I'm just fine. When I get like that, it's—it's just part of my depression. It makes me tired."

Beth clasped her thin shoulder affectionately. "You and your depression."

It was a little after seven p.m. the next evening when Beth came to an abrupt halt outside of Vala's door. She had been looking for Vala off and on for almost an hour. Vala had not attended her last two classes of the day. Nor had she met Beth at the library as promised. Nor had Beth found her at the dome, the cafeteria or in the video room. So . . .

She rapped quickly on the door and entered without waiting for a response. What she found was Vala sitting in bed, knees pulled up under her long flannel nightgown, eyelids drooped over dull lackluster eyes. It was just as she had expected. The depression was back.

She cast a stern glance at Vala's bedside table, where an almost empty aspirin bottle sat next to a partially filled glass of water. Beside that was a stack of saltine crackers, Vala's mainstay when her stomach was acting up. Still further evidence of illness was exhibited in the small bowl of water on the floor beside her bed and the damp washcloth Vala hastily removed from her forehead and dropped into it. The only light in the room was the desk lamp which cast odd shadows over walls and ceiling, leaving the bed in unrelieved gloominess.

The room was scarcely a decorator's delight.

Vala kept it neat but bare, save for pictures of her mother and father and a few knickknacks—a copper cup for pencils, a tassle from graduation—still, Vala's personality had been captured in some undefinable way.

Vala shrank deeper under the covers, avoiding Beth's stern eye.

"The music students," Beth said lightly, "are having wine and Beethoven in Jennie Dobbin's room." In the slight pause that followed, she wondered if Vala had comprehended either word; wine or Beethoven.

"I think," Vala managed finally, "I'll go to bed early. If you don't mind."

"Early? It's not even seven-thirty."

Vala's huge pupilled eyes tried unsuccessfully to focus on Beth's face. She tried to say something, failed, then made a small aborted movement to swing her legs over the side of the bed. She shivered.

"What's the matter with you?" Beth frowned. "Something's wrong, goddamn it. I can see that, so don't try to deny it. You're about half conscious. What in the world—"

She was interrupted as fingers brushed against Vala's door and a moment later, Georgia Urie's golden head poked inside. The usually cool eyes brimmed over with concern. And something else. Curiosity? "I wanted to see if . . ." Georgia's voice died off as Vala lowered her head to her pillow. "She fell," Georgia went on, turning to Beth. "Did she tell you? Jesus, what a thing. One moment, feet on the floor. The next thing you know, it's acrobatics in the hallway."

Beth, glancing from Georgia to Vala, had the sudden thought: What do you know, Vala's made friends with the reclusive Georgia Urie. It was true that Georgia had begun to drop by occasionally and even shared with them a magnificent cherry cheesecake acquired from a woman in Rosemont who sold bakery goods out of her own kitchen. But now, there could be no doubt: this was clearly a case of friendship. Vala had bagged her second friend and was making headway.

"Thanks for picking me up, Georgia," Vala murmured meekly. "I'm such a klutz. I didn't get hurt at all."

"What made you fall?" Beth queried.

"If you're thinking of a lawsuit," Georgia offered, "there was nothing suable. I checked. No wet spot, no banana peel, nothing slippery. The way you dropped, Vala, I could have sworn you fainted. You went down in that I-don't-give-a-damn-how-hard-I-fall style of tumble."

Vala stirred uneasily as two pairs of eyes affixed themselves to her face. "No," she stammered, "It wasn't—it wasn't anything like that."

An amused interest flashed in Georgia's wide eyes. "There's no disgrace in passing out, you know. Not unless you're . . ." Then a sudden thought made her stop to take a closer look at Vala, who miserably allowed herself to be examined. "Well, there's a hot shower waiting for me down the hall. In case you haven't noticed, I'm a fiend for hot showers. Two or three a day. I'll be a prune by the time I'm forty, don't you know, but who cares, right? Nothing wrong with prunes." She stopped at the door. "Incidentally, I saw your face when you fell. I never saw anything so peaceful in my life. You should have seen yourself. You were . . . quite beautiful. You were so surrendered." She grinned, the sudden mischief out of place on her elegant face. "To falling over your own feet, as it were. Well . . . see you later . . ."

When she was gone, the room was for a moment without focus, as empty as a stage after the star had made her exit.

Beth dropped onto the edge of the bed and waited until Vala finally gazed into her eyes. "You did faint, of course."

"No, really, I . . ."

"You need to see someone, Vala. A doctor."

"A psychiatrist," Vala joked weakly.

"Oh, God. What will I do with you? If you could only believe in your own mental health, then maybe we could get somewhere. Will you at least see a doctor, a regular nonshrink medical doctor? Will you do that much for me? Just for the hell of it?"

"I'll see."

"I'll find a doctor for you in Rosemont."

"Not yet."

"When?"

Vala hesitated. "Do you remember how we thought the admission physicals were strange? Do you still think so?"

Beth was taken aback by Vala's sudden shift in gears. "Shane doesn't think so. None of the parents think so, although Jennie says her mother called LeSabre about it. I'm just not sure what I think. I suppose the truth is I hardly think about it anymore. Why? Were you—"

"If you really thought something was wrong," Vala said casually, "you probably wouldn't come back next semester. Would you?"

"Would you?" Beth returned. "Of course not. As it is, I have to ask myself will I be coming back."

"Oh. Well, I'm sure nothing is wrong. It just crossed my mind all of a sudden." Vala sat up straighter in bed as though she had just found new strength. "I'm feeling better. Much better," she mumbled after a moment as though aware Beth still sat waiting for some further comment. And indeed a faint color had swept across her pale face.

In the days that followed, Beth sensed that Vala was deliberately hiding something from her. There were long periods of time when Vala was not to be found and then when she did show up, she went straight to bed and slept for long uninterrupted stretches. And something else . . . if she didn't know better, Beth would swear that during these times Vala had been using drugs. Sometimes now Vala appeared to be not only exhausted but actually out on her feet; so woozy that she stumbled as she walked.

Anxiously Beth confronted her. Drugs? Alcohol? What? Vala, what?

"Nothing," Vala said meeting her gaze candidly. "I give you my word, Beth. I wouldn't be that stupid. I'm just—I'm . . ."

"Tired," finished Beth unsatisfied. "I know, it's your famous depression." But she was unconvinced. What brand of depression made you walk crooked and dilated the pupils of your eyes?

SEVEN

MEMO

Highly Confidential

TO: Harlan Tyler St. John
Chairman of the Board

FROM: Alan Randelar, M.D., Ph.D.
Project Leader

RE: Five White Mice

Mr. Chairman:

Here it is as you've requested it, in layman's terms. I believe you will have no trouble in understanding what we have done here. Please observe:

1. A white donor mouse was injected with .04 percent solution of gene strain B.

2. After allowing suitable time for genes to become part of the genetic machinery, egg was then removed from white donor mouse.

3. Inner cell mass removed and separated into individual cells.

4. Nucleus extracted from one cell.

5. Sperm was then removed from a black mouse.

6. Nucleus from cell of white mouse fertilized with sperm from black mouse.

7. Hybrid egg, cultivated in nutrient solution where cell multiplied, became embryo.

8. New embryo was placed in incubator.

9. White mouse, genetically superior to genetic profile of white donor mouse, born alive. Both mother and offspring show no signs of adverse effects.

This procedure was repeated successfully five times. We're definitely on schedule and ready to proceed!

Cordially,
Alan Randelar

Randelar's face was tightly controlled as he read through the memo one last time. And then in his upright precise small letters he signed his name merely "Alan," knowing the familiarity would annoy the Chairman.

The information contained in the memo was accurate enough, but incomplete. Yes, incomplete was the right word.

For just a moment Randelar let his guard down. In that moment he let himself think—really think—exactly what he had done to those embryos.

EIGHT

"If you ask me," Georgia stated defiantly, "somebody's filling her full of drugs."

For the last half hour Beth had struggled to keep up with Georgia's long-legged easy gait. Now, breathless, she could hardly comprehend Georgia's words.

"Drugs," she murmured, glancing sideways at the huge black skeletons of old trees that lined the Triesius walks like listening sentinels. "She says she's not on drugs. Besides, who—?"

"She goes to the infirmary every other day."

Beth lifted her head to meet Georgia's direct gaze. "Are you serious?"

"Don't mention it to her. She sank fifty thousand leagues when I brought it up. Maybe she's seeing a shrink and they've got her on one of their antidepressants."

"Oh, yes," Beth sighed. "That would be it. Vala loves shrinks."

So did many of the others and they were provided here. Free shrinks. Free antidepressants. Free couches to spill your most intimate guts into. And yet . . . Triesius was not paradise and no shrink could change that fact.

"Could you buy me a milkshake?" Georgia asked, striding up the dome's short entrance stairs. "I left my wallet back at the dorm."

"Likely story," Beth laughed.

As they neared the entrance, something caused Beth to glance back. For an instant she thought she saw Vala standing alone at the top of the hill overlooking the infirmary. Standing there among the shadows cast by the overhead lamp against the thick trunks of aged trees, but no, it must have been a trick of light. There was no thin rigid body among the oaks, no head tilted to one side, forlornly watching Beth and Georgia's every move, listening to their laughter.

"Hey," Georgia said, nudging her. "You coming?"

Beth nodded. But she remained uneasy.

The next few days quietly slipped into brutally cold evenings; most dorm lights were turned off by eleven p.m. Here and there a light remained on; a yellow beacon shining in an otherwise black November landscape.

Bleak.

On the coldest night thus far, Beth slipped into her long-sleeved navy lounging pajamas and thought: *Tomorrow I'll be with Karl.* It was something. Most of the girls had nothing at all. She shook her head. Triesius—so well-planned, nothing left to accident, and yet there was the possibility that the whole thing was going to be a bust. She could feel it. Triesius, whose very name to Beth seemed akin to a modern-day Atlantis, where impossible excellence could be aspired to . . . yes, Triesius was subtly developing a sore spot which might or might not be malignant.

A mistake had been made. Not educationally. Educationally, it was A-number one. That was a given. The intellectual heart of Triesius was gold. But what about its soul?

For to Beth, it was precisely this that Triesius lacked: its very soul. And without a soul comes the soft spot of rot. What a negligent thing . . . no, a forgetful thing . . . or perhaps the conceivers of Triesius just hadn't realized how sterile an existence they had arranged for their twenty-five young women whose only crime was a certain precocity of the grey cells.

At Triesius there was isolation, the sort that eventually turns inward and, berserk with hunger, devours its own innards.

Beth gathered toiletries, reached for a fresh towel and moved quietly into the hallway headed for the shower. Immediately she could feel the scrutinizing gaze of Mrs. Fazio. With thin long torso, low-slung in the tush department, and free-floating egg-size breasts obviously wrung dry of the milk of human kindness, the woman hung in the hallway like the warmed-over ghost of Christmas past.

"Oh, Beth—have you seen Vala Hayes?"

"No. Isn't she in her room?"

"Not at the moment."

Beth shrugged. "Probably at the library."

"If you should see her, tell her I've got a package for her."

"Will do."

Beth ducked quickly around the corner and made her way to the end of the hall.

Doris Encoda went by lost in a thin brown book.

"Hi, Doris," Beth murmured and the other girl lifted the fingers of her left hand in a half-wave, never bothering to raise her head.

Beth felt a thin pulse of curiosity which rapidly evaporated. Doris was fine again and her usual self. On her heels followed Lovetta Rheinhart. Boring. The same people every day. The same buildings. The same everything.

Where was Triesius? Nowhere. Well, fifty miles out of New York City, but still nowhere. Manhattan was not accessible, given that Triesius students were denied the right to keep cars on campus. Ten miles away was the do-nothing town of Rosemont, to which the college provided transportation twice a week. Rosemont was good for a second-run movie, a barbecue sandwich, token shopping. Rosemont's young men were garage mechanics, college drop-outs, low-paid clerks in grocery stores and small businesses. Thank God she had Karl.

"Hey, Beth."

"Yeah." She raised her head to confront Willa Bishé, who was the pushy type.

"Rate me!"

"No, thanks." Beth avoided letting her eyes travel over Willa's plump broad-seated figure. ("Rate me," as though she expected a ten, for Chrissakes.)

"I'll rate you," Willa offered. "I'll give you a nine. Maybe a nine and a half, with those clothes. Now rate me."

"You're a ten, Willa!" sneered a sarcastic voice from further down the hall.

"*Really?*"

"No, not really. Umm . . . about a seven."

"A *seven?* Shit."

"What's wrong with that?" asked another voice as Beth pushed her way into the shower room. "I'd rate almost all of us that. Some less. Georgia's a ten. A ten plus."

This game of rating each other face-to-face had excited a

new viciousness among the girls. It was, Beth thought, the most brutal fad she had ever seen. There was talk that one of the lower-rated students had attempted suicide. This speculation had been met with a muffled giggle.

The slow swing of the shower-room door gradually closed off the shrillness of the girls' voices. Beth inhaled hot steamy air and reflected that critics abounded everywhere, the primary difference being that professional critics got paid for driving people to suicide.

Whatever makes you happy, I guess. She shrugged and headed toward the sinks, carefully avoiding a succession of puddles. At the first basin stood Georgia Urie, barefoot and in her frayed white terrycloth robe.

"Hey, Georgia," Beth said. "Did you know you got the only ten rating in the school?"

"That kind of thing makes me sick," Georgia said briefly, her flat clipped tone leaving no doubt that she wanted to drop the subject.

"But—"

Georgia's lips tightened. She shook her head impatiently as though to clear it from even the remembrance of such pettiness.

"It's just that I don't even want to dignify that bull by talking about it," she said. Then with one of her small cryptic smiles, she made a gesture of apology and glanced back into the depth of the room.

Steam poured from the tops of the two private shower stalls; the communal shower was vacant.

"Who's in there?" Georgia bellowed back toward the enclosed stalls.

"Carmel, here," floated back a languid voice from under the heaviest cloud of steam.

"Shh!" Beth hissed as Georgia threw a murderous glance at the stall.

"You know she'll be in there a half hour."

"I know, but I don't want to be here a half hour arguing with her."

"Who else is here?" Georgia called out.

"None of your frigging business," said another voice. "And don't hold your breath. I'm giving myself a steam treatment."

"Give your ass a steam treatment," muttered Georgia.

At that moment the outside door opened and a dark-robed figure entered quietly. It was Marguerite O'Brien, a serious girl who kept to herself and spent her time studying. Beth had a vague idea that Marguerite would have been an outstanding student elsewhere. Here at Triesius, merely adequate, no matter how hard she worked.

Slowly the girl removed her robe and slipped into the communal shower. Georgia and Beth murmured hellos; she inclined her head in a passive greeting. She withdrew to the far end of the shower and stood silent, the fine spray of water enveloping her.

Georgia went on: "There was a string of limos over at Research today. In the middle of all the hubbub, guess who I recognized?"

Sweat had begun to pop out on Beth's brow. "Who?"

"Four Star General Harris Weiss. From the Pentagon. I was impressed."

"What do you suppose he's doing here?" Beth murmured, interested.

"Hobnobbing with Alan Randelar. The General certainly doesn't like students. Remember that quote of his: 'Ninety-nine percent of all college students have the retention span of a chicken.' " Georgia chuckled. "I can't even dislike a man that crude. It wouldn't serve any purpose—he could care less if the whole world hated his guts . . ."

"But what kind of interest could Weiss have in Randelar's research?" objected Beth. "I mean, genetic research? Talk about strange bedfellows, those two men are as opposite as salt and sugar. Weiss would like nothing better than to cause a goddamn nuclear war . . ."

"And Randelar," Georgia finished softly, "is trying to improve life, not destroy it. I respect Alan Randelar. I really do. His breakthroughs in birth defects, operating on unborn infants—well . . ." She shook her head. "Put it this way. He's one of the Peace Prize recipients who deserved it. It's one of the reasons I wanted to come to Triesius—his being here. But wouldn't you know they won't let us close to the man? *C'est la vie*."

"Is that what you've been trying to do? Get close to the man?"

"What do you mean?" Georgia's face was faintly flushed.

"Well, I notice you've been going to the infirmary every now and again."

"They dispense sleeping pills like Solomon's gold."

"Sleeping pills?" Beth queried mildly. "I hope you're not—"

"I know, I know. Just every once in a while. Trust me."

Georgia glanced toward the private showers one last time. "Well," she sighed, "I'm not going to stand here all night. I want to see those crater slides in an hour. Are you going?"

"No, I'm going to skip it," Beth said and felt Georgia's unvoiced disappointment. "Ask Vala."

"I will," Georgia said, brightening. In the next moment she had quit the room.

Watching her tall frame disappear through the door, accompanied into the hallway by drifting steam puffs, Beth had a sudden and sharp realization.

It had happened.

Never before had she felt the same sense of belonging to a friendship that she had begun to experience first with Vala and now with Georgia. To go a step further, they were the only real friends she'd ever had. And in that friendship, they had given her something no one else ever had—liberation from the onus of being Shane Allen's daughter.

They never treated her like the daughter of a star. Neither did they cling to every mention of Shane. Neither did their eyes pop out of their heads when his letters and phone calls came.

With a shock, Beth suddenly realized something else. That she *liked* being less beautiful than Georgia, less intelligent than Vala. It eased some deep-harbored guilt.

Still wrapped in thought, Beth stepped out of her lounging pajamas and glanced at her nude body in the mirror. She decided she'd lost a few pounds. It suited her, although Shane would tell her she looked like hell. She leaned forward, hung her towel on a hook, then reached down to arrange her soap containers on the ledge of the shower stall.

A startled cry escaped her lips. A few water droplets had splashed on her hand. At first she thought it was her imagination. Impossible—the water simply couldn't be that hot. Scalding.

Confused, Beth glanced at Marguerite O'Brien, who continued to stand silently, almost limply, in the shower.

Now Beth plunged her hand directly into the force of the spray. Pure fire bit through flesh and nerves. She gasped and pulled back. Stared at her hand. The skin was burned red.

"Marguerite! The water! It's scalding—"

But Marguerite did not respond, did not even turn to look at Beth.

Only a moment now, another fraction. Beth was going . . . she was going . . . to start screaming. Heart pounding, she was seized by the fierce temptation of hysteria. A spasm of sickness shook her as Marguerite blanched and took in a sudden sharp breath. She seemed for a moment to calculate, to remember, worrying about something . . .

It all seemed to be happening now in Marguerite's eyes.

The grey orbs dilated suddenly, then expanded enormously, as if all the blood beneath her skin were madly boiling up, obscuring her vision, blocking out all of her senses.

"Marguerite!"

Ironically, the girl stretched both arms upward in a primitive gesture of worship.

Steam rolled from the shower as the water seemed to run faster. A thundering sound as it met concrete. Too much water to drain quickly; it backed up until the girl was standing in an ankle-high flood of scalding water.

"Marguerite!" Beth shrilled. "For God's sakes, the water's boiling. Get the hell out of there."

In the midst of a steam-cloud, Marguerite looked out at Beth inquiringly. Her mouth gaped open.

"Marguerite!" Beth pleaded. "Get out! Please . . ." She pounded her hands together, helpless to do anything else, as seconds went by. "Marguerite!"

The girl was almost totally lost in steam now. Her voice drifted to Beth over the heavy moisture. "The water's all right," she murmured. "Everything's all right."

Suddenly the valve was closed and Marguerite waded from the shower basin to stand beside Beth.

"But—it was—you saw the steam," Beth stammered. "Didn't you *feel* it? How hot it was?" She held up her hand where blisters had popped up on either side of her first finger. "Look. It burned me."

Marguerite stared at her. A strange gaze. Their eyes locked. Some sort of message was being communicated. Then Marguerite's eyes reddened and there was a sudden gush from her nose as blood mixed with the water on the naked girl's face and flowed over her open mouth and down her chin.

"You've got a nosebleed," Beth shuddered, handing her a towel.

"I'm all right," Marguerite said almost crossly. In the next instant, she had slipped her damp and sweating body into her long dark robe and disappeared from the room.

Dazed, Beth turned back to the shower.

"What's going on out there?" drawled Carmel Ritchie, emerging from her shower stall in the back. She stood dripping water onto the tiled floor, running her fingers through her long wet hair.

"Nothing, I guess." The other private shower was suddenly turned off, leaving the room silent. In the pause that ensued, Beth knelt and touched the concrete floor of the basin. Hot. Still burning hot.

"What are you doing?" Carmel asked.

Beth turned to stare up at her. "Marguerite was just . . ." She broke off. She could go no further with the thought. There was no place else to go.

NINE

Narrow slits of fading sunlight wavered through slats in the shutters, hesitated, then began to withdraw, leaving a slight chill in the atmosphere. Flecks of ash from the stove, drifting lazily across the room, were set into a frenzied motion by Karl's sudden movement. Rising from the cot, he quickly donned shirt and trousers.

"Where are you going?" Beth asked.

"Out."

"Why?"

"More wood," he snapped.

Beth sat up and swung her legs over the side of the cot, her body connecting with the chilled air. She covered herself with the blanket.

"Are you mad?" she asked.

No answer.

"Karl, why are you so angry?"

Again, Karl refused comment. He put on his jacket, zipping it in front before moving to the door.

"I guess I'll get dressed then."

"I guess you should."

"Christ!" Beth snapped, reaching for her jeans.

"I can't help it, Beth. I thought we agreed to spend one night without mentioning Triesius. I'm not kidding. It's bugging me. We can't talk about anything else."

"I thought it was odd, that's all."

"What's so odd about a girl suddenly leaving school? It happens every day."

"Not just any girl. Marguerite O'Brien."

"Depressed, they said. She had been depressed."

"And that day in the shower?"

"What about it?"

"She should have been burnt half to death. That's what about it."

"Please, Beth. Would you mind if we just dropped it?"

Beth shrugged. "I don't mind at all."

Karl slowly shook his head, mellowing a bit. "Look. I'm sorry. But it comes down to a simple equation: Two people plus one continuous topic of conversation over and over again equals boredom."

"Well, okay," she said simply and began to throw on her clothes in an abandonment of frustration and anger. "My goddamn purse. Have you seen my goddamn purse?"

He hesitated, then took a step closer. "Does this mean you're not going to be spending the night?"

"I have to be at a lecture," she lied. "I have these things that come up. Like you do on every other night except Thursday and Sunday."

"That's your right," he said stonily. "Just like I have my rights."

She was silent, standing now at the window, her back to him. The scenery blurred before her eyes, then steadied. All at once she began to perceive her environment on two separate levels.

On the one hand, there was Beth the student who owned the campus and strode about confidently on her way to classes or the dormitory. On the other hand, as now, there was Beth the voyeur peering out on a rolling landscape that had nothing to do with her. Lonely. Confused. From her stance at the window she could see part of the campus lake and far away in the distance the round, lit building that was the dome which sat like a sentinel, watching over all things.

"It's all changed," she murmured, her mind grappling with why she and Karl were so edgy lately.

"What's changed?" Karl said, not as though he were paying much attention.

"The atmosphere. The atmosphere at Triesius is different."

Karl let a short tense silence go by before saying, "On our last night together, it was people watching each other. LeSabre watching the girls, the girls watching each other, even that guy, what's his name—?"

"Alan Randelar," Beth said patiently. "I said he finally gave a seminar and he was nervous as a cat. Why should he be? Talking about monkeys and cats and watching us as if we were supposed to, I don't know, *react* in some way. I can't explain it."

"I guess you know how nuts you sound."

"Okay. Forget it. But this thing about Marguerite O'Brien, it's really getting to me. Something was wrong with her, Karl. Believe me. It wasn't just depression, like they said. There was something really wrong with her. And then she just disappeared. Look. I'll tell you what bothers me. I know of two girls who have what I consider to be physical problems. Both of them are written off as cases of depression."

"Who's the other one?"

"Vala," she said almost angrily.

She heard him sigh and met his gaze directly, a long friendly stare that let him ask the question that she knew had been bothering him. The question that was, no doubt, making him tense about Triesius.

"Are you coming back after Christmas break?" he asked softly, the words barely audible and it was all there in his face, that this was already the fourth of December and that semester break was coming up on the nineteenth.

"I don't know," she whispered and tears stung her eyes because she ached with the need to continue their relationship and ached with the need to end it. Because they were going everywhere and nowhere together. Because they couldn't keep going on like this. Hiding out together in a flimsy grey cabin and Karl never saying the words that had to be said if they were ever going to go anywhere.

His face. His wonderful face. It seemed to her she had never before seen his face, not really, until this moment. She grew to a sudden awareness of her own body, to the flush of having been loved. She still felt it, standing there across the room from Karl. Incredible. Her skin felt fever-warm, open-pored in its vulnerability. So sensitive to the touch, it ached. But then—she sighed and thought that everything had a sharper significance now, the way it does when things are coming to a conclusion.

Beth now shuffled slowly through the fast-growing darkness dimly aware that there was a chilly moisture in the air, somewhere between rain and mushy snow that melted before it reached the ground.

The emptiness of her stomach reminded her that it was dinner time, but she made no move to veer left around the circular driveway and up the steps to the dome's cafeteria. Instead, she continued on.

The walkway ahead of her was deserted save for a lone man who had come swiftly up the hill from the direction of the instructor cabins. His downthrust head and raised collar shielded his face from the electric lamps. It was a moment before she recognized him as Angusi, professor of languages and composition. He was so thoroughly replete with his own thoughts that he would have bumped into her had she not stepped to one side.

He squinted down at her, uttered a jerky apology and kept walking.

"Evening, Professor," she murmured, letting him pass.

"Evening," he returned, already disappearing back into his own head. A book was tucked under his arm. Were it lighter outside, she knew he would have been reading.

She turned to watch him go. On his way, no doubt, to a greasy hamburger at the dome, but very likely he would be oblivious to the taste. She thought Angusi was one of the loneliest people she had ever seen, but luckily he probably didn't know it.

The moisture in the air began to commit itself to being snow and the thought passed through her mind that if the temperature continued to drop perhaps the lake would freeze and, at last, she would skate.

She picked up her pace, consciously using the muscles in her thighs to push forward faster. Arriving at the dorm, she shook herself like a wet dog, stamped damp boots on the mat, then walked through the periphery of Mrs. Fazio, who sat at the front desk and pretended to read a magazine.

With the distinct feeling of being "Allen, Beth, present and accounted for," she checked her mailbox to find she had no mail, then with declining spirits trudged up the east staircase. Alone, she thought irritably, which was a one word way of saying what an ass she'd been tonight. *A lecture!* she mocked herself bitterly and wished like hell she'd taken the lie back. Pride. Damnable pride! It would be three days before she could see Karl again and that was too bad because she knew that time was no longer endless, something one could get lost in.

At the top of the steps, she paused beside a silver prefabricated Christmas tree hung with blue balls. The floor rang with unbroken quiet. The silence overwhelmed her. She felt bolted into place like an inanimate object. Even her eyes found themselves locked into focus on the small artificial tree. It sat on a hill of sparkled cotton, at the base of which was a wooden Nativity, its figures small and indiscernible of features. The baby Jesus was not a separate figure but was rather carved into the piece that was the manger.

"Somehow Jesus got left out," drawled a sardonic voice over her shoulder.

Beth jumped. "Georgia, in the name of—"

Georgia leaned forward over Beth's shoulder, her silky hair brushing against Beth's cheek. It was the closest to making physical contact that Georgia had ever come. Beth realized this as a fact she had subconsciously known for some time—that Georgia avoided touching—but had never actually expressed.

"I can just see a raised carving where his head should be and no body at all, just a blanket," Georgia continued squinting. "This has got to be the worst Nativity I ever saw. I'm sure Fazio picked it out personally. Also that cheap tree." She turned to Beth and added, "What do you want to bet they gave her two hundred bucks to decorate—she bought this, stuffed that old jug full of holly and put a hundred and fifty bucks in her pocket. What do you think?"

"More like a hundred and sixty bucks in her pocket," Beth decided. "She could have picked the holly. But wouldn't you say it's a little early for Christmas?"

"Hey, we don't want to let the rest of the crass commercial world get ahead of us . . ." Georgia pulled cigarettes from the pocket of her black coat and paused to light one. The click of her metal lighter was startlingly loud.

Beth turned to stare at her and wondered where Georgia had come by such a disreputable coat, ill-fitting and as shabby as sewn-together rags.

"By the way," she remembered, "where in the world did you appear from just now? You crept up like a spirit."

"That's me—light on my big feet. You on the other hand were like a statue. Dense. Unmovable. Lucky for you this isn't

Manhattan. Five minutes like that, you'd have found yourself a permanent fixture in the Museum of Modern Art."

"Sorry, I was drifting."

"Karl?"

Beth nodded.

"I wondered what you were doing back here on a Thursday night."

Beth sighed. "Not a good night."

"Ah, well . . ." murmured Georgia compassionately.

"It'll be better next time. Did you check the call board? Were there any calls for me?"

Georgia moved her head in negation, her eyes fixed once again on the Nativity as though the absence of baby Jesus were not only perplexing but had become a sudden annoyance.

"I've had a call into California for three days now," Beth explained, glancing at her wristwatch. "Since I've been in this school, I don't think Shane's been home two weeks back to back."

"What does that mean?"

"It means," Beth said, following Georgia slowly down a corridor that seemed suddenly too long, "that he's probably drinking too much. That he's got something on his mind. Or maybe it just means he's got a new girlfriend."

"What happened to the old girlfriend—the one you said you liked?"

"Sara? He and Sara seem to be off these days, but I should have figured that couldn't last—she's not much more than twenty years younger than him. A mere child of thirty-odd years. Plus she's smart—knows her ABC's and everything."

"Whoo," Georgia said expressionlessly and Beth grinned seeing that she intended to say nothing more. Georgia had an undeniable ability to know when to stifle herself.

The sudden silence between them drew them into the more pervasive hush. The atmosphere of the dorm tonight more resembled a church or a hospital late at night. Even the lighting was dimmer, as though some of the bulbs were out; as though one of Shane's better light designers had created the proper atmosphere for a deserted hall. Hold it. Yes, the test shot looks very good. Now let's shoot the scene.

"Where is everybody?" Beth wondered out loud. "There wasn't anything scheduled tonight, was there?"

"Inoculations over at the infirmary. Didn't you see the notice on the board? Flu shots—"

"Oh. Well, forget that. I don't believe in flu shots or cold shots. Pretty soon we'll have such sophisticated bacteria, nothing will kill them."

"That sounds like a pretty damn good reason to not take a flu shot," Georgia assented. "Me, I just wanted to take a hot shower. Goodnight," she added not coolly, but with just the edge of reserve that let Beth know she planned on spending the evening alone. Beth watched as Georgia's long body ducked into her room with some undefinable gesture that bespoke relief. It was plainly one of those evenings Georgia needed to put herself into solitary confinement. There were many of these evenings and it was part of their friendship that neither Vala nor Beth ever challenged her on it.

But the hall seemed twice as empty without her, twice as echoingly silent. She wondered if Vala had gone to the infirmary with the others. Perhaps and perhaps not.

Beth paused by the door marked "Hayes, V."

"You there?" she called softly.

When there was no answer, she inched open the door and found the room dark, save for the desk lamp left burning. In the shadows, Vala lay face down on top of the bed covers fully dressed as though she had intended merely to rest for a moment and instead sleep had crept up to claim her. It was a game Vala played with herself far too often now.

Beth withdrew from the room soundlessly, shutting the door behind her. If Vala couldn't be persuaded to see a doctor . . . but she must be persuaded . . . and soon.

Restlessly Beth changed into her robe, tried calling California again. This time even the housekeeper was out and the answering service picked up.

"Tell him," she said, "it's nobody important. Just his only daughter."

Back in her room, she submerged herself in physics for the next hour, so intensely that at first she didn't hear the tapping at her door until a hoarse voice demanded, "Hey, Allen! You there? Hey, Allen!"

"Come in," she murmured, attempting to hold a complicated pattern of thought, but she was too far into the theorem, there were too many steps to retain and even as she spoke, she could see the process breaking apart in her mind like old smoke rings. "Damn."

"What's your problem?" Carmel Ritchie said after Beth had jerked open the door, then added: "Don't look at me, I'm a mess." She held a mentholated cloth around her neck. Under her gown another cloth showed itself to cover her chest. "That God-awful flu. I've had it since yesterday. One hundred and two fever. Oh, Jesus—"

"That's too bad," Beth said automatically, noting that despite Carmel's sickness, her eyes burned with excitement, her lips smiled despite herself. "What can I—"

"Your father's on the line," Carmel said with malicious triumph.

"What?"

"I'm surprised you didn't hear the phone ring. My God, it's so close, it's practically the same as having your own phone—"

"I was studying," Beth said coldly and strode past Carmel into the hallway muttering over her shoulder. "You sure took your own sweet time in telling me."

The steady padding of high-built satin slippers that followed after her plainly told that Carmel was undaunted. Beth snatched up the phone. "Shane?"

He was joyful. He had had an inspiration. "Baby, let's have Christmas at home this year. Forget Aspen. Who needs snow, right?"

"Where are you calling from?" she demanded.

"Bel Air. Where else would I—why?"

"Then . . . you got my messages?"

"Oh, well, sure. Naturally." The slightest of hesitations had occurred. He hurried on. "Anything special?"

"I just worry about you," she said evenly.

"You do that?"

"You know you're the kid of our household, Shane," she said with some significance.

"Am I?"

"Much younger than me," she said, listening closely.

"Jesus, I'm homesick for you, baby," he said. "Why don't you come home, see, and we'll have Christmas out here in California." And then it happened, what she had hoped to prevent. He said it brightly, as though it had just occurred to him. "I tell you what. Why don't you bring your friend, that girl I met, the one who just answered the phone. Miss Carmella. Plenty of empty bedrooms."

Her mind jumped in alarm, but she managed to keep her voice neutral, noncommital. After all this time, God, he still had Carmel Ritchie on his mind. "I don't know," she said. "I'll see."

Carmel had sidled in close, now sat facing Beth at the counter, hugging herself, teeth chattering slightly.

"Will you do that?" Shane asked.

Beth said, "Maybe."

"Sure, why not? You tell Miss Carmella I'll spring for the plane. What else is money for if it can't make my little girl happy."

"Goodnight, Shane."

"Goodnight? What's the matter, baby? Did I say something wrong?"

"I can't hold a conversation with you when you've been drinking."

"I haven't—"

"Your voice is slurred. You've been drinking."

"Oh, is it? I didn't know that. You've got the trained ear. Have to hire you for the AA circuit—see who's been sneaking the corks out of the bottles. You're not mad at me, are you?"

"No, Shane. Just go to bed, okay?"

There was a long pause she didn't like and then when Shane spoke, his voice was wobbling all over the place. "Tell me something," he said. "Will you tell me something? Are you all right?" Unexpectedly, he spoke lower, almost whispering. "I mean . . . really all right. Because if anything happened to you, baby, I mean anything . . . well, that's something I just couldn't . . ." He cleared his throat.

"Shane? You're not blubbering, are you? Come on, that's one of the old drinking rules. No blubbering."

"Hey, you know I never blubber. Not unless it's in the script."

"Okay," she smiled. "And stop worrying about me. I take care of myself."

"Yes, but . . ."

"Shane, I'm fine."

"Well . . . that's good. That's good then. I love you, baby. You're everything in the world to me. That's what I was trying to say."

"You are to me too. And we'll have Christmas in Bel Air just like you want it."

It seemed almost against his will, but he said it anyway, as though it were his obligation to say it. "And you tell that girl—what's her name? You tell her to come."

"I'll see. No more booze tonight. Get some sleep. Call me this weekend."

"Okay. Goodnight. You tell her . . ."

"Yes, I'll tell her."

She hung up and Carmel said, "Tell who? What?" Her eyes had come alive—she knew.

Beth groped for the right words and then from over Carmel's shoulder Vala appeared like a weary sleepwalker, rubbing her eyes with her fingers, stumbling forward on bare feet. "What?" she mumbled groggily, repeating Carmel's question.

"Why, Vala," Beth said, getting the idea. "I mentioned to my father you were born in California. He said why not come for a visit this Christmas. We'd love to have you, we really would."

"I wasn't born in California," Vala said puzzled.

"Oh, weren't you? I thought you were. It doesn't matter. Come anyway."

Vala had regained a semblance of minimal alertness, but now she swayed slightly. "Thanks . . . but, you see . . . Christmas . . . it's been so long—"

"Then next spring," Beth urged. "Come next spring."

"I don't know," Vala said in a voice that wobbled precariously. In a kind of personal despair, she whirled around and half ran down the corridor to shut herself into her room so decisively it was as though she had hung a "Do Not Disturb" sign on the doorknob.

Beth had made a move to go after her; now she stopped. Nothing, she thought, absolutely nothing was right tonight. Everything was at least a shade off of how it ought to be. This utterly deserted hallway wasn't the least of it.

Snow made a peppery sound against a nearby window and she guessed that bad weather had detained the girls from walking over. Still she found it hard to shake the almost dreamlike state of mind that had claimed her, that gave her a sense of things dissembled.

Maybe it's me that's off.

She turned back to see Carmel still in her chair, listlessly folding a piece of the material from her robe around and around her finger. She looked so completely alone that Beth could not but feel a jab of pity.

"Why didn't you go for the flu shot?" she asked, her tone bordering on civil.

"Oh, that," Carmel returned barely glancing up. "I had it days ago. It didn't do any good."

"How—"

"I went to the infirmary for codeine. I had one of my headaches. So they went ahead and gave me the shot just in case I was coming down with it. God, I'll be glad to get away from here," she added and then clamped her wide lips together as though she had said more than she'd intended. Her eyes grew remote.

Just when Beth decided that Carmel had forgotten her existence and would say nothing further, Carmel glanced up and asked with a shade of bluntness, "I suppose you're going to Forum tomorrow night? Connecticut men tend to be so—so advantaged," she added vaguely. "Although I suppose that sort of thing doesn't matter to you. What in the hell would you need a rich husband for?"

"Connecticut men?" Beth repeated blankly.

"Forum night. We're hosting the Young Republicans from Hartford, Connecticut."

"Oh, yes. Well, I suppose I'll have to go, won't I? It's mandatory, as I recall."

"Mandatory," Carmel nodded, relapsing into indifference.

Slowly Beth moved away leaving Carmel sitting there, hair straight and in need of a shampoo, dark circles under sunken eyes. Her fingers beat a tattoo on the long telephone table. It seemed part and parcel of the night that Carmel too would be other than her normal self.

Her mind went back to Shane. Who had been—damn him—not only slightly intoxicated but lying. Three days' worth of messages all marked "Please call back today." She could almost imagine the housekeeper, writing down each call and spearing the pink telephone message slip through the spike that kept Shane's messages. That he had not seen the messages had come across clearly. It had been there in that infinitesimal pause that had escaped him when she'd asked about them.

But if he wasn't in Bel Air, then where—? She rubbed away

the frown that had settled between her eyebrows. Long ago she had come to realize that fathers, especially fathers like Shane, could not be controlled. One of these days she'd stop trying. Which would show some sort of progress.

She stopped at the window and stared out. A nearby lamppost showed that the ground was already covered with a crust of white powder. Even as she watched, however, the snow wore itself out and stopped as abruptly as it had begun. Surely the girls would soon leave the infirmary and head back to the dorm. Farther up the hushed corridor, she heard a door open and glanced up to see Georgia disappear into the shower room, a towel over her arm, shampoo and soap in her hand.

Faint voices drifted up from the lobby. Headmistress LeSabre's light airy tones: "Oh, Mrs. Fazio, could I have a word with you please?" and Fazio's lower whiney assent that tried to be pleasant.

Then more silence, uninterrupted until Beth could hear her own heart beat. The emptiness in her stomach caused a rolling sensation—or was it a premonition of what was to come?

Indeed, later it would occur to Beth that a sort of plummeting downward had occurred at that moment and from then on nothing was going to go exactly right. It was as though dominos were lined up and waiting to fall and that already a teasing finger had flipped backwards, then forwards, upsetting the first domino which upset the second domino which upset the third domino and then it got too fast, too confusing to call. Even the weather was part of it. That it was so cold, unbearably cold.

The next evening, December fifth, the temperature dropped to zero.

It was, in fact, zero hour. As good a place as any to begin.

PART II

Forum Night

ONE

He liked best the early mornings at Rosemont when a dense cloudy mist hung over the town and the town became anonymous, hidden away between Albany and New York City, completely surrounded by high timber and rolling hills, divorced from the world.

But when the fog lifted, it was a different matter. Then the tension began to build. Days slipped into nights as he sat there waiting. He was good at that—waiting.

Now he took the flask from his coat pocket and lifted it to his lips. Unflinchingly, he took a long swallow of straight whiskey, then another. In a matter of seconds, he felt its calming effect. His thought process slowed, the tension in his stomach unknotted and mixed with the chemistry of his blood, and his agony of indecision left him.

In the black stillness, standing on his solitary hill overlooking the campus, he laughed.

A loud raucous laugh, not quite human.

The world was not an easy lay. No, it could not be won by courting and hand-holding. The essence of it all was elusive. Could only be seen by the raw eyes of a man on the one and only make. Could only be taken by force.

His eyes fastened on the dome, a giant glass eye of blazing light. A seeing eye, he fancied, his brain heady from the liquor.

As God is my witness . . . no, only this white electric eye. He was God tonight and no other.

Again he drank, this man who was orgasmic God. Along his thigh ran a drop of liquid fire. He shivered, feeling the throb inside him become a burn of need.

He would be ready for her. He would not fail to be the best. No, not for her the average fate of an average woman. Endless nights in bed with a sliver of a man—some pale-faced, soft-armed, soft-penised accountant.

Anything average is nothing, he mused. Moments later, he was striding down the hillside. He knew exactly where he was going.

And what he had to do.

TWO

Beth Allen stood alone beside the frozen lake, her skates slung over her shoulder by the laces, her back against a slender birch tree whose branches were still faintly starred by a few remaining dead brown leaves.

She watched as the fog lifted slowly, until all that remained were diaphanous puffs of vapor far out on the ice, which soon were caught by the wind and blown away to nothingness.

She filled her lungs with cold air and wondered what Shane was doing tonight. Some vague worry about him lingered since his call. Something . . . Where was he, she wondered, and who was he with and was he telling whoever it was about her. Perhaps clinking goblets of imported champagne . . . "Oh, by the way, here's a picture of my daughter." Or lying in bed (she flinched) after lovemaking (she never thought about his lovemaking before or during, just after) . . . "You're so special, I'd like you to know about Beth. I'd like you to meet her." She'd met a lot of them, a maze of them. Soft-haired, crafty-eyed, sweet-smelling, hungry, clinging, greedy goddesses. All wanting Shane.

Losers. All losers. They'd lost the game of winning Shane too and, since she was being truthful tonight, she knew she had been glad when they disappeared, one after the other, leaving no trace of themselves in her world, hers and Shane's.

Still there was Sara; Sara who was not like the others; Sara, who had far too much substance and too much unguarded expression leaping from her eyes and not quite enough beauty to fit the mold of a Shane Allen love object. If Shane wasn't going to make this one last, well, that was too bad, but none of her business. She wasn't going to butt in.

Butt in? She reminded herself that she had her own problems, but refused to consciously allow thoughts of Karl. In a kind of blind anger, she pushed him out of her mind. Tonight is not your night. I'll think about you on Sunday. That's your night. You picked it.

The wind was really whipping across the lake now. Beth sighed, pushed herself away from the tree. She had come to the lake hoping to see ice. And now that there was ice, she knew she shouldn't skate on it. Not tonight.

She leaned forward to stare. The thought played across her mind that maybe the ice was at least hard around the edges. The danger of the thought made her shudder. To be alone in the dark of night—to fall through the hole in the ice—to bob up at the wrong spot, to find a roof of frozen death over her head . . .

She wandered down, picked up a branch, and jabbed hard at the ice. She listened for sounds of give. It seemed solid. Felt good.

It's been so long. I'll just go around one time, that's all.

She was shaking now, her fingertips and toes stinging, getting really cold. Still she walked up and down, pushing against the ice with the stick, stepping on the ice, letting it bear the weight of her body. Strange how suddenly time had stopped being defined. Right now her whole life seemed to have become compressed.

If I were dying, she thought smiling, I'd say my life was passing before my eyes. Flashbulbs and her first pair of diamond earrings, watching Shane make footprints at Grauman's Chinese Theatre, squeezing his hand hard when he didn't get the Oscar for *Silent Song*, his best film, walking on private beaches, breathing high, heady, expensive air. It was good living, incredible living. Perfect? No, but then nothing was perfect.

Naturally there were things she wished. She wished that she knew where her mother was, that her father would spend more time being famous alone with her, and that she could win the Olympic gold medal for figure skating. And she wished that on the first day of school she had not seen her father staring at Carmel Ritchie with that certain look in his eye.

Since Shane's phone call last night, she had all sorts of pictures in her head. Carmel in the back of the Rolls Royce, naked under a chinchilla fur. The slate grey Rolls, a bonus from Paramount, making Shane bonus baby of the year. Dinner in Vegas. Sweeping over the black desert in Shane's helicopter, coming without warning upon the blazing, eye-aching lights of Vegas. Having breakfast in the heart-shaped bed with the red-velvet bedspread. The special bedroom reserved for Shane's special lady guests. Never were the lady guests surprised by the maid in Shane's bedroom. He had more class than that. No, they slept in the Valentine bedroom. That's what she had always called it in her mind.

It was sickening, but, of course, there was no possibility that it could all actually happen. That her father could take Carmel Ritchie—she made herself say it—for his lover. Ridiculous.

But why had he asked the question? Damn it, she added mentally, concluding the whole thing with those two words. Damn it.

Beth gave one last push against the ice and then tossed the stick aside. I'm going around one time, she thought, and in the back of her mind knew she had been going to do it all along. Had come here to do it.

The zipper on her right boot stuck. She pulled off her gloves to work with it and pinched her finger. Damn. She fumbled with the laces. She felt miserably cold and bereft of exhilaration. She forced her frozen feet into the skates, which were new and painfully tight on her feet, the way good figure skates should be. She felt constricted instead of free, angry, and her fingers and toes ached. She took the rubber guards off her blades, stuffed them inside her boot tops.

I'm out of my mind, she thought, walking over the hard ground toward the ice.

Jaw set, she eased herself onto the lake and heard the ice give under her weight. A deadly crunch, way down deep. She waited, unable to move, listening to the thumping of her own heart. Under her skates, the ice was firm. It didn't give, didn't cut too deep under the blades. She told herself she'd imagined that crunch. The wind teared her eyes, blurred the ice until it was nothing but shimmer.

She was a Taurus. A stubborn, bullheaded Taurus. She had come to skate and she was going to skate.

Slowly, cautiously, she slid out onto the ice.

THREE

By the time Georgia Urie's wristwatch said seven o'clock, Triesius' Forum on Worldwide Consciousness of Young Republicans, Part I, had already been meeting three minutes and forty-two seconds because Triesius made punctuality an inflexible rule and because Headmistress LeSabre had a computer watch that had been synched with the world clock, and the world clock was three minutes and forty-two seconds faster than Georgia. The story of her life. The rest of the world was always a little ahead of her. Which left her always out of breath, jogging along trying to catch up, and always with a problem.

Like right this minute, the young man who sat next to her had his elbow sticking in her right breast. She felt guilty about that. Her fault, definitely her fault, for slouching down in her seat. She was fair game. How was he to know that she slouched not to make her chest more accessible but out of good manners because she was six feet tall. She glanced toward the end of the row where old frump Fazio was sitting. If Fazio were to notice what was going on, the wrath of God would come crashing down all over the place.

Nervously, she wished Beth would come to occupy the seat to her left, which she had covered with her clipboard to reserve it. She strained to hear the quick muffled steps of Beth striding confidently down the aisle, coming to save her from designated mingling night. But already she was sensitive to her inner belief that Beth was not going to show. No, Beth decidedly had left her alone to be devoured by the Hartford, Connecticut wolfhounds.

Georgia now cast a sidelong look at the young man sitting next to her. A Young Republican. Probably wealthy, if he followed in the tradition of good Connecticut Republicans. The pressure from his elbow intensified. Truthfully speaking, it didn't feel bad, that elbow, not bad at all. That one spot was hot as a branding iron.

The young man stared straight ahead at the Vice Chairman, who was introducing the speaker.

Damn you! she told him silently, forcefully, not looking at him, feeling the stillness, the heat of his body. Complacently he sat and stared ahead, regardless of condemnation and damnation. A jerk, she decided. Probably didn't even know he had his elbow in her tit. It occurred to her that she could just let him keep it there if he didn't know. But if he knew, it was cheap.

Pardon me, do you know your elbow's in my tit? I was just wondering, because if you don't know, it's perfectly okay.

She tried to focus on the Vice Chairman, a short-haired, prematurely middle-aged young woman who would without a doubt get her law degree and go into politics. She'd aspire to the Presidency, of course. All politicians did, especially women these days. It was human instinct to climb.

Georgia shifted her eyes to the guest of honor's chair, which stood vacant, explaining why the Vice Chairman had a slight edge to her voice and a nervous tick above her right eye.

Humm. Most likely the guest speaker hadn't kept his eye on the world clock. Or possibly it was a case of a missed train. Or senility of the appointment book, or laryngitis, bursitis, phlebitis, cancellitis . . .

All at once Georgia felt a faint interest in the Vice Chairman's dilemma. How best to handle the situation . . . But it seemed the Vice Chairman had the situation well in hand. Like most Presidential hopefuls, she had a long-winded speech ready and lost no time in hurrying into it. One of life's golden opportunities.

"Today's lack of political concern," the Vice Chairman was saying, earnest, perspiring, close to the mike, "is a blot on our national conscience."

National conscience, Georgia thought, humbled. And here she was worried about her right boob being felt. Too insignificant to even mention. Too insignificant to even think about and she tried, she really tried, to settle down, to listen to the speech. The problem was that she couldn't seem to think about anything except that the entire right half of her body was on fire. Georgia sighed because life was complex and because she was being frivolous with her brain cells again.

It worried her that she wasn't a deep person, a serious thinker. She'd never really thought of herself as very bright, even though they kept giving her all kinds of tests and telling her that her I.Q. was 175 sometimes and sometimes, depending on the test, as much as ten points higher.

No matter what they told her, she knew she was just taking up space. She was just a very normal girl who should never have been born a genius. The responsibility bored her just like classical music and modern art bored her. She was confused. Was it possible to be too stupid to use one's genius? Strange how for so long it hadn't bothered her at all.

The elbow was still there, finding its way deeper into the softness of her breast, pushing, intruding, but she wasn't thinking about it anymore, wasn't hot anymore. She was thinking about that contest, that stupid goddamn contest that had changed her life. Body Beautiful. The spring of her junior year.

A thought pressed itself upon her. That she would have been happier if the meaninglessness of her life had never occurred to her.

Her body was good. Georgia had known that even before the contest. Thin and tight in the right places, overflowing in the places it should overflow. Maybe it was being a giant that kept you skinny and tight.

Body Beautiful. She'd wanted that title, really wanted it. Standing there in the line of five finalists, she waited for the emcee to call out the winner, heart pounding, wanting to be Body Beautiful, please let it be me.

"Georgia Urie," announced Joe Skelton, who had sold her chocolate milkshakes from Skelton's Drug Store ever since she could remember, and she'd walked out proud in her black string bikini and her stilt heels that made her six feet four inches. Joe had made everybody laugh by not knowing just how to put on her Body Beautiful banner. His fingers felt like adult fingers on adult flesh. He whispered, laughing a thin high-pitched laugh, "I feel as young as springtime tonight, Georgia. Do you feel any older?" You're a dirty old man, Joe

Skelton, she thought, not caring, smiling, letting him get away with it. Taking her red roses, stooping for the gleaming-with-rhinestones crown to be placed on her hair, blinking from the flashbulbs.

And then, at last, down the ramp, the winner, swaying to music, looking into a sea of faces—her brother winking, her father with both hands clasped over his head, her mother crying. That was the first time the voice whispered in her ear. "Crying over being Body Beautiful, for Chrissakes? Come on, Georgia, wise up." A tiny little line came between her eyes. She could feel it there as she went on smiling, nodding, waving. It's an honor, she argued back to the voice who said nothing at all. As if the point was not to be argued, as if the absurdity of the situation was self-evident. Just like it was absurd that she'd refused to skip grades in school, refused to be elevated above her friends.

Angrily she smiled broader, her jaws aching, her lips dry and stuck to her teeth. I'm proud, I tell you. I have a right to be proud if I want to. Halfway down the ramp, she had the thought, Maybe it isn't such a big honor. "Uh, oh," said the voice. "Too late." Shut up, she ordered it, trembling a little. Shut up. She was at the end of the ramp, waving, feeling the spotlights flooding her with pastel colors. Oh, Jesus, this is silly. This is embarrassing and silly. That was when she panicked, pictured herself falling off her high heels. Falling into the audience, into some giggling adolescent boy's lap. He'd stare into her eyes and breathe sour breath into her face. She wouldn't want his red-dotted face to touch hers, afraid that his acne was catching, that he'd give her zits, that the zits would spread like poison ivy all over her body. She could feel him out there, waiting for her. Her ankles were weakening and her left heel turned sideways, almost pitching her headlong over the spotlights. Where was he, the boy who was going to catch her when she fell? I'm making a fool of myself, she thought, rooted to the spot. Everybody's laughing at me and I'm ridiculous, ridiculous to be out here in a black string bikini, to be Body Beautiful. Her jaws locked, she couldn't feel her mouth, couldn't tell if she was still smiling or making a face, doing something really bizarre. I'm so cold, she thought all of a sudden. So terribly cold. Goosebumps popped out in slow motion all over her long body. How come you look so proud of me, Daddy? I didn't do anything. Her hair felt wet around her face, wet and sticky from hairspray. "Don't let them know how you feel, Georgia," whispered the voice. "You've got to keep up a good show. Come on now. Walk!" I can't, she answered, her teeth chattering. I can't move, can't move from this spot until somebody comes and carries me away. "Then you really are an ass," said the voice contemptuously, dismissing her. She hated the voice for saying that, for giving up on her. I hate you. I hate you so much. Spitting snake venom, that's what she felt. It was the hate that got her going again. Right leg, left leg, right leg, left leg. She lost track of time. She thought about getting through one step at a time, as if she was learning to walk all over again. A tall baby, tottering along, refusing to fall. Loud cheers penetrated her mind. They're cheering because I'm learning how to walk. Come on, Georgia, take another step. Past Mom and Dad and the unknown boy with the acne. She was almost to Nasty-Old-Joe Skelton now. Get away from me, Nasty Old Man. Whatever you do, don't lay a hand on me or I'll . . . I don't know what I'll do. Joe Skelton let his arm fall back to his side. He looked pale and concerned under the bright lights. Cold water ran down from the roots of her hair, rained down her face and she thought numbly that now she understood what a cold sweat was. Past Joe Skelton, past the startled envious line of runners-up and also-rans.

By the time she got backstage, she was shaking so hard that nothing could make her warm no matter what they did for her. Sitting in a chair, wearing her coat, drinking hot coffee, she thought, I'll never be warm again. Not really. I'll never be able to function like a whole person. I'll never be the same.

Of course, she was wrong.

By the next day, she was fine, just fine. Everyone told her she was fine. That she was the old Georgia Urie, that the color had come back to her skin, that her eyes had lost that glassy stare. "Really?" she'd said, thinking what a cool spring it was. Her body temperature had dropped by a fraction of a degree. She knew that it had because she started measuring it by a thermometer every morning. It'll never go back to normal, she thought detachedly. But she was fine, wasn't shaking anymore. It'd been the shock, her mother said—winning the contest. She started wearing looser clothes, didn't feel like going to the beach that summer. She felt ridiculous, noticeably insignificant. She was scared. Scared that her mind was frivolous, that she couldn't get interested in world politics and economics and the women's liberation movement. She spent her energy in pretending to be more than she knew she was. She stopped dating, refusing to end up as a happy housewife. She was teetering on the brink of disgracing womanhood by having a useless destiny, an empty brain. An empty brilliant brain.

The young man's breathing was shallow now and rapid. The sound of a male animal aroused. Georgia could feel his body trembling in the intimate spasming of a man in need, nervous system overheated, and she thought, *I've really done it this time.*

Slowly, experimentally, she pulled her body to the left. The elbow wedged in tighter, welded itself to her body.

She felt claustrophobic, panicked. He was crowding her territory. She hated male sexuality. Men lost their identities when they got hot. She looked at the young man and then away. Away from his glittering blue eyes. His face was made of sparse lines, as if it had been drawn in outline and hadn't been filled in. Straight black eyebrows, thin, even, whitened lips, high pronounced cheekbones, dark hair.

She turned her eyes to the guest speaker who had stepped suddenly from the wings and, moving awkwardly across the stage, acknowledged the Vice Chairman with an embarrassed nod of his head. He wasted no time in hurrying to his chair where he sat. A lock of light brown hair had fallen across his forehead.

Georgia's memory stirred. He had spoken at the opening assembly. Just a few words, but she remembered him. He had a nice quality, considering he was a politician. A Councilman or something, she couldn't remember just what. With the town of Rosemont. What she did remember, strangely, was his name: DeWitt. James DeWitt. There was no accounting for what trivia the brain chose to retain. She studied his kind-looking rather than handsome face, trying to guess what was going on inside his head.

Again Georgia felt the boy beside her move closer.

"Do you want to go someplace?" he whispered, his breath hot in her ear. "I know where we can go after the meeting."

"If you don't stop touching me," she said, "I'm going to start screaming my head off."

"What?"

"I said I'm going to start screaming."

"Shh!" In front of her, Lovetta Rheinhart turned frowning to remind her that a speech was going on. That her problems couldn't possibly be as pressing as the Republican Party's.

The jerk didn't move.

Christ, Georgia thought. I hope I don't really have to scream.

His outline face turned. Only his blue eyes were alive, watery. "Don't you like me?" he asked. "Don't you think I'm good-looking?" The vein in his left temple throbbed with blood.

Be careful, she told herself. *Be very careful.*

"You got me excited," he said, looking down at himself. "You shouldn't have let me get excited if you weren't going to ball me."

She must have short-circuited after that, blanked out, something, because she couldn't remember just exactly what happened. If she'd said anything or slapped him or what. Couldn't remember hiding her body in her billowing black monster of a coat. She was running, that's all she knew. Falling over people's legs, being cursed by voices belonging to the legs, stepping on leather bags and coats, racing up the aisle, down the stairs to the main floor of the dome. "You shouldn't have let him get excited," said the voice, "if you weren't going to ball him." Her long shapeless coat cast a flowing, trembling shadow on the floor. He's back there. He's back there somewhere. I can hear his footsteps. Somebody's footsteps. Or was that the echo of her own footsteps? She couldn't stop running, couldn't take the time to find out. On a hunt, someone had told her, a fox seldom lives to get caught. He dies, most usually, of a heart attack, poor fox. Killed by his own fear. Her heart was racing.

Run, Georgia Urie, just as fast as you can, because the heat's going to catch up to you. You'll give yourself to the man with the outline face, just like you almost did to the man at NASA, who was kind enough to give you the special guided tour last spring. Like you almost did to the man who was at the gallery. The one who knew so much about painters. El

Greco and Degas and Rembrandt. Or how about the time—no. No, none of that's true. Or, if it is . . . I'll never quit running, she thought, her heart thumping faster and faster.

She slipped through the door of the dome and went running through the blackness of the night, her feet slipping over the frozen ground, her legs bounding along.

Nobody, she thought, can run as fast as me. *Nobody!*

FOUR

There were no lights on the Triesius lake; only the wash of a pale moon outlined the ice-encrusted shore.

Beth skated slowly and without joy. She skated, her head lowered against the wind, feeling cheated and deprived of the feeling she'd been expecting.

Famous star's daughter found dead in campus lake. She saw the headline, imagined the sensation. For everyone except her, of course. She wouldn't be around to enjoy it. Poor Shane, he'd never come up out of his bottle. And Karl . . . But she didn't want to think about Karl. Not tonight.

She blinked. It wasn't good, this ice. She knew what good ice was and this ice was bad. It had no depth to it. This ice could open up and swallow you. She cast her eyes over the lake, looking for proof of its weakness.

A vast crystallized shelf lay stretched about her. A wilderness of silence rang in her ears. Even the wind sounds were silent rushes of the force of nature rather than sporadic howls of confused velocity. Then for a moment even the air around her seemed to stop and she was caught in suspension, held there, a nonentity . . . a spirit floating above an endless sparkling landscape.

And then, she saw it. The break in the ice. It was midway across the lake. A ray of moonlight hit it, showing the waves lapping against the whiter lip of ice. It was all the reason she needed for getting out of there. Except there was a catch, as there almost always was in life, and that catch was a long object she had just spotted lying beside the break. It was a log or something. It couldn't be anything else, except . . . Except that down deep she knew it wasn't a log. It was that simple. She knew that the object was a girl, her long wool coat blowing slightly in the wind. Another skater, probably. Somebody like herself, stupid enough to skate over untested ice. Somebody who went out too far and freaked out when she saw that break. Somebody so scared, she'd just laid down, right where she was.

"Hello?" she yelled, her voice sounding too loud, scaring her. "Are you all right? Hello!" The wind blew wet and cold against her face. Snow, she thought numbly. It's snowing. "Hello!"

The girl lay silent, close to the water.

Beth wasn't going out there. It was too dangerous. She would go for help, but she wasn't going out there. She turned to go and couldn't, not until she'd answered the question that kept buzzing around in her head like a pesky insect. Was the girl freezing and if she waited to go for help would it be too late? Was it a question of minutes, seconds? If she didn't go out there and if the girl died, she'd never know if it was her fault. She felt a rush of anger. It wasn't fair that she was out here alone and that she had to risk her own life and that she was so painfully cold, so cold that the pain of it was almost unbearable. Damn the girl who was putting her through this.

She began to walk, feeling her way, fearing the blades of her skates. "Hello! Hello!" She could have sworn that somebody was listening to her. She could feel it and yet the silence was unbroken by human response. Her throat was aching from swallowing cold air. Could the girl be listening to her and not answering?

The ice cracked under the blade of her left skate. Shuddering, she jerked her foot up. A line of water bubbled up through the crack. She watched it trickle along the ice, creating a line of weakness. It was madness to be out here. And the further she went, the deeper the water, the greater the danger. Why had the girl gone out so far?

I'll never make it.

But she was so close, so damned close. She was not going to give up, now that she was so close. Quickly, trembling, she lowered herself onto the ice and began to crawl toward the girl, knives of pain stabbing through the palms of her hands, needles of pain pricking her whole body. The pain was worse than her fear.

And the fear was bad.

She blinked cold tears out of her eyes and squinted. There was something about the girl's coat, blowing open in the wind—why was the coat open? Why not buttoned up to the neck? The girl was close enough to touch now. Beth was positive that she recognized that coat. Dark plaid wool, with fur around the sleeves and neck. Oh, Jesus, she knew that coat.

"It's me," she whispered, trembling. "It's Beth. Are you okay?" The girl lay there, not moving. Not alive, Beth let herself think for the first time. She was afraid that the girl was dead. Violently, she took hold of the girl and began to shake her.

The moonlight shone thinly upon a blood-soaked dress.

Beth's hands slid slowly from the girl's body. She stared and then she turned her head to one side and began to vomit. She heaved for a full minute before she could begin to scream. The girl's head had been neatly severed from her throat. It bobbed up and down in the waves, sightlessly, silently, like a child's rubber ball, its blond hair wet and streaming over the water.

Beth turned away, her scream, high-pitched yet throaty, rising into the night like an evil vapor, its final choked note cut off in mid-tremble by a sudden rush of frigid air. Then all was silent.

Beth's heart raced in her chest as she moved away, tried to move away, crawling her way back to safety. Behind her the silence was broken by a harsh cracking of branches and the hasty shuffling of a form moving through the trees. Beth's body slackened as the last of her strength, her control, began to desert her.

The form of a man emerged suddenly from the trees. Beth turned, saw slivers of moonlight move across his face, saw the girl's head bob upright, eyes still open in a horrified gaze, saw blood frozen to her cheeks and the corners of her mouth, saw . . .

She reached out, fell. Saw nothing.

FIVE

The patient was dead. The organ was not.

Randelar had been informed. He was ready, gowned in white, masked, careful.

The youngest doctor, who seemed more boy than man but who possessed already some remarkable credentials said: "Fortunate, isn't it, that she was in the Control Group. Did she get both strains B and C? This is the girl, isn't it? My God, to think it happened to the one girl . . ."

Over his mask, Randelar's muddy-colored, deep-lined eyes glanced up briefly. He said merely, "Bring the basin."

The head O.R. nurse lifted her gloved hands, but before she could reach toward the indicated receptacle, Randelar's key assistant, Dyer, had lifted it himself. In the bright lights of the O.R., Dyer's fortyish, square-cut features were dead-white, almost corpselike. Over his mask, his eyes were exclamation points of caution. His hands on the soft pliable container were rock steady, gentle as a woman's.

"Sideways," Randelar murmured, "now move in under me."

Dyer grunted, his smaller, plumper body molded into Randelar's. The two men had been a team for almost fifteen years. After this amount of time together, they could almost read each other's minds. Randelar's motions were a split-beat ahead of Dyer's. This was Dyer's sole deference to Randelar's authority. *You first*, he seemed to say and at the same time he was watching. Always watching. As if someday, he would lead a team.

Absolute quiet was maintained then as the two doctors

worked as one, first in depositing the organ into the basin and then in rapid transference into its prepared environment case.

With his first show of nervousness, Randelar gestured questioningly toward the blood feeder.

"I typed her myself," Hamilton, the staff doctor said reassuringly. "Just to make certain. She was O positive. Some of her blood was still in the body. Frozen. We added it to our plasma supply."

Randelar nodded and attached the feeder.

Hamilton and Dyer stood aside until sterile isolation had been secured. Only then did Randelar speak.

"Close the skull," he said. "I have a meeting."

It was an unprepossessing room: an old desk, a few chairs, a row of books on the wall. The rug was still in the corner rolled up and tied with a cord.

The voices droned on. Coffee was spilled on the desk.

Yes, they had all been given strain B. Promising. But then without warning the cell structure had begun to collapse. Fatality seemed a definite possibility. Strain C was out of the question. Could not be administered.

"And yet," the man from Geneva said with some distaste, "strain C was, in fact, administered. Your own test clearly showed that." He paused to study his fingernails. "By whom?"

To that, no answer was given.

"Only this one girl?" he frowned. As though aware his question would again go unanswered, he said in his thick accent:

"An interesting coincidence, am I right, that this girl who was injected with strain C was . . ."

A smooth voice entered the conversation, placating him. Adding the necessary compliments. A pat on the back, a few words about the good work they were doing in Switzerland and, finally, somewhat mollified, the scientist from Geneva said:

"This strain C. Ah, it's too bad. There's no way of recalling it now that you've released it. The best you can hope for is a protective antiagent . . . We in Switzerland were more cautious, still . . ."

The American scientists asked him their questions, and then when he had gone, slunk from the room, they looked at each other. They knew the Geneva scientist wouldn't want to be bothered again. He was paranoid about American reporters.

In the heavy silence, Randelar voiced his opinion. He was calm, relaxed. "Strain C saved the organ. Endowed it with superhuman strength. We were afraid of strain C. But it was strain B that did the most damage. C strengthened." He paused for a moment, then chuckled.

"What's funny?"

"I was thinking of the tests we never administered. If the girl had been a rat or a dog or a monkey, we would have done so, but not to a human animal. Tests of cold, perhaps running with a heart thumping close to explosion. Tests of emotional control. Reaction perhaps to a secondary wound, even a third or fourth, before the mortal insult. Even sexuality. But someone administered those tests, after all, didn't they? In a way, didn't they? Of course, I don't suppose we'll ever find out the results. More to the point, I don't think we're likely to meet the—scientist?" He laughed wryly.

A pause and then a cold response. "We certainly didn't kill her, if that's what you're insinuating."

Randelar shrugged. "Well, the organ lived. That's all I need to know."

SIX

Somebody called, "Man in the house!"

A scream, bare feet running.

"Oh, Christ," somebody said. "Jennie's caught nude in the hall again."

"Did he get a good peek, Jennie?"

"Bet your ass he did."

"No, your ass. It's your ass he's thinking about now, Jennie."

"Oooh, that turns me on. It's too bad they sent those young Republicans home early. I haven't gotten laid since I've been in this nunnery."

"You're locked in tomorrow, Miss Dobbin!" snapped Fazio curtly, her voice revealing a thin line of hysteria under its military crispness. "As is the next young woman to interrupt the silence."

A frigid wall of blankness went down the corridor. "Shit," said a subdued voice, consoled by no one. Into the strained void, a low male voice uttered several terse words to which Fazio gave a little gasp. The man's voice rose, admonishing Fazio to calm herself and at once two sets of footsteps hurried down the corridor and disappeared echoingly into the stairwell. Silence born of caution maintained itself behind them.

"Thanks a hell of a lot for the support," Jennie snapped. "Although by the way, your silence is very revealing. Just as much as your speech. Remember—according to Swami Prabhavananda—"

"Take that book and ram it, Dobbin."

"Fuck you."

Fuck you, Vala Hayes repeated mentally from behind her closed door. It must be wonderful to vent oneself as easily as that: Fuck you.

Outside her door a delirium of sound—mad patterns of movement—approaches, retreats, doors slamming—giggles. Then silence.

Vala sighed and reached for the aspirin. (You've had enough, Vala. Fuck you, I'm having a bad night.) She popped three tablets and wondered who the man in the hall had been. He had spoken so low it was hard to make out his voice. Maybe Dr. Hamilton. If it was Dr. Hamilton who had caught Jennie nude, it wouldn't be quite so exciting as, say, if it was a plumber who wouldn't be so used to seeing naked bodies.

She wondered how it would feel to have a strange man looking at her with her body bare and vulnerable. At least she knew how she felt when the doctor looked at her during an examination. She hated that. But being caught naked in the hall would be worse. It bothered her that she was so modest, even after three months of dorm living.

Still she reminded herself that she was getting better, that she'd started running around in short nightgowns and she didn't blush now when she had to take a shower with the other girls. She'd changed in other ways too. From the awkward Vala whom nobody liked, from the oddity who had been almost out of another time, to an accessible girl, a girl who lived among other girls, a girl who had lost some of her self-consciousness.

A lot of it was due to Georgia and Beth. They had gotten to her. She had observed them and through her observations she had learned. She knew that they came from different worlds. Absolutely fascinating, sampling those worlds. Smoking Georgia's short unfiltered cigarettes, listening to Beth's stories about Hollywood, laughing at jokes she was just learning to understand. It was making a different girl out of her.

And yet . . .

Tonight. Like other nights, it still happened. Was still possible. She could feel the tension building, herself breaking into jagged pieces of raw nerves.

Calm down. You can handle it. You're just having a bad night. Fifteen years old, the youngest girl in the school, and having a bad night.

She ran her hand across her forehead. The wind-up clock

ticked loud and fast, having a nervous breakdown, no doubt. Ten o'clock, tick, tick, tick. She wasn't sweating like she'd thought, not on the outside.

It wasn't the worst of nights. No, not the worst. But bad enough.

She placed her hands flat on the desk. Dead white skin with blue veins on dark solid wood. She hated looking at veins. She looked at her desk instead, at books and pens and carved initials and her high school tassle hanging on the top knob. She remembered high school graduation as an almost meaningless experience. She hadn't gotten her full height yet. She was tiny among the graduates and the youngest girl in the class, barely twelve years old and even so, it was a laugh, everyone had said, that she was in the school at all. But she hadn't wanted to go away to a special school and she'd been right, because when they sent her to Yale on that special program right after graduation, it hadn't worked out. She'd had to come home. Nothing had worked for a while, not until she was fifteen and feeling stronger and then they'd heard about Triesius and all of a sudden she'd wanted to try again.

Now Vala cast a thoughtful glance at her English comp papers, all piled up. No A's, because Triesius didn't operate on the grading system. Just remarks, analysis. She flipped through the papers. You have a unique mind, Ms. Hayes. You have a remarkable way with words. A talent, if I may.

No, you may not, Professor Angusi. You wish you could, but you may not.

The way she thought—daydreamed?—about him was odd. So many times she had almost mentioned him to Beth and Georgia, just casually like when Beth was talking of Karl. And then would think: He has nothing to do with me, nothing. And could not say his name.

A curious man, Philip Angusi, she had thought more than once. His eyes made her anxious. Always fastened on her in the most intense way. It sometimes made her breathless, almost as though he had physically touched her. She was drawn to fantasize about what it would be like if he had, in fact, touched her. If he had perhaps stroked her hair or run his finger down the curve of her cheek. Once she had even imagined that his thin downcurved lips had brushed hers. She could hear herself sigh: Philip. It gave her an odd sick sensation.

Stay away from me, she had thought after that. Whenever

she saw him: Just keep your distance, Professor. Stay away.

And yet. She studied his hands. The nails were chewed down to the cuticles, just like hers. She noticed the pallor of his skin and wondered if, like herself, he had never had a suntan. She could feel his sadness, felt she knew it. Hadn't she experienced something similar her entire life?

And—yes, she was curious to know what it would be to hold him, that strange alone man, almost as alone as she herself.

But all the yeses did not add up to the noes. She knew she must stay away from Philip Angusi.

She pushed the papers away. Faces smiled at her. *Good girl, Vala.* Her mother in a silver frame. *Atta girl, Vala.* Her father, framed in black. *Don't let that professor get any wrong ideas.* She smiled at them because she loved them and she didn't want them to know she was having a bad night.

She pressed her hands firmly against the top of the desk. She had to keep reminding herself to keep her fingers outstretched so she wouldn't make fists. She sat there staring at them, at how suddenly relaxed they were.

She was handling tonight really well. Really well. Three months ago, it would have been—no, she would have been different. That first day. Headmistress LeSabre as she entered the room, her spike heels clicking on the marble floor. Her hair swept up and away from her face and her features delicate, clean and elegant.

"I'm the headmistress, Yvonne LeSabre, Vala. I wanted to welcome you personally, because we're especially honored that you decided to be with us."

Vala had stared into the grey eyes thinking, but you don't know how alone I am. So terribly alone.

Now just thinking about it made her feel a little sick in the pit of her stomach. Her right fingers crawled toward her palm, but she was in control. No, you don't. No fists, no screaming, no crying. She'd really made an ass of herself that first night. Cried until she'd made herself sick and then she'd had the dry heaves in the john for an hour with strange girls staring at her.

Later, washing her face in the sink, she lost her left contact lens down the drain and had to wear glasses her first week, orientation week. The school had presented her with a new one and an extra pair as a backup.

Poor girl, thought Vala, thinking about that girl as if she were someone quite separate from herself. Vala, the homesick girl. Thin brown hair, blue eyes, white skin. Who hated to be seen in bright sunshine. Who had a terrible sense of direction and got lost on the grounds of Triesius. Who never smiled in the beginning. No, never smiled.

All at once a draft of cold air blew across Vala's neck. She got up and shut the window. December the fifth, she thought, and as cold as Christmas. Something in the air when it blew as cold as this reminded her of a land she had never seen. Piercing, pure in its cold brutality. She pictured herself at the heart of a polar storm. Stepping barefoot, virginal, naked from a safe warm cocoon into a mound of icy whiteness. Being taken swiftly, totally, into frozen infinity.

Lord, it was cold. Beth could get some skating in finally. Even in the midst of her isolation, the casualness of the thought struck her with reassuring warmth. If only her father and mother could see her now, she thought. In the middle of a real friendship. Two friendships, she reminded herself with some amazement, thinking of Georgia. The fact that she was relating to other girls, reaching out as much as she could, meant that she was improving and if her mother could only see her, she'd see how adjusted, how very well adjusted she really was.

Although there were times when the panic came back, when her mind turned dark and she couldn't make it light again and her chest would get so tight, she couldn't breathe, couldn't get the air down far enough. It will pass, she'd learned to tell herself. And it did. Only tonight it was taking longer than she knew it should.

"I'm sick," she said out loud, totally surprising herself. "I'm really sick." She hadn't even known she was thinking it. Way back in her mind. Her complex mind. Sick, physically sick. The glands and the throwing up and the tiredness. Maybe she had an ulcer. Maybe she had mononucleosis. And the way she looked. Too thin, too white, too baggy-under-the-eyes. And the rash. Maybe the rash was the measles or something, instead of nerves, like she'd imagined. Another thought. It would also explain the infirmary, why they kept calling her back for more and more tests. They knew something was wrong with her too. She had a right to feel bad. She was sick and it had nothing at all to do with nerves. She felt suddenly and joyously triumphant, giddy in her relief.

It was at this high and powerful moment in her psyche that a knock sounded on her door. It was Fazio, a weeping and slightly hysterical Fazio, wearing a grey robe, a pink hairnet incongruously atop her silver hair. The woman pushed her way into the room blindly, breathing panic.

"Vala," she stammered. "It's . . . I'm—"

"Yes?"

"I'm afraid . . ."

Other girls now pressed into the room behind Fazio and awaited her final pronouncement. It had been a grand summoning, herself the last to be called. Vala could feel the air leave her lungs as Fazio said:

"It's Carmel Ritchie. She's dead." The woman hesitated and then added, "Beth Allen just found her body."

SEVEN

Beth was on a sandy beach tossing a golden ball back and forth with Vala. Both girls wore blue string bikinis and the sun was blazing high in the sky but the ocean was frozen.

"Why is the ocean frozen?" Beth asked, throwing the golden ball.

"Water freezes at thirty-two degrees Fahrenheit," Vala answered as the ball floated into her hands. "Or at least that's the theoretical point. In actuality, experiments have proven it impossible to freeze water, especially sea water, at so high a temperature. Unless, of course, the water is in contact with ice." Vala tossed the ball.

"But the sun is shining," Beth said.

"Only on the outside," said Vala. "On the inside, it's below zero."

Someone tapped Beth on the shoulder. "Pardon me," said Carmel Ritchie, who wasn't wearing a head. "As soon as you finish tossing my head around, I'd like to have it back."

Beth reached up and caught the golden ball by the roots of its hair. "Why, certainly," she said. "I have to go anyway. I'm going to ice skate on the ocean."

Pinpoints of light penetrated her eyelids and Beth floated up a level of reality. Some functioning observer inside her mind knew that she'd been heavily drugged. What a strange dream, she thought groggily, keeping her eyes closed. Carmel's head being tossed back and forth like a . . . Something inside of her hesitated. What was it about Carmel's head that she was trying to remember, trying to forget all at the same time?

"Has she come out of it yet?" asked a woman's voice and a man said, "No, not yet. Soon."

Beth wondered what she was supposed to be coming out of. What kind of drug? Colors seeped through her flickering eyelashes as she smelled a familiar musky fragrance and knew that the woman had moved closer to the bed. "You're awake now, aren't you?" the voice asked persuasively.

Obediently, Beth opened her eyes. Two out-of-focus faces stared down unblinkingly at her. Drowsily she fell back into grey blankness, but a hand was rubbing her shoulder and a voice kept saying something and finally, she tried again, propped her eyes open and this time a cameo face appeared clearly inches away from her face.

Headmistress LeSabre was looking at her with deceptively soft grey eyes. She was saying something about shock. Dr. Hamilton's face appeared beside her, nodding, and he added something about a sedative, and all Beth could think about was whether or not LeSabre was having an affair with Dr. Hamilton. It was somehow strange to think of LeSabre having an affair with any man. There was something about her of castrating razor-blade sharpness in back of the calculated softness.

"How do you feel?" asked LeSabre, looking so cool and well put together as to make Beth struggle back toward her own well-being.

She opened her mouth, but it felt swollen and numb, and she closed it again. Her body felt heavy and weak and everything was too much of an effort, yet there was something she had to ask about, if she could only remember . . .

"Are you thirsty?" asked Dr. Hamilton, his eyes evasive somehow.

"Yes," she said fuzzily. "I'm so thirsty." Experimentally, she moved her tongue up and down. It felt numb too and enormous, but some of the sensation was coming back, bringing with it a bitter nauseating taste.

An arm was supporting her neck, a straw was put between her lips and she drew in cool water. She wanted buckets of water; water to pour over her body, to rinse out her mouth with, to gargle with, to saturate her dry inner tissues with. But she was allowed only a tiny sip, was made to rest, another sip, rest, when she was really desperate for at least one big satisfying swallow. She tried to reach out and hold the glass. She was too weak. LeSabre's well enunciated, almost musical, voice kept telling her that she could have all she wanted, but just a little at a time. Finally exhausted and nauseous, she could take no more and lay back on her pillow, tears welled up in her eyes.

"Don't cry," said LeSabre, running a long thin hand through Beth's tangled hair. Shudders ran through the girl's body in spasms. "Why are you crying?" insisted LeSabre, her lips shimmering with gloss, her slender fingers untangling the girl's waistlong brown hair.

Suddenly the faded picture in Beth's mind dropped into focus and she came into full dizzy consciousness. She gave a gasp that came from the depths of her interior. "Who would do such a terrible thing?" she said fiercely, clutching at LeSabre's wrist, her fingernails making vivid red slashes on smooth perfect skin. LeSabre paid no attention to either pain or blemish. Her eyes were fastened on Dr. Hamilton, who was making a note on Beth's chart, seemingly absorbed in his own thoughts.

"What terrible thing?" asked LeSabre softly, still staring at Dr. Hamilton.

"As . . . as to murder . . . as to kill . . ." stammered Beth, but LeSabre was already saying no, she was wrong, Carmel Ritchie had fallen on the lake, been knocked unconscious and had died of exposure.

"A terrible fateful accident," went on LeSabre, sighing delicately, a caution light flickering in back of her eyes.

"It's something we have to help you deal with, Beth." Dr. Hamilton looked up for the first time."The shock of finding her like that."

Beth's wide-open eyes were disbelieving and then blank as the world turned upside down. She fell once again into a deep stupor of sleep.

EIGHT

It was now Saturday, December sixth, and the town of Rosemont was quiet. Only the wind swirled through the hedges and trees, compelling them to bend to its will.

Harlan Tyler St. John, Chairman of the Triesius Board of Directors, sat back in his silver-grey Rolls and waited for the chauffeur to open his door. That he was disinclined to open his own door indicated that he had put himself under the discipline of patience.

"Here you are, sir," murmured the familiar face under the visored cap.

The man had been driving for him for over a month, St. John thought idly. He really should make an effort to put a name to that face . . . instead the Chairman stepped briskly from the car with a word of murmured thanks and made his way up the courtyard steps.

On the second floor, he turned right and tapped on the first door. James DeWitt, Head Councilman of the Town of Rosemont, answered the door himself. He was nervous as shit, the Chairman noted with matter-of-fact disgust and smiled.

"So how are you, young friend? Tell me."

Jimmy seized on the opportunity for small talk. The Chairman listened. It was his job to listen. He had come to talk with DeWitt about the taboo subject and now it was just a matter of waiting around until Jimmy's fine sweat subsided and he could tolerate speaking about something that, to his mind, was at least unorthodox and possibly criminal.

The Chairman sat relaxed, his legs crossed, a two-dollar Jamaican cigar between his teeth, a sympathetic smile hovering around his full sensuous lips, and let Jimmy rattle nervously on about the Mayor's press conference last Wednesday, the Landmark Preservation Committee and cutbacks in education allocation. The latter made him stutter because education was too close to what he didn't want to talk about. His voice cracked, he slowed, he couldn't look into the Chairman's eyes, then he stopped. The Chairman puffed appreciably at his cigar and let the silence continue until he saw Jimmy's shoulders rise and fall in a resigned shrug and the tension slide moodily out of his body.

"Jimmy," he sighed gently, "why are you so hard on yourself? Always asking yourself, 'Did I do this right?' 'Did I do this wrong?' 'What if somebody finds out I did this?' It's no good, Jimmy, running through life like a scared rabbit. If you want to get somewhere, you have to dare to fail, don't you see?"

Jimmy's thin face, pale to the roots of its eyelashes, was suddenly devoid of expression. "Is that how you think of me, Harlan? A scared rabbit," he mused softly and the Chairman raised his hands placatingly toward the heavens.

"You misunderstand me," he said smiling; a transition smile. He remembered how long it had taken him to bring Jimmy to a first-name basis and away from the dumb respect of "Mr. Chairman." Perhaps he should have left well enough alone. "It's just that this Triesius thing," he continued warmly, "has made you nervous from the beginning and I feel guilty because it was my choice to involve you. I'll be honest, Jimmy, it didn't have to be you. You didn't have to be in on it. But if Triesius turns out the way I think it may, it could be good for you. Good politically. If it works . . ."

"Good press?" smiled Jimmy bitterly.

"Controversial press. It'll help you start developing your political image. Right now, you see, you're a political blur." The Chairman smiled to take the sting out of his words and Jimmy couldn't help smiling back because he liked Harlan St. John and because he needed him if he was ever going to be able to climb. Harlan was the goods and if Harlan said he was a blur, he was a blur.

The phone rang and Jimmy reached for it, overturning a tarnished silver cup filled with pencils, pens, erasers and paper clips. "Damn."

The Chairman shook his head wryly and settled back comfortably in his uncomfortable chair. He had the knack for being comfortable anywhere, whether in a hard chair or in an awkward situation, and it gave him the edge over others who from time to time turned up with stiff backs and tension headaches. He was also at ease in his life as one who has found just the exact niche he is best suited to fill. His was an amiable low-key personality and he was one of life's likable victors. He was also an attractive victor, perhaps a little too much so. The men called him a man's man and the women whispered, panting, that he was an animal. He had had to take care to never get caught in the wrong woman's bed. It was hard sometimes; he had a sensuous nature and was attracted to intelligent beautiful women, some of whom were dangerous.

He stirred restively and Jimmy's eyes now jerked in his direction. Harlan St. John smiled, radiating calmness and optimism. Jimmy had been handpicked to help with the project because Jimmy was a small fish and controllable. If this Triesius thing blew up on them, they'd need a goat to throw to the press and Jimmy was it. In the meantime, Jimmy had to be coddled and hand-held and lied to and, above all, he had to have his strings pulled—his mouth strings and his hand strings and his morality strings. For that purpose, the Chairman now sat in Jimmy's cramped office, sipping not-so-terrific coffee out of a styrofoam cup, flicking expensive cigar ashes into an overflowing ashtray while Jimmy answered his own phone because he shared a secretary with three other men down the hall, spilled coffee on his tie and lost his temper with an outraged consumer.

"Ah, Jimmy," sighed Harlan, seeing that his young friend had slammed down the phone. "That could have been a vote you just hung up on."

"Damned woman deserves to be hung up on," said Jimmy, mopping at his tie with a crumbling Kleenex. "Maybe if more people would hang up on her, she'd stop being that way."

"What way is that?" asked the Chairman, handing Jimmy a snow-white handkerchief from his suit pocket, which Jimmy distractedly pressed against coffee stains and handed back again, crumpled with brown streaks.

"The way she is!" snapped Jimmy. "Concerned consumer, my hind foot! She's just looking for a platform to raise hell on and a schnook's ear to raise it in and I wasn't in any mood to be the schnook. Accurate feedback, that's what I gave her." He reddened suddenly. "Sorry, sir, I . . ."

The Chairman laid the handkerchief on the edge of the desk next to a withered plant. "Is it woman trouble, Jimmy? Is that what's the matter with you today?"

Mutely Jimmy shook his head, shifting his eyes to gaze out the window. Tiredly he wished that he had a secretary who answered phones, that he had some of the Chairman's savvy and that he could start taking life a little less seriously. Maybe then he wouldn't feel that raw burning spot at the bottom of his stomach that hinted ulcer like a flashing red warning light.

"So it is woman trouble."

"Hardly."

"Jimmy, we're friends. We can lay it on the line to each other. Am I right?"

Jimmy shook his head.

"Is it the divorce, is that it? I was deeply sorry to hear about that."

"Oh, don't be sorry. Monica's having a wonderful life. She's vacationing in St. Martin's just now. Jogging on the beach. Bathing in the salty surf. I wish to hell I had her life. Although I'm thinking of upgrading my life in that direction. As much as I can afford, that is. I'm thinking of buying myself a sunlamp."

"Don't be bitter."

"Being bitter," Jimmy said without rancor, "is the only luxury I can afford." He forced a chuckle.

"I'll give you some advice," the Chairman said gently. "The least you can do is take care of yourself. You don't mind my saying so, you look a little, well . . ."

"Seedy?" Jimmy filled in. With delayed self-consciousness, he ran his hand through his hair.

"The idea of the sunlamp," the Chairman shrugged, "is not half bad. A few pushups, a massage. Life is better up here . . ." he tapped his head, "when you stay physical."

"I'll try. I'm sorry to—it's just . . . it's not easy."

"Don't take it so hard. The truth is, perhaps marriage is not such a good thing. I've noticed it seems to change people."

"It sure changed Monica. She had a nervous breakdown or something. One night she swallowed a bottle of aspirin. That was the first night I knew there was anything wrong. It cost me thousands of dollars to a psychiatrist to find out it was my fault she swallowed the aspirin. That's how big a headache I was giving her."

"That's a goddamn shame," the Chairman said sympathetically.

The two men sat silent for a moment, absently nodding their heads.

"About this Triesius thing," Jimmy said at length.

The Chairman raised his eyebrows, kindly permitting the question.

Jimmy exploded suddenly and without warning. "Have you read the goddamn newspapers this morning, Harlan? Not a word about the murder, for Chrissakes. Not one word. Then you come here and you don't say a word about it. I thought that's why you were here. It's like it never happened. How do you keep something like that out of the newspapers?" He slapped the back of his hand against the newspaper spread open on top of his desk. For the first time he looked directly into the Chairman's eyes. "How in the name of . . ."

"An accident," said the Chairman softly, blowing smoke toward the ceiling.

Slowly Jimmy sat back, feeling his blood chill. "Harlan, I saw the girl. I was there last night speaking, remember? The girl was lying on the ice decapitated. Do you understand what I'm saying to you? I mean, it was the worst-looking thing I ever saw and she used to be an attractive girl . . ."

"It was an accident," repeated the Chairman regretfully, looking into Jimmy's eyes.

"But her parents—"

"It's all been taken care of. The girl is being flown back to Salt Lake City, where she will be buried in a closed casket on Monday." The Chairman sighed and rose to his feet. "Like the casket, Jimmy, the matter is closed."

Jimmy stared back for a long time and then slowly, carefully, he nodded.

It was then that the older man began to talk very earnestly, stressing how important it was that Triesius continue its valuable work, and what a fine opportunity it was for Jimmy to be affiliated with Triesius. In fact, the Chairman was now suggesting that Jimmy's ties with Triesius be strengthened and it was even possible that he would be chosen as the figurehead sponsor for the school. In that regard, he would henceforth be speaking almost weekly at Triesius. The way it was all said indicated plainly that the Chairman thought Jimmy was a lucky son-of-a-bitch and when all was said and done, it gave Jimmy a little thrill to be getting on such a personal basis with a man like Harlan Tyler St. John. Just being with him was a step in the right direction. Yes, if things worked out the way he thought they could, Triesius was going to be the best thing that ever happened to him.

After the Chairman had gone—lint carefully brushed from sleeves, tie straightened, his footsteps crisp and measured in the hallway—Jimmy sat silently behind his desk. He felt nothing. The momentary excitement was gone, evaporated in the absence of Harlan St. John. The emptiness inside him now was vast, too deep to explore.

For a moment, he tried to summon up the image of Monica and the kids. Even the pain would be better than this emptiness. But the image was incomplete, boring, and he whispered, "So that's how far we've come, Monica."

His mouth twisted strangely. He wondered if he was smiling. He had thought of something that pleased him. Getting his body back in shape, the way the Chairman had suggested. Pushups, sweat, his body hardening, defining itself. The image lingered in his mind in a pleasing way.

He sat back in his chair and closed his eyes. He was seeing himself, hard and lean from exercise, tanned from a sunlamp, walking toward a tall blond young woman.

"Georgia," he whispered. Georgia Urie. He knew her as he knew all the girls at Triesius. He had seen her photograph countless times. Now he strained to see her in his mind's eye.

She came toward him, smiling and holding out both hands.

Nine

It is a curious psychological fact that a sufficiently strong mental image will bring with it a proportionate physical force. That's the way Carmel Ritchie's death had hit Georgia. First mentally—the image was blond whiteness on ice—then physically. Her whole body ached.

The ache wasn't—it certainly wasn't—grief. She and Carmel had enjoyed a mutual dislike for each other. What she felt was more pain in the center of her being, a morbid sense that it was she who had died, and a taste of truth as to who she was to the world. Nobody, that's who she was. A big zero. And if it had been her body they had found last night, not many people would really care. One mother, one father, two brothers. Two new friends. And a partridge in a pear tree. Oh God.

She knew, of course, why it was hitting her so hard. Because she and Carmel had had a common factor. Threads of beauty, threads of gold. Threads that wear out. Snap. Georgia's lip curled scornfully. She'd never been one of those beautiful girls who believed it was going to last forever. She'd always been sensitive to time passing, always known that from bassinet to ashes happened fast, too fast (but sometimes she thought not charitably fast enough). So she had never been one to flaunt youth and beauty the way Carmel used to, and thank God, because there was something about that that was really sickening. Always with the hairbrush in the hand, the toilet paper between the toes so as not to smear the freshly applied polish on the toenails. That image now filled her mind and she stood chewing on her lip, forgetful of her surroundings.

"May I help you?" The voice was not in the least helpful, but annoyed.

Georgia stared coolly across the reserve desk into the eyes of the male librarian. He was stuffy, adenoidal. Very much in the Mr. Belvedere genre. Asexual, thank God. At least, he had that much going for him.

"A week from Monday," she said, "I am supposed to speak aloud for one hour on the subject of the physiological development of man and how this relates to his mental and social evolution."

"Um," the librarian said with cold fish eyes.

"I would like three easy volumes on the physiological aspect, one on archaeological history, and two conflicting volumes on evolution with the emphasis on scientific versus religious."

"It isn't that easy," stated the librarian with satisfaction.

"Shit," she said. "That sounded easy?"

"You see," he said, "everything is always intermingled."

"Isn't it always?"

"What did you say—mental and social evolution?"

"Yes. You know, from an ape to an ape."

"You could spend a lifetime just on theory."

"I have a week, but then I'm bright."

He lost all interest. "Start in the back section, in the 1100 series. There's at least a hundred books to get you started."

"Thanks," she said. "You've been a big help." A big fucking help, she repeated silently, heading for Section F. Casually she scooped an armload of books from the shelf and dumped them on the table.

One of the books was of captioned photographs. She thumbed through. Stopped on a stark white landscape. Bare. Its icy sameness went on and on. A simulation of how it used to be.

The chill factor in evolution. The deadly ice. Towering prehistoric creatures flashed before her eyes. Seemingly indestructible and then—ice. She closed her eyes.

Froze to death, she thought. It should have been me. That would have been very appropriate. Me freezing to death. She could imagine the comments: Did you hear Georgia Urie froze to death? No kidding. Well, I always said she was as frigid as a witch's twat, but I never thought it would kill her. Amen, brother. Amen.

Georgia tried to concentrate on the evolution of man. First

there was a cell. No, first there was an atmospheric, circumstantial plane of energy that was hospitable. She sighed.

From simple to complex, that was evolution, revolution. A simple discontent that grew strong enough to tempt an apeman to deal with it. An action more easily done. A lifting of the head, of the arms, the torso. Development. Let's hear it for the thumb, the wheel, the tongue, the bomb. Let's hear it for oblivion.

Georgia glanced up. Where the hell was everybody tonight? Oh, Saturday, right, with the bus making its usual round trip to Rosemont, but even so there should be more action than this. There were usually at least half a dozen resident bookworms. But tonight, no one. It was cold, that was it. So goddamn cold. She couldn't get Carmel Ritchie out of her mind. Who would have ever pictured a girl as hot as Carmel freezing to death?

Moments later she stood at the counter waiting to check out her books (she certainly couldn't work in this deserted tomb) when she looked back to see Vala. Vala sat alone at the last table staring absently into space. She had apparently materialized from nowhere. Soundlessly.

Georgia shook her head at the dazed expression on Vala's face. Now what? she wondered with helpless concern.

She had accompanied Vala to the infirmary earlier that day in an effort to pay Beth a visit only to be told "No visitors . . . She's in shock . . ." and a few other words that added up roughly to "get lost."

On the verge of leaving, Vala had stopped and turned back to face the nurse.

"Can Doris Encoda have visitors?"

The nurse frowned. "Who?"

"Doris Encoda. I heard she was brought here this morning. E-N-C-O-D-A. Encoda."

Hesitating in the hallway, the nurse glanced back toward the offices, then at Vala. "Oh, yes, I remember," she answered belatedly, as though the infirmary had a thousand patients. "No. No, Doris can't have visitors. She's contagious. Flu."

"What were her symptoms?" Vala asked, a slight but suddenly immovable object.

"Ah—" The nurse shifted her gaze to Georgia, who moved closer to Vala, now rather interested. "Glands, I think. Fever. The usual sort of thing."

"Did she have a rash?"

The nurse shrugged, having apparently remembered she was under no obligation to answer questions. "No rash," she threw over her shoulder, disappearing.

But Georgia said, "Yes, she did have a rash, Vala. Jennie said so. She's getting one too and she's worried she caught something from Doris. Why?"

Vala's hand had wandered to her throat. She turned an exhausted face downward until she stared at the floor.

"Why?" Georgia repeated.

Vala shook her head. "You're too much like the Walendas," she said with the ghost of a chuckle. "You'd think nothing of telling the whole campus to go to hell and you'd do it all without a safety net."

Georgia turned to stare at her. "What's that supposed to mean?"

"It means . . ." Vala hesitated, her eyes still studying the tiled floor, "that I'll tell you later. When I'm sure. Listen, I . . . I'll see you tonight. Okay?" And she had been gone before Georgia could add another word to this rather remarkable conversation. She had watched Vala go, almost running, her feet awkward and flat in her cheap tennis shoes, her hair thin flying wisps.

Poor strange little Mouse, Georgia now thought and began backtracking in Vala's direction.

Vala, however, was no longer alone. Opposite her, leaning over the table, was Angusi, the comp and languages professor.

"Tomorrow then, at four," he was saying and Vala said, "Yes, all right," in a voice that struggled to be indifferent.

Deliberately Georgia edged closer. Angusi seemed to feel her eyes boring into the back of his head. Swiftly, he turned and nodded.

"Good evening, Miss Urie," he said in even tones.

"Good evening, Professor," she said acidly. She waited until he was at the door before saying, "I went back to the infirmary. Beth can't see anyone until Monday at the earliest."

Vala nodded. "I know. I called twice."

"Oh."

Both girls remained silent for a moment. Vala twisted uneasily in her chair. Finally she sighed deeply and said, "Professor Angusi . . . he's—"

"Be careful of that man, Vala," Georgia interrupted.

Vala's neck turned red. "What do you mean?"

"Oh, come on, Vala," Georgia whispered affectionately. "I see the way he looks at you in class. And did you see him now? His book marker was twitching, for God's sake." The color continued to work its way upward into Vala's face and Georgia grinned sympathetically. "Just be careful, that's all."

Vala, totally embarrassed, pretended not to understand. Fixedly, she eyed several of the girls just entering the library.

"Well, anyway," Georgia said letting her off the hook, "want to go for a milkshake?"

"I would, but I need to do some reading."

Georgia glanced down at the books stacked neatly in front of Vala. The top volume was a large expensive book on DNA. Its author was Alan Randelar.

"Randelar," Georgia began enthusiastically. "Did he write that recently? I'd like to take a look at it when you—"

"It's an old book," Vala said swiftly. "And not very interesting. But after his seminar, I was interested in reading about . . ." She hesitated, but continued with a slight reluctance. ". . . *E. coli.*"

Georgia nodded. "I found that interesting too. That a bacterium can crossbreed . . . that's like a cat mating with a canary. Of course, my excitement abated when I found that for the most part we were talking about achieving mutations in the corn plant. I mean, I'm truthfully not into corn that much. A nice asparagus, maybe . . ."

Vala smiled, but her earnestness, if anything, increased. "Why didn't you take the laboratory tour?" she asked.

Georgia shrugged. "I'm squeamish about experiment animals. I couldn't face being taken around a bunch of cages of desperate abused animals."

"Oh. There weren't any."

"Then I guess the corn mutants haven't progressed to monkey mutants. Thank God."

"I guess not. But then they didn't let us see all that much."

"Was *E. coli* used in the original corn plant experiment?"

"DNA carried by *E. coli*," Vala nodded. "The first experiment took place in the late 1960s," she said, glancing at the book. "They found that the high mutation rates were definitely due to the insertion of large segments of DNA. They were able to label four main blocks of insertion sequences. The genes that were affected became unstable and produced mutants."

"Good God," Georgia said lightly, "if they were doing that in the '60s, can you imagine what they can do now?"

Vala glanced up, unexplainable fear written all over her expressive white face. Then she tore her eyes away, focusing her energy on the stack of waiting books. "I've really got to read for a while," she mumbled.

"Okay. Well . . ."

"Georgia?"

"Yeah?"

"Do you remember any other symptoms?"

Georgia stared at her. "What?"

"Doris Encoda. Did Jennie say if it was anything other than a rash? I mean, were there any other—ah, changes . . ."

"Why?" frowned Georgia. "Listen, are you sick?"

"No. No, I was just—I was wondering, that's all."

"She only mentioned the rash. That's all I know about."

Vala nodded and lapsed back into her own thoughts.

"Hey, are you sure you're all right?" Georgia asked.

"Oh, sure—I'm fine."

"Well . . . goodnight then." Georgia hesitated and then made her way to the door.

All the way back to quarters, trailing in the wake of a trio of laughing girls, Georgia found herself thinking of Vala. Vala who seemed to be wandering in a barren time warp. Limp, defenseless, awkward Vala who was at the same time strangely appealing, eager. Struggling to be free. Georgia decided that anyone who struggled to be free was worthwhile. She shuddered suddenly as a gust of wind penetrated her coat and hastened her steps. By the time she reached the dorm, she was breathless.

Continuing her quick pace, she passed Fazio at the front desk and ran lightly up the one flight of steps. She was almost to her door when the phone rang at the far end of the hallway.

"Phone, Georgia," Jennie Dobbin said. She giggled. "He sounds sexy."

"Oh, Christ," Georgia said, grabbing the phone away from Jennie. "Hello."

"Georgia Urie?" said the man's voice in her ear.

"Yes?"

"Who is he?" whispered Jennie. "What does he look like?"

"Get lost, will you?" Georgia hissed. "Hello?"

Silence.

"Hello?" Georgia repeated, watching Jennie duck into her room in a huff.

"You ran away from me last night. Is that the game we're playing?"

Georgia's brows grew together. She could feel her thought process slow as it always did when she was zeroing in on something. "Listen, creep—"

"Did you say creep?" A hollow laugh came over the wire.

"That's right, creep," she said rudely. "Now if you don't mind . . ."

"I take it by your attitude that you don't wish to make it? Is that it?"

"Geez, you're fast."

"The joke's on you, sweetheart. I'll hang up now, but I want to leave you with something to think about. Sort of a riddle."

About to slam down the receiver, Georgia hesitated. Goddamn curiosity, she realized.

"Here's the riddle then. On the subject of making it . . . in a sense, we already have." The voice was odd and raspy, she noted mechanically. She quickly tried to determine his age. An older man? No, about thirty. The truth was, she wasn't sure. "Tell me," he went on, "was it good for you?" He laughed as though he'd made a funny and very private joke. Then a breathless whisper: "Give us a goodnight kiss, all right?"

"God, you're sick, did you—"

The soft sound of kissing interrupted her. She jerked the phone away from her ear as though she had been personally violated. Then as the man began moaning obscenities, she slammed the receiver onto the hook.

A moment later she sat slumped on her bed full of self-loathing because there had to be something wrong with her to have attracted such a man.

It wasn't until hours later, after she had taken two sleeping tablets, after she had crawled into bed, after she had fallen into a deep sleep, that she awoke suddenly in a profuse sweat and wondered how her caller had known her name. And what did he mean—that in a sense they'd already made it?

It wasn't until that precise moment that her feeling of being vaguely sick turned to fear.

TEN

Beth awoke slowly, trying to block dream fragments from her memory. She felt curiously sodden and, from the quality of the light, she was unable to determine what time it was. She glanced out the window. The tops of the trees were white, but that was all she could see. Just twisted bony-white fingers pointing at her.

"Where's Shane?" she croaked. Was that her voice? The nurse came to her bedside. "My . . . father. Where is my father?"

The young nurse pointed toward a huge cream-colored vase. It contained roses—dozens of them.

"Is . . . is he coming?" Beth asked, too exhausted to lift her head.

"There's no need." The nurse flashed a smile. "You're fine. Just fine."

"Did he call?"

"Oh, he certainly did. Rest now."

"But . . ." Beth could feel her eyes begin to close. ". . . but he always . . ."

She slept. A spacey narcotic sleep. She went in and out of it, hardly able to distinguish consciousness from unconsciousness. Thoughts drifted across her mind and dropped off the edge. Something was wrong. A face. She was trying to see a face, but the face was always in shadows watching her and, yes, there was something about that face that was very familiar. *Forget it. Don't try to remember.*

Shining needles glinted in the bedside light. She was rolled this way and that as deft fingers gave painless shots in either hips or upper arms.

Why am I being punished?

Beside the bed there was a silver stand holding an upside-down bottle which released regulated drips of glucose into her vein. The needle in her wrist held her prisoner.

"Let me help you to the bathroom. Walk. Lean on me."

She leaned on a blue-uniformed shoulder as she shuffled back and forth from bed to bathroom to bed. The machine was wheeled beside her. A rattling stainless steel ball and chain.

"Easy now," murmured the nurse. "Easy."

Beth was angry. She was very angry. Her hands curled into helpless little fists and she rained feathery blows into the mattress. Shane. When Shane found out what they were doing to her, he'd take her away from this place. Away from Triesius.

A hand slipped under her head; cool water was spooned past her parched lips. A moment later, a needle was slipped into her arm and she cried out, not because of pain but from fear of the darkness that was descending upon her once again.

Sometimes in her sleep, she whispered the name "Karl" and then a certain face wandered across the movie screen of her mind. She smiled to herself when she saw that quiet face with the straight nose and the eyes that were the color of faded denim and that little quirk in the corner of his mouth that reminded her how wonderful life could be. That face was somehow dearer to her than she had ever realized. The face crinkled its eyes at her and, smiling, slid out of her mind. She wept to see it go.

Time passed—how much she couldn't begin to calculate. How many hours, or was it days . . . no, it couldn't be that long . . . how many bottles of glucose made up a day? She woke up; she sipped water or sometimes clear broth or tea; she slept. How long had it been? As long as a whole day? Longer?

Usually someone was with her when she woke up—sometimes the nurse and sometimes Dr. Hamilton or LeSabre. She couldn't understand why LeSabre was there so often. Why did she matter so much to LeSabre? She was fascinated with LeSabre's mouth. She stared at it through a narrow center of white with black walls around it. Ripe red lips. Glossy wet lips.

As if they'd been dipped into a glosspot of blood. Sometimes when LeSabre was lost in thought, she would roll her lips outward like the beak of a bird.

"The operation's beginning," whispered a voice at the door and LeSabre turned sharply and disappeared.

I don't need an operation, thought Beth, fighting her way up from the depths of the drug. An unreasoning fear hit her. They wanted her mind. What else could it be? It was her brain they were operating on. Don't let them do it, Shane, she cried out silently. Don't let them take my mind away. The walls of black closed in. There was only a glimmer of light. She fought to stay awake, knowing that, when she slept, they would perform a lobotomy because . . . why? Because they thought she knew something, something she shouldn't know. What?

"I won't tell," she whispered, tears slipping down her face. "I promise I won't tell."

The darkness was too seductive and she slept and dreamed that she was walking through a white room, vast and empty, except for a glass table beside a huge window. Upon the table was a goldfish bowl with fish inside it swimming to and fro and nibbling on their food. She walked closer because she wanted to see the pretty goldfish. Her footsteps rang as she walked across the marble floor, the kind of bigger-than-life sound that footsteps make in a movie. She felt as if she were in a movie and that people were watching her. She smiled for the cameras as she reached the goldfish bowl.

LeSabre appeared suddenly from a dark doorway, her lips red and huge and grotesquely distorted. She was laughing. Other voices laughed too and then she saw Dr. Hamilton. His pipe was clenched between his short white teeth, his lips twisted in mirth. Behind him stood four men in white, one of whom was holding a blood-covered scapel. All of them were laughing.

Beth turned and stared down into the murky water. The fish—they weren't goldfish at all. They were piranha and the food they were devouring was her brain.

She tried to scream but no sound came. She watched in confusion as the pulsating organ floated in the water, the fish thrashing around it, their voracious mouths and teeth ripping it to pieces. She placed her hand to her forehead and found it had been sliced neatly across. That was the way they had left it when they scooped out her brain. Now at last she could make a sound. She screamed.

The night was especially black with the merest glimmer of moon. It reminded Randelar how intensely tired he was. Sleep was no longer in his schedule. He slept only when he was overcome with fatigue, wherever he happened to be. Tonight it was in the faculty dining room at the dome.

He had eaten quickly, his senses reeling, the food barely palatable, the coffee too weak. From the others around him, faculty and researchers, flew the usual pesky questions, as annoying as a swarm of insects one cannot brush away. Sometimes Randelar wondered if there would ever come a time when just one human being in the world, only one, would approach him without the word "genetics" puckering at the lips. Even in the middle of all-night sessions, one or the other of his researchers would come, most likely Dyer, his partner for years now, and the topic was genetics by the light of the overhead gooseneck lamp. Sometimes there was an open bottle of whiskey between them. Always the same. Mouse embryos and the insulin gene in skin cells and the work of Illmensee and Hoppe.

The question came now from the table to his right: "Can we alter the genetic code of a human being?" He had no idea who had asked it. At the table were four faculty members, none of whose names he had bothered to learn. Numb with exhaustion, he heard himself begin to answer in the dull lay terms necessary when addressing a foreigner in one's country, one who doesn't know the language.

No doubt he had fallen asleep mid-sentence. He never remembered exactly where he had stopped speaking, had no memory of lowering his head to the table, his cheek against the white tablecloth.

He was sleeping.

A much younger Alan Randelar materialized and tapped him on the shoulder.

"Do you remember how it used to be when you were like the others?" this younger Alan said, easing into the vacant chair beside him.

Yes. It was a good deal easier.

"Less lonely, you mean?"

Shh. Alan Randelar is never lonely. Alone, yes. Lonely, no. There's a big difference. The one is permissible to a man of my responsibilities; the other, never.

"But just between the two of us . . ." his visitor persisted. "Have you never thought about—well, a woman? Children? A *life*, for God's sake."

My life is my work. It makes as much sense to me as a woman. Or substandard offspring.

The visitor chuckled. "Substandard offspring . . . where did you read that?"

I never read my thoughts. I think them. And it is my opinion . . . In any case, I have no time. No time, no time at all. Even to live.

In that timeless vacuum, his despair rose to taunt him. His emptiness. His fear of eventually dying alone.

"Any last words?"

I won the Nobel Prize, you know.

"Any family to survive you?"

At the word family, he wept, thinking of the only family he had ever had: his mother who had died when he was seven, his father who had died when he was thirteen.

No family, he answered. No one at all.

"Dr. Randelar? You're needed at the infirmary. It's an emergency. Dr. Randelar?"

Randelar came into full alertness immediately. Blinking, he looked around. After years of practice, he had no trouble going headlong into wakeful reality.

"It's an emergency," the black-uniformed waitress repeated, stuck on the phrase.

He nodded reassuringly. "I'm on my way." And with a sense of relief, he was indeed on his way, his long legs carrying him swiftly across the room toward the only thing that would ever matter to him: his work. It mattered deeply. One could use the word love. And, yes, it would survive him.

Beth awoke in the blackness. She had sweated through the sheet. She lay there shivering violently, penetrated to her bones with chill. She felt a terrifying blankness, as though she'd lost the words to think with. She was crying and she didn't even know why. She was frightened in a way she'd never been frightened before in all of her life. She was frightened as a creature who had lost something vital to its whole existence, something central to the creature's identity; she felt as a bird would feel with a clipped-off wing.

Her mind. They'd taken her mind.

"Harvey," she whispered, tasting salt tears, and suddenly she was fully conscious and alert. "My name is Beth Allen," she whispered shakily. "I'm nineteen years old. There's nothing wrong with my mind." She raised her right hand to her face and wiped away her tears. "There's nothing wrong with my mind. My name is Beth Allen. I'm nineteen years old . . ."

Far up the hall, there was a noise, a rattling that reminded her of a grocery shopping cart. Yes. Something was being wheeled across the floor.

She felt trapped in the cold sweat-soaked bed. She couldn't get up, couldn't even move much because of the needle in her left wrist. Emotions converged, coming together from all directions. She felt relief because her mind was all right, but then there was depression because she was alone in the dark. Worry over why she was here. Panic. Unreasoning panic.

She focused on the thin sliver of light beneath the door. Suddenly it was urgent that she get to that light.

Swiftly, unthinkingly, she dug her nails under the tape that held the needle in place and with a single rip she tore it off and pulled the needle out of her flesh. A tiny trickle of blood leaked out of the puncture. She put her wrist to her mouth and sucked. Shuddering, she swung her legs to the ground.

Now she could hear voices and the rattling sound seemed to have started down the hallway. There was something hectic about the atmosphere. Even from here she could feel it. Something had gone wrong in some way.

She stood up and had to catch hold of the bed for support. Maybe she had really been sick. Maybe they hadn't been punishing her after all, hadn't given her a drug.

Shakily, she moved across the floor, still off balance, her damp hospital gown stuck to her back. She felt as though she were in a time and space somewhere outside of reality. Maybe it was the dizzy light feeling in her head or maybe it was the strangeness of the room, dim with vague atmospheric lighting from the window. The room was sparsely furnished, just the bed and nightstand, one chair and a small chest against the wall. Wind rattled the window and howled shrilly around the building. She figured that she was in a wing of the infirmary, someplace she'd never been before. She couldn't seem to steady herself, to get her bearings.

With her fingers on the handle of the door, she paused, suddenly reluctant to be seen. Maybe they'd be angry with her for taking the needle out of her vein. Maybe she shouldn't have done that. Cautiously she inched the door open and put her eye to the crack. The sudden glare of light sent an ache shooting to the center of her head, somewhere in back of her eyes.

At the end of the hall several people were gathered around an ambulatory stretcher. Two women, probably nurses, Dr. Hamilton, and two other men who had surgical masks, now untied and hanging from their necks, and who looked like they'd been through an exhausting ordeal. They still looked tense, as if the problem hadn't been resolved. Beth immediately guessed that the patient on the stretcher was in a life-or-death crisis. The person she stared at the hardest, however, was Alan Randelar who had come swiftly through a large swinging door. Dr. Dyer followed behind him. Randelar was wearing a suit, but the jacket was flung over his shoulder and held by his left fingertips; his collar was open and his sleeves were rolled up.

A murmur of voices as all four doctors began to speak, interrupting each other as though each was anxious to exonerate himself to Randelar.

The scene swam before Beth's eyes. She couldn't make sense of what they were saying. The only voice she could plainly hear was Randelar's as he cut off the others by making a matter-of-fact statement.

"It isn't at all unusual that skin suffocation would occur, regrettable though it is," he shrugged. "The body was ill-equipped to handle the very armorization it was developing. In a sense then, her own self-defense mechanism turned against her."

An unmistakable stir of relief as the surgical team turned to follow Randelar into a side room, leaving the two nurses alone with the patient.

"I'll be in very shortly," Randelar said over his shoulder, handing his jacket to one of the other men.

Beth's eyes were fixed on the stretcher, which had been

partially blocked from her view. One of the doctors had apparently pulled back the sheet, because the figure now lay exposed, scantily covered in green. Her eyes automatically went to the face. It was swathed in gauze. Only the eyes were exposed. Something strange about the closed lids over the eyes. The eyelids were coarse and multi-layered as though thick membranes overlapped.

Beth hung onto the door, taking quick shallow gulps of air. Her brief clarity of mind was fading. She was seeing things all wrong. Optical illusions. *Get hold of yourself.* She straightened. Her vision seemed clear now as she focused on the two women in uniform, one of whom was reaching to pull the sheet over the still figure. Beth allowed herself to focus on that body. She could feel herself focusing, so burningly that her eyes teared. And still she couldn't arrange what she was seeing into coherence. She stared harder.

All at once she felt a flutter in her chest that spread outward until her whole interior trembled.

The body's skin. It wasn't human. Instead of soft pliable human tissue, the body was covered with a series of bony plates similar to but shorter than the sort found on an armadillo. Hard, brown, animal skin.

Not human. The figure was not human. But yet—two legs, two arms—a human torso. Around the chest was a small patch of softer skin, minus the plates. Across this vulnerable skin open sores oozed fluid as though volcanic boils had exploded. Around the outer edges of the infected area, the skin was coarser. Some sort of transformation had begun.

"Where are you taking her? Which room?" Randelar had appeared suddenly, now smocked, an instrument of some sort in his hand. It glinted, seemed hooked at the top.

"One hundred one," the older nurse replied. "It's all set for—"

"No. Take her to one-thirty," interrupted Randelar. "And I want her isolated. Code red. Set up the room, then set one-twenty-eight with a portable O. R. unit. She's going to need emergency surgical procedures all night."

"Yes, sir."

"Go on. I'll stay with her."

Beth withdrew somewhat as the nurses pressed their way toward her, soon passing her door, the quickness of their stride saying it: Emergency. She could still see Randelar clearly from where she stood. He was bending over the body.

"I never lie," he said distinctly as though the creature could understand. "There will be pain. A lot of it. But possibly life as well. Possibly. No promises."

So saying, Randelar took his instrument and began to scrape, and to dig, and to endeavor to pull at the horny coat around the creature's throat. The sound was metallic, nothing that had anything to do with living matter. Scraping. Scratching. Prying at a door that refused to open.

Beth gasped. It could not be happening. He could not be . . .

But the hook had caught and one of the plates seemed to be giving. Randelar twisted the instrument, braced himself expertly, and began a pitiless assault that must end in a prize torn from the creature's throat. The sounds were of Randelar's exertion. His quickened breath, his grunting, the erratic roll of wheels as the bed moved this way and that, and under it all . . . a strange gurgling . . .

Now Randelar stood there, an immense boxy plate dangling on the hook of the thing he held in his hand. The throat was an open bleeding wound.

Beth shuddered and glanced again at the creature's face. Its eyes began to open. Wide. Wider. Frightened pinpoints of yellow light darted around behind dull tightly wrapped gauze.

Suddenly, as though an alarm had gone off, the body shot forward and began to curl together into a ball, cowering like a frightened animal.

Randelar pulled the sheet forward to cover it. Abruptly the gurgling sound stopped. At that moment the two nurses came past Beth's door and entered her vision, their rubber-soled shoes squishing rapidly down the hall. She paid no attention to them. Her gaze was riveted on Randelar, who now turned back to the room he had come from. Casually, as though that piece of matter he held, dripping red from the bottom, was a lid from a can of stewed tomatoes.

Beth closed her eyes and leaned against the door, fighting a tidal wave of sickness. She felt herself moan as it rolled over her and left her hanging there, the bitterness of gall in her throat. *It can't be.* She banged her fist against the door frame. *Can't be.* When she opened her eyes, the stretcher was being rolled toward her. Beside the stretcher was an upside-down bottle and another machine on wheels on the other side. Beth quickly moved back into the darkness, away from the partially opened door. As they passed her room, she heard a nurse's scared voice.

"She won't die, will she?"

"I don't know," said the second nurse indifferently. "It might be better if she did."

"What a shame. She's so young. So helpless."

"Listen, you can't get involved. We agreed . . ."

"First the Ritchie girl and now this. And both of them in the Control Group. Five girls and two of them . . . don't you think that's odd?"

"Precisely," the second nurse said. "That's why you should leave it alone."

"But Dr. Randelar assured us—"

"We all make mistakes."

"Mistakes! I'm afraid it's a bit more than mistakes," she said. "I know this sounds crazy but—"

"Hurry up. I'm getting a very weak reading."

Beth stood frozen, listening to the stretcher move away down the hall. Then all was still. Too still. Heart pounding, she managed to get back to the bed. She had begun to weep again.

Behind closed eyes she felt the pressure build. A metallic dull clicking of heels hurried down the corridor and disappeared. Violently, nausea filled her world. Everything seemed to stop now, drawn out in flashes as she managed to cover herself with the blanket she had gathered from the foot of the bed.

Then sleep, a stupor of sleep; deep, black. But from somewhere she imagined that yellow eyes peered at her. The amber eyes of a frightened animal in the dark.

ELEVEN

Vala Hayes stood looking from a window at the front of Philip Angusi's cottage on Instructor Row. The window afforded a clear view of the campus lake, white-swept and still in the fast-fading sunlight; a wilderness of isolation where death had occurred only three short nights ago and left no trace of itself.

From the mantel, there was a sudden metallic twang that made her jump. A small cheap mantel clock had announced the half-hour. Four-thirty. Still time left to get out of here, but not much. No, not much time. Despite the crispness of the air, Vala cracked the window. She needed to breathe deeply. She needed to clear her head.

It was now Sunday, the seventh of December.

Behind Vala, sitting in a leather upholstered chair, Angusi was playing professor. Wryly, she watched his reflection in the window, watched him make his busy professor scribbles in her composition notebook.

She knew what those scribbles represented. He was reducing her last theme to her simpler statements, such as:

Into the tragedy of mankind, I bring my own inappropriate joy. I investigate. Where does it come from, this air bubble I ride . . . some new chemistry of my blood?

The chemistry that had been caused by having looked into his eyes one day in class. A boiling cauldron of chemistry, that; his and hers; mingling all over the place.

Later, reading her own words, she had thought: *How weird of me*. But she knew what was happening when he'd come up to her in the library; could read beneath his words: "If you'll work with me, Vala, I think you could start publishing . . ."

All so much bull, but the point was, she was here.

She continued to study his reflection. Anxious. Georgia would have said: Scared shitless. Vala observed his body hunch in tighter, saw the tightly corded tendons in his neck, saw his eyebrows draw in face-center. She thought: No, not exactly scared. That was not the right word, somehow. She sighed. Her gaze shifted slightly to include her own reflection in the glass next to his and it was only too obvious, the ludicrousness of the whole thing.

I'm a child, she thought tiredly. An old child, but a child nonetheless. Tonight with the ribbon in her hair, the thin-ribbed white sweater that emphasized her small breasts, her shining lips from the gloss of a schoolgirl's first makeup, she seemed younger than ever. And he older.

He looked up. She met his eyes in the glass. There was that look again; that crazy chemistry happening. She was oddly breathless. Desperately she focused out the window, but the light was all but gone. Quite suddenly a veritable cloud of black swooped over the lake and swallowed it.

"It looks like a storm," he murmured, his first words in the last half hour.

"Yes," she said, facing him at last, "it's that kind of black calm right before it hits. I like storms. I don't know why."

"How about a cup of hot coffee? Or tea."

"No, thank you."

"Wine?"

"No, I don't—"

"I set out cheese and crackers."

She swallowed hard. The pain in her throat mixed in with the slight nausea she had felt for so long it was the norm. He was offering orange juice or hot chocolate now as, swaying slightly, she made her way to the sofa and sat facing him. The room was softly lit by lamps but on the seaman's chest that served as coffee table there were flickering candles beside the cheese board and wine glasses.

"I really don't want anything, but thank you."

He laughed, as though she had said something enormously funny, and helped himself to wine from the decanter.

"What's so amusing?"

"Nothing to do with you. Just enjoying a joke at my own expense. Well, here's to your 'inappropriate joy,' " he said, raising his glass, and drank.

She waited trembling, thinking only that she had never felt so nervous in her life, so awkward and tongue-tied. So horrible and ridiculous.

The irony was what he said: "You're more comfortable at night, aren't you?" Proving that he knew nothing about her, nothing at all.

She stared at him. "Not particularly."

"Oh, yes, you are," he insisted. "You know how I know? It's something you do usually. Something you're not doing now."

"What?"

"You always keep your hand on your face during the day. Like this . . ." He propped his chin in one hand, his fingers hiding his chin and mouth. "Or like this . . ." He shifted his hand to his left temple and, frowning, rubbed at an imaginary spot. "Or like this . . ." He placed his thumb and index finger on the bridge of his nose and stared up at her over them cross-eyed.

"That's a lot of stuff," she said, not laughing.

"Stuff? You mean bullshit?" he asked, but his voice was gentle rather than derisive. The boldness had gone. Now he was tentative. "I care about you, Vala. I think you're special." He reddened and hurried on, his words running together. "A special student, that is. Teachers, you see, ah, we need special students. If we don't get special students," he said into his wine glass, "then, ah, we can't deceive ourselves that we're special teachers. That session we combined composition with languages was my idea. But who except you could have actually, you know, broken my heart in so many languages." A slight laugh that mocked his own words. Hurriedly, he added, "With your theme, I mean. It was a passionate theme."

"It was a good idea you had," she said.

"I thought it was. Not that, by and large, I think I'm anything special. I know—I know too well—that I'm not equipped to help you, but—"

"Stop that," she said unexpectedly.

They stared at each other. It started out to be a neutral silence, each wary of the other but not hostile, and then it warmed a degree. At the last moment, she tried to reach for the indifference she had always used to shield herself from him, but that game had played itself out.

"What I said to you," he said finally. "It's true. I'm not fit to teach you. You must know that." He did not take his eyes from hers.

"I never came to school to get smarter," she said. "I came because I hurt. Inside," she added and tapped her finger against her chest with dead-on accuracy as to the exact location of her heart.

"Everybody hurts in there," he said.

"Oh. I didn't know that."

"You still didn't answer me. Why do you hide your face in daylight?"

"I don't know."

"Do you feel like you're not pretty in a bright light?" he asked bluntly.

She drew a sharp breath. "I'm not pretty in any light."

"Oh, yes, you are," he said, staring at her. The dull red that stained his neck and face told her he knew that he had crossed an invisible marker, that he was being far too intimate with her. He must know he was way out of line.

She knew she should go no deeper into this vein of talk and yet she could not resist the question. Incredulously: "You think I'm pretty?"

He said, "Yes, I do. I'm not lying to you. I'm just—I can't seem to get you out of my mind."

She couldn't look at him anymore but she could feel him there, trembling slightly, as from a chill. She wondered if his heart was beating as fast as hers, if that could be possible.

"Oh, Jesus Christ," he said abruptly and reached for her.

She tried to resist, but could not. She had not forgotten her fear or that he was her teacher, or the most important fact that he was perhaps forty and she was fifteen. But with his body next to hers, an incredible spiral of warmth radiated the center of her being. She felt herself sigh, releasing the core of her resistance. Then she felt his hands pulling her still closer, felt her body pressing harder against his as though independent of her own will.

He slipped both his hands under her sweater and up her back. When she made no protest, he moved his thumbs forward to stroke the curve of her breasts. She was embarrassed for a moment; she had always wanted larger breasts. Then heard his murmur: "You're beautiful, Vala. Beautiful."

Tentatively, she put her hands behind his neck and was surprised to find his skin so warm beneath her touch it seemed to give off sparks.

She thought: *I've never been less alone in my life.*

Confusion then as he pulled her sweater over her head. Her first thought: It's less wonderful now. We should have stopped. No, don't stop, let's . . . She hated the awkward movements he made as he freed himself from his own clothes. Disliked the way he trembled. Loved the way he smelled. Of salt and aftershave. She cried out. He had opened her jeans and pushed them down. He was rougher now, less sensitive to her needs. His open mouth smothered her sound of protest. His tongue in her mouth was unpleasant. Was this what it was all about? This mystery of life she had missed.

"Vala doesn't like the boys." Her mother had perfected that phrase until it was singsong, a song of love for her daughter, the ugly duckling.

Angusi lifted her in his arms, was carrying her up to his bed, she knew. She clung to him, surprised at how strong he was. Put me down—no, too late.

His bed was made up neatly—did he know he was going to do this—brown sheets. She closed her eyes.

Felt him lower her to the bed. Felt his naked body press against hers. He was not as tender as she'd thought he'd be. He was all over her. His hands. His mouth. She kept her eyes screwed closed. Wanted to scream: Don't. I don't like it, I don't like it. I hate it. I hate you. His body on top of hers was a hot seal of passion. She trembled. Shock as little live-wire spasms shot up from her belly.

"Vala doesn't like the boys," she repeated to herself in wonder as Philip parted her legs, a curiously easy task. They felt like jelly.

His fingers tried to be gentle but they pinched. She gasped. Revulsion struggled against passion. Strokes. Pinches. Her breath quickened. Fingers were inserted in her. She said, "No—don't . . ." Then, as he penetrated her, pain. No, I don't like, I don't . . . "Oh, my God, don't . . ." she almost screamed.

"Hush."

"But—"

"Hush."

His eyes rolled up in his head as he concentrated. Not looking at her now because she was trying to force him off and he was no longer to be denied—then a flow of sweat, a deeper concentration, a deep black silence and it was done.

After it was over, she thought about how she was going to feel once the numbness wore off. And wondered if she could be unlucky enough to get pregnant the first time.

"I'm so goddamn sorry, Vala," he said into the silence.

She glanced down and then swiftly away. The blood . . . she withdrew to her side of the bed.

"Are you all right?" he asked. "Oh, Jesus, fifteen years old. I deserve to go to prison."

"Don't say that."

"You must hate me."

"No." But I should. Why don't I? Why don't I hate myself? The answer came easy. Because he's the only man who'll ever want me. Ever in my life. She pushed away a sadness that threatened to overtake her and closed her eyes.

Then in the silence: "Vala, your skin. What's wrong with it?"

"Oh, the rash," she mumbled. "Some of the other girls have it. I don't really know . . ."

"Rash? But it's rather more than just a rash, wouldn't you say?"

Puzzled, she let her fingers go to her throat, then wander down. She felt the swollen craters; startled, she opened her eyes to stare down. "What are they—boils?"

"I would say."

"It just happened. I asked the doctor about the rash during this week's physical, but—"

"Physical? Are you sick?"

"I have an examination every week. Just routine."

"Routine," he repeated and took a moment to consider. "In these exams," he said at length, "what do they do to you?"

She hesitated and then she told him what she had never told anyone. "I'm not sure what they do. They usually put me to sleep first."

She saw the surprised look that flitted across his face before the expression was controlled into inscrutability. He said nothing. For some reason, that angered her.

"I don't like it, what they're doing," she said with emphasis. "I'm thinking of seeing another doctor. Somebody in New York."

"Oh, I wouldn't do that. The Triesius doctors are first-rate." He had sat up on the edge of the bed. Now he tossed her a robe. "Time to be getting yourself together." He was wrapped in his own thoughts, almost forgetful of her presence.

It was only when she was dressed and leaving his cottage, a resentful flush high on her white cheeks, that he came out of his revery to put his arm around her in a close hug. "We have to be careful, Vala, but . . . later this week? Thursday?"

"Thursday," she agreed, relaxing somewhat.

"I want you to remember," he whispered, "how special you are to me. Always remember that."

She nodded gratefully. "Even if I leave Triesius—"

"Leave Triesius? But that's something you can never do, Vala. You belong here."

The conviction in his voice, on his face, stilled any protest she might have made and mirrored back an impression of herself that she carried away—clearer than any image of their love-making. Of herself once again on the fringe of normality, a curiosity even in her lover's eye. Better to be at Triesius than in a nuthouse was the message, clear and simple.

She walked faster through the darkness. Comforting, that darkness. No reason to shield her face from the light. Here you are, Vala Hayes, breathed the very path she walked. Here you are and here you will stay.

Here I will stay, she thought obediently. It seemed the inevitable thing to do.

TWELVE

Georgia Urie's anger built along with a certain frustration. Her obscene caller could have been anyone—anyone at all. An instructor at Triesius, a motley boy out of Rosemont or her primary suspect—El Jerko from Forum night.

The question: Would she recognize the voice if she heard it again? It had not been a well-defined timbre or vocal distinction that had transmitted itself through the wire, but rather a quality of raw sexuality. It was even possible that she'd heard the voice before; she imagined that there was something vaguely familiar about it.

Sunday morning, over scrambled eggs and bacon, she decided she would definitely not recognize the voice. Shit. She scraped her uneaten breakfast into the garbage. Alone in the laundry room that night, she thought she could. In her elation, she absently plucked her laundry from the dryer and brought it back to her room still half wet and limp.

The next morning, she began to have doubts. Yet, sitting in Horowitz's class, "The Laws of Chance," that afternoon, she decided to hell with it. She was going to be positive. She would know the voice.

She forced herself to relax. Almost definitely the caller had been the boy who'd sat beside her on Forum night. He could have found out her name easily enough: Who on earth was that girl sitting next to me—you know, the one who ran out during the Councilman's speech. What's her name?

I'll kill him, Georgia thought, teeth gritted. Because she was sure he'd be back for Forum, Part II—tonight. He wouldn't be able to resist coming back and then—

"What do you think, Miss Urie?" The instructor's voice penetrated her consciousness with a dry craftiness that told her she'd been caught in a squeeze trap.

She observed the piece of chalk in Horowitz's hand, saw that his arm was half-raised and his body angled toward the blackboard.

"Well, I pondered the question last night," she murmured.

"Oh, did you ponder?" he responded caustically.

"Yes, sir."

"*This* statement?" He jerked his head toward the blackboard.

"Yes, sir." What the hell had he written, anyhow? She tried to read behind his strategically placed body. No luck.

"Oh, good," he smiled. "I'm sure we'd all be interested then in hearing if you came to any conclusions."

Jennie Dobbin giggled behind her.

"Conclusions," murmured Georgia. "Oh, absolutely. I discussed them in depth with Miss Dobbin. She has our notes on the subject, I believe."

The giggle changed to a gasp and then a sigh of relief as the bell rang.

The instructor rose. "All right then, young women. We'll continue this better prepared tomorrow."

The girls were already on their feet laughing and Jennie was yanking playfully on Georgia's hair. "I'll kill you for that," she hissed.

Only Georgia still sat staring straight ahead at the blackboard.

"Chance alone cannot account for the events of one's life," she read thoughtfully. Was that true? She shrugged. She was already thinking: Tonight. Forum night, Debate, Part II. Tonight, you son-of-a-bitch. Just be there.

The debate was a bust. The social afterward was an equally lackluster affair. Smooth organization, a well-set table, and not enough spark to light up the rear end of a lightning bug.

Georgia stood by the all-glass wall of the dome's reception hall and divided her attention between the grounds of Triesius on the one side and the bullshit of society on the other.

Milk and cookies hour at the kindergarten, Georgia thought wryly. Hartford boys looked longingly in her direction, their lust sliding over her like sweet sticky syrup. She stood there in her black ski pants and black turtleneck sweater, stunning instead of understated as she'd tried to be, and wanted nothing more than to be naked under a hot shower. And then to bed, lying comfortably under two blankets and a quilt. Instead here she was, the blond gleaming point of attraction within the room, society drawing at her like a high-powered vacuum cleaner moving across a shag rug. She folded her arms across her chest and hugged herself protectively. Living in her body was like living in a goldfish bowl, she thought.

Scanning the room now, she thought she had never seen such a crowd of conformists. Boys in identical sports jackets of different colors, all in highly polished shoes. Her attention shifted to the male chaperones. They all looked exactly the same as the students. Same jackets, same carefully combed hair, same shoes. Just filled out a little and no longer in the prime of their adolescence. She studied the Triesius girls and was glad to see they fared a little better. They had more individuality in dress, more style, more class.

She moved further into the room, making her way easily through the guests, her eyes carefully searching for Mr. Obscene Phone Caller. Where are you, you little bastard? she thought vindictively. Just let me find you and I'll show you what obscenity is. Your ears'll be in sailor knots by the time I finish with you.

Over by the door she caught a glimpse of Vala just hurrying in. She would have joined her save for a quick frown Vala tossed in her direction, clearly a signal to stay away. Georgia made a mental note to confront that frown back at the dorm. Her conviction was strengthened by the fact that Vala looked far from well as she stood clinging now to the back of a chair, her eyes curiously intense as they went from girl to girl as though she were compiling some sort of data.

Willa Bishé appeared at Georgia's elbow. "What's happening with Beth?" she demanded with no preamble. "Good Lord, can you believe we went right on with the Forum like nothing happened on Friday? As though Carmel hadn't—"

"I don't suppose there would have been much purpose in cancelling. There's the memorial service tomorrow at the Chapel."

The girl's small pale eyes narrowed still further. "Is Beth going?"

Georgia hesitated and then said with her customary bluntness, "Beth is under wraps. The infirmary says shock-shock-shock like a broken record."

"Oh." Willa's body lifted and fell in a pleasurable flurry. "Listen, what do you suppose Carmel was doing out on the lake? The grapevine says she had a date. What do you think?"

"Not being a grape," Georgia murmured, "I couldn't say."

Willa persisted. "She was dressed up like she was having dinner with Prince Charles. You want to know what I think happened? I think she was going off to the back section of guest cottages when she fell. That's why she was taking that short cut over the ice."

"Does anybody know who Prince Charles is?"

"Nein. Only that he isn't a student. You can bet your ass on that."

"Do you think it was something serious?"

"Serious? Carmel? Everything was serious to Carmel. As for me . . ." She leaned forward and whispered, "I always felt that her life was nothing more than a series of trivial events in meaningless juxtaposition. Her death was the first important thing that ever happened to her." She winked. "Gotta run."

Georgia watched her trot briskly away through the half empty hall. The social was not as well attended by the Triesius students as was usual. There were at least three young men for every young woman. And less than the usual amount of older visitors. Over by the long table Councilman DeWitt stood chatting with a man she recognized as Harlan Tyler St. John, the Chairman of the Triesius Board. Next to them the man at the piano played on while Jennie Dobbin with white yarn around her dog tails ladled out punch. Mrs. Fazio came from the kitchen carrying a tray of sandwiches.

And Mr. Obscene Phone Caller was nowhere. Georgia released her breath in a deep sigh of frustration.

"Hi, Georgia." The boy had materialized on her right leaning forward to study her name tag. "Dwayne here." He indicated his sticker. "And you look sensational."

"Thanks," she said, peeling her name tag from her sweater.

"May I get you some punch? Or cake?"

"Nothing."

"Well . . ."

She allowed her lips to curve in a brief smile. "But maybe you can help me though."

"Sure thing," he said eagerly.

"Tell me, Wayne . . ."

"Dwayne."

She squinted at his name tag. "Sorry. Dwayne. Nice name."

"Thanks."

"Were you at Forum last Friday?"

"I was."

"I don't suppose you—you didn't happen to see where I was sitting, did you?"

He smiled. "Are you kidding? Third row, fourth from the left."

"Did you happen to notice third row, fifth from the left?"

"No. Why, is she as pretty as you?"

"He."

"He?" Dwayne shrugged. "Not my style."

"Oh."

"Why?"

"I just wondered who he was."

"What does he look like?"

"Uh, black hair, black straight eyebrows . . ." She paused. "Very blue eyes. Jewish, I guess. But very delicate features."

"He sounds darling."

"Do you know him?"

"Not offhand. You sure he's a Young Republican?"

Georgia stared at him. Come to think of it, he didn't fit the image. Jesus. Georgia drew a breath. She had never thought of the possibility that he was not a Young Republican. Images merged. What the hell was he doing there?

"No, I'm not sure," Georgia sighed and noticed Jennie Dobbin waving and pointing to Dwayne. "Send him over," said her finger very plainly.

"Dwayne," Georgia said. "I think that young lady over there wants to see you."

He turned, smiled. "By God, so she does," he said with a playful growl. "She and I discovered last Friday that we have very compatible politics. But, listen, are you sure you wouldn't rather . . ."

"I'm sure I wouldn't rather . . ."

"Right," Dwayne said philosophically. "See you later."

Georgia let her eyes keep wandering, past Jennie and Dwayne, to where Vala now sat hunched over in a hard straight-backed chair. Across from her was Philip Angusi, his back against the wall, drinking punch. They were trying not to look at each other, Georgia guessed shrewdly, but every once in a while their eyes collided like a Mack truck running into a brick building.

Vala, my girl, she thought suddenly worried. *I hope that's not what you've been up to.* Oh, Lord, wouldn't that be a mess? She was beginning to think sex should be strictly reserved for the purpose of propagation.

"Would you like some punch?" asked a young man whose name sticker said "Charlie." His hair was too short, his nose was too long and he had various raw flaky red spots on his face like windburn, the kind of skin condition attained by using too much zit cream. Charlie had missed a whole fuzzy row of light chin whiskers while shaving and Georgia stared at them, fascinated by how long they were. They grew just slightly under the baby flab of his chin at what must have been his shaving line.

"Get away from me, Charlie," Georgia said kindly. "I have V.D. and I can't trust myself with men."

He stumbled away, his face red as a ripe tomato, no doubt hoping that she really did have the syph so that he wouldn't have to deal with rejection. Georgia gazed pityingly at his retreating rear. She'd rather be a nun, she decided. And withdrew into the isolation of a fantasy of a solitary life, calm, peaceful and alone. A life that would be a long straight line without curves or surprises. Yes, perhaps that would be best. For a while, lost in her imagination, she let herself relax, let the tension drop from her face . . .

Across the room by the punch bowl Jimmy DeWitt stood with Harlan Tyler St. John watching the tall blond girl who kept turning the boys down. He would have known her anywhere. Georgia Urie was the caption under the black and white glossy photograph that preceded her bio in the private Triesius directory.

"That's a breathtaking girl, Harlan," Jimmy said in an undertone.

"That's not a girl, Jimmy," said the Chairman warmly. "That's a woman. She's easily the oldest woman in this room."

"How old do you think?" asked Jimmy.

"About nineteen going on thirty," said the Chairman.

Jimmy was suddenly thirsty and he drained his cup of punch in one swig. The lime sherbet was cool and delicious as it slid down his dry throat. He set down his cup, carefully blotting the foam from his lips. The thought occurred to him that he'd been ungracious to drink so fast and he hoped the girl hadn't noticed. "I saw that girl Friday night when I was speaking to the Forum," he said. "She ran out of the hall in the middle of my speech."

The Chairman laughed. "Did you speak so badly, Jimmy?"

"That wasn't it," Jimmy said indignantly. "My speech was all right. I didn't even talk that long. By the time my introduction was over, I only had fifteen minutes left. No, it didn't have anything to do with me. She had a fight with her boyfriend and left."

"Were you making your speech, Jimmy," drawled St. John lazily, "or were you making eyes at that beautiful girl?"

Jimmy blushed and quickly changed the conversation. "You were in a meeting with Headmistress LeSabre tonight. Did she mention the investigation?"

"Investigation?"

"The murder of Carmel Ritchie."

St. John turned his gaze from the girl and looked at Jimmy irritably. "It's being taken care of. But how many times must I tell you . . ."

"Okay. I won't say it again. Just tell me if she said anything, that's all. When I think . . ."

"Not here," said the Chairman. "As to your question, nothing at all."

"Nothing," repeated Jimmy dryly. He knew that once again he was being maneuvered, and probably more successfully than he allowed himself to admit—but then again, they were all in the same boat, weren't they? If anything was wrong about Triesius the Chairman was taking a risk too. So what was the big problem.

"Has everyone been alerted to our problem here?" Jimmy asked meekly.

"Those that count."

"And that's pretty high up, isn't it?"

St. John gave him a quick direct glance. He saw just a shade of worry on St. John's face and that told him a great deal. So if he was stuck, St. John was stuck too. Jimmy was comforted by the thought. St. John was a hell of a lot bigger fish to fry than he was. Chances were if things broke the wrong way, nobody would look twice at James DeWitt, Councilman. But if it turned out lucky, James DeWitt, Councilman, would certainly splash greedily in the glory. Damn it, it was going to work, no matter what. He would personally see to it. This time he was going to think big. Because deep inside of him was this very sharp, innovative and powerful man who just might be capable of something fantastic.

"I have an idea," St. John said suddenly. "Let's go take that girl some punch."

Jimmy roused himself from revery and stared at his older friend and then all at once he was laughing and he couldn't stop. Gasping, he slapped St. John on the back in a gesture of comradeship that was totally inappropriate for their vastly different stations in life. For a moment, St. John was silent, his lips twitching, and then carefully he set his cup of punch on the white linen tablecloth next to a plate of pink and green mints and then he laughed too, his dark head thrown back and his laughter full-bodied and unrestrained.

The girl kept staring around the hall even when Jimmy was talking to her. Jimmy knew he shouldn't give a damn, but he did. He was jumpy as a schoolboy. She was dynamite. The kind of dynamite that could blow up his career and restructure his entire life. Except this girl was nobody who could ever care about him. He kept talking to her and she kept looking from face to face.

"Why didn't you send us away like you sent all the other boys?" Jimmy blundered, trying to exude the power of intimacy.

She glanced at him oddly and said nothing, but the message was clear. She wasn't going to play games.

Jimmy's face reddened as St. John stepped smoothly into the awkward little pause he had created. Georgia turned her full attention to him as somehow he swiftly turned the conversation to the Middle East, smiling at her with hidden significance.

"You are, of course," he said, "especially interested in that topic, I believe."

"How did you know I—" She hesitated.

"That you wrote a thesis on the issue of diplomacy in the Middle East? I read it."

"The whole paper?"

"The whole one hundred and thirty pages. What would you say if I told you we were thinking of sending it to the Secretary of State?"

"I would say how sensible of you." As both men laughed, Jimmy's laugh a bit louder to his own ears than the Chairman's, she chuckled too and added, "That was one of my infrequent little jokes. Actually, there's nothing there that hasn't been tried. There is no diplomacy until each side longs to lay down arms. Just now, I'm afraid each side longs only for the other side to lay down arms."

The Chairman smiled. "Would you like to hear a bit of philosophy on the subject of killing one's enemy? In that instant, killing becomes joy. In that act, there is a force that denies the existence of matter. Spirit becomes all. It's the only way of coming together they have, the only true peace. As the bull who dies in the arms of the matador who has killed him. At that moment they even love each other a little." He hesitated, reflecting on his own words with almost reverent delight. "Now that's a bit of poetry for the soul, wouldn't you say? Yes, it gives me pleasure, that image. Two enemies, their hate running from their wounds as surely as their life's blood. At peace at last." His eyes glittered strangely.

"I'd rather stay at odds and live longer," she returned, "but I see your point."

Her eyes were deadlocked with St. John's now as they went on talking. Jimmy stood by miserably, holding her cake on a white napkin as she broke off crumbs and ate them one at a time, favoring the icing. Jimmy had a sudden ludicrous image of himself as President of the United States and Georgia, lovely and brilliant, his First Lady. He pictured her standing beside him as he made his acceptance speech, her face glowing. The first night in the White House, they would celebrate with champagne and make love lying before the fireplace on a fur rug. Highly exotic love, Jimmy fantasized and imagined her legs wrapped around him, holding him tighter and tighter. He hastened forward in the scenario. They would lie in each other's arms and make their plans. The world would be intensely real, engulfing them in quiet meditation, and he would be peaceful, feeling her heart beating against his chest.

Jimmy glanced at Georgia now, this girl whom he had just made violent love to, who stood nibbling cake and nodding at something St. John had just said, and he felt anew a strange raw pain around his heart. He imagined that they were waiting for him to leave so they could make their plans.

Christ, he thought. He couldn't concentrate on whatever it was they were talking about, but he couldn't tear himself away either. He kept standing there, listening, until he could no longer keep his hands off the girl.

He took her by both shoulders and turned her away from St. John to himself, because he had to have her full attention, if just for a moment, no matter what the cost in embarrassment. The palms of his hands were burning where he held her and he thought with satisfaction that that kind of heat couldn't pass between two people unless both of them felt it.

Georgia gave a little gasp, her lips falling open, her eyes looking into his with a little shock and he felt the yielding softness of her body for one fleeting moment. Then abruptly she pulled free of his hands and moved swiftly across the room without a backward glance.

At the door, she seized her coat from one of the racks and would have disappeared into the darkness of the night, except for Vala Hayes who caught her by the arm and talked rapidly for a moment. Georgia nodded finally, touched Vala briefly on the shoulder and then almost flung herself through the door.

Down by the lake Georgia wrapped her arms around an elm tree and put her cheek against the cold bark. She noticed that the tree was dying of white elm blight and for some reason that made her feel a kinship with it. Blight, she thought blankly, running her hand down the smooth bark.

She was ashamed now because by this time she was convinced she'd played a game tonight. She'd known she was driving DeWitt crazy by ignoring him and she'd loved doing it. She couldn't help herself. That she had taunted him showed the shambles of her mind tonight. Or perhaps, she thought with painful honesty, it was just another sick aspect of her relationship to all men.

Let's talk about frigidity for a moment. In this cold bleak landscape.

Well, I feel hot at the beginning, almost always, when an interesting man comes on to me—a mature man. But then somewhere along the line, I'd like to axe off his sweaty rude fingers. Men would be a hell of a lot nicer without fingers.

Have you always felt like that?

No. But since that damn contest—

It changed you.

Yes, it changed me. Now sometimes I do things. . . . I can't explain why . . . but it hasn't anything to do with the man.

Do you think you're . . . ?

Yes. Yes . . . Frigid.

Georgia pressed her face harder against the elm. She was so involved in her own thoughts that she never saw the man who had crept so silently down the bank and stood behind her. Waiting.

It was the man's breathing that she heard first, deep and heavy, as if he were out of breath. She froze, still holding the tree with both arms. She had no doubt as to who it was. The boy from Forum night; the boy with the outlined, formless face. He hadn't gone to Forum tonight, instead he had waited for her in the dark.

She felt him come closer, heard the crunch of his shoes in the snow and still she couldn't look up. Then suddenly two hands placed themselves on her shoulders and she turned to look into the eyes of James DeWitt.

"I'm sorry," he said softly, "if I did anything to—"

She silenced him with a quick shake of her head. His eyes seemed very bright in the dim moonlight.

He took a hesitant step forward. "Georgia—"

But she was gone, so quickly that it might only have been the ending of a brief spell of magic.

Somewhere out there in the void of night, he knew she was still running.

PART III

The Break

ONE

Unforgiving ice, Beth mused, gazing from the window of the infirmary. It had snowed on and off during the night and now the campus of Triesius was covered with mounds of billowing whiteness. But Beth could still imagine the ice below. Glassy, brittle, crystalline forms of water that could kill as easily as not.

Diamonds were called ice in slang, she reminded herself, and her mind started to play word games. Iceblink, iceboat, icebound—she felt that way—icebound. Iceage, iceberg, ice-cold, and she shivered at the thought. Ice skating. She had been ice skating when . . .

She broke off and stared at the bowl of soup on her tray. Cream of tomato soup, her favorite. And saltine crackers. Wearily she lifted the spoon, attempted to eat. Her hand still shook a little and she spilled soup on the sheet and on her chest.

"Whoops." The young nurse uniformed in blue set aside her needlepoint and dabbed at Beth's gown with a hand towel.

Beth smiled at the girl and passed another spoonful of soup between her lips. Her hand was steadier.

"Are you feeling stronger?" asked the girl, pressing a napkin around Beth's chin.

"Yes, thank you." Beth motioned for the tray to be taken away. "No more soup, okay? Just a cracker."

The girl set the tray on the bedstand and unwrapped a package of saltines. "Are you sure you can chew? Can you sit up straighter?"

Beth chewed, she sat up straighter and talked small talk with the girl. She found out that the girl was from a small town in North Carolina, that she was a registered nurse, that she was twenty-four years old, that her name was Shelby Paul and that she was a Shane Allen fan.

"Shelby's a nice name," Beth said, taking another cracker from the package.

"Thanks. I don't look like a Shelby though, do I? I mean, a Shelby ought to be blond with skin like a peach and she ought to be a surfer, don't you think? Not like me with a hundred freckles and kind of jolly and cute. I ought to be a Betty or a Nancy or something." Shelby had a pleasant Southern accent and a pretty smile but she wasn't an especially attractive girl, not if you looked at her features one at a time. Her beauty was her gorgeous gleaming light-red hair.

"I think you look like a Shelby," decided Beth.

Shelby shrugged.

"I was wondering—were you here when my father called?"

"He's called several times. But, worst luck, they didn't put through the call. You were sleeping. And me—I missed my big chance to speak to Shane Allen."

"When he calls again, I'll let you talk to him."

"Really?" squealed Shelby.

"Really." Beth managed a smile into the excited eyes of the young nurse. She stared at her with something approaching the beginnings of a friendship.

Beth wanted very much to talk to Shelby about things that she couldn't get out of her mind. She wanted to talk about Carmel and to ask if they were still calling Carmel's death an accident. She wanted to share with Shelby the horrible moment when she had found Carmel and how the image had burned itself into her brain. Because if she could talk about it, then maybe the whole experience would be easier to bear. Going it alone was hard.

And, too, she wanted to ask about the body she'd seen on the portable hospital bed. Had she imagined it—the scales, the dozens of open sores that oozed fluid, the pinpoints of yellow light that darted frantically behind a mountain of gauze.

"Listen, you can't get involved. We agreed . . ." the nurse had said.

"First the Ritchie girl and now this. And both of them in the Control Group. Don't you think that's odd?"

"Precisely. That's why you should leave it alone."

Slowly Beth pulled her body upright to a more solid sitting position. No, she was not crazy, she had not imagined what she saw and heard. One of the two nurses, the youngest one, had been genuinely scared. And she hadn't even seen what Alan Randelar had done to the patient.

Beth turned to glance at her reflection in the mirror which hung over the white hospital table: Her face was pale and drawn, hair disheveled. Her mind raced. She was strong enough now not to begin all over again doubting her own sanity.

Her sureness was abrupt, sudden.

She was remembering a man, his face in shadows. A man who had stood watching her from across the lake. A silhouette. Tall, familiar. Then the light was gone. Flipped off. Only the darkness had remained. She had seen his face and yet she hadn't. His features were so clear, yet a distant scrim in the back of her mind clouded the image.

Who had the man been?

A peculiar sense of numbness gripped her, and she welcomed it. Every part of her wanted to sleep. But she knew she had to stay awake, alert to what they were trying to do to her.

She turned suddenly and stared at Shelby, who looked back at her curiously.

Then just as suddenly, Beth turned away. Away from the red-haired, curious onlooker who now moved closer to brush cracker crumbs from the coverlet.

"It was terrible about that Ritchie girl, wasn't it?" she murmured.

"Terrible," Beth said faintly and closed her eyes. *Don't talk. Whatever you do, don't tell them anything.* Strong flashes of light swirled behind closed eyelids.

"And you found her?"

Beth whispered, "Yes."

"What did she look like?"

All Beth could remember now was the blood. *Blood!* Slowly she opened her eyes. Very, very consciously, she forced herself to relax. "I don't remember."

"Really?" the nurse murmured with a faint shake of the head. Her face was pink. Like a flower or something, Beth thought.

"I don't remember," she repeated softly with finality and drifted off into her own thoughts. She wondered what time it was. What day, even.

She must have asked the question out loud because Shelby said, "Tuesday. It's Tuesday morning, Beth. You've been here going on four days."

Tuesday? From Friday night to Tuesday morning. Could she have really lost track of all that time? Suddenly one thought moved out of her confusion: Karl. She was supposed to have seen him again on Sunday. Thursday night they had argued. Damnit! If only she hadn't . . . "Tuesday," she breathed.

"Nine-thirty." Shelby moved closer. "But don't worry. We're going to help you now."

"I'm cold."

"I understand. You'll feel much better once—"

"No!" Beth snapped. "I'm all right now. I feel much better, really. Ready to go back to the dorm." *Don't panic. Don't panic.*

Faintly she heard Shelby's voice: "Oh, good morning, doctor."

Beth looked up and was surprised to find Dr. Hamilton standing inside the doorway observing her. He had stopped by—when?—to examine her. No, question her. Was that yesterday?

Hamilton's dark well-sculptured face turned briefly to Nurse Paul before he said, "Beth. How are you feeling today?"

"All right. Much better." She hadn't thought she'd have to face the man again. Surely not more questions?

"Your color seems to be returning." As he walked up to the bed he signaled to Nurse Paul, who rose and walked out of the room. He waited for the door to close before asking, "And how is your frame of mind?"

Beth hesitated. "I—I don't understand."

"What have you been thinking about since we last talked?"

Beth considered for a moment. "Nothing. Just that I'd like to go back to my classes."

"That's understandable." He laughed. "A hospital room isn't very conducive to learning, is it?" He paused to flick loose strands of black hair away from his forehead. "Do you recall what we talked about yesterday?"

"Yes." She couldn't—not all of it.

"Good. Good."

Now he was probing her eyelids, shining a small light into her eyes. His face was so close she could see the stubble of his beard. "I'd like you to relax now."

The light flickered, penetrating into the darkness behind her eyes. Now he was touching her at the throat—pressing. She caught her breath. "Does this hurt?" he asked.

Beth shook her head.

He quickly slipped his hand inside the sheet. His fingers pressed into her stomach. She tried to control her shivering. Suddenly the coldness came to her again like a flood, throwing her without warning back onto the lake, face down, hands reaching out for Carmel.

"Any pain?"

"No."

Now he ran his fingers down each leg, pressing viciously into her skin. "So . . . tell me, Beth, have you had any new recollections about Friday night?"

Christ! It was going to be more questions. "Not really."

"You haven't had any new thoughts?"

Beth shifted restlessly under the sheets. "No. When can I go back to my classes?"

He took a while answering, seemed to be studying her closely. Finally he said, "Beth, I think we'd like you to spend a bit more time with us. So we can continue to counsel your recovery."

She looked at him sharply. She understood the meaning of his words and that they weren't through with her yet. That the questioning would go on, would not stop, and that they weren't going to let her return to a normal life on the campus. "Has my father been informed of this?"

"Of course. He approves of our decision." He was talking very calmly. "We all understand how you feel. But you must understand you have suffered a very stressful traumatic experience. Physically, you will recover quickly. But your psychological recovery may not come as easily. That's why we'd like you to spend more time with us. I assure you, we will make it a very tranquil experience."

Beth shook her head in annoyance. "No. I just want to get back to class. I'll be all right once I'm back with the other girls."

"Beth, you have to trust us. Your father concurs with our judgment. We feel you will need a little more time, a little more counseling."

Beth watched as again the man flicked loose hair away from his forehead. Somewhere within her a small voice whispered: *He is not to be trusted. No one here is to be trusted.*

"Why won't you let me go back to the dorm?" Beth asked.

"We will."

"When? I feel fine. Why not today?"

He didn't answer her right away. Just studied her in a detached way. Then: "Beth, I'm afraid you don't understand yet what has happened to you. You have suffered a severe psychic trauma. Here you have a pleasant environment, proper care. A place that is secure. Where you can relax. In a few days—"

Beth sat upright and thrust her body into what he was saying, to make him understand. "But I don't feel relaxed here, Doctor. I don't feel secure. I'll be all right as soon as you allow me to return to my classes and my friends. And I still don't understand why I haven't heard from my father."

He kept on talking in flat tones, telling her she shouldn't concern herself about her father right now. He reassured her that Shane Allen was fully aware of her progress and would be in touch with her shortly. That she should get her rest, and that he would be in again to see her soon. That what she needed most was to rest and to collect herself, not burden her mind with classes.

"Is there anything else you'd like to tell me?" he asked from the doorway.

Beth let her head drop once again to the pillow, saying nothing. When he turned to go, Beth didn't acknowledge his departure.

She rolled over on her side and stared from the window as Nurse Paul came back into the room.

"Isn't he handsome?" Nurse Paul whispered, giggling.

"I guess," Beth murmured and she was sure of only one thing: she would never, never let them question her again. No, the next time Dr. Hamilton came back into her room, he'd find an empty bed.

Dr. Hamilton stared thoughtfully at Shelby Paul. "So she says she doesn't remember. Do you believe her?"

"She's a spoiled rich bitch," shrugged Shelby disdainfully. "I don't guess she'd know enough to lie."

Hamilton returned the arrogant gaze. "She's a tested genius, Miss Paul. Never let yourself forget that."

"It's Dr. Paul. Never let yourself forget that. And I didn't join this project to give baths and carry soup bowls." Shelby no longer looked like the nice girl next door. There was something not quite normal in the hard shine of her eyes as she turned on her heel and swung out the door.

Almost immediately, Dr. Hamilton reached for the phone and began to push buttons.

TWO

The complexions of the students whitened almost overnight, perhaps as a result of the unrelenting cold that had gripped the campus like a tight fist. Perhaps it was also the cold that had altered the expressions on faces, squeezed the vitality from the youth of Triesius.

Certainly, the girls' health had declined.

A nasty bug was going around; fully half of the students had contracted it. But Georgia Urie had not. It was a victory of sorts, she guessed, and congratulated herself on her own continuing good health.

Breathing somewhat heavily now, she entered the TV room in a half-run. The room was totally deserted. She flipped on channel five and lowered herself into a white vinyl chair. She was a few minutes late for the Villines interview even though she'd jogged back from the infirmary.

She waited for the set to warm up. Even the TV was suffering from frostbite. She shook her head.

"No. No one is allowed to see Beth Allen," the nurse had said.

"But why? It's been four days now and—"

"Talk to Dr. Hamilton. He's in charge here."

"I've tried. He's always—"

"If you'll excuse me . . ."

Georgia had fastened her seat belt and gathered all her courage. "Listen, if you don't let me see Beth Allen this instant, I'll—"

"May I help you, Georgia?"

Headmistress LeSabre stood in the doorway like a sentinel,

her lips parted in her usual congenial smile.

"It's Beth Allen," Georgia muttered.

"Yes. What about her?"

Georgia shrugged. "I'd like to see her."

LeSabre looked at her curiously. "Perhaps tomorrow. Beth is doing fine. Just fine. We wouldn't want to do anything to jeopardize her progress, now would we?"

She stared at Georgia for an extra second, and Georgia knew that the subject, at least for the moment, was closed.

So too was Vala Hayes's room. Closed. Locked. Vala nowhere to be found. All Georgia knew for certain was that Vala had also gotten bitten by the dreaded old bug chewing up half of Triesius. Suddenly Georgia felt like one of the three mice who ran up the clock.

Hickory, Dickory, Doc.
Three mice ran up the clock.
The clock struck two
And one got away with minor injuries.

The TV picture finally came into focus as the sound raised a notch in volume. Rob Villines, the interviewer, was already engaged in conversation with his guest, Dr. Jonathan Dyer of Triesius College.

The camera was close in on a face she recognized: the slightly rounded, ambitiously congenial face of Dr. Dyer, key assistant to Alan Randelar. Georgia tried to concentrate.

Dyer was now speaking: ". . . so that scientists in the U.S.S.R. could indeed produce a species capable of performing feats incredible for most of us to even conceive." Dyer's words almost rippled in the stir of his enthusiasm.

The camera view widened to include Villines, who took a moment's pause to choose words to heighten the sensational aspect of his interview. "What sort of feats?" he asked finally, smiling slightly. "Do you mean physical feats? Like a bionic man or woman? Is it that farfetched?"

"Well, I wouldn't use the term bionic," said Dyer. "It would be more accurate to say that through generations of selective breeding, exceedingly bright and physically fit children would evolve and, incidentally, much more rapidly than you would imagine."

"Not another attempt at the super race, doctor . . ."

"That would certainly be one aspect and the simplest aspect, at that. But even more interesting would be what I'll refer to as the modifications. I'll give you an example. Human beings require special equipment when they dive to great depths in the ocean. To the other extreme, they also must be outfitted with temperature-controlled space suits and oxygen-support systems when they travel into outer space. The Soviets' research program is believed to have already modified problems such as the ones I have just named and, in time, it may even eliminate them altogether."

"That's incredible," said Villines, his eyes wandering slightly to the left.

"Incredible, perhaps," nodded Dyer. "But very probably true. This species will be adaptable beyond anything man has ever imagined."

Villines had a station break coming up and was now concentrating on timing. He wanted to get to an interesting point and leave the observers hanging. "What does this new super race have to do with us, doctor? I suppose for one thing, Russia will be setting up space colonies." He laughed slightly.

"That, yes," Dyer said. "The Soviets will be capable of populating outer space with a species of creatures who adapt themselves as easily to alien atmospheres as we of earth breathe oxygen. I'll go further." Dyer hesitated and sipped from a glass. For the first time, he seemed almost reluctant to proceed. "In the event of a worldwide nuclear war," he said finally, just when Villines would have spoken, "nuclear fallout would endanger life over the entire span of the globe. This specially bred species, however, would be totally immune. They could live above ground and breathe what would be to you or me lethally poisonous air. Even more importantly, they could serve the interests of Soviets, who could have been safely removed to subterraneous caverns, perhaps even before the first button was pushed."

"These people . . ." began Villines, now grim-faced, unminding of his approaching station break.

"I never called them people," Dyer cut in smoothly.

Villines's face was in close focus, grim, chalky under its tan makeup, as the station went unannounced to a break.

Georgia leaned forward to lower the volume. She could feel the incredulous set to her own face: the sardonically angled brows, the twist to her lips, the wideness of her eyes.

"Space colonies," she muttered. "Alien atmospheres . . . species of creatures . . . Shit."

It struck her as especially ironic that a man like Dyer would engage in this variety of cuckoo-bird conversation to further Villines's purpose of making an interesting interview. In any event, the hoped for dialogue on fetal birth defects was obviously not going to take place.

Georgia stirred restively. Any other ideas on how to fill a typical evening here at Triesius? she inquired of herself. Oh, God, a person could die of ennui under the moon. Tell me the truth, doctor, how did Georgia Urie die? Was it too much introspection? Ah, yes. Too much being left to her own thoughts.

Great, just great, she sighed and unzipped the front of her ski parka. The short jog from the infirmary had left her wide awake but unrelaxed. She could feel the dreaded tension in her back, working its way up into her neck. If she was going to sleep tonight, she'd have to take a pill. No. No more pills, she thought decisively.

The Rob Villines interview had come back on the air, but Georgia was too preoccupied to listen. She heard disassociated words such as "gene exchange" and "cell substitution" and, frequently, the name of Alan Randelar. She finally glanced up just as Villines was beginning his windup.

"In these experiments," he said, "you've stressed that Russia is believed to be far ahead of America."

"Some say so," responded Dyer neutrally.

Georgia turned the volume louder.

"How far would you say?" continued Villines.

"There are those who say as much as ten years. Some say as little as five."

"But I'm not interested in any of those obscure people," pressed Villines. "What does Dr. Dyer say? Better yet, you work closely with Dr. Randelar. What does the Nobel Peace Prize recipient have to say on this subject?"

Dr. Dyer smiled, puffed up with self-importance. "Well, I can't speak for Dr. Randelar, but as for myself, I would say our experimentation is not far behind."

"Thank you, Dr. Dyer," said Villines with satisfaction. "Now, one last question, if you please."

Dyer inclined his head.

"Randelar's research at Triesius College for young women

of 170-plus I.Q. . . . does this work have to do with what we've talked of tonight?"

Dyer's face was once again in close focus. His infinitesimal pause was made obvious by the camera, by the wry expression on Villines's face as the camera panned back to include him in the shot just as Dyer began to mutter, "No, no—I didn't say that. Dr. Randelar's field of genetics is geared toward finding and eliminating birth defects while the fetus is still in the womb—"

"But that's related, isn't it?" said Villines innocently. "We're talking about gene snipping, aren't we?"

"Not necessarily. You see—" began Dyer, frowning.

"Thank you. Thank you very much. Your comments have been most provocative," concluded Villines triumphantly. "Ladies and gentlemen, unfortunately our time has—"

Georgia's wide eyes were locked on Dyer's dismayed face as he attempted to interrupt Villines, to protest, but it was to no avail and his attempt only made him look worse. Guilty almost. Imbecilic.

And then, mercifully, the interview ended.

Feeling almost dizzy, Georgia snapped off the TV just as two of the other students wandered in, still wearing their coats and red-cheeked from the cold.

"What's happening, Georgia?"

What's happening, indeed, she repeated to herself, almost drawn to laugh because the whole thing was too absurd, just a nut's interview. Aloud she said, "Going off to bed. I've had it for tonight."

But in bed she lay staring at the ceiling where odd shadows fashioned from her desk lamp had gathered. Strange shapes on a smooth surface, she mused as simultaneously her thought process cracked, her subjects intermingled. Carmel . . . Vala . . . her obscene phone caller . . . Beth . . . super race? No. Sleep. Just sleep.

Obediently, she closed her eyes. But sleep was far away.

Chill. Waves of it washed over her. It started with a general coldness beneath her skin, then grew into a spasmodic rush to the surface. Then came a numbness, a deadening of her senses.

Blankly, she looked at her watch. It was almost ten o'clock.

The dorm was totally dark except for a small light that shone from Georgia's window.

The pace of her heart quickened. Vala supposed by now she should have been used to Georgia, but there were still times—like now, when she thought of her with something resembling awe.

She shook her head. No, she must not tell Georgia about Philip Angusi. That she had found it necessary to go to him again tonight. As before, he had been passionate. Tonight, she was almost on automatic. Her mind raced past the lovemaking. Randelar. The laboratory. Why had he—no, what was . . . She had tried to talk to Philip. Perhaps he would say something that would bring the whole thing into focus. He had. Without knowing it.

"You are using something for birth control, aren't you? When is your next period?"

She felt herself freeze. Her period. And realized it was late by at least two weeks. Her mind strained to think. Hadn't she heard some other girl mention . . .

What have they—

Tears suddenly flooded her eyes. What is wrong with me? Why do I distrust Triesius so much. Why do I question all the time?

Her questions were unanswerable.

Her eyes shifted to the laboratory sitting back among the trees. Gloomy and dark. Her thoughts skipped backward. Why had they shown the students so little of the laboratory? They'd certainly had a right to see more than just a few offices.

Slowly, she felt the numbing sensation reach her fingertips. What an odd feeling. Lord, I'm so weak. Exhausted—drained. Georgia. I must speak to Georgia. She was just about to move inside the building when she saw Georgia's light go out.

She froze—rigid, confused.

Against her will, her eyes roved again to the laboratory. Secrets, she thought, and knew there were things moving under the surface of the water that no one knew about.

Dim memory . . . somewhere . . . long, long ago . . . lying in the infirmary? "No, not that needle, this one." And the substitution had been made.

Startlingly clear image: Dr. Dyer smiling as he left the room.

But had it been an hallucination? A vivid dream? What if I'm wrong? What if I tell someone and it isn't true? Everyone will blame me, accuse me . . . Of course, that's the way people are. They pretend to be kind and understanding to catch you off guard. Then they cut you into pieces with accusation.

Did you hear? Did you know? Vala Hayes is saying the oddest things. Strange girl, don't you think? Well, poor child, she's only fifteen years old. What did you expect? Children do fantasize, after all.

Vala's eyes shifted rapidly back to Georgia's window. Blackness. Everywhere—blackness. And the itching and tingling of her skin and the terrible pain, which for a moment, crazily, became pleasurable, then reverted into pain again.

She was on fire now and the fire was consuming her. She struggled for some reason, any kind of reason, but none came. None came . . . none came . . .

Her eyes moved once again to the laboratory.

It was there that her mind stopped.

THREE

(Excerpt from an interview one hour after *The Rob Villines Show* between Dr. Jonathan Dyer and James Megan of CBS News, New York.)

MEGAN: Could we have a further comment, something to clarify your remarks on the Rob Villines interview.

DYER: No comment!

MEGAN: Were you expecting the media response? Surely, you must be surprised—

DYER: *(Interrupting)* To be honest, I'm somewhat annoyed. That is my response.

MEGAN: Why annoyed?

DYER: Because of irresponsible journalism. For years now, research has progressed in Geneva, Switzerland, without the media exploiting their work . . .

MEGAN: You mention Geneva . . .

DYER: Their replicas of mice—exact living copies of mice.

MEGAN: Does this relate to the research going on at Triesius College?

DYER: Of course not! No matter what Mr. Villines has inferred. If you're interested in sensationalism, why don't you put Geneva on your newscast? They're vastly underexposed. (*Moving away from the camera*) Excuse me . . .

MEGAN: (*Following after him*) Dr. Dyer, one last question. Do you have any response to the petition that is to be brought before the President's Committee on Medical Ethics concerning stricter guidelines on genetic research?

DYER: I know of no such petition.

MEGAN: It is our understanding that there is such a petition. In the event that our source is correct, could you give us a comment?

DYER: My comment is that I wouldn't give a thought to the matter. Our research at Triesius is only concerned with gene defects in unborn children. That's all.

MEGAN: Dr. Dyer . . .

DYER: Excuse me!

Fifteen minutes later, a recording of this interview was played by telephone to the Chairman.

St. John listened and said, "Again."

The recording was repeated.

"All right. Put a call in to Randelar."

"He's upstate at the Hilton."

"Not there. I don't want to go through a goddamn switchboard."

"Well . . ."

"Did Randelar know about the Villines interview?"

"No, sir. None of us did. Apparently, Dyer took it upon himself."

"You mean the son-of-a-bitch broke ranks without telling anyone?"

"Apparently so."

"I'll be goddamned . . ." The Chairman caught his breath. He felt the blood rush to his head. He felt, for an instant, somewhat ready to explode.

"We've sent word for Randelar to remain under wraps until we can pick him up."

"Right. Call me as soon as he gets back on campus." The Chairman dropped the phone on the hook and thought: A disaster. The Villines interview had been a disaster. Almost immediately, he had another thought and picked up the phone again and dialed. At once the receiver was picked up.

"And as for that son-of-a-bitch Dyer," he said, "I want his

mouth shut once and for all. Any other reporters get to him, I want only two words to come out of his mouth. 'No comment.' Got it? 'No comment.' "

"Right."

The Chairman dropped the phone on the hook and made a small grunt of disgust. For the time being, the Triesius people were going to be expected to operate on a much more conservative level. That was absolute. He personally would control the research department. Randelar would have to answer for Dyer.

His anger, however, did not as yet quite include Alan Randelar. The man's genius was too impressive.

Thoughtfully, he reached for the photograph file and spread eight color pictures across his uncluttered desk. On the weight of these pictures, he had made his original decision to back Alan Randelar's research. Four of the pictures were of partially formed fetuses which had aborted from their mothers' wombs. Two of these laboratory mothers had died, having been poisoned from substances expelled from the fetuses. The fetuses, small as they were, bore evidence to what Randelar had been attempting.

The Chairman picked up a magnifying glass and studied the face of the most developed fetus. He was still fascinated with several aspects, although he had looked at these photos countless times. The tiny scales that covered most of the face and the neck, the huge skull and, most interesting, the modification of external sexual organs in this male specimen.

He thrust aside the picture of the fetus and turned his attention to the four remaining shots, of babies who had actually come to term. By God, he had thought in reluctant admiration, Randelar had almost achieved goal one. Two of these babies had been able to withstand sustained inhalation of carbon monoxide and to injest various modifications of infant milk.

He had asked Alan Randelar one key question. Not in person; he had chosen to deal through a middle man. The question was: "What is the greatest danger that this sort of positive genetic engineering represents?"

Randelar's response: "There are several dangers, including patenting life forms (who would be in control of seeds, etc.), religious rebellions and problems of creating a form of biological warfare between nations. The latter, however, has been already begun by the USSR and we have no alternative but to catch up. The greatest danger, however, is in unleashing new life forms that result in a new classification of human being. The trouble with this is once it has been introduced into the lifestream, it cannot be recalled. It will be with us for as long as we continue to people the earth."

This had troubled the Chairman, but he was a realist. The Russians had begun this research. If they were doing it, then the United States had to do it too, no matter how damn controversial it was. His opinion on this remained unchanged.

At this moment, his aide knocked twice on the door and then let himself in.

"I've talked to Washington, sir."

"I don't have to know about that, Ray," the Chairman said gently, putting the photographs back into the folder. "I'm sure everything was all right."

"The Senator was very insistent on speaking to you directly."

"I hope you were very blunt."

"I'm sure he understood," the aide said impassively.

"Good." Very slowly, the Chairman stood up. He raised his glass to his lips and drank several swallows of whiskey. "Have the girls arrived?" he asked, a portion of his mind still on the photographs. Another portion still on the Rob Villines interview.

"Yes. They've been in the east bedroom for an hour." The aide paused indecisively for a moment and then added, "Shall I have them leave?"

"No. Have a hot bath drawn for me. I'll be up in a minute. Is one of the girls a blond?"

"One is blond and one is red-haired." The aide's well-trained lip did not curve, but there was a flash of contempt in his eyes.

"Make sure they understand what I want," the Chairman said without a trace of embarrassment.

"They understand."

The Chairman chuckled. "Do you know what your trouble is, Ray?"

"What is that?" the aide asked impassively.

"You've no respect of quality. For example, you look down on these girls merely because they're call girls. You look down on me for enjoying their services. They're artists in their own way—in the art of making love. Excellence is something to admire wherever you find it. Remember that."

"As you say, sir." The aide paused for a moment and then judging from the Chairman's silence that he intended to say nothing further, let himself from the office without excusing himself.

The Chairman stepped leisurely to the sideboard and helped himself to a dozen or so clams on the half shell and another half glass of whiskey. He was calmer now. He was thinking of the girls who were waiting for him. He knew they would be very young, certainly under twenty, because he liked young women.

Absently, he licked his lips. Already his sizeable organ was pushing up, growing to immense size. He chuckled. In the elevator, he fantasized for a moment how he would please both young women. He knew it wasn't an act. Women always were attracted to him despite his solidly square, barrel-chested body. They, like everyone else, were drawn to the power that seemed to ooze from his body like a lubricant. Women liked bathing in this precious oil, loved filling themselves, any orifice he chose to fill, with his huge tool, almost fainting when he would shoot his essence inside them.

For just a moment he could see past his physical need and he felt curiously alone. A negative feeling he rarely allowed himself. The women in his life were all fleeting shadow figures. Never a life companion. But quality women, he reminded himself. They had given him intense physical pleasure. He had no room in his life for anything more.

Now he stepped from the elevator and knocked lightly on the door before opening it. Moments later, he was in a warm tub. The blond was washing his back, her long hair falling over his face. The redhead was propped on the edge of the tub, legs spread, her mouth open and ripe and smiling.

The Chairman settled back and luxuriated. He could easily see how much she liked him.

FOUR

She had been thin to begin with. Now in four short days she had grown shockingly thin and white. The effect was to make her look younger, almost a child inside her designer jeans, her white cashmere sweater, her high-heeled suede boots. Her skin, bare of foundation, gleamed from the days of near-fasting and long hours of sleep. A touch of lipstick and mascara were the only cosmetics she had bothered to apply; her hair hung scrupulously clean but uncurled like a long veil around her small solemn face.

Beth moved slowly, stopping often to catch her bearings, occasionally pressing her palms against supporting oaks when she got waves of dizziness. At the clearing, she paused to glance at the grey cabin. A sob caught in her throat. The light that burned in the kitchen told her that Karl was here and that time, after all, had stood still in this one spot.

Then she was running, snagging her jacket on bushes; branches reached out to catch in her hair, to lash across her skin. Her steps rang out across the porch and at the same moment she reached for the doorknob, the door flew open and Karl was there.

Blue eyes shining into hers, hands reaching to catch her before she could fall.

"Beth? What—what's happened?"

Beth could not speak, could only stare a moment longer until with desperation she threw herself into his arms and began to cry.

"Beth, are you all right? What is it?" Awkwardly he guided her inside. Before he could close the front door, her arms were reaching out for him again. He eased the door closed and pressed her body close to his.

"It's all right, Beth. Take it easy."

Beth drew away and wiped her cheeks with her hands. "I'm sorry. I didn't mean to act like this. I'm sorry."

"What's happened?"

She crossed to the cot and sat without removing her coat. The curtains in the room were drawn, the dim glow from the fire in the stove sent red splotches here and there, and the reddish tint that fell across Karl's face gave him an odd look, lips dark and thin, eyes set too deep, too hollow.

Karl dropped on the cot beside her. "Beth, tell me what's happened. You're shaking. You're sick."

"No, not sick. In shock. At least that's what they tell me."

"Shock? From what?" His eyes narrowed. "Is your father okay?"

"He's fine. It's not that. It's just—something that happened. To one of the girls." Unexpectedly tears again gushed from her eyes. She wiped her cheeks.

"Hush," he said, taking her into his arms. She was stroked, comforted and kissed, her tears dried, before he leaned back to say, "I was worried when you didn't come. I thought maybe you'd written me off."

She shook her head. "You knew that wasn't it. A girl at school died." She heard the word escape her lips smoothly; why hadn't she said Carmel was murdered? She hadn't realized it was going to be difficult to get it out, hadn't counted on having to deal with her own curious reluctance.

"Was she a friend?" Karl was murmuring.

She shook her head. "Carmel had no friends."

He hesitated. "I'm sorry . . ."

"I found her body."

"God," he said putting his arm across her shoulders.

"I think—"

"What?"

She drew a long breath. "I think she was murdered, Karl."

"Murdered," he repeated blankly.

"Her head was—" She swallowed heavily. "Karl, she was decapitated."

"Jesus . . ."

"That's not all. They don't want anyone to know about it. They've been keeping me doped up. Fooling with my mind, like they think I'm such an idiot I won't remember what I saw. They kept telling me Carmel's death was an accident. That she slipped on the ice. Froze to death. But I know what I saw."

Karl stared at her. "I don't understand."

Beth began to laugh, almost hysterically. "Jesus, Karl, what's to understand? They're covering up a murder. They weren't going to let me leave the infirmary. Afraid of what I might say. So . . . I left on my own. By this time, they're probably looking for me."

The feeling of fear came back, stronger than ever, as Beth described how she had come to find Carmel's body out on the lake.

"It was terrible seeing her like that with her head gone, as if it had just been lifted off her body or as if it must be an optical illusion. As if the head must be there somewhere, I just wasn't seeing it. You know the first thing I thought of when I saw her, when I realized what had happened? I thought about a doll I had once and its head came off. I felt like I murdered that doll because I used to carry it around by the head. It had blond hair like Carmel." She gave a sharp little sigh, then continued.

Karl listened for a moment longer, then rose to put water on the stove for coffee. He digested her story in silence.

"I can't exactly understand why they would want to do such a thing," he said in a moment. "Bad publicity, I guess, but would they really take such a risk . . ."

"But I'm telling you they did!" Beth persisted, making a helpless gesture with her hand and then letting it fall weakly to her side. "Well, it doesn't matter, does it? What I have to figure out is who I should tell. The police or maybe my father." She slid back on the cot, settled her back against the wall and closed her eyes. "It's unbelievable how weak I am. I could hardly get here. I had to keep stopping . . . and I ripped open my thumb on the barbwire fence." Her eyes blinked open; she glanced up at him.

Karl gave her a rather intent look, but said nothing. He took the kettle from the stove and poured water into a bowl. He began to clean the wound. When he had finished, he applied a small bandage and stepped back to look at her.

Beth glanced at him nervously. "What do you think I should do, Karl?"

Silently he poured the rest of the water on instant coffee.

"Do you think I should go to the police or do you think I should tell Shane and let him handle it?"

"Have you told anyone else about this?"

"No."

"Not even Vala? Georgia?"

"No, I—I didn't chance going back to the dorm. I came straight here." She paused. "Do you think I should go to the police?"

Karl picked up a spoon and began stirring the coffee. "Did you at least think about the possibility that . . ." He hesitated.

"Yes?"

"Well, that they're right. That the girl's death was an accident?"

"What?" she asked on a long breath.

"I mean, you could have seen it wrong, Beth. It's possible, isn't it? Lord, they wouldn't lie about a thing like that. It wouldn't make sense for them to lie."

Beth stared at him incredulously. "You don't believe me either," she said in a flat voice. "You don't believe a word of it, do you?"

Karl shifted his shoulders very slightly and then in an even unemotional voice as if they were discussing a scheduling change or talking about the weather, he said, "I'm really not sure what I believe."

Beth sat staring at him. "Are you trying to insinuate that I imagined Carmel was decapitated? That isn't possible, you see, because I actually . . . I took hold of her and the blood was all over her and her head was floating in the water. Like a rubber doll's head."

"Have you ever envisioned your own death?" Karl asked.

Beth shrugged, angrily dismissing the question. "I'm sick of all the analytic bullshit. I heard enough of it from them. This has nothing to do with my mind. I believe that you think it does, but you're wrong. I didn't see Carmel as myself lying there and I didn't imagine that she was killed for some deep-seated psychological reason. Her death in no way pertains to my analysis and I am not interested in discussing it on that basis. Now either talk about what is true or don't say anything. And if you think I don't know the difference between fact and fantasy, just remind yourself that I'm Shane Allen's daughter. I'm a specialist at recognizing illusion."

Karl nodded, encouraging her to continue, the way he

always did and it was such a natural thoughtful nod, such a familiar nod, that she was suddenly very confused. She felt like she was being pulled between two poles.

"Carmel was murdered," she said defiantly and heard the doubt in her own voice. Was it possible that she had really imagined it? No, it couldn't be, because she remembered taking hold of the body and shaking it and that was her first real warning that something was wrong. The body had felt so strange in her grasp; the torso too light, off balance, because the head was . . . She tried to cast her mind back, even though the effort made her flinch. Had the thought come to her about the head before or after she had seen the mutilation? She was irresistibly drawn to follow the thought to its conclusion. Could she have possibly made up her mind in advance that Carmel's head had been severed and then imagined the rest? Of course, she had been very scared already and that could have made her hallucinate. But she had been so sure.

Resentfully she thought that she was falling under Karl's spell, believing as he told her to believe. "What about the blood?" she asked. "I'm sure about the blood," she said warningly. "Her dress was soaked with it." Unbidden the thought came that maybe the dress was wet. If Carmel were wearing a red dress and if the material had gotten wet, would it have looked like blood? Perhaps, but there was something wrong with the image, something she couldn't put her finger on.

"What color was the dress?" murmured Karl, as if he were reading her thoughts.

"Burgundy, they said!" She almost screamed the words.

"Why are you angry?" he asked mildly.

"I'm angry," she said, her voice laced with acid, "because I was just ready to believe you instead of what I know to be true. And I'm angry because you sicken me with your mummified listening; I'm angry because I was kept a prisoner and I'm angry because they told me Carmel Ritchie was wearing a burgundy dress when she never wore red or burgundy in her life!" Something had clicked in a chamber in her brain. "Only," she counted on her fingers, "blues, greens, yellow, brown, black or white. Nothing beige and nothing crimson or too bright. Beige was too blah and crimson was too overpowering. Carmel wanted to be the flower face, not the face behind the flower. Any more questions?"

He concentrated on putting sugar and powdered milk into the coffee.

"Goddamn it, answer me!" she said furiously and a faint flush stained his lean young boy's face. He hadn't shaven that day and the dark bristly stubble made him look tired.

"Okay, so I believe you," he said, not meeting her eyes. "Now let's drop it for a while. You should be resting. Here. Have a sip of coffee. It'll warm you up. It's cold in here."

"No, it isn't."

"I'm cold, okay? Is that all right?"

Furiously she stared at him.

"I don't want the police nosing around here," he said. "Is that enough for you?"

"No. It's not even close to being enough."

Karl's face became slightly confused, concerned as though the situation had gotten out of hand, gone in a direction he hadn't expected.

"It's just that I came here to be left alone," he said in a softer voice. "If you call the police, they'll come swarming all over the place and it'll be ruined. All of it—ruined."

"I won't tell them you're here then. That I spoke with you. I won't say a word."

"It won't take much leg work to find out I'm the only person inside of ten miles who isn't part of Triesius. They'll probably accuse me, for Chrissakes!"

For a moment he stood perfectly still, his mouth in a slight twist, as if his own words had left a sour aftertaste.

"What's the matter, Karl?" Beth asked in a tired voice as he sat down beside her.

"I guess—I guess I'm trying to protect what I have here. What I feel. At least . . ." He broke off.

"What?" she faltered. "What is it you feel?" Whatever other problems she had, the loneliness of the last four days without Karl suddenly seemed more important. It was as though Karl had pressed a button; he began to talk, his voice relatively expressionless at first. Beth didn't mind. His body was pressed close to hers and felt good.

"I'm all fucked up, Beth," he said. "I . . . I don't even know why you want to have anything to do with me. I mean, why do you bother with me at all?"

What could she possibly say to that? She tried to focus on the word "love." A tricky word. She was going to cry again.

She could feel the subtle stinging behind her eyelids. She *refused* to cry again. She thought that if she could have one wish granted at that moment it would be to rid herself of Triesius forever. To erase it from her mind as if it had never existed.

She was getting cold now and she wanted Karl to put his arms around her, hold her, tell her God only knew what. She turned to look at him. She felt helpless; she had no idea of how she looked to him. He went on talking, never really looking at her directly. His left hand gripped the side of the cot. With his right he pulled on his earlobe.

She closed her eyes. Remembered the day her mother had left when she was six years old. She had watched her go. She had been sitting on the stairway, peering from between the white posts, staring, staring, as her beautiful young mother went storming down the stairs and out the front door. Her mother had been angry. That's all she could remember about that day. A lot of confusion, a lot of tears. Maybe that was why she had often thought with some kind of vague hope that her mother had forgotten to say goodbye.

Beth turned suddenly and opened her eyes. Karl had taken hold of her hand.

"Poor finger," he said. "Look at it."

"Poor old finger," she echoed.

Tenderly he brought her hand to his mouth and began kissing each finger, from the bottom to the tip. Only when he had finished did he let his eyes meet hers. He leaned over and kissed her. Beth let her body sink against his chest, her mind revolving on a slow tilting axis while images revolved in the opposite direction.

Faded brown prints in a torn photo album: her mother's beaming face, Harvey seated on the hood of his first car, Shane in a beach chair . . .

They moved back so they were propped against the wall, in each other's arms. They started to make love, stopped to undress each other, then made love with painful pleasure. The sensation of his entering her was so intense that the heat spiralled up inside her and she gave herself up to it, working for the one incredible shattering moment of throbbing pulsations.

Afterwards she fell deeply asleep but even while she slept there was an image of Karl's face over hers, as he moved inside her in slow deep strokes, the sweat rolling down his face and then dripping on hers like pellets of hot rain.

Much later, she awoke and reached for him, but the space beside her was vacant and cold. She opened her mouth to call for him, but something stopped her, warned her to stay quiet.

Across the room, the firelight from the stove shone on a nude white body. The well-formed body of a young boy.

"Karl," breathed Beth so quietly that he did not hear her. He was standing perfectly still, staring out the window. It seemed to her that there was some sort of anguish on his face.

In a moment he walked across the room to where a knife was slung over a kitchen chair in a worn leather holder. He hesitated and then unsheathed the weapon and held it, blade downward, in a vicious attack position. For an instant he appeared as a young hunter of ancient time. She thought that the beauty of him was incredible but savage as well. He frightened her somehow. And then she realized he was shaking violently.

All at once he took a few steps to the kitchen window overlooking the porch. Intently he stared, his hand straining around the knife's handle, and then turned back toward the bed. Beth closed her eyes as he came nearer, knife still in hand, and a moment later she felt him lower himself to the cot and climb under the covers. There was a slight clatter as he dropped the knife to the floor and slid it a few inches under the bed.

After a while Karl's breathing steadied and she knew that he slept. She kept her eyes closed, but remained awake. An old memory drifted through her mind. It was right after her mother left and she wouldn't let Shane read to her out of her book of fairy tales. She never told him why, but it was because she no longer believed in happy endings.

As on that night, so it was tonight. She closed her eyes and silently cried herself to sleep.

When she opened them again, she was lying on her back and her face was wet. What is this? she thought. Droplets of perspiration began to roll down her face. She needed to swallow and saw red flickers of light dance across the cabin ceiling.

"Karl?" Her hand reached out. She was alone. She lay quite still and thought: *I am not alone. Someone else is in the room with me.*

"Karl!" She sat up in bed. She was immediately seized by a fit of dizziness that swept over her in waves until she felt exhausted and spent. Everything in the room seemed to waver in her tired gaze.

Figures standing by the doorway. Two men. She wasn't sure who they were because she couldn't get her eyes to focus.

"Who's there?"

She said this helplessly, covering the upper portion of her body with the sheet. She heard faint noises of movement in the bedroom. Then running water. Then she came around to stare at the two men standing by the doorway.

"Who are you?"

They neither answered nor looked at her directly.

She thought: I'm still asleep. I must be.

Behind her someone said, "We've come to take you back, Beth."

Beth turned to stare into Headmistress LeSabre's eyes. They looked at each other and she felt her face twisting out of shape, felt the tug of her facial muscles as they produced an agonized grimace, and at the same time the identical grimace appeared on Headmistress LeSabre's face.

"Get dressed, Beth." She signaled to the two men at the door, who turned and left the cabin.

"Karl . . ." Beth murmured uncertainly.

"Karl who?" asked LeSabre, her lips made up too red on her white face. "You seem to be alone."

Beth covered herself with the sheet, tried to regain a trace of composure. Karl was no longer in the cabin. That, at least, made things the least bit less awkward. Nevertheless she wished he was here to help her.

The headmistress's hand gently removed the sheet from Beth's nude body. "It's time now. Get dressed. We'll take care of you. You're confused, but we'll help you. You'll see how much better you'll feel. Trust me."

Slowly, hesitantly, Beth lowered her feet to the floor.

FIVE

Shane Allen sat beside his glass-enclosed swimming pool drinking tonic, no gin, and feeling edgy. He sat with his elbows planted on the glass tabletop, his head tilted to one side, thinking about Carmel Ritchie.

He had tried not to think about her. Jesus Christ, how he had tried. Five days and still the image of the girl persisted.

Suddenly from the depths of his heated pool emerged a disembodied head. It shook violently, flinging water here, there and, most specifically, in his direction. The head grinned and began to thrust upward. Now a thin neck emerged, followed by two shoulders, the beginning of a torso.

"Watch this!" cried the girl and dove sideways, body zig-zagging, performing her version of amateur water ballet.

He thought: *By God, I'll never be able to feel a damned thing for a woman again.* There was no further despair at the thought; despair already saturated him, he could not hold a drop more. It was simple truth. If Sara, who was so special, could do nothing for him, then he was beyond help. Sara. Carmel. Sara.

He'd met Sara almost exactly two years ago in Phil Rosen's office at Paramount. On the day that, for him, this whole thing had begun. Two topsy-turvy years ago. Right before he'd gotten the lead role in the movie *Ecstasy*, which had immediately sky rocketed him to the top of box-office favorites. A spot he hadn't occupied for quite some time.

He had just walked through the door to the outside reception area when she came out of Rosen's private office. She was wearing too much makeup, he had noted absently and flashed a smile at Rosen's secretary, before his eyes wandered back to the girl. The girl wore a plastered-on smile which never wavered. She reached for the door and Shane made an impulse decision.

"Catch you in a minute, Bea," he grinned and made a U-turn right on the girl's heels.

The instant she hit the hall, her control snapped, as if she'd had just enough courage to get this far and not an inch farther. Even if she felt his presence it didn't matter because she was exploding inside. She threw herself against the wall and hung there, wailing aloud, really going at it like a kid who'd just fallen over the handlebars of her bike after a bad skid.

Shane watched her cry for a minute wondering if he hadn't ought to go in there and beat the hell out of Rosen for whatever the hell he'd done. Hesitantly, he took his handkerchief out of his jacket pocket, tucked it into the girl's fist and said soothingly, "Now don't cry like that. Believe me, I have good connections. We'll put a hit on the S.O.B."

She hiccupped, somewhere between a laugh and a sob, and spun around to face him. At once recognition flooded her face and a panoply of emotion flitted after. Shock, respect, uncertainty and all of the emotions Shane had seen on so many other faces. But there was something else mirrored on her face, something he'd never seen before. A strange sort of regret that seemed to have something to do with him directly, because she couldn't take those drowned grey eyes off him and the harder she looked, the more she cried, until Shane was seriously worried about her.

"What's the bastard done?" Shane asked gently. He pulled his handkerchief from her clenched hand and tried to mop up the flood draining down her face.

She still had that look about her of profound regret.

"Whatever he did, it can't be worth this," Shane said blotting carefully under her eyes. "Even rape can't be worth this." His eyes narrowed. "Is that what he tried to do—rape you?" If that's what it was, then he was damned well surprised because he had always assumed that Rosen was a fag. "I could understand if he tried to rape me," Shane said doubtfully, "but—"

Unexpectedly she laughed. "It wasn't rape." Her voice was low and rich, despite the tears. "It was worse than rape. He told me to take acting lessons."

Shane stared at her. "The lousy bastard."

"Why? He was telling the truth."

"Phil Rosen wouldn't know an actress if he broke his ass tripping over one," Shane said, putting a reassuring hand on her shoulder. He detected the deep tremors in her body and he felt a murderous hatred toward Rosen for saying such a thing. From nowhere, as if it had been yesterday, he remembered an old woman agent who had once said much the same thing to Harvey Allen. "Is it my talent you don't like," he'd asked in a blaze of temper, "or my bulbous nose?" She'd said nothing, only smiled a superior smile. "How about my ass?" Harvey had said furiously. "I hope you like that because you're welcome to kiss it!" Even today as Shane Allen, a legend in the business, the memory of that cruel old bitch made him furious.

Shudderingly, he was forced to another image. Harvey going through the windshield of the cab he was driving . . . the blood and the nose that had shattered into pulpy jelly . . . and then the better face they'd given him, the new nose and Shane, the new person he'd invented. Harvey couldn't have made it in a hundred years. Shane made it in eight months.

The girl was gazing at him questioningly.

Abruptly, Shane reached for his wallet and removed a white card. "Around one-thirty this afternoon," he said and slipped the card carefully into the corner of her shoulder bag. "Do you want to drive or should I send a car for you?"

"I have a Volks," she said, her eyes widening. "But why? For what?"

"Acting lessons," he said winking. "Wear comfortable clothes, jeans or something. And bring a bathing suit. My acting classes are usually held underwater. What's your name, for God's sake?"

"Sara." She reached up and straightened a tendril of hair.

"Sara, you look better now that you've cried off all those black lines around your eyes. I think we'd better have a makeup session after scene study."

He watched her go, turning three times to see if he was still there or if possibly she'd imagined him and then disappearing around the corner after one last backward glance and a small tentative smile. He was curiously sorry to see her go and savored his last image of her with those little red spots burning on her cheeks and her grey eyes beginning to shine with something other than tears. Then he went straight into Rosen's office and gave Bea a hug.

"It's not your fault you work for an asshole," he whispered sincerely into her ear and Bea's honest face mirrored the startled truth. She knew she worked for an asshole.

Shane strode through Rosen's private door.

"Shane, baby," gushed Rosen, a plastic smile flitting across his smooth baby-soft face.

"Can it!" Shane had an odd amount of power when he refused to smile as he was doing now. There was something almost dangerously quiet about his face, chilly and isolated for the moment, but with a feeling that the animal in him might be waiting for just the right moment to spring.

Rosen's smile faded, his diamond-studded fingers flying to his face. "Dear man, what's the matter?"

"Do something for me, Phil." Shane sat at the edge of Rosen's desk. "Tonight, just before you go to sleep, say to yourself, 'I'm a worthless little faggot who has forgotten I'm a member of this sad old human race. Instead of trying to bring hope to the disspirited, I seek to destroy dreams. Instead of reaching my pudgy little hand out to a man in the middle of a rope bridge, I cut the cord. I stand for nothing. I believe it's my right to be nasty to whomever I choose.' "

"Shane!"

"Shut up. I can't imagine what sort of pleasure it gives you to utter those goddamn poisonous phrases of yours . . ."

"What kind of—"

"I said shut the fuck up. I'm going to tell you something about those little phrases of yours, Phil. Phrases like 'go take acting lessons' to a woman who's condemned herself to a life of poverty for the chance to act. Who was probably so nervous giving her little audition for a creep like you that she didn't even do herself justice. Those little phrases take about five seconds to spew out of your mouth, but some of the people you say them to will agonize over them for the rest of their lives."

"I can't use every actor who walks through my door, Shane," Rosen said stiffly. A trace of pomp had returned to his manner.

"I'm not telling you to cast the girl, Rosen!" Shane yelled at the top of his temper. "I'm telling you not to send her into a hot bathtub with a razor blade! Me, you can tell to take acting lessons. But you can't hurt me, you fucking creep, so it's—"

"Just who," shouted Rosen in sudden retaliation, "in the hell do you think you are, Shane?"

"Bigger than anyone you handle—"

"Were," interrupted Rosen. "You were the biggest at one time. Not anymore. Placate him, the studio tells me. Put him off. Buy him lunch every once in a while. He's good for a cameo. Maybe even a guest shot on TV if he'll do TV. Not much more than that." Rosen leaned forward for emphasis. "He's over the hill. That's what they tell me."

Shane stared him dead in the eye. "It's over for you, Rosen."

"Bullshit," scoffed Rosen, studying his well-manicured nails.

"Listen to me, faggot. I give you a month. Better get in a lot of expensive lunches."

Shane didn't even wait until he got home to make the phone call. Three days later he had the starring role in the motion picture *Ecstasy*. He started filming two months later, a month after Rosen was fired from the studio. Ten months later Shane was numero uno once again. And Sara had indirectly started the whole thing.

Now watching her carrying on in the pool, he told himself he'd done the right thing two years ago. *Ecstasy* had also given Sara a niche in the business, a name for herself. Shane had seen to that. And with any luck and a few more phone calls, she would be on her way to stardom.

His plans had been running so beautifully, so damn beautifully, and now it all seemed to be crashing down around him. Anger erupted and rushed through him, gripping his face with pressure.

"Do a drunk snake," he called laughing nervously and Sara began to wiggle through the water in a jerky motion. "That's just great," he said. "Remember Phil Rosen? You should have auditioned for him in a pool."

"Hah."

"You know, there's something I never asked you. About that day."

"What's that?"

"The way you looked at me. You kept crying and looking at me. That look—what the hell was that?"

"Oh," she said, paddling about in a slow thoughtful circle.

"Just something about coming face to face with a dream you just lost."

"Ah."

Sara stopped swimming and flipped lazily onto her back, floating in water close by where he sat. He smiled and lowered himself from his chair to the side of the pool. For several minutes neither of them said anything, just comfortably let the silence go by.

"Why did you mention Phil Rosen?" Sara finally asked.

"What?"

Sara came out of her floating position and stood up in the water, facing him, crossing her arms on the side of the pool. "You still think about that? His getting fired?"

Shane answered at once. "No, why should I? The bastard got exactly what he deserved." He gazed at her a moment longer, then leaned closer and gave her a friendly warm kiss on the mouth, liking the wetness of her skin with the water still running down from her hair.

"I'm not so sure," Sara said, pulling herself from the pool.

"Of what?"

"That Rosen got what he deserved. After all, he was only being truthful. A bit crass, but truthful."

"Hey, we've been all through this." He put his arm around her and stroked her back. "You're a good actress. A damn good actress." With his free hand he drew a towel from the chair. "A good actress," he repeated dreamily, intoning the words in a seductive chant.

All at once he felt her body stiffen against his.

"Is that why Copolla never bothered to call me back after the test?" she said.

"He will. You'll see."

"Yes? And who will get fired this time?"

Shane gently patted water away from her cheeks with the towel. "Kiddo, I love you. I don't intend to let anyone hurt you. Ever again."

She lowered the side of her head against his shoulder. "I don't know . . ."

He said, "Well, I do know. Soon we'll be on our way—"

The terrace door slid open. "Mr. Allen?"

Shane turned. "Yes?"

Mrs. Zucco, Shane's housekeeper, entered the glass enclosure. "Phone call. Long distance."

"Who is it?"

"I think it's Mr. St. John."

"Oh, shit," Shane groaned. "Sweetheart, I'll be right back."

Shane took the call, standing in the den, easing a cigarette from his pocket, his sixth in an hour.

The Chairman spoke easily, but bluntly. "We're having some difficulties back here in the east."

"Beth?" Shane said sharply because, although he'd told himself a hundred times not to worry (hadn't they said she was fine), he was worried, damned worried, and why in the hell wasn't he there instead of—

"She's still in the infirmary," St. John said, a frown in his voice.

Shane felt his knees give way and he sank into the leather chair. "You said there was nothing wrong with her."

"Shock. Although we have explained to her very carefully—what she saw, you understand?—she doesn't remember it that way, apparently."

"I thought she did," Shane said. For some reason he felt cold, chilled to the bone. He shuddered.

"If she did," the Chairman was saying, "would she have run away? Don't worry, we found her, but—"

"Where? Where did you find her?"

"I'll talk to you about it tomorrow. Here."

Shane hesitated, drawing in smoke, his heart speeding from the rush of nicotine into his system. "There?"

"I'm afraid I must ask you to be back at Triesius tomorrow. You understand it's urgent or I wouldn't bother you like this." The Chairman spoke a moment longer, choosing his words carefully, obviously not wanting to discuss the matter over the telephone.

When the Chairman had finished speaking, Shane gave a blank nod at the receiver as though the other man could see the gesture. The silence served, because the Chairman said with a certain gentleness, "You'll be out here tomorrow then? I need to count on that."

"Right," Shane said in a voice he hardly recognized as his own and dropped the phone on the hook. He sat there for a long time, his cigarette laying forgotten in the ashtray.

"My little girl," he murmured and covered his eyes. He felt the tears leak past his hands, felt the jerks of his lungs as he tried to put a lid on his weeping, and still the tears kept coming.

"Shane? What is it? What's wrong?" Sara stood in the doorway now, bathed in sunlight. She looked clean and wholesome, her hair still damp and her face glowing from her workout in the swimming pool.

Shane went to her swiftly. "God, I need you," he said and put his head on her shoulder. Gently, she ran her fingers through his thick dark hair. "It's all right, Shane," she said. "Now it's my turn to be here for you."

SIX

Vala Hayes was trapped. She wondered if she was dying. Insane how she'd never been aware that she was in the least danger. She felt perspiration running down her cheeks or perhaps she was crying. She couldn't decide which and, in any case, it didn't matter. Most probably she was dying and nothing mattered anymore, not even the fact that she hadn't been the woman she'd hoped to be. She hadn't been charming or pretty or even successful in her studies. All those brains and she had only a high school diploma to show for it. A second rate high school, at that. She hadn't been popular. Hadn't been a daughter who brought joy to her parents. She hadn't been anything. Except, finally, a lover. A pathetic lover of one man. Her head swam. Perhaps she slept; she couldn't be sure.

Shadowy faces seemed to gather oppressively close around her bedside.

She tossed on the sweat-soaked sheet, the blanket knotted around her legs. She was too sick to rise from her bed. They had control now. "They" were ruthless and extremely clever. She could feel their looming, this indefinable they. United, strong.

Vala moaned. From somewhere beyond the walls of her room, others moaned. A chorus of sorrowful sounds like mourners at a wake.

Suddenly her eyes opened. She couldn't remember what she had just been thinking—or had she been dreaming? Outside the wind was howling, the sound seeming to intensify the coldness of the room. She shivered and reached for the blanket.

She had been on fire and now she was chilled again. From hot to cold to hot, that's the way she had been going. Each time, she went a little further each way. Hotter. Then colder as her fever broke and the sweat poured off her. Teeth chattering, lying in her cold soaked bed; then hot.

She ran her fingertips across her breast, shuddering with disgust as she felt the soft and swollen craters in her skin, oozing with liquid that ran together with her sweat. She wiped her fingertips on the sheet, knowing she was spreading the poison everywhere, lying in it, drinking it with the pores of her skin.

There was something she had to do, but she couldn't quite think what. Her thoughts, her memories, were ghostlike and fleeting, taunting her. She was too high on the narcotic of illness to care about chasing them.

Dammit! she thought, head reeling, she had to care. She had to force herself to care or everything would be lost. She pushed herself up in bed and pulled the blanket up to her neck. Stale sweat dripped from her chin.

She was trying to remember something. Something she had to do. The laboratory, that was it. She had to find out what they were doing at the laboratory. She didn't know exactly what it was she would look for, but something tangible. Something she could take to somebody and say, "Look, here's what they're doing. Here's the proof that these people have gone off the deep end."

Cautiously now, she let her feet touch the floor. Her mind blurred as a sharp pain gripped her stomach. She didn't want to get nauseous again. Already she'd spent a good part of the day with her head over the toilet bowl. She felt better though, just now.

Yes, much better.

She was beginning to remember clearly. She could almost see the chart in her mind's eye. A hospital chart with a heavy metal cover and sloppy doctor's writing inside. Dr. Dyer had stopped to chat with her during one of her physicals at the infirmary. He had placed it on the cabinet. Left the room for a moment. She'd stood there looking at it by the light that had just begun to shine through the window. Although the jargon had been unfamiliar, she'd gotten the impression that unfertilized eggs had been removed from five girls. Suddenly she had felt a rush of approaching danger. Swiftly she had closed the chart as Dr. Dyer stepped back into the room. Moments later Dr. Dyer was on his way to the laboratory.

That damned chart, Vala thought now, moving slowly across the room. She believed that if she could only get it into her hands, could show it to the right people, then maybe she could put an end to it. The Triesius nightmare.

Groaning, Vala began to change into street clothes. Her pajama top was soaked and stuck to her neck. The surface of her skin was gritty with salt. What the hell, she thought recklessly, the unpleasant sensations were beginning to feel normal.

Unconsciously she had begun to play a game with herself. She would force herself to be strong for a few hours and then she would never have to be strong again. She knew there were things she had to accomplish; things that she couldn't put off. It had to be now while she was cool, because she wasn't lucid when the fever went past a certain point. There was the fear too that next time it wouldn't break but just keep climbing like an over-stoked furnace gone wild. She imagined the mercury in her own bodily thermometer climbing past caution into danger; warning, warning, boiling, and then a thin deadly ping as it exploded through the top, flowing like molten lava.

A plan of action was already forming in her mind, curiously detailed, as though she had known for some time what she was going to do.

She took a flashlight from her top bureau drawer and shone it briefly to test the battery. She noticed that her fingers were gripped tight around the handle of the flashlight and she started talking to herself, reminding herself to relax. Tension would just make her stumble, make her mind stumble. She began to dress, wincing as she substituted the heavier material of a warm blouse for the soft flannel of her pajama top.

She hesitated and then gathered together school records and several of her admission papers, whatever she could find that looked official, and stuffed the whole into a large envelope which she carefully sealed. Next she typed a label.

It was nine-thirty when she left her room, locking the door behind her almost ceremoniously. She had a feeling in her gut that she was never going to see it again.

The night was clear and she guessed it was cold although she wasn't sure. Her own chill had nothing to do with the weather. She walked quietly, wondering if anyone had been watching her, but she didn't think so. She didn't blame them; she was easy to forget.

Outside the low white research complex, she paused to wait. Several lights were still burning in the back, toward the curve of the building. She had brought a half-empty pack of stale cigarettes—Georgia's cigarettes; short, unfiltered—and lit one. She supposed it was bad for her to smoke, maybe it would even make her sick, but it made waiting tolerable.

She found a seat on a large cold rock and smoked, trying not to scratch, trying not to think about the passage of time. Above all else, trying not to think about what she could do if the lights didn't go out, if there were scientists working throughout the night. Wryly, she reflected that if she had been in any danger of surviving, the exposure she was getting tonight would take care of that.

At eleven, the last laboratory light went out, except for the lobby light where the guard sat. Minutes later the front door swung open and voices sounded, an old voice and a deep flat voice. A tall figure, careless of posture, emerged from the building, walking slowly as though lost in thought.

Vala recognized the man who was the last to leave. Randelar, the famous researcher himself, had been working alone late into the evening. The watchlights shone on Randelar's face, illuminating it perfectly. Vala noticed the satisfied smirk lurking at the corners of his exhausted mouth. Something must be going very well indeed. Vala closed her eyes for a moment, realizing how deadly afraid she was of Randelar's genetic research. She wondered if moral ethics ever entered the mind of a man like Randelar. She thought not after considering it. Probably it was only the weak who found it hard to live with guilt.

When she opened her eyes, Randelar stood less than ten feet away, out of the light, separated from her only by the blackness of the night and part of a tree trunk. A deep line dragged down between Randelar's brows and the stillness of the man indicated deliberation. Vala froze. The cigarette smoke; the goddamn cigarette smoke had given her away.

Randelar stood motionless for a moment, seeming to weigh something in his mind, and then abruptly moved away, his footsteps fading. Vala's lungs flattened, the pent-up breath gushing between her lips. The silence Randelar had left behind seemed desolate, heavy-hung, and for a moment Vala wondered if she wasn't merely a passing thought in Randelar's mind and, if so, would she now cease to be as Randelar's computer brain reprogrammed itself.

Phase Two, Vala told herself firmly, but she was shaky under the improvised bravado. She had seen the enemy and she was afraid. Courage. The biggest test was still ahead.

She stood, her knees feeling like rolling water. She took her time in approaching the low white building. Her senses were hypersensitive. Even the air seemed shrill, as though some high-pitched alarm had gone off that only she could hear. Five times she stopped, but ultimately she knew she had only one choice. Only one choice, she thought resignedly and pressed her finger against the buzzer.

The old watchman's face was whiskery and grey, his tiny eyes darting back and forth between Vala's face and the manila envelope she was extending. As the old man waited, he wetted his index finger against his tongue and touched it to his lower lip, the saliva shining on a dark spot which looked like a stain, perhaps nicotine from countless years of smoking cheap cigars.

"Dr. Randelar's waiting for this," Vala said importantly.

The watchman's hands closed around the envelope. "Well, I'll see to it then." He held the envelope to the light, squinting at the label.

"You'll see that he gets it this evening?" Vala pressed.

The guard grinned, showing several short brown teeth and a long vacant space on his upper right gum. "I'll see to it," he repeated.

Vala cursed inwardly. The old man was too senile to even realize what he was saying. For a moment she considered the incredible failings of otherwise intelligent beings. Some person in authority had actually hired this senile old geezer to stand guard over priceless controversial research. She shook her head, thinking of the scores of people who would love to be invading this building tonight and just how God Almighty easy it would be.

The old man started to close the door.

"Excuse me," Vala said, "but I was told to deliver the envelope directly to Dr. Randelar. Could I see him, please?"

"Heh?"

"Could I see Dr. Randelar?" Vala shouted, reflecting that what appeared to be stupidity might be deafness.

The old man's face lit up. "He ain't here. Nope, he left."

"He was supposed to wait for the envelope. Headmistress LeSabre said he'd be here till eleven."

"Eleven," repeated the old man doubtfully. Then after a long pause and a glance at his watch, "Well, he was here all right. Yessir, you just missed him." His face was more trustful, as if the eleven o'clock element had established beyond the shadow of doubt Vala's right to be here. "You couldn't have missed him by more'n five minutes, I'd say," the old man confided.

Vala's chest itched maddeningly. She felt her knees buckle and wondered what would happen if she just passed out here on the floor. Her mouth was absolutely dry, as if not a drop of saliva remained.

"Are you all right, Miss? You got a terrible look about you."

"Just worried about . . ." Vala paused desperately, unable to remember her own story.

"This here envelope," the old man filled in. Thoughtfully he continued, "If it's that important, I'll tell you what I'll do for you. I'll take this here envelope up to the doc's office, so's he gets it first thing. How's that, now? Because I won't be on duty when he gets here in the morning and I wouldn't trust that day man for nothing. I'll take it right up there. You just sit yourself in that green chair, the one by the door." He trudged off, his body at right angles to the floor, his finger darting into his mouth to begin the lip-wetting ritual which was apparently something he did to fill the time.

Vala wondered longingly where the kitchen was, wishing for water or, better still, cold beer, if they kept such a thing. The sudden heat of the room had begun to make her sweat. The sweat ran over her sores, burning and itching intolerably until she was ready to start tearing at her clothes and screaming for help, for relief, but then there was just this one chance left, she thought dizzily, before the end of the world.

She quickly edged down the hall into a darkened doorway, feeling her way with wet slick hands, leaving perfect sets of fingerprints in a trail down the hall. Once into her hiding place, she waited for the guard's stumbling footsteps to approach and retreat; waited further for an exclamation or alarm when she was found to be missing, because there was no reason for her to be getting away with this and, anyway, she half wanted to be caught, wanted it to be over, so she could stop being strong and could scratch and writhe with the intolerable pain, but that was not to be the way because silence and darkness maintained.

Edging once again down the hallway, she realized she wasn't sure where Dr. Dyer's office was. Her senses were confused. Maybe she'd passed it or maybe it was that room just ahead. Did she dare put on a light? She stumbled into a dark room, her eyes burning as the sweat dripped into them, and fumbled for the flashlight in her pocket. The thin beam of light showed an empty brown desk, a row of books on the wall, a rolled-up rug in the corner, nothing. She began to move down the corridor again, less careful now not to make noise, hurrying, feeling that in some way time was running out.

She went into three more rooms, ran past several more. She wasn't thinking anymore, just hurrying, rounding a curve and then she saw it, a simple bronze nameplate on whose shiny surface was etched: DYER. She drew a deep breath. She was shaking slightly at her own success.

The office was cold and impersonal. There wasn't a touch of life; no plants, paintings, or photographs. Only a solid steel desk with chair and a row of filing cabinets.

She approached the cabinets almost silently, her soft-soled shoes moving rapidly, gracelessly, across the tiled floor.

After several minutes the spark faded from her eyes, replaced by a cloud of confusion. Most of the drawers were empty. Those that weren't contained nothing more than medical articles, carefully categorized and bound in plastic.

That damned chart, Vala thought, it must be here. Her eyes moved swiftly to the desk as her nails dug into pus-swollen flesh. Some kind of letting go was happening inside her. She could feel it. A weakening of defenses. Hotter. She was getting hotter. She had to hurry. She was losing her strength.

The top main drawer of the desk was empty save for a pair of sunglasses and a razor blade. She quickly opened the middle side drawer. Folders. Twenty-five carefully labelled folders. Beth Allen, Willa Bishé, Jennie Dobbin, Doris

Encoda; one for each of the girls at Triesius. She examined each one carefully. Odd, she thought. Some of the folders were marked with a red letter A. Others were marked A, B, and C, as was Vala's own folder. The C was circled in red ink.

She stood completely absorbed, fascinated. A, B, C. What did it mean?

Clumsily, she removed the twenty-five folders. Her fingers were shaking so violently that two of them slipped sideways and fell to the floor. To her highly tuned ears, it sounded like a loud crash. She laid the other folders on the desk and fanned them out. She felt lost. Disoriented. She could make no sense of it. None.

Suddenly she heard footsteps. Quickly she put out the flashlight and knelt behind the desk. The footsteps paused outside the door for a moment and then retreated. Instantly she rose from her crouched position and made her way to the doorway. She peered out.

A light went on all at once at the far end of the hallway. Now she heard voices. Low, muffled voices followed by laughter. Men laughing until she thought they'd never stop. She took several steps toward the desk, then stopped irresolutely. Time to find a way out of here. Perhaps the window in Dyer's office.

Weakly she drew her hand across her forehead, staring at the light and then she felt her legs moving, taking her to the doorway even though her mind was ordering them to stop, because this was really suicide, but she couldn't stop. She had to see even if she wasn't to be allowed to tell it. She had a right to know, didn't she? She had a right to that much. She was walking an invisible line down the center of the corridor.

A sudden thought almost made her turn; the file folders still lay across Dyer's desk. Two of them on the floor. She kept moving.

She came at last to a whole suite of rooms, entered by double doors that were propped half open by door stops. She stepped closer. Right up to the entrance. She felt shrunken in size. The doors seemed immense.

Through a mist, she saw two attendants in white coats sitting at the end of a table sipping coffee. There were papers scattered along the table and heavy books and a separate unit where there was a sink and clamps and various containers.

Throughout the room was the noisy sound of an air pump.

Uncertainly, Vala inched forward, her eyes seeking she knew not what, and then there was suddenly no doubt; she was seeing something more incredible then she had ever wanted to see, because that was a living brain she was staring at, wasn't it? A living human brain? A brain that rolled and twisted with the same agony and confusion that she had felt inside her own head. A drumming pulse began to throb in her temple. Maybe it was her own brain that she was seeing, some kind of horrible practical joke that all of Triesius was in on, everybody except her. And then she felt herself begin to slide down onto the floor and the light was going out and she had one illogical unconnected thought. That life was goddamn sad, but there was nothing she could do about it. Desperately, she grabbed hold of the door frame for support.

Moments later, she was staggering toward the exit door, the last ounce of her strength carrying her into the awaiting arms of darkness.

SEVEN

There were eight men in the board room and two women, Yvonne LeSabre, blond and gaunt, and Shelby Paul with her freckles and red hair. They were all gathered around a long table spread with papers, pens, cups and saucers and crystal ashtrays. The air smelled of early-morning men smells, shaving lotion and cologne, and underneath that was the rich aroma of fresh-perked coffee.

Despite the social smell, the people in the room were cold and separate from one another as if each was attempting to say, "The business at hand has nothing to do with me, nothing at all." But, of course, it did. Every person there had a professional stake in Triesius, and something personal as well that went right down to the morality of the issue; and how each man and each woman regarded the latter revealed the moral fiber of each of their souls, who they were as human beings.

Each was vitally concerned.

This was true of Dr. Randelar, the distinguished genetic scientist, and it was true of the Chairman, Harlan Tyler St. John, who was the wealthiest and, quietly, one of the most powerful men in the United States. It was true of Head Councilman James DeWitt. It was true of Yvonne LeSabre and Shelby Paul (who was actually a much smaller cog in the machine than she considered herself to be) and of Dr. Hamilton and the other scientists who were committed to Randelar's research. It was true of every individual in the room. They all had a great deal to lose and they all had a great deal to gain.

The light in the room was unexpectedly dim. This was fortunate because today, Thursday, December eleven, fourteen days before Christmas, no one felt like looking anyone else in the eye.

Dr. Randelar had been speaking for some time in his tired monotone. Jimmy DeWitt, watching him and doodling on his yellow legal pad, thought it was amazing that Randelar wasn't attempting to put a bit more emotion into his voice since it was his research that was at stake. The most important goddamn research of Randelar's life. Jimmy was caught by the fact and stopped doodling to watch Randelar closer.

Rhythmically, the man's words continued, each following the one before without inflection or force. Jimmy marvelled. It was incredible, but the man was making absolutely no effort whatsoever to sell his proposal. His voice was perfectly flat and disinterested, his face bland and tired. Only a slight satisfied gleam shone from his deepset eyes and Jimmy thought that was another surprising thing, because the man ought to be worried as hell right now.

Randelar was now stating, "I have concluded that it would be inopportune for any of the students to leave the campus. Therefore the Christmas recess must be cancelled."

"Cancelled?" the Chairman interrupted sardonically. "How would you suggest we manage that?"

"Easily enough," stated Randelar calmly. "The majority of the campus has been inoculated with a virus. I've seen to it that the symptoms are unusual enough to warrant a quarantine."

In the undercurrent of surprise, the Chairman's voice emerged clearly. "Who gave you permission to do such a thing?" he asked furiously.

Randelar paused. "Permission?" he repeated, eyebrows raised. "Well, in any event"—negligently—"what's done is done, wouldn't you say?" He glanced into his notes and picked up his place in the speech, concluding without a word of apology or further explanation.

Incredible, Jimmy thought, just incredible. At that moment, Randelar's lips curved slightly, an arrogantly self-confident smile and Jimmy thought, so that was it. The man must be such a conceited bastard that he had absolutely no concept that anyone could disagree with him, could possibly not accede to his desires. And then on second thought, Jimmy decided that it had to be more than that. Randelar was too intelligent, had risen much too far to be blind to men like the Chairman.

The Chairman stirred, adjusting the lapels of his imported silk suit. A carnation was affixed fashionably to the left lapel and he bent forward slightly to sniff its fragrance before he took a handrolled black cigar from his pocket. The room was silent, waiting, as he went through the ritual of rolling it on the table, removing the band and loosening the tip, then burning it with a match to assure an even smoke. Randelar seemed perfectly at ease, sitting quiet and relaxed in his chair. Perhaps it was this that irritated the Chairman. That there was a man apparently immune to his force. Abruptly he thrust the cigar to one side, not bothering to light it.

"I thought I gave you an order," he said, the color rising in his cheeks. "And, by God, Randelar, I'm not the man to ignore. I'll see that you never get another government grant! What in the hell made you think you could go against my orders?" The room exploded with the Chairman's anger.

"What orders were they?" inquired Randelar innocuously. "I don't remember any specific . . ."

"Low profile!" screamed the Chairman, a vein in his forehead throbbing. "I said keep it low profile! First it was the goddamn Rob Villines interview . . ."

"Dr. Dyer is no longer with us," murmured Randelar.

The Chairman's scream rose higher. ". . . and the next thing I hear is you want to slap a quarantine on the entire campus!"

"My purpose is to maintain seclusion," Randelar said smoothly. "The quarantine supports that."

The Chairman controlled himself from making a quick retort. He was the kind of man who could abandon anger when it seemed to serve no purpose. Also he was no fool. By getting angry in the face of Randelar's composure, he was becoming less powerful than the scientist. He sat for some moments in stony silence.

"Let me try to explain my position, doctor," he said finally in a reasonable voice. As he continued, a folksy quality crept in, another approach he used from time to time. "Let us say that I'm a man who planted an illegal tree in the park. I did it more or less secretly, because there are a lot of people who might fear this tree, might call it an evil tree. Well, just between you and me, I don't give a damn what these people think because the majority of people are jackasses, you see.

But on the other hand, neither do I want to be caught in a circle of charging jackasses."

There was an uneasy laugh from most of the people at the table, which the Chairman rewarded by a thin chuckle of his own.

"So you see the position I'm in," he continued. "I go against public opinion, I plant the tree, but I try to disguise it a little. Maybe I call it a flowering chestnut or something. Low profile, doctor, you see? But now all of a sudden, the damn tree starts growing all over the place and people start to whisper, 'By God, what kind of a flowering chestnut grows like this?' The damn tree is a monster. About this time, I begin to get very nervous.

"Now one of the people in my organization takes it upon himself to get into a public controversy. At the same time people are gossiping about my tree and I'm really on the barbwire fence, caught by the seat of my pants, wouldn't you say? Somebody says the tree is growing poisonous fruit. Somebody else claims that something's evil about the tree. While this is going on, I'm still trying to be low profile, I'm still claiming it's a flowering chestnut, but I'm in a hell of a mess." He paused to light his cigar, puffing lightly, three little audible puffs that somehow accented his words. "Now the final straw," he said quietly. "Somebody builds a fence around the tree and quarantines it. The jig, doctor, is up. You want to call attention to something, just build a fence around it and say it's got a rare disease. That goddamn tree would be on the front page of every newspaper in the country. Probably with me hanging from its top limb. And, of course, my various . . . accomplices . . . from lesser limbs. Is that perfectly clear?" He blotted his forehead with a monogrammed blue linen handkerchief. His gaze was fixed significantly on Randelar's face, meaning that he had already made up his mind.

"The best thing to do," the Chairman concluded, "is to let the girls go home for Christmas. How can that possibly hurt the research program? In three weeks, they'll come back and suspicions will be forgotten. Normality will have been restored. It will give us the necessary breathing space."

Randelar responded that for one thing it was, well, a known fact that the school was in danger of losing Vala Hayes. They absolutely could not let the girl leave the campus, because she would never return.

"How do we know that?" interrupted the Chairman.

"We know," stated Headmistress LeSabre, speaking for the first time.

Randelar continued. "Within two months, we will be ready to perform a major chromosome operation on the girl, but until that point . . ."

"Chromosome operation," repeated the Chairman distastefully. "What's involved in that?"

Randelar began a discussion of the operation, an operation much too technical to be understood by laymen. Jimmy DeWitt studied the faces of the other scientists while Randelar spoke and he was convinced that something other than Vala Hayes was at issue here. Impatiently, he shifted in his chair, irritated by the babble of meaningless words.

"How many girls were given the inoculation?" Jimmy asked hoarsely and felt himself trembling as he waited for the answer. He was thinking about Georgia Urie and wondering if she'd gotten the shot. It worried him more than he cared to admit.

"Most of them," muttered Shelby Paul.

"Beth Allen?" snarled the Chairman.

"Certainly not." Dr. Hamilton leaned forward in his chair. "She was given the preventive vaccination."

The Chairman glanced at Randelar. "That, at least, was a wise decision. Her father is here on the campus. He's taking her home today." He hesitated. "Any objections?"

Randelar shook his head. "None at all."

How nice for the movie star father, Jimmy thought bleakly. His daughter gets exempt. No, they wouldn't want to get the rich and famous Shane Allen mad at them.

Jimmy sat back and listened, his pencil making harsh lines across his yellow pad. What was Randelar up to? He could feel sweat begin to bead on his forehead. Not a cold sweat though; warm sweat as images of Carmel Ritchie flickered through his mind. Why wasn't her name mentioned during this meeting. Why hadn't anyone thus far alluded to what had happened the night of Friday, the fifth of December. It was goddamn nerve-wracking that no one had mentioned it, that the killing was simply being ignored, as if it had never happened. Before he knew he was going to say it, the words had slipped out of his mouth. "Why is Carmel Ritchie's murder being covered up?" he said, apropos of nothing.

Randelar stopped speaking and there was an embarrassed silence. The Chairman gave Jimmy an exasperated glance.

Jimmy persisted. "Why is it being concealed?"

The Chairman shrugged. "Murders happen every day. Every damn day of the week. Some crazy man who sneaked onto the campus with hot pants . . ."

"We couldn't afford to be involved," Headmistress LeSabre said coldly.

Jimmy said incredulously, "So you never reported it. All the time, I kept thinking you'd called in the cops and they were keeping it quiet. Low profile," he added sarcastically and the Chairman's eyes sparked gently, just a warning signal.

"There were other people to consider," the Chairman said. "That particular evening there were a great number of influential people on the campus of Triesius. We had guaranteed their right of privacy."

Jimmy faltered under the ice in the Chairman's eye. "I understand that, sir, but . . ."

"We had guaranteed their right of privacy," repeated the Chairman. "Privacy does not mean being questioned about or being linked to or being charged with a murder." He studied the ash on his cigar. "You have nothing further to concern yourself with." It was clearly an end to the subject.

Jimmy slumped, red-faced, in his chair.

"Christmas recess is at hand," the Chairman resumed after a suitable interval. "We will see that the young women are treated for this—ah, virus—and released to go home."

"Actually, the situation is more complicated than that," Randelar said.

The Chairman's shrewd eyes took a moment to stare directly at Randelar. "Am I missing something?" he said at last.

It was suddenly a two man debate.

Randelar shrugged. "It's the four remaining girls in the Control Group—the girls who were originally given strain B."

"What about them?"

"We can no longer deceive ourselves. The girls are dying." He paused, then added, "The cell structures can hold up another two weeks, possibly three, not more. It is our belief, however, that strain C can save them. We'll need at least three more weeks to prove this theory."

"No. No more experimenting."

"We all know that Carmel Ritchie carried strain C. What

we have found in the autopsy is staggering. Strain C definitely strengthened. Strain C will save those girls if anything can."

"Strain C cannot be further introduced into the lifestream. The Geneva scientists said—"

"I'm afraid it's too late. I felt it absolutely necessary that strain C be administered to the remaining four girls. Now we wait. They must be observed. Here. And they must be anonymous. The quarantine will accomplish this. All anyone will see is one health problem, not two. The symptoms are quite similar."

"So the anonymity of four girls must be preserved at the cost of the health of an entire campus?"

"A small enough cost, in my opinion. The virus is harmless and our research is at stake. In three weeks we will know if we have won or lost. It's a double or nothing situation."

Jimmy's eyes moved to Randelar's impassive face. He now understood completely why Randelar had been so sure he'd have his way. No one could change things now, not even the Chairman.

The Chairman's hand shook visibly as he laid his cigar in the ashtray. He glanced from one scientist's face to the next. Last and most scathingly he glared at LeSabre. "You knew they were doing this." It was a flat statement, not a question. "You had an obligation to keep me informed."

"The inoculation?" murmured LeSabre. "I certainly thought it had your approval, Mr. Chairman."

"My approval," he stated coldly, "is apparently not so important as it was. Once before I gave the order to stop."

"And we did," Randelar said. "The research had failed. But one girl had already been given strain C. Come now, we all knew that Carmel Ritchie was given strain C. If she had lived, the results would have taken weeks or months. Too late to help the other girls. Too late to help the research. But—" he coughed, "you see, she died. And when I saw the autopsy results—" He rose to his feet, excitement richening his voice for the first time. "Then as a scientist, I simply had to proceed." He paused, then added, "When you see what I shall show you, I believe you will concur."

EIGHT

The brain was covered with a film of fluid. As it agitated, it expelled drops of this liquid, but a fine spray from the top of the plastic container renourished the brain continuously. The brain looked vulnerable and, somehow, pathetic. There was something convulsive about its pulsations, indicating panic.

A machine whooshed noisily as the sides of the plastic container moved in and out.

The Chairman shuddered. "What's that sound?"

"It's an air pump," Randelar explained, his eyes curiously alive in his haggard face. "Without oxygen, the brain would die."

"It's alive?" The Chairman withdrew somewhat.

Almost reverently, Randelar's fingers touched the outside of the container. "Perfectly alive. Possibly in a great deal of panic. It may be in a state of trauma more advanced than anything any living person has ever experienced."

The Chairman, standing between Yvonne LeSabre and Dr. Hamilton, struggled for control. "Do you mean it knows what has happened to it?"

The four people stood perfectly still, watching, as the brain writhed.

"Picture the computer of all the senses removed from the organs of sense," Randelar said in a rich voice. "It knows only that it is alive. It can no longer see images or color or even darkness, Mr. Chairman. It is worse than blind. Its audio facilities have been removed. It can no longer even try to hear. It is in a vacuum. It has no taste, no feel, no perception of where it is. It is open, lying on a sheet of wet porous human skin, removed from its body. It is without perception of any kind and yet, theoretically, its memory banks are completely intact. It remembers. It knows what was. But it has no way to compute what has happened to it and we are unable to tell it. It is impossible for it to communicate to us and it's impossible for us to communicate to the brain."

The Chairman's eyes bugged, but he was unable to keep himself from staring at the pulsating organ.

"The brain of Carmel Ritchie," said Randelar. "Beautiful, isn't it? In itself, void of the sensations it remembers. And yet, I know a way to make it feel once again. Pain . . . even pleasure. I can do that," he said, patting the container as gently as though it were a woman's body, one he knew intimately.

The Chairman's face was a model of reserve. He was quite suddenly seeing a new side of Randelar, one that made him uneasy, but one that at least showed Randelar's vulnerability. Here with his work, Randelar was as sensitive as a lover. Inappropriately so. If he were thus vulnerable, he could be controlled. Now that the Chairman knew this, he would be watching Randelar even more closely.

Covertly, he shifted his focus to LeSabre, who interestingly enough in this particular setting was least accessible to decipherment. She was staring expressionlessly at the container. One hand smoothed back her sleek blond hair in absent strokes.

"Why is this necessary?" the Chairman asked, gesturing vaguely toward the receptacle.

"You have some objection?" Randelar's voice was mildly surprised.

"In some departments, this would be called extreme and unusual cruelty," the Chairman said drily. "But I don't suppose you look at it like that. I'm not certain I would concern myself with it either, if I were you. You and I are different from the majority of mankind, Randelar. You understand my meaning, I'm sure. There's a quality we have in common. I recognized it in you immediately. We are superior to the average man and, therefore, exempt from the laws that govern him. At least, that's always the way I've seen it. And if I'm wrong to feel the way I do and to do some of the things I've done, frankly I don't give a damn, doctor. Even if I were convinced I was morally in the wrong, I would still proceed as I have proceeded and hang the morality. Nevertheless, arrogant though I am, I'm glad this particular blot lies on your immortal soul and not mine."

"Immortal?" Randelar queried, his mouth wry.

The Chairman smiled gently. "I'm interested to know how this applies to genetic research."

Dr. Hamilton seized this opportunity to make his presence remembered. Hurriedly, he flipped open the metal chart that lay flat on the table beside the container. "It's all rather technical," he said importantly. "The electroencephalograph tests are here, the sensitivity probes, the pain threshhold and adaptability monitoring . . ."

"Pain threshhold," murmured the Chairman. "But in its current state—"

"We have our ways," stated Hamilton.

The brain pulsed, its thoughts for the moment contained within its plastic walls.

"It's the center of it all," Randelar said softly, staring into the container. "In time, I will have performed hundreds of experiments on this brain. I will know it intimately. Unfortunately, it will never know me. Sad, wouldn't you say?" Although his voice sought to mock, there was a spark of genuine regret there. He shrugged it away.

"In the end," he continued, "when I can afford to lose it, I'll begin the most important part of my work. If I achieve the results I anticipate, we shall see cell-toughening. Adaptability. If I can tamper in such a way with a mature brain, then similar experiments will be conducted on our test embryos. These embryos will probably be almost worthless. But the second time around, we should do a great deal better and so on. And, of course, they'll be conceived of the best genetic stock available."

"It's incredible," gushed Dr. Hamilton and both of the other men lapsed into cool silence. Hamilton turned awkwardly away, aware that he had been remonstrated for his inappropriate outburst of enthusiasm and, in a moment, the Chairman said:

"How was it possible to save this organ? I understand the girl had been dead for some time . . ."

"It couldn't have happened more ideally for our purposes," Randelar said. "As the head was decapitated from the body, it fell into the ice water and was frozen almost instantly. Fortunately for us, of course, the brain was frozen as well and this prevented the vital fluids from draining away. This is the memory fluid, the blood food, the sugar solution and so forth."

The Chairman glanced toward LeSabre and Hamilton, who were conversing quietly together in front of the plastic container.

"Do you mind if I change the conversation for a moment, Doctor?"

Randelar shrugged.

"I believe I have radar," the Chairman said. "It's saved me a lot of money from time to time. I'll hear a convincing talk, everything will be in order right down the line—literature, credit references, everything. I'll have my fountain pen in my hand. But then that radar clicks off in my mind and I won't sign. Something was wrong, that's what I felt and it wasn't based on anything."

"Interesting. But what is this leading to?" Randelar asked politely.

"Your audacity. It's your goddamn repugnant audacity that's putting us all in danger. That's my sixth sense."

"I believe if you'll look into my background . . ."

"I know every pimple on your ass. And I also see now that this research is a little too important to you at this time. It makes you forget your discretion. It's screwing up your timing. Be honest for a moment. Will you admit that six months, even a year from now, would have been a better time to begin fertilization?"

"I'm completely familiar with the process," Randelar said stiffly. "And this time there are no laboratory mothers involved, so the whole risk element has completely changed."

"Artificial everything, eh? Is that brain artificial?" he said, glancing toward the tank. "Was the girl's death artificial? Someone killed that girl. Convenient, wasn't it? Her death. Had she not died . . ." The Chairman broke off as Randelar actually laughed.

Yvonne LeSabre and Hamilton glanced at him in surprise wondering what could have possibly evoked a laugh from the man who seldom smiled.

Randelar paused for a moment, then said simply, "Please understand. There is nothing—nothing—I won't do to further this experiment. Everything that I do as a scientist for the rest of my entire life relates to it. Who killed the girl—why she died—really isn't my concern. If it served the project's best needs, I would contribute my own life. It would be a trivial contribution actually, if it furthered the research."

"Very laudable," the Chairman said dryly.

Randelar placed his hand on the Chairman's shoulder. "We are so close, Mr. Chairman. Strain C has performed a miracle. You can see that. Without it, this organ would never have survived. I'm convinced strain C will save the other four girls. If not, well—we had lost anyway, hadn't we?"

He paused and looked intently into the Chairman's eyes. In the sudden silence, the air pump sucked rhythmically. Strained understanding flickered behind the Chairman's eyes.

"I don't believe I want to hear anymore," the Chairman said.

"That's up to you. If you'll excuse me, there are a few things I—"

Just then the door to the isolation room opened. A neatly clad guard entered and went quickly to Yvonne LeSabre. A moment later LeSabre shook her head.

She waited for the guard to leave the room before stating, "Mr. Chairman, I'm afraid I have bad news."

"What is it?"

"It seems someone broke into the laboratory here last night. Went through the files. From the description the guard on duty gave—the person was Vala Hayes."

NINE

It was rolling now. Georgia could hear a faint roaring in her ears like a wind shaping itself into a black funnel or like a bowling ball spinning dead center down the lane toward a pale silent array of awaiting pins. Georgia was certain that momentum was building. There was a force and there was a target and there was a D-Day.

This morning the note had come, slipped under her door sometime before daylight. "Take the afternoon bus to Rosemont. Please. Vala." And then as an afterthought: "Destroy this note."

Carelessly Georgia wadded the paper into a ball and tossed it toward the wastebasket. "Shit," she murmured tolerantly, meaning that she wasn't going to play Vala's game, but at two p.m. she found herself, after all, trudging through slush to the parking lot where the Triesius bus sat waiting.

Vala was already aboard, sitting alone, third row on the driver's right, looking limp and bony and unattractive. Her complexion had gone yellow and her hair lay flat and lifeless against her skull.

Ghastly, Georgia thought, pausing in the aisle. "007 reporting for duty," she hissed down at Vala, a grin tugging at the corner of her mouth. But Vala barely glanced up, her eyes distracted as if they were seeing inward rather than making any real contact with the outside world. She seemed to be concentrating on some thought that had nothing to do with Georgia; an unhealthy concentration, the way a dying patient sometimes concentrates on death and refuses to focus on life.

A doctor recognizes that concentration as an enemy that can kill.

Once Georgia had even seen that same distracted quality in the beady eyes of a bird. It was on the six o'clock news. The bird had gotten covered with oil during a tanker leak. There it stood on the beach while rescuers worked over it. Trembling, saturated, doomed. Concentrating on death. That was what Vala reminded her of. That bird. Georgia felt her heart roll sickeningly and it was at that moment that she began to hear the roaring in her ears.

"I'll see you in town," Vala whispered and turned her head to stare out the window. It was a dismissal.

Obediently, Georgia moved two rows further back and sat down, also alone. Aloneness was becoming a common factor at Triesius lately. There was also a different feeling in the hallways, less talking, less laughing. Wait a minute. She tried to remember accurately. Was there really less laughing or was that just her own unsettled state of mind, her paranoia?

All at once she had a clear image of Jennie Dobbin standing in the shower this morning. Just standing there, her eyes round vacant circles as the water flowed over her body, soaked her hair, even flooded her unprotesting eyes and still she didn't blink. A red rash covered her neck and the thought had mechanically crossed Georgia's mind that the rash looked like an infected case of poison ivy, but how could Jennie have poison ivy in the winter? The main thing Georgia was thinking, however, was how strange it was to see silly, chattering Jennie Dobbin standing there in the shower, just standing there, frozen into a trance like a zombie. And only Monday at Forum she had been fine.

Georgia felt the bus take off and turned to see that most of the seats were deserted. Curiouser and curiouser, as Alice in Wonderland would say. The bus was usually loaded with girls going to Rosemont for dinner and a movie or shopping and now here she sat on a practically empty bus, with a few silent girls scattered here and there, shivering and staring out cold frosted windows.

Ass, Georgia cursed herself silently, knowing she was making up things to worry about, seeking distraction from her own deeper thoughts. These thoughts were confusing lately. This morning there had been two messages. One from a man who had not left a name. One from James DeWitt, Councilman. Georgia closed her eyes briefly and let her mind settle momentarily on Jimmy DeWitt. It was a shameful image and her mouth curved down slightly. She remembered him at the social—stumbling over his words, self-conscious, and how she had felt strangely willing to toy with the man. Like a cat toys with a mouse, she told herself. And then later, down at the lake, the way he had looked at her. So humble it hurt.

A slight bump and she opened her eyes.

The bus rounded a curve rapidly and Rosemont came up on the left, the shabbier part of Rosemont with squat little grey houses on dirt lots. Brown paper over the windows and falling-down roofs and big cars in the driveways. Food out of the mouths of babies to put gas in the stomachs of the cars.

These houses were scattered far away from each other, too poor, they seemed to say, even for the purchase of society. Georgia stared past the transparent image of herself into these invisible lives and, because she was so removed, it seemed to her that there were aspects of these lives she could see better than the people who were actually living them. Perhaps if they could see her, they could also make correct observations. From their separate world, perhaps they could tell at a glance the secrets of Georgia Urie.

She imagined a dirty-faced acre farmer looking at her and saying . . . what? In his hick voice, somehow proud of his own ignorance . . . What could he possibly have to say to her? Nothing, actually. He would only laugh. And in that derisive laugh there would be an accurate observation. In the bus window, her pale lips smiled in cynical agreement with the acre farmer.

Finally the houses grew closer together, the properties became better cared for, the houses nicer and the cars, in some cases, more compact. They passed a gas station and an auto parts store and a spacious white house with an adjoining doctor's office.

The bus slowed, turned right and right again and stopped to unload. The girls signed out silently, one by one, and climbed from the bus.

Downtown Rosemont was four blocks long with the main street severed by a railroad track. Twice a day, trains stopped traffic and interrupted conversation.

Georgia had always found Rosemont people standoffish and watchful. In superficial contacts made with them in shops or the cafe, she sensed a strange mixture of coldness and piety. One thing was for certain, they didn't like strangers. It was also obvious that, being from Triesius, near though it might be, was still being a stranger and the students were treated with reserve over a layer of distrust.

People now turned to stare at the girls who filed down the street, especially the blond beautiful girl who towered over the thin ugly girl who looked dazed and sick. They wandered aimlessly down the main street and finally ended up in Sanders Cafe where they ordered barbecue sandwiches, which were greasy and delicious. Georgia ate hers ravenously and Vala took two small bites and then sat with her mouth covered with a white scratchy napkin. Except for ordering, they had not spoken, but the silence was compelling rather than awkward.

Georgia pushed her plate back and sipped coffee thoughtfully, wondering whether her role was to continue sitting and waiting or whether she should ask questions, such as, what was the big mystery and why had she been summoned. (And I hope to fuck you make it good, she added mentally, but actually she wasn't angry at being here.) "Are you going to get in some Christmas shopping today?" she murmured finally, thinking the question safe, but Vala's eyes were bleak. She swallowed painfully and lowered the napkin from her lips.

"I haven't thought about it," she said tonelessly.

"Why not, for God's sake? I thought you were big on Christmas."

Vala averted her eyes. "Have they given you your injection yet?" she countered.

"What kind of injection? I was scheduled for the infirmary this afternoon, but I didn't go. I came here."

"Don't go back. Don't let them give you that shot."

Georgia pinched her eyebrows together. "Are you going to tell me what . . ."

Vala looked at her directly for the first time. "I want you to see something." Suddenly she pulled up her hair and leaned her head forward over the table, one hand pulling at the neck of her sweater, partially exposing the back of her neck.

Georgia stared disbelievingly and then it was she who was almost sick.

Ulcerated sores oozing with fluid dotted the back of Vala's neck, starting from the hairline and disappearing into the black neck of her sweater.

"God, Vala," Georgia said hoarsely and Vala let her turtleneck settle back into place and sat slowly up, swaying slightly in her chair.

"It goes down the front too. And my glands are swollen and the inside of my mouth is filled with ulcers clear down my throat." Vala's words were slurred as if it were hard to enunciate and Georgia suddenly realized that was probably why she had spoken so seldom.

"I believe they're doing something to us," Vala said. "Injecting us with something."

"Who?"

"The doctors at the infirmary. I believe we're all in danger. That they're experimenting on us."

"Lord, Vala, do you—do you have any idea what you're saying?"

"Haven't you noticed the rash some of the girls are getting around their necks? That's the way mine started too. And girls are getting sick. And look at this." Hands trembling, Vala pushed up both sleeves, then laid her forearms on the table, wrists up.

Georgia gazed and then met Vala's eyes sharply. "When did this start? God*damn* it!"

"Just yesterday. It looks like scales, doesn't it? I—I took a razor blade and I tried . . . to dig into it. Into my wrists. But . . . the skin is like concrete."

"Jesus. And you think they did this?"

"Alan Randelar," Vala whispered. "His research. How's this for a theory—" She paused to cough, a throat-wracking sound. Blood dribbled from her lips and she blotted it away with the napkin.

"What's the theory?" Georgia said after a moment's pause.

Vala shrugged dismally. "He's using us like laboratory rats. That's what I . . ." Her voice died off. She sagged.

Oddly, after the first dizzy moment, there was no doubt in Georgia's mind that Vala's theory was accurate. Vala was Triesius' most brilliant student and Georgia believed in the intuition of genius. Intuition was usually based on intellectual reasoning too subtle and swift to be on a conscious level. The memory of the Villines interview boiled up. Dr. Dyer. Super species. Inhuman.

"Are you sure they're doing this to other girls?" she asked bluntly.

"You believe me then," Vala said relieved, and then continued thoughtfully, "I thought it was just a few girls at first . . ."

"Doris Encoda . . ."

"Yes. I guess. They were always doing all sorts of psychological testing on me. And all sorts of new tests to determine different aspects of the I.Q. Not the cube, probably nothing you ever heard about. They froze different parts of my brain . . ."

"What? You let them do something like that?" Georgia felt the fine hairs on the back of her neck rise.

"I didn't know at first what they were doing. I was so used to being tested by that time, I didn't think much about it. I mean, people have been probing into my brain cells since I was six years old. But having my brain frozen . . . It's the strangest feeling, Georgia. The most imperceptible numbness—like a pinpoint. And when they were doing it, there wasn't any real pain, just a little sting. Dr. Dyer used a surgical needle."

"How did you discover what it was they were doing to you?"

"It was the last time they ever did it. Dr. Dyer said. 'I found it! Look at this!' like he was really excited about something and a woman in a white coat said, 'How can you be sure that's it?' and a man who always ran the machine said, 'Because we froze her brain, every inch of it, piece at a time, until we isolated it.' Dr. Dyer told him to be quiet, but by that time I knew. What I don't know is what they found."

Shakily, Georgia lit a cigarette, noticing two people at the next table who were glancing at them. She had seen that sort of glance before from Rosemont people. "Two crazies from Triesius," the glance seemed to say.

"When you found out what they were doing, what did you say?" Georgia asked, lowering her voice. There was no need to warn Vala to speak softer; she seemed to have only the energy to speak slightly above a whisper.

"I didn't say anything," Vala said painfully. "I never felt in my life that I had a right to say anything. That's one of my weaknesses as a human being." She considered that briefly and then added with a little shrug, "I guess I've always just sort of done what people told me to do."

Once again Georgia seemed to hear the rumbling of the bowling ball and at the end of the alley stood Vala, waiting patiently for her own destruction. So little time, Georgia felt unreasoningly. She was somehow sure there was so little time.

"Don't forget," Vala said suddenly, as if she knew what Georgia was thinking. "It's you too. It's all of us."

Georgia heard the bowling ball go whoom! against the pins and heard the voice in her head say, "Got them all, poor helpless bastards."

"I won't be going back to Triesius, Georgia," Vala said, leaning closer.

"Won't be going back?" repeated Georgia blankly.

"I have a friend. He's promised to take me away from Triesius. He's meeting me behind the courthouse at four-thirty."

"Who is this friend?" Georgia asked suspiciously. Vala glanced away, avoiding the question. "Vala, it's not that I doubt you, but—but was it this friend who suggested we all might be in danger?" Vala still refused to comment. "Vala, please—I want to be sure how this whole thing really got started. Maybe it's just a bug that's going around. Maybe your friend wants—"

"I know what they're doing. It's no bug." It seemed impossible, but Vala's voice grew even fainter, almost soundless, a mere flutter of air passing through trembling lips. "I broke into the laboratory last night. I saw records . . . They're keeping daily medical records on each one of us here at Triesius. I saw something else. A disembodied organ. A brain. It was alive. I swear it was—" She swallowed; tears had filled her eyes.

"What was in the records?" Georgia frowned.

"I didn't have enough time to read them completely. But they're marked A, B and C. Most of the folders were only marked A. My folder was marked A, B and C." Again she paused, then resumed uneasily. "Georgia, you have to believe me. All the girls I've noticed who have the rash. They all had injections about three days before they broke out. There's something else that worries me. Beth's disappeared."

Georgia felt a sudden hollowness in the pit of her stomach.

"What do you mean—disappeared?"

"I asked to see her this morning. They still said no visitors. I waited until the nurse's station was empty. I went to her room—room one hundred twelve. That's the number they gave me when I sent a note. She never answered the note.

When I got to room one-twelve, she was gone. The bed was stripped. Her clothes were gone. I've checked everywhere. She's nowhere on the campus."

"Vala—"

In the wake of Vala's dismal gaze, Georgia's voice fell away. She thought irrelevently: It's dark in this place, as if they've turned out the lights. She shivered. "Vala, let's get out of here. Let's go to the courthouse and wait there."

Light clicking of spike heels sounded on the floor and a musky odor of fragrance suddenly filled the air. "Vala, this is very foolish of you," said a woman's precise voice. Yvonne LeSabre sounded very sympathetic and a little remonstrating and in back of it all, pleased as a purring cat. "You're much too ill to be away from campus, my dear, and I think we did explain that to you, did we not?" Firmly, she dug her red nails under Vala's thin arm, forcing her upwards out of her chair. "Have you paid your bill? Perhaps Georgia would . . ." LeSabre paused, caught in thought.

"I'll pay the bill," Georgia said swiftly. Her eyes were on Vala's terrified face.

But Vala's gaze eluded hers, darted past LeSabre's swept-up blond hair, settled on the source of daylight: the heavy oak-framed door that stood ajar.

Vala whimpered. "You . . ." she gasped. ". . . you told them. Why? *Why?*" A small groan of agony ripped her being—an internal cry that linked her to Philip Angusi, who now stood in the doorway, his head lowered. His presence carried Vala closer and closer to the point of hysteria.

Georgia turned back to Vala. "Is the professor—is he the friend who was going to help you?"

"Yes!" Vala screamed as a pair of hands seized her. Instantly she closed her eyes and moaned. Mourned. There seemed little else she could do.

LeSabre glanced sideways at Vala and then back at Georgia. "Forgive me," she said in a soft, concerned voice, "but are you sure you're quite all right? You look a little pale. There's a bug going around, you see, and . . ."

"I'm fine," Georgia stated firmly. "I'm going to do a little Christmas shopping and then maybe I'll see a movie . . ." You can't stop me, she thought, staring at LeSabre without fear.

LeSabre smiled. "I believe we can all go home a little early today."

"I don't want to go home early."

"I'm sure," LeSabre said softly, "that you're not going to be unreasonable, Georgia."

"I'll be anything I please," Georgia began angrily and then broke off.

Over LeSabre's shoulder she saw Professor Angusi back out the door, his slight frame replaced by the burly bus driver whose square face was set and determined as a bull. Behind him were two of the school's security guards, wearing similar steel-colored uniforms, the same determined expressions.

Slowly Georgia turned away, frightened by the looks on their faces. The depth of her fear amazed her. She was even more amazed when the two guards began moving slowly in her direction.

TEN

Beth rode a long wave of dizziness. Sometimes it seemed like a dream. But Headmistress LeSabre had showed it in her face, Shane in his behavior, in the way he moved about the room and scarcely looked at her. She could hardly believe it was happening.

"Shane, I don't understand—"

"Please, baby, for everything there is a time and, believe me, the only thing it's time for now is for me taking you by the hand and getting you the fuck out of here!" He forced a grin. "When I say I'm in a hurry, I'm in a hurry. I didn't even take time to rent a good car. I'm driving a Pinto. Can you imagine me driving a Pinto?"

Beth looked up at her father from where she sat on the bed. She thought he looked like a giant. And so healthy, she thought drearily, her throat aching with tears again. "God, it's terrible, Shane," she whispered, listening to the silence of the halls. "Am I the only one—the only one—who got vaccinated in time?"

Mrs. Fazio appeared suddenly at the door, wearing a purple wrapper, her blue-grey hair awry. "It's awful strange," she whined, "how you get to leave the rest of us. I never heard where one gets to leave during a quarantine. A quarantine means nobody leaves."

"Beth, put your coat on," Shane said swiftly, ignoring the woman who hung in the doorway, nervously playing with the buttons on her wrapper.

"I haven't packed yet." Beth stared at Mrs. Fazio with

haunted eyes, at the redness of the woman's flabby throat.

Shane picked the silver fox jacket off the bed and lifted Beth with his other arm. "So who needs to pack? You'll be back after Christmas vacation, isn't that right?" He smiled mirthlessly into her eyes, telling her, Baby, baby, don't you know we're running a bluff? Don't you know we've got to get out of here before they change their minds? Any moment, somebody else may be standing at that door and then I'll have to slug our way out of here.

"What's happening?" Beth whispered with trembling lips.

Shane stopped and hugged her suddenly, so hard that he hugged the breath out of her. "I don't know what's happening," he whispered back in anguish, his lips against her hair. "All I know is I'm getting you the hell out of here."

She felt rather than heard his voice, because he had barely spoken, barely released his words into the air. But with her head nestled against his chest, she felt his vibrations. Fear, she thought. Shane was afraid. She accepted the urgency then.

"Okay, Shane," she said on a shuddering deep breath. "I'm ready to go."

Mrs. Fazio blocked the door. "Take me with you!" she begged, unconsciously clawing at the rash on her neck. A trickle of blood ran down from an opened sore. "I'm too old to go through this. They'll kill me. I could tell you plenty about what's been going on here. If you help me, I'll tell you everything you want to know."

Shane's eyes were fastened on her hands, spotted with age and bulging with dark blue veins. They were reaching out to grab his wrist. Under the nail of her forefinger, right hand, was a well of infectious blood. Shane motioned her back. Puzzled, she stumbled back and then, almost sobbing, came toward him again, reaching. Her words droned. As she spoke, she retreated and advanced, an aging bull uncertain in the ring.

Beth watched her in fascination. She thought she had never seen anything so pathetic and ugly as Mrs. Fazio at that particular moment. Never beg for anything, she thought. Not if it looks like this. Not if it sounds like this. The sound was as terrible as the sight of the woman herself. Every once in a while, she would hit a word for emphasis. These sounded like little screams. Please, please, please, please, please, please, please,

please. After a while, that's all she was saying, Please, in a series of little screams like a fly caught in a web watching the spider advance.

Shane interrupted gently. "Would you like to go with us? No, now you mustn't touch me, you see, because you've been scratching yourself. If you'd like to go with us, you'll have to go get dressed. You can't go in a robe, now can you? Hurry now and be sure to wear gloves."

Distrustfully, the woman still blocked the door. "You promise you'll wait for me? You have to promise. You have to give me your word as a . . . a gentleman, you know. I'll believe you then. You know, I always watched all of your pictures. I always was a big fan of yours."

Beth felt the knot of tension in Shane's body that was a solid wall between her and Mrs. Fazio, but he spoke cordially, unhurriedly. "Is that a fact? Well, Mrs. Fazio, I give you my word as a gentleman then, if that's what you want. Now hurry, if you want to go."

Simpering, the woman hurried away down the hall, scratching now at her arm, contaminating a new area of her body.

Shane waited at the door watching and smiling as she kept looking back over her shoulder for reassurance. His hand was like a vise around Beth's wrist, cutting off her circulation, but she hardly felt it because all of a sudden she had picked up Shane's panic and it was building inside of her, blocking off everything else, every other emotion except the panic, and so, when Mrs. Fazio at last disappeared into her room at the end of the corridor, Beth would have bolted from the doorway, carried by the force of her terror.

Shane held her back. "Wait, baby, wait. Don't you know human nature? Just wait, you'll see."

Craftily, Mrs. Fazio's blue-grey head popped from the door, her eyes searching their way to where Beth and Shane stood waiting. A selfish smile beamed across her lips.

"Old biddy wouldn't care if she spread the pox to half the population," Shane muttered, returning her smile and motioning her to hurry. When her door closed again, he waited a moment and then said decisively, "Well, that's it. Let's go," and he was leading her down the back steps out the fire door like he'd planned it. The parking lot was not far, but Beth's legs were trembling so that she stumbled and Shane picked her up and carried her.

It seemed to her that it couldn't be happening. The strangeness of being carried by Shane for the first time since she was a little girl. His being strong and her being weak, when for so long now she had felt like the strong one. Even the oddity of seeing Shane behind the wheel of a cheap car threw her into a state of vagueness. There was nothing to hang onto except the continuing feeling of panic. It was the one thing she could pinpoint that felt solid. She could feel herself shivering, so she supposed she must be cold, but she didn't even feel that on a conscious level. She tried to picture Karl in the cabin over by the lake, but at that moment, Karl seemed like someone she must have made up. She felt the car stop, heard Shane's voice and another man's voice. The other man sounded a bit uncertain, Shane very sure. She felt the car take off. She kept testing herself. Nothing, nothing, nothing. Just the panic, the fear.

"Did you hear the old witch scream?" Shane asked after a while.

"No. No, I didn't."

"She pushed open the window and yelled bloody murder. Christ, I can't believe you didn't hear that. 'You gave me your word! You gave me your word as a gentleman!' " Shane laughed.

"You did, you know."

"Good thing she didn't ask for my word as a rogue and a bullshitter. I might have been stuck then."

Beth laughed uncertainly and the laugh caught in her chest and throbbed in back of her breasts. "Shane, am I doing what you said Mrs. Fazio wouldn't mind doing? Am I spreading germs to everybody?"

"You had a vaccination, didn't you? If anybody's spreading germs, it's me."

"Shane, they didn't give you the serum?"

"I didn't deliver my hide into their hands, baby." His profile was virile and strong. And determined, she thought. Most of all, determined. He reached over and covered her hand with his. An unexpectedly tough hand for an actor and hot with California sun. "I'm stronger than any piss-ant bug you ever heard about," he said. "You believe that, don't you?"

"I believe you, Daddy," she whispered and tears burned her

eyes because he was so goddamn wonderful strong. Staring at him, the panic started to drain out of Beth. In a rush of grateful emotion, she felt pain again, felt alive again, began to come back to who she was. It was like she was thawing. She must have been in shock, that's all. She remembered Chip, her puppy when she was a kid. Chip had run across a busy street when she'd opened the door of the car. A taxicab had run over him and Shane had said, putting his hand over her eyes, "Well, honey, that's the end of Chip, I'm afraid," but then the taxicab went on and Chip was standing there all right. The cab had missed him altogether, but he was just standing there frozen from shock. Shane had gone out and picked him up and Chip didn't move, couldn't move. For an hour he was a statue and then he was all right. That was shock and that's what she'd had. Shock.

"Are you okay, baby?"

"I'm fine now, Shane. I'm really okay."

At the airport, he took her to the Executive Lounge. He had coffee and she had a Coke and they both had steak sandwiches. She was beginning to relax a little now. Her appetite was back. She found herself laughing, listening to Shane telling about a silicone starlet who ended up with one breast two sizes larger than the other and no time before the picture started filming to get a repair job.

"What did she do?" Beth asked chewing.

"She made it with the cameraman."

"Why did she do that?"

"In order to get his word of honor to favor her right breast. We'll go see the film when it's released. I want to see how good a job she did on the cameraman."

"Shane!"

"You want another steak? Dessert? You're all ribs. You scare me letting me see you like this. Have a milkshake or something, for God's sake."

"What time does the plane leave?"

He glanced at his watch. "Ten minutes," he said quickly reaching for his wallet. "We'll have to make that a milkshake to go."

"Never mind. I'll eat another lunch on the plane. That should make you happy."

"Yay!" he said pushing money under his empty plate.

"Come on." He put his hand under her elbow. "You concentrate on walking. I'll concentrate on talking."

"What are we going to talk about?"

"Ach—ach—you're supposed to walk—I'm supposed to talk. Get it?"

"Got it."

"Good," they said in unison.

"Now," he said, dragging her along. "Do you know what I'm getting ready to do?"

"What?"

"You won't like it."

"What is it?"

"Faster, faster. You're going to miss your plane."

"I'm running now and I can't keep up with you. What am I not going to—wait a minute." She stopped dead. "Whose plane am I going to miss?"

"Your plane."

"You mean just my plane? Not our plane?"

"Baby, it's one of those goddamn things. I can't leave New York right now. I've got business up to my eyeballs. I'll be home in a few days." He was hurrying her along again.

"I'm not going," she said at the check-in counter.

Shane winked at the blue-coated check-in attendant. "Don't worry. She's going."

"I'm not going," she said at the first-class boarding terminal.

"You're going, all right." He held her gently as she tried to bolt past him. "You can either walk onto that plane or I will personally carry you onto that plane."

"I'll throw a tantrum."

"You know me," shrugged Shane. "I never minded a good tantrum. It's you who always wants to avoid scenes. Get going."

"Do I have to, Shane?"

"Well, you're of age, but I'm stronger than you." He crushed her against him for a moment and then pushed her forward. "I love you, Baby."

"I love you too, Shane," she said coldly, not moving.

"Okay," he said and scooped her up into his arms as the door were being prepared for closing.

"What are you doing, Shane?"

"I'm showing you I've still got a lot of muscle." He deposited her inside the plane and told a grinning stewardess, "Make sure that young lady eats her lunch. See you in California, Baby."

The door closed behind her and the stewardess had taken her ticket before Beth had time to decide if she was angry with Shane or not.

As she retreated toward her seat, the stewardess's voice trailed after her. "Nice to have you aboard, Miss Allen."

"Thank you," Beth murmured and felt cut off, felt both silly and depressed; it was the solitude—no, it was the isolation she now felt that bothered her the most. Running had been necessary to escape, but from what, from what?

Instead of finding an answer, she sat motionless in her seat and found the journey a long scream through a dark tunnel of thoughts that seemed to go on forever.

ELEVEN

Georgia had kept her eyes fastened on the sharp shining steel as it punctured the skin of her upper arm, stinging a little.

The odd thing was not being at all sick and yet knowing that she'd been infected. Georgia hadn't even bothered to fight the needle or to argue with the nurse who honestly seemed to believe the nonsense she was saying about a flu vaccination.

Smiling, the nurse emptied the contents of the hypodermic into Georgia's bloodstream and withdrew the needle, leaving a bubble of blood which she hastily dabbed with alcohol on a ball of cotton.

"Sorry," she said.

Georgia glanced dully from her arm to the nurse. "For what?"

The nurse laughed slightly and held up the blood-stained cotton. "I should have done a better job."

"Oh, you did a good job," Georgia said tonelessly, putting her hand over the injection. It burned hot under her fingers. "You did it just fine."

Now, many sleepless hours later, she lay in her bed in the student infirmary imagining the silent army that was moving through her body. The enemy had invaded her. She waited. Waited to be sick.

Beside her in the only other bed in the dimly lit room was Vala Hayes, who was a frightening picture of what she herself would soon become. Eaten up with infection, no strength left to fight.

Nervously, Georgia made claws of her fingernails and

dragged them time and time again across her scalp, down through the strands of her thick blond hair. Vala's raspy breathing filled the room and the sound both depressed and reassured her. Depressed her because the sound reminded her how sick Vala was and reassured her for another reason, something her mind kept refusing to acknowledge.

No, she would not allow herself to think . . .

It was Vala who said it first. Sometime in the middle of the night, she said in a calm, crisply lucid whisper, "Do you suppose I'm going to die, Georgia?"

"No, of course not," Georgia said crossly. "You're going to be fine, Val. Don't try to talk. Sleep."

"I've just been lying here thinking. I don't know how my parents could handle something like that. If I should . . ."

"Val, please don't keep talking about that," Georgia said desperately.

"I can't help it. I keep seeing their faces, Mother's and Dad's. They've been through so damn much with me."

"All parents do," Georgia said carefully. She remembered all of a sudden that Vala was hardly more than a child. Only fifteen. Fifteen goddamned years old, she thought bitterly.

Vala lay silently for a moment and then said, "In a way, I ruined their lives. I did that to them. I made them just as sick as I was, because I kept pulling on them, dragging them down with me. I could see it in my father's face sometimes, but I couldn't help myself. Everything kept falling away and I had to hold on to something and so I held on to them."

"That's what being a parent is, Val."

"It wasn't fair," Vala said obstinately. "It shouldn't have to be that hard. There should be some joy or what's the point of it? The questions they had to try to answer when there weren't any answers, when even the questions scared them. Think about that, Georgia. I could tell sometimes that they were terrified, dreading to think what I'd come up with next. And I couldn't help myself, I'd say it anyway. Some of it was really bad. Some religious things. Other things too, weird things. Obsessions."

Georgia's hands clenched, her nails digging into her palms, and the voice inside her head, which had been silent now for some days, laughed mockingly. *What's the matter, Georgia? You're not scared, are you? You're not letting her get to you, are you? Are you, little Miss Cheesecake?* Georgia groaned between tightly ground teeth.

Vala was saying something in a more casual voice, as though she were telling a mildly amusing story.

"What? I can't hear you," Georgia said, a pain trapped inside her skull like a weight.

"I said there were two weeks once when I was obsessed with the process of my body." Vala actually laughed a little, a tiny uneasy laugh that caught in the mucous of her throat. "I could picture the whole thing," she went on hoarsely. "I could see the blood going through my veins and arteries, picture my heart pumping, feel the capillaries in my eyeballs. I couldn't eat because I started thinking about the digestive enzymes in my saliva and how food was broken down in the digestive process."

"Jesus," Georgia said weakly.

"Dad had to take off from work because Mother couldn't take care of me alone. You see, someone had to be with me every minute." Vala stopped to clear her throat and then in a moment, she whispered, "Georgia, did it ever happen to you?"

"Not that."

"No, of course not that, but . . ."

"Other things," Georgia said reluctantly.

"It's because of our minds." Vala's voice was eager. "They're able to concentrate longer and deeper than a normal mind. They get trapped in trouble areas—"

"It doesn't happen to—to every genius," Georgia said, having trouble vocalizing the word. She felt like a fraud.

"You know there are logical geniuses and there are emotional geniuses, Georgia. The logical geniuses are the lucky ones. Everything's an equation to them. They don't actually *feel* the vastness of the universe, they aren't frightened by it. They're intellectually fascinated by it. It gives them joy to prove theories and make hypotheses."

"Like how there's no God," Georgia said caustically.

Vala hesitated. "Yes."

"What about Carmel Ritchie? Which category of genius was she in?" Georgia heard the name slip from between her lips without much surprise. Carmel kept lingering in her mind somehow, bubbling up to the surface at odd times. "What about Carmel?'' she continued unsteadily. ''She wasn't intellectually stimulated and she didn't seem to feel much either. Except depressed if her hair was messed up.''

''Carmel was obsessed,'' Vala said instantly. ''It takes one to know one and I knew she was obsessed. With her beauty, don't you see? And she was also sensually obsessed. Boys, food. Did you know she would sometimes eat four banana splits at one time and then come back and stick her finger down her throat so she wouldn't get fat? She would have been a suicide case if she'd lived.''

''I'm the opposite,'' Georgia said. ''I plan to be very happy. That is, if . . .''

There was a brief strained silence and then Vala whispered, ''You never told me. When they took you down to the examining room. Did they . . .?''

''They gave me the shot,'' Georgia said, hot stinging tears filling her eyes.

''Oh,'' breathed Vala tremblingly and she fell silent, not even bothering to suggest the possibility that perhaps the injection hadn't been what they were both so certain it was. Their common certainty united them, as did their fear, their entrapment. They seemed so close at that moment it seemed they could read each other's minds, as if their thoughts had become transparent images breathing through the walls of their minds. So it was that Georgia suddenly knew without question that Vala was crying in the darkness, not making a sound, but crying, releasing her pent-up feelings in a flood of little-girl tears.

''Hey,'' Georgia said softly, getting up, feeling her way between the two beds, shivering as her bare feet touched cold tile. ''Don't do that,'' she whispered, sitting on the side of Vala's bed, and hesitantly, feeling repulsed at the physical contact, she leaned down and slipped her arm under Vala's shoulders.

''It's almost Christmas,'' Vala said in a strangled voice.

''The bastards.''

''Why did they have to do this at Christmas?''

''Why did they have to do it at all?'' Georgia returned bitterly, lifting Vala's body up against her own and noticing that she was on fire with fever. ''I wish you wouldn't cry, Vala,'' she said softly. ''It isn't good for you.''

Vala wept louder, putting both arms around Georgia's neck, and for some reason, Georgia felt less awkward now about the feel of Vala's body against her own, just a very faint numbness in her upper chest where a slight strain of resistance remained.

"Why?" Vala gritted out, her voice breaking. "Just tell me why. Why are they doing this to us? What is Randelar trying to do with his research?"

"I don't know, Val, and yet . . ."

"It is Randelar, isn't it?" finished Vala in a small voice, but her body was already quietening. Georgia settled her carefully back on the bed, drying her eyes with the edge of the sheet. Vala's hand was locked around Georgia's wrist, her eyes staring up at her in the dark, sparkling with tears.

"I'm sure it's something to do with medical research," Vala said after an exhausted moment of thought. "But I swear I can't see my way from one end of it to the other."

"They're in big trouble," murmured Georgia. *"We're* in big trouble."

Vala lay more relaxed in bed, her hand loosening around Georgia's wrist. "Triesius," she said with sad irony. "It was supposed to be wonderful. I thought maybe I'd get stronger here, and in a way, I did, Georgia. I was starting to talk with other girls and I was handling my own fits of depression and it was starting to be a lot better for me. But now—"

In the next moment, the strength seemed to be seeping out of Vala's body and a relaxation almost dangerous in its deepness had set in.

"Can you sleep?" whispered Georgia, brushing strands of hair from Vala's forehead, and Vala nodded, blinking heavily, trying to stay awake.

"There was something else I wanted to tell you," she murmured, her words slurred as though she'd been drugged.

"Just sleep, Val. Don't worry about anything, just sleep."

"It's about Philip," Vala breathed softly. "I didn't tell you—" A slight smile curved her thin lips. "I figured it out. Why he did it, you know. He and I . . . we're so much alike. We don't have the strength to go against the tide. Philip couldn't betray Triesius."

"He could betray you though, couldn't he?" Georgia retorted and then regretted her bluntness. "I'm sorry."

"Don't be. You just don't understand weak people. Philip and I—we're putty in the hands of strong people. It wasn't me he betrayed—it was himself. Don't you see? Try and . . . forgive . . ."

Her eyes fell heavily and she slept.

Frowning, Georgia stared down at her, feeling suddenly lonely and frightened again. When there had been the two of them, all at once nothing had seemed quite so unsolvable. But now she wasn't sure again.

Gently, she smoothed the sheet across Vala's chest and rose, following her own restlessness to the small high window. The outside of the building was flooded with light and she wondered if there was a guard. Maybe if she got a chair, she mused, she could climb up, use something to break through the window and . . . Nervous exhaustion tugged at her, making such plans impossible.

Maybe tomorrow after she had slept. Maybe tomorrow she would escape and get help for Vala and herself. And the others. How many others; would it be all? Where was Beth and where was Jennie—and all the others? Oh, God, why was she trying to pretend she didn't know that the other girls must all be here in the infirmary, side by side in rooms like this one, up and down the corridor. What are they telling our parents? What lies? How long before someone doesn't believe them? Insists on coming to see their daughter. Insists . . .

Vacantly, she stared out at the line of trees facing the window, feeling incredibly lonely. It was a completely new feeling for a girl who had in the last few years sought solitude, shunned companionship. If she could only go on with her life now, she'd be able to reach out more. People would be more important to her. Then in a rush of cynicism, she thought that probably that was all bullshit. Crisis over, she'd freeze back into indifference and nothing would matter.

Georgia's eyes shifted suddenly, attracted by a flutter of movement beside one of the trees outside the window. It was as if her gaze all at once found itself telescopic and adjustable, able to focus itself on the most selective of images.

The shadow had appeared first. Thin, wavering, falling across the shrubbery and onto the icy clearing just ahead. Then, cloaked in shadow, his back to the moon, he stepped forward from the bushes into view. He paused for a moment, only his head rotating slightly as if to survey the grounds that lay crystal-white and sparkling before him.

Strange, Georgia thought, and moved still closer to the window, standing on tiptoe to see better. The boy's hand moved abruptly and Georgia felt her throat constrict. Something metallic caught the moonlight and glinted. A knife. The boy was holding a knife.

Georgia's mind began to race, her heart pounding in quickening thuds against her chest wall. She wasn't sure now—was it a knife? Her breath was beginning to steam up the window. She smeared her palm across the cold glass—squinted, watched as the boy stepped forward, his face looming up at her. And then their eyes locked.

Georgia put her hand across her mouth and frantically stepped backward, stumbling slightly away from the window. The boy's face, she thought. His face. It was the tenseness of his face and something about his eyes that caught her, made her start to remember something. Something about that face, she thought numbly, staring and then suddenly she heard quick, soft-soled steps approaching and arms pressed themselves upon her. Voices spoke, but no one seemed to understand what she was saying. The boy, she kept trying to explain. The boy with the outline face. The boy who had sat next to her on Forum night and who had called her over and over again. He was waiting out there for her. Even now, he was waiting out there for her, with his sharp hunter's knife.

Something heavy was binding her. She couldn't move her arms. She hated that claustrophobic feeling of being trapped. And then suddenly she heard someone screaming and, confused, she wondered who it was. The screaming continued until the world seemed alive with the shrillness. It's me, she thought in wonder, I'm screaming. And she felt her throat straining, her vocal cords vibrating painfully, and still she couldn't stop. She never felt the needle, never felt herself sinking, just fell suddenly into a blackness that was complete and perfect.

Sobbing, Karl Immer sheathed his knife and sank to the ground, his head between his knees. He sat this way for a long time even though he was long since due at the laboratory. The way she had looked at him—the fear—the hate. She didn't understand. Just as the laboratory people didn't understand. They thought he was some sort of weirdo, he could see it in their eyes. *I'm just hired help*, he felt like telling them. *Just like you. It's not my research. I don't know anything about it.* But he did. He knew too much.

His sobs began to abate. His anguish was lessened by the dry choke of sudden fear.

He wished he had taken care to know less. But now that was all too late.

Panting, he hastened to his feet, wiping his cheeks with both hands. He was suddenly in a hurry. Not wise to be late. Act like normal. Give them what they wanted.

And wish to God he hadn't been born a genius. A higher I.Q. than Beth, for God's sake. One hundred and ninety. His sperm, tampered with, had fused with a test-tube egg. That egg had been implanted in his girlfriend Joyce, who "needed the money." Too bad that Joyce, the surrogate mother, had absorbed an alien substance from the fetus she carried. It had killed her. Too damned bad, that. But that had been the beginning and now he was in too damn deep.

Karl Immer, male donor, superb genetic stock, began to run to Research. He knew they were waiting for him.

TWELVE

Many years from now, she was sure, when she looked back on her life, she would remember the last few days of this week, this day of this week, really, and would consider it as a landmark, a turning point in her life.

What she felt inside was a sense of sadness. It was, above all, a painful sense of betrayal.

Seven hours ago she had sat in the room she had occupied for three and a half months, the room she had studied in, slept in, laughed and entertained friends in.

Now, in the pale wash of twilight, cool for a California evening, she walked alone in her garden, trying to release herself from the nagging cocoon of introspection, from the nagging thought that she had betrayed her friends.

Beth stopped suddenly and glanced down. She had come upon a lizard. So grey was its color to match the stone it sat upon that she almost stepped on it. In alarm the lizard went skittering, changing colors as it went: brown to match the scattered cork, green to match the grass, grey again as it blended into the sidewalk.

Beth thought as she watched it go that Triesius was such a lizard, different in every light. It changed even in her mind as she tried to see it, to capture the last days spent there in her imagination. Here in California, amid tropical splendor, it was possible to pretend that Triesius was merely a novel she had been reading and all its people merely characters, shadowy sketches drawn from the pen of a confused author.

But Vala and Georgia had been more than that. They had been of real flesh and blood, and Beth felt anew, with a sickening lurch, that they were still back there, locked away and perhaps seriously ill.

With what? What kind of a virus?

That's what Sara had asked Beth on the way home from the airport. A reasonable question.

It doesn't have a name. Virus X. How's that?

What symptoms?

Who knows. Who cares.

Now in frustration, Beth banged her fist against the bench's armrest. *I care,* she thought. *I care! I care!*

Dammit! She had allowed Shane to segregate her again. Single her out as someone who was not part of the norm. But she had been part of the norm, hadn't she? Hadn't she shared herself with Vala and Georgia? Hadn't they reciprocated in kind, confiding in her their most intimate emotions, thoughts and feelings? Vala, who had been alone, always alone, and Georgia, one of a kind Georgia, both special. Together with herself, they had formed a strangely compelling threesome.

And what about Karl? Oh, God, Karl. She groaned.

Things had moved so fast at Triesius. One minute she had been with Karl, the next she wasn't. Questions chased after each other. Where had he gone that night? And why? And when he came back, were they waiting? Did he know they had taken her away? I felt a hundred miles away from you that night. Lying there, staring at you across the room. You were somebody I didn't know. I think that was somebody's fault. Yours? Mine? Maybe it doesn't matter whose fault it was, but dammit, I thought I knew things about you. Like how it was to experience the Grand Canyon on a motor bike. If I could see you right now—

The thought trailed off. She couldn't. She was banned from Triesius. Locked out. They were locked in. She was out.

Forget Triesius. It doesn't exist.

But if so—if Triesius didn't exist, then nothing existed. And there was going to be a deadly silence over the rest of her life. The kind of silence an only child sometimes feels on a rainy day when left to play in an empty house. A frightening feeling, that aloneness, almost like living in mortality, which according to Shane was a terrible mistake. "Live," Shane always said, "in *im*mortality. Die in *mortality*. That's the only way to have any fun."

Beth rose from the bench and walked, kicking up pieces of bark. Tomorrow perhaps she would go into downtown Beverly Hills for a facial. Then to Ivar's for a haircut. Then to the skating rink. Get down to the business of making the faces disappear. Vala's scared face, Georgia's sad face, Karl's remote face. Make them go away. For lunch, maybe she'd call some of the old gang. Fellow movie star kids. They could all sit around and complain about how tough it was to be rich and privileged. Tough.

And Triesius didn't exist. Rosemont, New York, was a million miles away. Just a hick town frozen into a single image in her mind the way she had seen it that night out on the lake . . . dark, bleak and, most of all, icy. She settled on that. A rolling landscape sealed in ice. Soon to be obsolete. Such was the effect of an ice age.

And then it appeared. Out of a single grey square block of ice, a face emerged. Still in shadows. There and yet not there. One step closer and she would see it clearly. The blades of darkness that fell across the man's forehead and cheeks, that shadowed his eyes and his lips . . . those blades of darkness would part and she could gaze at him. At last, she would see him.

Before her gaze, the setting sun blazed red. Bright red. It dissolved into blood that ran down from the girl's neck. Drenching her dress, her coat, Beth's hands as she shook the body by the shoulders.

The man was gazing at her from across the lake. Running now. She could see the moonlight break over his face.

The head bobbed up. Blond hair. Vacant eyes. All gone now. The life's all run out of me, said the eyes. He did it. That man. Can you see him?

Beth leaned over, her whole body heaving. Screams were driven from her.

The man stood watching. Beth straightened. For a moment their eyes seemed to meet. And then by the off-center angle of her body, the wailing of her screams that had no focus or direction, her head that was raised up to the dark sky, by all of this she was telling him . . . I don't see you. Not at all. You're nothing more than a shadow to me.

The man waited for a moment. Then he was gone.

Beth stopped walking now. Her eyes were burning with unshed tears. The California sunset had never been so bright. Almost bright enough to see through a memory of the grey frozen landscape of Triesius, three thousand miles away.

THIRTEEN

Vala had no illusions about the situation. The danger was tangible—she could feel it surging through her veins, could smell it in the air she breathed, hear it in the subdued voices around her bed. Dr. Hamilton's head shook from side to side. Not good.

"Ah, well, we'll see," murmured LeSabre through dry lips, watching her.

In a moment, they were gone. Immediately, Vala struggled to a sitting position and glanced at Georgia's empty bed. How long now since they had taken her away? And where? Time. Time was of the essence.

Dizziness flooded her as she thrust both legs over the side of the bed. Her eyeglasses rested beside her contact lens case. She put on the glasses and strained to see the wall clock. It was four a.m.

She was burning hot, a dry heat that built insidiously. Higher. Higher.

Her hand shook as she drew Kleenex from the box on the bedstand and soaked them in the pitcher of cold water. She wrung the tissues over her head, felt the water saturate her hair, trickle down her face and neck. Then she plunged both hands into the water, brought them still wet to her forehead, her upper arms. A moment later, she was burning up again.

She had to get out of here. Before it was too late.

In a moment of bravery, she let her body fall forward, thrusting her weight entirely upon her legs. They buckled. She cried out as she fell forward, sprawling the length of her body on the tile floor. Her glasses flew across the room with a resounding clatter. Hopelessly, she lay there on her stomach thinking that at any moment they would surely come.

Seconds passed; minutes.

She had to get out of here.

The urgency of fear pushed her forward. She began to crawl toward the door. Looking up, she saw the blur of shining metal and reached for the door handle; used it to drag herself up. She stood there, flattened against the door, her breath coming in shallow quick gasps.

A moment later, she was limping back across the room; apparently she had hurt her right knee in the fall. No matter. Nothing would stop her.

She had no money, not even small change. She needed change for the phone. Her fingers explored the top of Georgia's bedstand. Nothing. She drew open the drawer and thrust her hand inside. A small leather pouch, heavy with change.

The room was nothing more than shadows to her unfocused eyes. A swift search for her glasses proved fruitless; she was in too much of a hurry to look further. She reached for her robe and slippers, both the same drab green as her hospital gown.

Again she was at the door, the handle cool beneath her fingers. Through the crack in the door, she gazed at an approaching figure. The nurse paused and glanced in her direction. Then checked her watch and hastened forward around the corner.

Vala slid from the room. The glare of overhead lights made her blink. She clutched the change purse harder and muttered through gritted teeth, "I'll make it. I've got to make it."

An increase of ventilation sent a stir of air under her thin robe. She hesitated, uncertain. Turned right and then back. She was totally disoriented, totally lost. One thought sustained her. *A phone. I must get to a telephone.*

She stumbled forward, almost falling, and steadied herself against the wall. Her hand touched a red line. A broken red line, she realized squinting. An arrow pointing to a fire exit.

Without hesitation, she raced forward, her fingertips brushing the wall. She fancied the nurse was behind her, running after her. Any minute. Any minute she would be there. Ahead of her the arrow thickened to a point. Here. Right here. She threw herself against the door. It opened so swiftly she was fairly catapulted into the night, so suddenly she had to run in order to keep her feet under her.

The coldness was delicious. Thin ice cracked under her scantily shod feet. The wind opened her robe, spread it around her like a billowing cape. Her hot skin collected cold droplets from the moist air. She felt like she was flying.

Under the dim shimmer of stars, she slowed, forced herself to seek the path. It was all so deceptively easy. An unseen hand seemed to take her by the arm. This way, now your feet are on the path. Catch your breath; you remember the way, don't you? *I remember.*

Past Research, down the curve toward Administration. If they watched her, she couldn't tell. Everything was a blur.

A small structure loomed ahead. She allowed her steps to quicken. She aimed her body at the structure. In a few quick strides, she collided with it. Almost sobbing, she clutched the wall of the phone booth and pulled herself inside. For an instant, she stood there, her head in her hands, both elbows on the metal counter below the telephone. The feel of the leather pouch against her cheek brought up her head. She unzipped the pouch and fumbled for change. She found a quarter, dropped it into the slot and dialed 0.

"Operator. May I help you?"

"Operator, I need the police."

"Where are you calling from?"

"I need the Rosemont police."

"You can dial that—"

"Can you dial it for me?" Vala's voice broke. "Please. This is an emergency."

The operator's voice hesitated momentarily. "Hold on."

A clicking as the connection went through and then a cheerful voice identified himself as Sergeant Carrolton of the Rosemont Police. Vala drank in the solidity of his no-nonsense tones, the certainty that at last she was doing the right thing. Sergeant Carrolton was going to believe her, was somehow going to save her. Was going to save them all.

"Triesius. Yes, I know it," he said. His voice was a shade less friendly. "What's the trouble?"

"I'll tell you when you come." Her voice sounded strange to her own ears. Garbled. She cleared her throat. The pain was catching up to her. A long time now since her last pain-killing shot. The pain—

His voice interrupted her stream of consciousness. "Now see here, where are you calling from?"

"From a pay phone in front of the—" Mucous choked her voice. She coughed.

"You don't sound so good."

"It's—my throat hurts. Please just send a car. I'll meet you outside on the main highway in front of the gate."

"What?"

"The highway in front of the main gate," she said, forcing herself to speak louder. "Pick me up there."

"I tell you what. I'll pick you up if you'll tell me what this is all about."

"I—I—PLEASE!" she screamed. "I can't stand here much longer."

"All right, calm yourself. Now I need to have your name."

She was whimpering now, great heavy sobs that caught midway in her throat. "In the name of God . . ." She broke off, unable to continue.

He hesitated. When he spoke, his voice was crisper, more authoritative as though he'd suddenly come to a decision. "Stay where you are. Stay on the campus. Where is this phone booth?"

"It's in front of the Administration Building."

"All right. I'll be there in ten minutes."

Vala was slow in returning the phone to its cradle. It was like cutting off an unseen life support system. She shuddered and once again lowered her head into her hand. A memory nudged her—she raised her head just a bit to stare at her wrist. Then at both wrists. She stared until her eyes burned. The scales had turned brown. Had climbed up her arms. Disappeared into her gown. Crawled along the backs of her hands. Down her legs.

She spun away from the booth. Gasped for air. The world shone yellow to her eyes. Everything yellow. She could feel herself changing.

She tried to scream. Heard a strange animal sound that fought with her own voice, before she could regain control.

"I'm okay," she breathed shakily. But she knew it wasn't so. She would never be okay again.

All illusions were gone. It seemed to her that an icy breeze was blowing through her head, forcing away the past, forcing her toward a moment that would be somehow unique. A beginning. Or an end.

Maybe it was the night, she thought. There was something

so mystical about the night. Banks of grey-white clouds over a black sky rolled above her up-turned face, kept reforming, blown by the wind to shape different pictures. She watched, trying to see God up there as she always secretly looked for His face in the clouds. She was not a person who didn't need God. She wished she was, because so many of her instructors had felt it their responsibility to prove to her He didn't exist. And still she looked for Him in the clouds.

In a quick ceremonial gesture, she touched herself on the forehead, the lips and, lastly, over the heart. The truth, she entreated reverently, as known by the head, as spoken by the lips, as felt by the heart. But once again God was silent.

She raised her hands to her face but shrank from her own touch. The skin was too hard. And deep down under the skin was an itching that was maddening. Nervously, she glanced around. Despite having stepped off to one side, she was still too visible. Any second she felt she would be seen. She tried to move closer to the building, away from the light which spilled softly from the overhead lamppost.

Time. She could feel it moving. Moving. It was no use.

Regardless of Sergeant Carrolton's orders, she couldn't stand there any longer. She would have to get to the front gate.

Quickly she ducked off the main walkway. She couldn't feel her legs any longer, only her forward movement as she darted into the darkness.

The path dipped down to the right, through a row of gnarled oak trees and twisted briars. The bare branches of the trees arched over the pathway, encasing it like a webwork of bony fingers. A thin sliver of moonglow shone over the wooded area just ahead of her. She dared not look back. Safety lay ahead; she could hide along the front wall beside the gate until the police arrived. She would be safe there.

The thought made her move faster. The briars snagged her clothing. She desperately tried to force her way through them. It was no use. She spun around, thinking there was an open space to her right. She had taken only a few steps before getting entangled again.

She was breathing faster now, gulping for air, and then she thought she might not make it. The deadly cold had taken hold of her, and despite her frantic movement, her hands and feet had begun to grow numb. It took all her existing strength to untangle herself, to put herself into motion again; running.

The closer she got to the wall the more difficult was her progress because it had grown significantly darker and because there was no discernible path to follow. She had to slow down, feel her way, taking one careful step at a time, blindly.

And then in the utter darkness, she heard it. A sharp crackling sound directly behind her. The sound of a heavy foot snapping twigs. Her breath caught in her throat as she stood motionless, listening.

Another twig snapped underfoot.

Quickly she knelt in the underbrush and waited. There was no sound to be heard now and no one in sight. Yet she felt a sense of helplessness.

A sudden little wind sent branches brushing against her cheek. She drew back, taking hold of them. And then she saw it, the shadowy figure of a man standing not more than twenty yards away from her. She could barely see him. He stood motionless, his body blending with the many tree trunks, his head rotating slowly as he scanned the surrounding area.

Vala carefully lowered herself to the ground. She could see between the rocks. The man paused a moment longer, then started walking in her direction. Vala instantly felt panic take hold. Ahead of her, not forty yards away, was the wall. Should she try to make a run for it? The highway was just beyond. And light.

All at once the man stopped, glancing back toward the campus.

At that same instant, Vala could see the headlights of a car as it slowly wound its way down the highway, heading in the direction of the Triesius campus. She was certain that it was the police.

"Please, God," she pleaded with closed eyes, "let it be the police." She could see light through her closed lids. She imagined the entire area flooded with brightness as she pressed her lids tighter, still pleading inwardly.

Some kind of letting go was happening inside her. She could feel her energy weakening; feel her grasp on life loosening. She was terrified. She who had always been afraid was experiencing the ultimate in fear as she pressed her body closer to the ground. But why was it so light, light that seemed to zero in on her, drawing the fluids from her body in a wringing sweat.

Her eyelids shot open. The surrounding area lay about her in grey-black shadows; the man had vanished; the brightness merely an illusion. Just token streaks of moonlight, plenty of darkness to lose herself in.

In the next instant she was up and moving again. Only twenty more yards, she reasoned.

The headlights drew nearer. She stumbled, almost falling to the ground; then, straightening, she regained her balance. But she was too late. From the darkness a hand reached out, took hold of her and began to drag her away into the underbrush.

She pulled free, turned.

She began to run now, her legs trembling, knowing already that she would never be able to run fast enough. When he was on top of her, his arm around her neck like a whip, his legs wrapping around hers, bringing them both crashing to the ground, he allowed her time for one last thought.

Her thought was that she had never really loved anyone in her life, merely needed them. She must have said it out loud because the voice answered her.

"Need is love," he said majestically.

And then—to her surprise—he slew her.

PART IV

Point of No Return

ONE

Somehow, each dream she had dreamt during the night seemed filled with blood. Now as she struggled up from sleep, the dream she had been living in her mind was still sharp behind her eyes . . .

On the dresser she saw a vase within whose porcelain shell grew an enormous white orchid. Straightaway the flower opened out, revealing its lush red center. "Be not afraid," someone whispered. The flower seemed to writhe in agony for a moment, then, with a final shudder, sent blood spewing from its center to gush upon the walls and ceiling of her room.

Each splattering of blood formed yet another flower. Brighter, redder—exploding, the flowers vanished, leaving reddish lip-gloss glows that came together, then fanned out to form a vaporous figure of a young girl. The girl smiled at Beth; then, as if being summoned, she slowly began to drift upward toward the ceiling, where she hovered for a moment longer, then vanished.

Beth awoke suddenly with a splitting headache. She lay still, trying to dispel dream fragments from her memory. The veins in her temples were pumping blood like a fountain gone berserk.

She sat up in bed and swayed. She tried pressing her fingertips into the pressure points to quiet the pain, but nothing close to relief was forthcoming. Certainly sleep was not forthcoming. Not with the confusion that had begun to mix with the pain, churning inside of her until she was driven to rise.

She turned to gaze at her clock radio. 4:30 a.m. The last

time she had looked, it had been 3:45, before that 2:00. Tonight sleep came in brief uneasy moments of surrender to exhaustion. Exhaustion that threatened to overwhelm her, drag her under. Then the dreams, the images, the eyes that seemed to gaze at her from every corner.

Her head continued to throb. In her short green nightgown, barefooted, she made her way into her private bathroom and, staring at herself in the mirror, swallowed aspirin. The expression on the young face was anguished.

Guilt, she realized, forcing down a glass of water. Guilt over being safe at Palmer, the estate in Bel Air, eating fresh salmon hollandaise and brandied peaches instead of school fare, being safely walled in and well when others were not.

Vala's face swam before her eyes. She had looked ill for so long. Depressed, Vala had insisted.

What kind of depression makes you walk crooked and dilates the pupils of your eyes?

If you ask me, somebody's filling her with drugs.

Despairingly, Beth turned off the bathroom light and wandered back into her room. No, not drugs. That was impossible. What then?

She dropped wearily onto the bed. Oh, God—would this night never be over? It seemed all she could do was keep track of the seconds, the minutes, each moment becoming a sort of a freeze-frame action, herself seeing herself, the others, suspended, isolated.

At Triesius, it would be 7:30 now.

Right after dinner, she had placed a call to the school. She had been unable to make connection with anyone save the switchboard operator. The dormitory was closed. The girls had been moved to the infirmary. It sounded like a prepared statement, flat, impenetrable. And then there was Karl in his cabin beside the lake and no way at all to get in touch. She had written a letter addressed only to Karl Immer, Rosemont, New York, but had no faith that it could possibly be delivered. The letter still sat propped on her dresser waiting to be mailed.

She flipped on her reading lamp, her eyes moving restlessly around the room. White furniture, glass shelves covered with plants, deep wine carpeting, white curtains threaded with green and red which were blowing slightly in the mild, almost tropical, breeze. At the far reach of the room was her favorite nook, an indention of walls, making a small room where there was a love seat and shelves of books. On a special shelf along the back were her old childhood books, worn, almost forgotten. Impulsively, she went to run her fingers across their covers. *Little Brown Bear*. Shane used to read that one until she knew it backwards. So well, in fact, that she would correct him on those occasions when he was in a hurry and tried to leave out a part here and there. *Cinderella. Sleeping Beauty*, her favorite.

Musingly, she removed this volume and opened it, her throat heavy with the sort of pain nostalgia brings. In a way, she thought, her eyes glued to the old picture of Sleeping Beauty's castle, Triesius seemed like that. Swallowed in a dense forest—encased in a wall of thorns. She felt the ache of depression and sank down on the love seat, drawing her feet up under her, her head swimming with images.

Karl, her lover; Shane, her father; Sara, her father's lover. People she had grown up with. Grandmother Allen, Raymond, in second grade, who had been thin and tall for his age with thick curling brown hair. All kinds of people loving, in love, or possibly pretending to love.

Beth turned the page, touched the sleeping face of Beauty, peaceful and undisturbed, waiting for the kiss of her lover to call her back into life. Loving was more than a risk, she thought. It was a race. Shed your love of your parents before they could die on you. Fall out of love before your lover could fall out of love with you.

And yet, she loved. Shane was responsible for that. She could not be Shane's daughter without loving. The way Shane loved her. The way Shane had loved her mother at one time.

Closing the book, she curled deeper into the love seat, almost into a fetal position. For a while, she seemed to slow down inside, ceased to worry out of sheer tiredness.

Time went by. Her headache seemed to fade away. Everything became clear. With no effort at all, she was able to see herself lying there on the plush love seat, her filmy green chiffon gown billowing about her. Beth Allen, who always had wanted a friend. Not just any friend. A lifelong friend. Someone really special. And she had made not one but two. Tears gathered in her eyes and began to seep from the corners. She lay here, the elite one, the one who got away and left her friends to their fates.

While at Triesius, there was the flu and something else—a

man. A man who had—she must not be talked out of this—a man who had killed. A man whose face was in shadows, but if she tried—just a little harder—she would be able to make the shadows go away.

Thoughtfully, she pulled herself to a sitting position.

Almost of their own accord, thoughts flowed through her mind like a river overflowing its banks. Things she had known—always known, she supposed. Even though she had heard others deny them.

She had sensed there was something odd about Triesius from the very beginning. Ever since the admission physicals. Why in the name of God had twenty-five healthy intelligent young women allowed themselves to be put through such a thing? Frowning, she tried to consider the question, but it brought itself to no reasonable conclusion. No, it was all in the psychology of the thing that the issue must be pursued. That once upon a time there lived the myth of Triesius. A deceptive myth of such power not to be challenged, certainly not by twenty-five young women so very proud to be there. Proud to be observed. Agreeable to be used. To give of themselves. If hair follicles and skin patches from the inner thigh were part of the bargain, it was not enough to dispel myths.

And besides, the parents had "signed something." Shane himself had admitted it in his first phone call. Beth nodded grimly, then followed her thought process to an inevitable continuation. If all twenty-five had allowed such liberties to be taken with their bodies . . . was it possible that just a few, chosen carefully for their emotional weaknesses, could have allowed a great deal more?

Words. Frightened ghostlike words. Wary, careful. What had she heard?

"First the Ritchie girl and now this. And both of them in the Control Group. Five girls and two of them . . . Don't you think that's odd?"

"Precisely," the second nurse had said. *"That's why you should leave it alone."*

Leave it alone, Beth repeated blankly to herself. Yet the number five stuck with her, turned over and over in her head. Five girls?

Faces slipped by her mind's eye. Carmel Ritchie, Marguerite O'Brien, of course! Beth caught her breath. Blankly, she stared straight ahead, unable to believe, unable even to absorb what she was now seeing. On the stretcher, the body had . . .

A creature covered with scales lurched forward. Hot water poured from the mouth of a shower. Marguerite! Get out of here! Marguerite!

Beth gripped the sides of the sofa, fought off an almost overpowering urge to scream. Her head was aching again, and her mouth was dry.

"But Dr. Randelar assured us—"

"We all make mistakes."

Five girls in the Control Group. Beth wiped large beads of sweat from her forehead. Five girls . . . Carmel Ritchie, Marguerite O'Brien. Beth flinched at the next thought.

. . . Vala Hayes.

Oh, dear God, that would explain it. That would explain Vala's sudden fits of depression. Her constant weakened condition. And Doris Encoda . . . hadn't she been ill long before the others? Yes, Beth was sure she had.

But . . . who was the fifth girl?

Beth couldn't concentrate, couldn't keep the images from puncturing her mind. Mrs. Fazio as she hung in the doorway like a frightened animal: "I can tell you plenty about what's been going on here," she had said.

But Shane hadn't let her finish. No, Shane hadn't . . .

In her agitation, Beth rose, her hands clawing in anguish at the expensive chiffon. Ripping. She felt the anger explode inside of her and surface cleanly as she turned to grasp the silver-framed photograph of Shane and confronted the smiling face.

Shane! Had taken her away! Shane! Was acting Shane-the-powerful! Making her weak, making her a coward who runs out on friends. Why? Why!

If her fingernails could have clawed through the glass, she would have ripped his picture to shreds. Instead she threw it face down on the bed and began to open drawers. She reached for clothes, tossed them haphazardly on the bed. Began to dress.

When she was dressed and heading from the room, she hesitated. She was still trembling, but the emotion was no longer anger. It was tiredness from the rushing about. The thinking. The anxiety.

Slowly she set her bag down and walked back into the room.

She reached for Shane's photograph, traced her finger lightly over his cheek and then hugged the frame against her chest. Then with an unsteady hand, she set it carefully on the table in its old place. She stared at it for a long moment, then turned and left the room.

Somehow she would make Shane understand why it was that she'd had to go back.

Back to Triesius.

Two

Early light broke over the town of Rosemont, the December morning cold, the night frost replaced by dry frigid air. A few people, shopkeepers opening up their establishments, trudged in and out of doors, pulled up venetian blinds and, with steaming cups of coffee in their hands, paused to exchange hellos with their neighbors.

One man, however, did not drift with the easy flow of the morning activity. He was edgy and in a hurry. There was an annoyance—even fear, perhaps—in his clean-shaven, thin-lined face, but no hesitation in the brisk pace that carried him up the steps to his office.

"Good morning there, Councilman!" The voice was obnoxious with early morning goodwill.

"Morning," Jimmy DeWitt grumbled, taking the steps two at a time now.

Before he reached his door, he could hear his phone ringing.

"Damn." His keys flipped out of his grasp and landed at his feet. Angrily, he retrieved them and found the right key to his office. By now the phone must have rung ninety-six times. Hell, it could have started ringing when his alarm clock went off at 6:45 a.m. Not that he had any reason to set alarm clocks these days. He never slept. Never climbed into bed. Never sat at peace. No, always he was moving and, when he sat, he was possessed of a monotonous rhythm that brought his fist striking down on wooden chair arms or tabletops. He supposed it was a way of relieving tension. Or just a damned habit he'd picked up along the way, the way some people doodled to pass the time or filed their nails. His thing was pounding his fist against hard surfaces.

He flung the door open and hurled himself toward his desk where the phone continued to ring like a demented robot. He took a deep breath before picking it up, preparing himself in the same way that a swimmer hesitates before diving into cold water.

"Where have you been? It's nearly ten o'clock, for God's sakes," the voice said with no preamble. "All hell's broken loose."

"Triesius?" asked Jimmy dryly. He felt strangely calm.

"Vala Hayes is dead," she said, almost whispering it.

"Dead?" Jimmy repeated. "Why? What does Randelar say? I thought strain C was supposed to . . ."

"It wasn't strain C," the headmistress said tensely. "She was attacked last night on the campus. She was stabbed."

Jimmy heard the words without absorbing them, just sat there nodding, letting them flow over him without relating to them. Stabbed. Attacked. Stabbed. And then by degrees, his calmness ebbed and he felt his fist strike dully against the top of his desk.

"Jesus Christ," he murmured. "Murder, then. Another murder. Didn't I try to tell you all . . . ?"

"This is solving nothing."

"Well, goddamn it," he muttered.

"I know. The point is, we've got trouble."

"I suppose," Jimmy said caustically, "the campus is swarming with cops by this time."

"No. What I told you about Vala Hayes is strictly between you and me. Only a handful of people know. They have her body hooked up on a life support system."

"WHAT?" Jimmy felt a coldness creep up his spine. "What are you trying to tell me?"

"They say she looks alive. If they decide to, they can do something about her wounds."

"Why are they covering this up?" Jimmy asked hoarsely.

"Time. It'll buy us some time until we decide what to do. We can't have the cops in on this, not yet. This thing is busting open too fast, much too fast. It's like treating rabies. We can't cure the whole problem at Triesius, so we'll just try to handle each situation as it arises. And I mean fast. I have something for you to do."

"Strike me. I'm getting out."

"Too late, my friend. No one gets out now. At this point, it begins to look as though we're all going to be strung up on the Chairman's tree."

"All that has very little to do with me," Jimmy said icily. "I'm beginning to realize something about myself. I never was cut out to be a politician. I was happier in law. So you can tell the Chairman—" He broke off.

There was a long silence over the wire and then LeSabre's voice said in a detached sort of way, "Do you know what happens to small fish when they go against people like the Chairman? They get fried. They start at the bottom of the ladder, Councilman, and work their way up. Do you remember how the Chairman said he'd be hanging from the top branch of the tree? Well, my friend, that may happen, but not until the lower limbs are laden with our carcasses. I can forget getting close to a school again. Not just a good school. Any school. I'll be finished if this torpedo goes off. You can forget ever practicing law again. That's just for openers. No, I'm afraid that nobody gets off the boat now. The only thing we can do is grab buckets and start bailing water."

Jimmy cursed silently, his mind caught in a circle. Every path turned back to point A. "What do I do?" he said and heard the headmistress's breath release in relief.

"The quarantine is now official. The parents are going to have to be informed. Handling the parents is going to be our job."

"Not my job," Jimmy objected. "That's hardly in keeping with my position—"

"It's because of your position that you've been elected. You sound important. For people like Vala Hayes's parents, that's key."

"Vala Hayes's parents . . ." Before he could further object, as he certainly intended to do when the faintness left the top of his skull, she had hurried on.

"We'll make the phone calls, try to calm everyone down. If they insist on coming in, we'll make hotel reservations. Stay calm. And whatever you do, don't mention Alan Randelar or his research or any kind of injections. This is Russian flu or Hong Kong flu—"

"Russian flu," he said automatically. "That's appropriate."

"Whatever you wish. Just so long as we're consistent."

"Consistent," Jimmy repeated and then laughed.

"I fail to see the humor."

"You know," Jimmy went on, "whenever I think of those twenty-five girls at Triesius, I can't help thinking of all those French and German girls in the thirteenth century who set out with the Children's Crusade, only to end up as slaves in Marrakech. The never-ending abuse . . . death at seventeen or eighteen."

Very quietly LeSabre asked, "What did you say?"

"The Children's Crusade. Where good Christian ship captains lured them aboard by promising them the Holy Land, only to find out later that they were to be sold to the Moors as slaves, as prostitutes." Jimmy sighed, then added, "But then most crusades end that way, don't they?"

"Councilman, my best advice at this time is for all of us to keep going—"

"Oh, sure. We always have to keep going. But that doesn't make it any easier. And I might add," Jimmy growled, "that if we go long enough, we become . . . what? Hell, I should have stayed in the Navy. I knew a guy who retired when he was only thirty-eight years old."

"In the meantime, you are—"

"At Marrakech."

"If you wish."

"What I wish is to hang up now," Jimmy said, smoldering with impatience.

"We've a good deal more to discuss. Including Sergeant Carrolton."

Jimmy glanced at the telephone with a wary thoughtfulness. "Rosemont's Sergeant Carrolton?"

"Yes."

"What does he—"

"He received a phone call last night. From one of the girls here at Triesius. We believe he spoke with Vala Hayes."

Jimmy hesitated. "Believe?"

"The girl didn't give him her name. Only asked that he come to the campus."

"For what purpose?"

"Carrolton didn't know. He just said she sounded like she was in some sort of trouble. He hung around last night asking questions. He was here again this morning."

"And—and what did you tell him?"

"That he had no legal power over the university. That he could not question the girls without our provost's permission. The Chairman wants you to go to Carrolton's office. Speak with the man. Convince him that the phone call was nothing more than the ravings of a sick girl."

"Carrolton is a very pigheaded, single minded man. He's not going to swallow that crap!"

"I'm afraid that's the best we can do. It might help if you mention the thirty or so jobs Triesius provides for the people of Rosemont. And the real estate, inventory and payroll taxes."

"What in the hell does he care about that? He's not a politician, he's the biggest pain in the ass in the Rosemont police department."

"Sorry, I have to run. The Chairman would like you present for a meeting at two o'clock today. Here at Triesius. Go to Carrolton, see what you can do."

"Just a minute. Are you sure the girl didn't tell him anything about what's going on? I don't want to look like an ass."

"Apparently Vala met her fate before she had a chance to tell him anything at all."

He hesitated and then said, "Oh, hell."

"Councilman?"

"I started to say—can you believe this—thank God she never got to the police. I've really turned into Triesius material, haven't I? The Chairman would be so proud."

"Stop rolling in the muck, Councilman. It doesn't make you any less guilty or the situation any less grim. That's my advice."

Before Jimmy could respond, LeSabre had given him very precise instructions of what he was to do and without further ado she then hung up the phone.

For the next half hour, he made notes, took phone numbers. In back of it all, he knew the boat was going down and that somehow the Captain had neglected to provide lifeboats.

THREE

At precisely 7:30 a.m., flight number six from Los Angeles to New York's Kennedy Airport closed its boarding doors and prepared to taxi down the runway.

Midway back in tourist, Beth sat breathless, knowing that in some way she was breaking all the rules. She was absolutely certain that if Shane knew what she was about to do—no, doing, as the engines roared—he would not only be furious, but would find a way to stop her. However, she wasn't doing things Shane's way. Not this trip.

"We're about to take off," the stewardess reminded her. "Please fasten your seat belt."

Beth gave her a nod, dutifully snapped the buckle over her stomach, and for the first time let herself ponder the unanswerable question. How had the Triesius people come to find her at Karl's cabin?

Oh, it was possible, certainly it was entirely possible they'd searched the entire area and just happened to find her. But there was something about the way it was done. Something about it being LeSabre who stood there staring at her. So well-groomed, on top of the situation, so capable and unshocked. It was LeSabre's lack of surprise that confused her the most. Karl? Had he called them? And if so—why?

She felt the plane lift, and she knew that the jetliner had left the ground.

A murder had been committed. To a girl who had been in Triesius' "Control Group." Physical experiments? Yes, and the man in charge was Dr. Randelar. But if Carmel Ritchie's death had a connection to the experiments, she couldn't see it.

Abruptly, Beth glanced at her watch, wondering if her absence had been discovered yet. Sara would arrive at Palmer first thing. She would find her absent without explanation (similar to guilty without explanation). Just plain gone. How long would she wait before sounding an alarm that would be heard clear to the East Coast?

Hello, Shane? She's disappeared.

Without seeing, Beth gazed at the airline publication, turned pages in a swift flutter that brought her to the end of the magazine. Then she folded her hands tightly on the cover and sat there full of nervous exhaustion. If only she could sleep. She needed it. Needed it badly.

They had been in the air now for approximately thirty minutes and the stewardess came for drink orders. Beth decided she would have a gin and tonic, and found herself drinking thirstily, rather than sipping. Almost as soon as she drank it, her eyes felt heavy, and she gave into it gratefully.

Not until the wheels set down at Kennedy did she stir, drugged for the moment.

The stewardess had paused in the aisle beside her. "We've just landed," she said.

"Thanks."

Beth groaned and sat up straighter. Stretched. She had slept too deeply to pull out of it easily.

"Excuse me." The stewardess slid in front of the vacant seat on Beth's right. Stood there staring down. "Aren't you Shane Allen's daughter?"

Panic set in. Sara had already called Shane. Shane had called the airline. There'll be a girl traveling alone. Nineteen years old. Long brown hair.

She forced a laugh. "Shane Allen's daughter? *The* Shane Allen? You've got to be kidding."

"Oh." The stewardess kept her eyes focused on Beth's face. To escape her stare, Beth bent to retrieve her carry-on case from under her seat. "Your picture was in the newspaper," the stewardess said. "I mean *her* picture. His daughter."

"Sorry. It isn't me." Beth stood, case in hand, purse slung over her shoulder. "Excuse me." She tried to push past the stewardess into the crowded aisle.

"I met him once," the stewardess sighed. "I was working

first-class from Kennedy to L.A. International. It was—what—the beginning of this month. He was—yes, I can do that," she interrupted herself to answer a short excited gentleman who was demanding his hang-up baggage.

The stewardess deftly entered the flow of passengers and hurried forward. Beth was momentarily at a loss, stood hanging over the back of the aisle seat facing her. The beginning of the month? Shane had been in New York this month? And hadn't called her? Impossible.

She stepped into the crowded aisle and was pushed forward.

At the door she was once again penetrated by the stewardess's keen stare.

Beth paused. "Are you sure?" she breathed. "Shane Allen was flying from New York to Los Angeles at the beginning of this month?"

"Of course, I'm sure." The woman laughed; a short, rueful chuckle that made a statement. "Would I forget a thing like that? It was a Saturday. The sixth, I think." The young woman's green eyes flashed. "You are her, aren't you? His daughter?"

Beth shook her head distractedly. "No, really, I—" Then swiftly she was making her way through the boarding terminal, her eyes moving ahead, trying to decide if she was being watched.

A man in blue stood at the final point of exit. Watching her? Yes.

Her heart in her throat, she came closer to him, walking as far away as possible. Not looking at him now. Eyes on the floor. Any moment an arm would take her elbow, a voice would say, "Beth Allen? Would you step this way, please?"

She walked faster, leaving him behind. She was breathless now, almost running, but she dared not pause until she reached a newsstand in the lobby, where she stopped a moment to catch her breath and to set down the brown leather carry-on case which had rested underneath her seat on the flight.

Massaging her hand, she glanced at the clock behind the cash register. Three-fifty, New York time. By the time she rented a car, it would be well after four. Too late. Too late to run off half-cocked today.

The pang in her stomach reminded her she had slept

through food service on the plane. She picked up two packages of cheese and peanut butter crackers and groped for money. Turning to pay the man behind the counter, she must have caught a glimpse of something because she found herself jerking forward, leaning across the newsstand, and there it was. The morning *Post* with huge black headlines: SCHOOL FOR GENIUS CHILDREN QUARANTINED.

In the lower right-hand corner were two pictures relating to the Triesius story. One photo was of Councilman James DeWitt, whom she vaguely remembered from opening assembly at Triesius. In the photo, he looked very pale and skitterish and it was labeled, "He sponsored the school." The other picture was of Alan Randelar and it was labeled, "He quarantined the school." The article began: "Let's speculate. Has someone been snipping genes after class?"

Beth froze, her eyes scanning the story, her mind racing ahead, seeing things the average outsider could not possibly see, feeling things the outsider could not possibly feel.

A hand suddenly placed itself on her shoulder.

"Miss?"

Beth turned with a start, stared at the man in the grey suit.

"You dropped this, I believe." He handed her a crumpled five-dollar bill.

"Thanks."

The man nodded.

Beth stood motionless for almost a full minute after he had left, her eyes riveted to the front page of the newspaper.

She muttered: "Jesus—"

Now as Alan Randelar removed the slide from the microscope, his fingers shook so that he dropped it and spoiled the smear.

"Damn it," he said tiredly. Only that and nothing more, but he could not perform the simple act of reaching down to retrieve the bit of glass.

It was a strange concept, working always alone now. There were plenty who would have taken Dyer's place; none capable of doing it. The rage in Randelar was built on something bordering grief. To lose Dyer was to lose the one man he had called friend for fifteen years. That Dyer's stupidity had jeopardized the whole project made the mourning process incomplete. Choked the memory of their partnership, leaving Randelar with a strange emptiness he would never have admitted.

He heard the clink of glass against the toe of his shoe and knew he had connected with the dropped slide. Slowly he leaned to one side.

"I'll get it." It was the red-haired girl researcher, Shelby Paul. Randelar had noticed her lately, primarily because she seemed always at hand, always bringing his coffee, keeping his papers straight. It was rather a bore and at the same time rather comforting.

He muttered "Thank you" now and buried his face in his hands.

"Shall I redo the smear?" she asked.

"No. I'll do it later." He sat there, an odd numbness spreading across the top of his skull. It was the tiredness, he knew. He had been tired many times, but not like this. Not this bewildering feeling of being alone in the middle of a railroad track, a racing locomotive of exhaustion right on top of you. It was due to the loss of Jonathan Dyer, without whom his burden was . . . Startled, he lifted his head, amazed to find that he had spoken aloud to the young woman scientist. "This research of mine," he had begun. "This obsession . . ." He forced himself to stop speaking. The exhaustion was making him do strange things, things that to Alan Randelar were unorthodox. Such as speaking to this young woman who was nothing to him.

She picked up the thread he had left dangling. "It happens," she said comfortingly. "Brilliant scientists become obsessed. When that happens, a miracle can take place."

"Or a catastrophe," he mumbled, alarmed that he was continuing the conversation. He clamped his lips tightly together.

"You don't mean that," she was saying. "You're just tired. Sometimes I try to imagine what it must be to live in a mind like yours. To think your thoughts for an entire lifetime. It's a frightening concept. When I imagine it, I think of a fire burning behind my eyes. It gives me a headache."

He had been massaging his temples with both forefingers. Now he actually laughed. "I was a very poor high school student," he offered. "Or perhaps average is more like it. Mostly B's. Enough to get into an adequate state university."

"What happened?" she asked wide-eyed.

"My brain woke up quite suddenly. I can remember almost the instant it happened. It was in a physics class—theoretical physics. And I sat there thinking, 'I shouldn't be here. All this is beyond me. Way beyond me.' And this stab of pain seemed to run through my skull. Like an electric current. And all of a sudden, it wasn't. Beyond me, that is. As for the rest of my life, that changed too. It seemed fitting that I change my name, and indeed I did. I had always used my first name—Frederick. I transferred to Cornell under my middle name, Alan, and I've never used the Frederick again. Perhaps it's a superstition. That if I were to call myself Frederick, the electric current would shut off."

He nodded to himself for a moment in the silence she let go by as she brought him black coffee in a styrofoam cup. Along with the coffee she unobtrusively deposited a sealed bonded envelope addressed merely to A. Randelar.

"Dr. Dyer came by the office today to pick up his things. We had them boxed and ready. He stood over there . . ." She nodded toward the glassed observer's room. ". . . and he waited for about an hour, but he didn't . . . ah—"

"He had better sense than to say goodbye." Without looking at the envelope, Randelar tore it across and flung it into the wastebasket. "We have nothing further to say to each other."

Tactfully she avoided glancing directly at him, merely stood there, her red hair gleaming under the glow of the overhead lamp.

But a vessellike container had broken inside him and the outrage came flooding out. "There was a silence in him," Randelar cried out. "I could depend on that. If there was a man born who couldn't be used, it was Jon. There was—a similarity between us. But something happened. Maybe it was the Nobel Prize. After that, he was perhaps . . . you see, it was my research. Always my research. Now in looking back I can hear him saying, 'I haven't had an independent thought in fifteen years, Alan.' "

"But that was his fault, not yours," she said severely.

"Naturally. And, goddamn it, so long as he answered to me, he had no right . . . no right at all to—" Dismayed, he felt the involuntary filling of his eyes, the swelling in the back of his throat that choked off his words. *What's happening to me*, he thought. *I can't lose control like this. Not now.*

She moved closer; her hand brushing his shoulder. It was reassuring, that touch. It said it was okay for Alan Randelar to be human every once in a while. Just so long as he confined it to the laboratory.

FOUR

Eight ball in the side pocket. A tricky shot.

Shane Allen stood aside and painstakingly chalked his cue. He and the Chairman had been shooting pool for almost an hour. Thus far the two men had spoken little.

The question now, on this final ball, was whether to go for the shot and take a chance of losing the game by a scratch or to deliberately miss the shot by applying the wrong English, thereby sending the eight ball down the side of the table where it might nestle itself against the thirteen, the Chairman's remaining ball. It would leave the Chairman badly set up. He would almost certainly miss the shot.

Shane shifted position slightly and tightened his jaw. Determination set in. He lifted his stick and settled it on the well-formed bridge of his fingers. An instant later the cue ball spun sharply, striking the eight ball just a degree off of what would have been perfection. The eight ball sank, yes, but the cue ball went careening backwards and disappeared into the opposite pocket. He had scratched.

"If I had been you," the Chairman said mildly, "I would have missed that shot and left me badly set up."

"That's your style," Shane snapped. "Not mine."

The Chairman chuckled, a short rueful sound that held no mirth. His eyes, almost hypnotic under the overhead lamp, held Shane's gaze captive. Shane could feel the irritation seeping away, replaced by a weak-kneed fear. He could read the relentless message that was being telegraphed. It was unpleasant, to say the least.

"Are we in that much trouble, Harlan?" he asked hoarsely and the Chairman's short terse nod only confirmed what he'd already known. "What in the hell went wrong?"

"Why bother to analyze broken eggs?" returned the Chairman with a shrug. "The point is, we're working as fast as we can to mop up the mess. What I want to talk about is a boy named Karl Immer. You know that name?"

Shane thrust aside his cue and reached for his glass of bourbon. "My daughter's boyfriend," he said, taking the seat the Chairman motioned to at the opposite end of the room by the fireplace which was lit and glowing with fire.

"She's mentioned him then?" asked St. John.

"She's preoccupied with love. At nineteen, everyone's in love. So what?"

"Do you know who he is?" murmured St. John. He stood at the liquor cart adding fresh whiskey and a dollop of milk to his glass.

"A young Thoreau, I understand. An initiate looking for a guru to emulate. You don't have to worry. He doesn't know a goddamn thing about what's happening at Triesius."

"It's the other way. Karl Immer is our—ah, male contributor. A highly paid contributor, at that. He knows a great deal, Shane. Too much. His mind is phenomenal. He actually supplied the missing part of Randelar's original theory. It was Randelar's way of rewarding him to let him—"

"Reward him!" Shane interrupted harshly. "Why in the hell would you—"

"To keep him silent," shrugged the Chairman. "I should think that was obvious. What we're concerned with is what he said to Beth."

Shane sat stunned, too much at a loss for words to answer easily. "She—Beth knows nothing at all," he managed finally. "I know her better than I know myself. The boy told her nothing. Goddamn it, Harlan! Nothing!"

"Take it easy. I'm just trying to tie up loose ends, that's all. What I *don't* want"—he stressed the word—"is for Beth to end up with the wrong information. People, oh, you know people, Shane. It's already a problem that she knows what happened on the fifth. It's even possible—just a theory, mind you—that she may actually have seen what happened that night. You see?"

Shane felt the blood drain from his head. "I'm sure she didn't," he said with less conviction than he would have liked. "Wouldn't she have said something?"

"Not if the boy had made her paranoid about Triesius. No, to the contrary, she could know a great deal and just be afraid to tell anyone."

"I don't think so." Shane stirred heavily in his chair. What was the man driving at? With so much to talk about, why dwell on Beth? Was the Chairman losing his senses; what, in fact, did he hope to find?

Some secret about Shane himself.

Some weakness.

"Well, anyway," St. John offered, "let's don't dwell on the subject." He had said the words quickly, but they came out of a shadow of close scrutiny. And suspicion.

A moment. Then he added quietly:

"You can take my word for it, the boy has been well paid to keep his mouth shut and he's rather a coward, so I doubt we'll be seeing much of young Karl after today."

He continued to stare at Shane; Shane wished he wouldn't. Seeing Shane's discomfort, he seemed to realize what he was doing, and moved away to settle in a stuffed chair opposite the fireplace.

Shane felt a surge of anxiety, hot at first, then icy.

"I still don't understand how this thing got out of control," he said. The palms of his hands were moist, cold; he felt himself trembling.

The Chairman hesitated, as if on a threshold. "Randelar," he said. "He's become a problem. His research has taken him over. Hell, it's taken all of us over. He's gotten in too deep—we've gotten in too deep—"

"But human experimentation? To remove a couple of skin patches is nothing too extreme. I could live with that—hell, I did live with it. A little blood withdrawn, that kind of thing. But how did this other stuff get started?"

"By degrees. Just the way you said it. A couple of skin patches, a little blood. Then he froze Vala Hayes's brain. Don't look so pious, my friend. It wasn't so horrible. Perfectly safe. She wasn't in pain. But then it was so easy to find a little problem, nothing serious, and to cure it, you know, with a well-tested drug that simply wasn't on the market yet. And it did work—a small neurological problem was cleared up and the Hayes girl was better off for it. She became more relaxed after that, began to make friends. She thought she'd begun to get better mentally, when actually it was a physical problem she'd had since birth."

Shane listened, soberly and quietly, his eyes never leaving St. John's face.

"It was in little ways like this," the Chairman continued, "that the experiments began—all you understand, to help, not to harm. The Ritchie girl had headaches. She came to the infirmary often for codeine. She thought it was codeine. Another girl was tense. She ran out of Librium. There were five girls in all. It was to these five girls that the original doses of strain B were administered."

Shane lifted a small protesting hand that said, Enough for the moment. Obligingly, the Chairman let a suitable silence go by before inquiring, "Have you eaten? I have a bewildering assortment of refreshments. Everything from oysters to prime rib. Perhaps corned beef on a roll."

Moodily, Shane shook his head, then turned to stare out the sliding glass doors to where a drizzly rain had begun to fall. The wind moaned, reminding him it was cold as hell out there.

"I hate to be cold," he muttered, as pissed off about that as if it were the weather that was the real bane of his existence.

"I like it," the Chairman said stoically. "I mean"—he clenched both hands into fists and made a hearty gesture—"I like *weather*! In the summer, I want to be hot. I sweat like hell in the summer. Love it. Then, you see, in the winter, I want to be up to my eyeballs in snow." He chuckled. "I'd winter in Alaska if there were any decent restaurants."

Shane shivered. Against his will, his mind had returned to strain B. "Was it really a weakened strain?"

"Oh, yes," the Chairman said, understanding his meaning. "So weak that in the first administration very little happened. Then, by degrees, the dosage was increased. There were various symptoms. One of the girls lost all sensation to hot and cold. Injured herself rather badly in a hot shower and didn't know it. Luckily, her skin had begun to toughen."

"But still a weakened strain."

The Chairman nodded. "It was not supposed to be capable of living outside the laboratory more than forty-eight hours.

Unfortunately, the viral agents in question apparently had the rather rare ability to cross species lines to exchange genetic information."

The Chairman stopped, contemplating his own words.

"You speak of exchanging genetic information," Shane said softly. "What does this mean?"

The Chairman's eyes swept over him. He seemed to pause to give his answer weight. Then: "It means that the virus used those two days to mate with other bacteria already present in the girl's bloodstream. The offspring are almost . . . indestructible."

All at once Shane felt an odd current course through his body. The Chairman sat very still. Indestructible? Shane thought. He had used the word *indestructible*, there was no mistaking it. The word continued to slosh around inside his head and then spilled over. He knew he had become part of a mad momentum, of inconsistent behavior that made no sense, of insane energy that would not be denied.

"But . . . strain C," he stammered. "Strain C was supposed to wipe B out. That's what you said."

The Chairman rose from his chair and seemingly brushed imaginary lint from his coat lapel. "Not exactly," he said, then moved slowly to the liquor cart. "Refine it, yes. Accentuate the positive. Build up the entire bacterial defense of the organism to make it possible to host strain B. But—"

"Jesus," Shane was muttering. *"Jesus."*

"Don't be so troubled, Shane," said the Chairman. "We're all working around the clock to straighten the matter out. By Monday, Triesius will emerge clean—spotless. The computers are on their way out—the records are half-burned and half-relocated—the staff is working as hard as they can . . ."

"But, Randelar—goddamn it, he had no right." Shane shook his head. "No right."

The Chairman said, "Men do what they have to do. I'm sure he believed it to be the best for mankind's future . . ."

"Good Christ!" Shane exploded angrily. His pulse quickened. "Mankind's future. What kind of future?"

The Chairman stirred restlessly. "We really don't have time for this . . . to engage in verbal harangues. This problem is our responsibility as well as Dr. Randelar's. He was only—"

Shane Allen looked at him defiantly.

"You can't defend him," he said rather shrilly. "You can't defend the son-of-a-bitch after what he has done, and you know it. So just let's cut through the bullshit, Harlan. But don't try to defend him."

The Chairman mumbled something inaudible. Then sighed. "As you wish."

"Because nobody in this world ever seems to do anything except for the best of motives," Shane persisted. "I've never known a problem yet in which all sides didn't claim, even as they annihilated one another, that they were inspired by the noblest of reasons."

Straightaway, with a smile: "What is this, self-righteousness?" the Chairman asked.

"Not at all."

"How ironic that you, of all people, should preach to me. There is more involved here than Randelar's research. Or have you forgotten, my friend? So far"—the Chairman's emphasis of the two words was slight but inexorable—"I've been able to keep you out of it. After all, you were on the campus the night of the fifth. The Ritchie girl was coming to spend the night with you. For all I know, she may have already spent part of the night with you. You argued, had a few drinks. She left your cabin in a huff, who knows—"

"I had nothing to do with what happened. Whoever killed her had to be the same man who killed Vala Hayes."

"Precisely." The Chairman laughed, his eyes looking at Shane without expression. "And once again you were conveniently present on campus."

"Goddamn you, Harlan!"

"Easy, my friend. I'm saying only one thing. You're in this thing, whether you like it or not. Now, what I need from you—"

Shane's eyes froze. "I'm sorry, Harlan, but—"

"It's not a request." Suddenly a spark of the Chairman's anger ignited. "Damn it, Shane, we bought your name! We bought your daughter! Have you forgotten the fancy price tag? A thirty-million-dollar picture that made you. That raised your dead reputation up from the ashes and made you a star again. A star, Shane. At a time when you couldn't get lost in Hollywood. Now, goddamn it, we bought you and we own you and you are sure in hell going to back us!"

Shane considered that in stony silence, the ghost of a smile creeping to his lips.

"You're planning to bail out, aren't you, Shane?" The Chairman spoke in low dreamy tones. He continued: "Let me try to think with your head for a moment, Shane. Maybe you're thinking something like this: What can they do to me? I'm Shane Allen, they can't take that away. My involvement is slight. Even if they think I had a thing going with the Ritchie girl, they can't prove it. Best of all, the picture is released. They can't get it back in the can. What can they do?" The Chairman nodded gently. "What can they do?" he repeated, his eyes intent now on Shane's defiant face.

"Let me make myself clear, Shane," he murmured in a voice carefully devoid of emotion. "We wouldn't have involved ourselves with you if we hadn't known we could control you. Let's start back a long time ago—several weeks before your wife left."

Shane felt himself blanch, felt the sickness in his gut. "My wife . . ." Already he knew what was coming, felt the old pain as though it were yesterday.

The Chairman sipped his whiskey appreciably, then continued. "She had been having an affair with the tennis pro at the country club. Such a typical thing to do. He was studying at the seminary, or so the story goes. Is that right?"

Shane sat nodding dumbly.

"He was a very young man, I understand," the Chairman continued. "In his early twenties. That made it even more uncomfortable for you, I would imagine."

Shane shrugged, his eyes on the crumbling red-black logs in the fireplace.

"Perhaps it was retaliation," offered the Chairman gently. "You're only human. And I feel very sure the young girl did lie about her age. She admitted that much, I understand. You were enraged about your wife. You were attracted to her. And possibly you'd had too much to drink."

"I was attracted to her. I've always been—"

"Attracted to young girls," said the Chairman. "Yes. I know that. Perhaps it would have blown over. But the girl got pregnant and insisted on having the baby. The worst thing . . . the thing that no one knew until much too late . . ."

Shane drank long and deep. "The Episcopalian priest," he

said in irony. "He's the one who had the filthy germ. He passed it on to my wife. And my wife was gracious enough to pass it along to me in her quick monthly gesture of charity. And I . . ." He shook his head hopelessly.

"The baby was born retarded," the Chairman murmured, as one who is appointed to state an unfortunate truth. "Hopelessly so. Little more than a vegetable. A little girl, I understand."

"You understand nothing," Shane said hoarsely. "You bought me. Yes, I was for sale. What you didn't know was that I would have done it anyhow. I was going to do it. I started reading about Alan Randelar. His research on prenatal birth defects. If I could have spared even one other person . . . My other little girl, she'll never be able to talk. Never be able to dress herself. Never be out of a diaper." With enormous effort he was able to keep the tears from overflowing their borders.

The Chairman let a tactful pause go by and then cleared his throat. "I know you made a substantial out-of-court settlement, Shane, and that you see the child and pay all of her expenses. It's been one of those well-guarded, well-paid-for secrets. But the fact remains that the mother was a mere fifteen years old when she had your child. Your retarded child," he reiterated gently.

Shane made no response.

"That's right, you think about it. Put your mind to it."

The Chairman's last remark had been spoken in a voice so soft it might have been coming from another room. Or did Shane only wish the Chairman was in another room. Anywhere, instead of standing beside his chair, hovering over him, waiting for his next move. Shane had the odd feeling that the Chairman would wait there for a long time.

"What is it you want me to do?" Shane said, his voice barely audible, his eyes cast to the floor.

The Chairman nodded. "Good, good," he said and hastened to light a cigar. When he next looked at Shane there was some small recognition in his eyes. Perhaps contempt. Shane wasn't sure. The Chairman stood with his back to the bookcase, the end of his cigar pinched between his fingers.

"Three things," he said. "First, some of the girls' parents have insisted on coming to Rosemont. Talk with them. Tell them how happy you are that Beth is a student at Triesius. People trust celebrities. Buy this, they say, and the people run to the supermarket the next day and buy it. It's amazing how little people question things when they are in the presence of a star."

Wrong, Shane wanted to cry, you are so wrong. He looked sixty at that moment and felt less like a star than he ever had since becoming Shane Allen.

"Secondly," the Chairman said and paused to puff appreciatively on his cigar. "I want you to question Beth further. I'm sure she knows more than she's been telling us. More than she's told you. It is imperative we find out just how much she does know."

Shane could already feel his head nodding and he thought: Sweet Jesus, what won't I do to go with the charade; the incredibly ludicrous charade of being Shane Allen? And for the first time, he had a strange curiosity. Who was this Shane Allen anyhow? But he was afraid to venture further in that direction.

"And thirdly." The Chairman hesitated. "There's the matter of six large containers . . ."

Outside the wind moaned louder.

It was two hours later and the Chairman had wasted the second of those hours arguing with Randelar.

In this crucial time, St. John noted with disgust, Randelar had begun to come apart at the seams and, like an old Teddy bear, begun to lose his scientific stuffings. Whether from tension or loss of sleep, Randelar was reduced to a whining emotion-ridden man who could do little more than repeat over and over again his one stuck-in-the-groove refrain:

"We cannot stop now. We must not stop. Not now when we are so close."

"We not only can stop, we have stopped. At some future date, we will begin again. We have the embryos. They will be protected. We have our various test results . . ."

"I beg you."

It was the wrong choice of words. The Chairman despised the pitiful concept of begging. "It's a bit late," he snapped, "to be begging me for anything. If your goddamn project was so important to you, you should have been more careful. In a matter of months—*months*—you have jeopardized your whole research program."

"It was only the culmination. Before this, I spent well over a decade on animal experimentation. And you knew fully well about the other off-the-record implanted impregnations."

"I don't give a damn what you did elsewhere; at Triesius you were supposed to conduct yourself as skillfully as your credentials suggested you could. Ethics don't concern me, but stupidity certainly does. I thought I was getting a goddamn scientist, not a man with hot pants for his research. I mean, good God, man."

Unsteadily, the Chairman sipped cold coffee from his styrofoam cup and stared over the rim at Randelar. They were alone in the boardroom. The long deserted table was coated with dust; the atmosphere was leaden and airless.

Randelar pressed his finger into the dust and vacantly observed the print he had made. "But we're so close," he said as though to himself.

Angrily, the Chairman reached for a folder which lay atop his attaché case. "Your preliminary papers," he murmured, "were filled with such phrases as stringent containment of potentially biohazardous agents and safe laboratories that should come equipped with air locks, a negative pressure environment, treatment systems to inactivate or remove biological agents that might be contaminants. Also mentioned were safety cabinets, Hepa filters. Protective laboratory clothing and showers at each exit from containment facilities." He opened the folder and began shuffling papers. "Here. Read it for yourself. It goes on ad infinitum. But you, goddamn it, you introduced test DNA molecules into warm-blooded vertebrates. I don't have to tell you the risk." He squinted down at the report. "I'm looking at your categories: Minimal, Moderate and High Risks. It isn't listed in any category. The risk is too great to be attempted, that's why. You say it yourself in your original goddamn meaningless report."

He threw the report on the table. "A bunch of words. You manipulated me, Randelar. Now it's my turn to manipulate you. Triesius is going to be as clean as your proverbial whistle on Monday. Or you, my friend, are finished. Your research, finished. The second Nobel Prize you long for, so much smoke up the chimney. The only thing I want to discuss now is choices. I've spoken with Shane Allen. He assures me he can have a private plane here by tomorrow evening. Now I want the research ready for transference by then. Otherwise"—he tapped his fingers on the paper on the table—"I will burn your fucking research. Is that clear? Your laboratory will be the hottest crematorium you ever heard about. Now can we do it?"

Randelar's face had gone an unbecoming sallow shade, almost yellow. The look on his face told the Chairman something conclusively, something that no other man would have seen with such clarity. He saw that an indescribable change had come over Randelar, the sort of thing that occasionally happens to a man, almost a chemical change from which he can never recover. The kind of change that takes a winner and transforms him into a loser.

At that moment the Chairman realized fully that until he had found a replacement for Randelar, the research could not go forward. Two unappealing names drifted across his mind: Jonathan Dyer and Karl Immer. He sighed.

Suddenly, out of control, Randelar screamed. "You don't understand! You don't understand what we're proposing. We are actually talking about improving genetic codes. This is our aim. We're not talking about cloning here. We're talking about creating a new type of human being who cannot be destroyed. Who can live through an atomic war, walk on the moon, without support mechanisms. Creatures who can grow arms and legs within minutes. Go without breathing for days, without food for years. Creatures who cannot be destroyed. We are proposing to speed up evolution a trillion times! Who knows what can be accomplished by creatures of this sort? We come—we go. But this new species—they will . . . they will not be so easy to get rid of . . ." His voice trailed away.

"Excuse me," LeSabre said in the deadening lull. She had opened the door and stood poised there, well-groomed, well-coiffed and yet, under the tidy facade, haggard from sleeplessness. "We are gathered now."

"Come in," St. John nodded.

Silently, they filed through the door. Dr. Hamilton first, his pomposity still intact, his dark handsomeness untouched by forty-eight hours of ceaseless effort. Behind him was Shelby Paul, moving like a zombie, clearly asleep on her feet. Clear too was her emotional exhaustion. She dropped into the chair on Randelar's right, her fingers just touching his sleeve.

Philip Angusi came next, his eyes nervously shifting about the room, here, there, anywhere save into other eyes. His lips moved silently and the Chairman, who was intuitive to such things, thought he might well be repeating a chant of self-hate.

LeSabre closed the door.

The Chairman loosened his tie. He knew he would be at it for some time.

FIVE

It was two minutes past eight when the big green-and-black truck with "Worldwide" printed on the sides nearly forced Beth off the road. The trucker sounded his horn and gestured with his hand as he sped by, the thrust of air from the passing vehicle nearly sucking Beth's small compact under its belly.

Nervously, she inched her foot off the accelerator. The rain had been falling steadily for almost an hour now and the monotonous rhythm of the windshield wipers was making her drowsy.

She lowered the side window slightly and took a deep gulp of fresh air. Fierce pellets of rain struck her face. She turned and peered through the windshield. The road ahead was a vague blur between rows of dark skeletal trees. A shaft of lightning pierced the sky, followed instantly by a single clap of thunder.

Beth drew back and realized that to continue driving in this weather would be sheer stupidity. At the next cut off, she braked the car, pulled over to the graveled shoulder, and stopped. She was shivering, more from fear than cold.

Too much was happening at once. The strength she needed was displaced by confusion; she felt constricted, short of breath.

Something wasn't right. Dimly, she remembered how she'd hesitated back there at the last intersection. That was it; she had taken the wrong turn.

Where am I? Where in the hell am I!

She glanced into the rear-view mirror and caught a glimpse

of her face. Her eyes were teared and her lips were drawn together in a taut line.

It was all going to be so easy, she mused. And now, sitting there on a strange road, cramped and tired, she realized how wrong she had been.

She tried to laugh, to relax herself, but she would not be comforted. She sat trembling in the chilled air, teeth chattering, all hunched in upon herself, confronting the deadly onslaught of her own exhaustion. Behind her she could hear the sound of an approaching car, then saw its headlights fracture the blackness. The car passed swiftly, leaving her utterly alone in the dark and the steady downpouring of rain.

The thing to do, she told herself, was to stay somewhere overnight, get some rest, and arrive in Rosemont tomorrow morning, fresh and alert.

Yes. Yes, that was the sensible thing to do.

The quality of light had changed, the clouds had shifted and the rain had begun to subside slightly. Beth wriggled forward into a more comfortable position behind the wheel and let loose the emergency brake.

Cautiously, she eased the car into a U-turn, drove under the overpass, struck the main highway, and headed back to the intersection where she had made the wrong turn. Mechanically, she ran her hand across the inside of the steamed-over windshield, stared unrelentingly at the road ahead, and resisted the impulse to close her eyes.

There were more cars now; more lights. A gas station appeared, then another. Ahead and to her right she saw the sign. MOTEL. The vacancy portion of the sign was lit. She left the highway. Now she could see people milling about in the motel's front office. She switched off the ignition and left the car.

The sudden contact with people brought instant relief.

"Looking for a room?" the thin, balding man asked.

She nodded.

"Single or double?"

"Single."

"Our single rooms are thirty-one-fifty. Plus tax," he said, placing a white registration card on the counter.

"Fine," Beth said and opened her bag. She handed him two twenty-dollar bills as he held out the pen.

Beth glanced down at the registration card, then wrote the name—*Susan Harris*—and the address—*New York City*.

"Need any help with your luggage?" The man handed Beth her change.

Beth shivered gratefully. "No. Thank you."

"Nasty weather, isn't it?"

"Yes. Yes, it is," she said with a nod and left the office.

Moments later she tossed the newspaper on the bed and flicked on the bedside lamp. The room was small, but bright and dry and warm. For the first time in days Beth found herself smiling. She opened her overnight bag and began to unpack. A hot shower. That's what she needed; that, and sleep.

She zipped off her boots, then raising her arms, pulled off her sweater. She had begun to remove her jeans, but stopped. She stared fixedly at the front page of the newspaper. At the faces of Alan Randelar and James DeWitt.

Tomorrow was Sunday; would anyone be available for her to speak with? She paused for a moment to consider the possibilities. Why have I come back here? she cried silently. What is it I'm hoping to accomplish?

Someone once said: *If I had to choose between my country and my friends, I'd hope I'd choose my friends.*

Remembering this, Beth felt a little more sure of herself.

She cleared a place for herself on the bed and sat. Outside her door she could hear the sound of retreating footsteps, then the click of a lock as someone entered the room opposite hers.

In the silence which followed, she picked up the newspaper. She sat studying the faces of the two men for a long time before reaching for the telephone.

It had been one hell of a day, but Jimmy DeWitt had not bothered to explain this to anyone. For one thing, he really didn't believe that people were interested in anyone's problems but their own. For another, no one had asked him how his day was going, which only proved the point.

It all kept coming at him until he had a blinding headache behind his eyes and a knot in the bottom of his stomach which had turned into fire. Parents, reporters and then the Chairman had called on the subject of Sergeant Carrolton.

"I'm not sure he bought my story," Jimmy had said.

"Not sure?" The Chairman hesitated. "What happens now?"

"Do I know what's going to happen? Do you think I know what's going to happen even five minutes from now? Good Christ!" Jimmy slid a Valium into the side of his mouth and swallowed it with gin.

"Take it easy, Jimmy. Just handle the business on your end. Forget the meeting this afternoon. I'll fill you in later."

That afternoon, more gin, the Budget Committee, the Elks Club and the Chairman again about Karl Immer. Yes, yes, Jimmy had muttered. He'd see to it that it was taken care of.

Somewhere around eight o'clock that evening Jimmy stumbled into his apartment. He undressed and lay down naked on top of the covers, extremely drunk, and tried to go straight off to sleep. But his mind refused to shut down.

He cursed Triesius, yet felt no anger against the school; on the contrary, he knew Triesius was his one and probably his only ticket out of Rosemont. Recalling current ambitions, he tried to smile.

If only Monica was here to see how her husband was making out in life! What I mean is, Jimmy, she would say, this is one hell of a way for a man to act, Jimmy!

Jimmy's eyes opened. He peered about him at his tiny bedroom, his disheveled bed, the filthy living room beyond and the kitchen with dishes piled a mile high in the sink.

He took a deep breath. Well, between you and me, Monica, this isn't too much to show for thirty years; this isn't any way for a Councilman to be living, I know. But—

Hey, Jimmy, let me ask you, are you ever going to amount to anything? Are you, Jimmy?

Jimmy smiled. You'll see, Monica. You'll see.

Just then the telephone rang.

As long as he had been living in this apartment, Jimmy still hadn't become accustomed to the telephone in his bedroom. It seemed out of place.

He reached for it. "Hello?"

"Councilman DeWitt?"

"Yes."

There was a momentary pause.

"Hello? Who is this?"

"Carmel Ritchie," a voice said with urgency.

The name brought Jimmy up to a seated position at the edge of the bed. He could feel his heart banging away. "Listen, is this some sort of a joke?"

"Is this question and answer time?" countered the voice, now shriller and louder.

Puzzled, he tried to consider why the voice was so distorted. He was fighting the inclination to feel caught in the Twilight Zone. There was certainly something inhuman in the tone, something of the quality of a funhouse-recorded laughing voice or a hyena screaming in the jungle.

"I have a question for you, Councilman!" screamed the voice.

"Who are you?" he shouted.

"Never mind! My question! Are you ready?"

Suddenly he believed he had solved the riddle of the voice. It was so simple really when you stopped to think of it. Someone—a girl, without a shadow of a doubt—was adopting this voice to disguise herself.

"Are you ready?" screamed the voice fiercely, and he shouted: "Yes! Go ahead!"

"All right, Councilman. Take down the question and then do your research."

"What's the question?"

"The question . . ." said the voice more gently, ". . . is who killed Carmel Ritchie?" Softly came the laugh. "Who killed Carmel Ritchie?" Singsong. Trying to irritate him. Trying to make the words stick. "Who killed Carmel Ritchie?" A sort of hesitation. "Or don't you care? Doesn't anybody care?"

"Who are you?" he was yelling now, forcing himself to stand. Who are you? he thought, staring at the oddly shaped designs on the wallpaper.

"What difference does it make?" the girl asked, now coating her words with ease and a tinge of not caring, as if it were all so simple. Carmel Ritchie, find out who killed her, what's the big deal. It was like a play; it was not difficult if you understood the plot. It was not difficult if you understood who the main actors were. But that was impossible now.

Jimmy heard the click. Then the silence. Whoever it was had hung up.

Beth sat on the edge of the bed, her hand still resting on the telephone. Suddenly she looked up, half prepared to rise, and the newspaper slid from the bed onto the floor. She had heard a noise, as though someone were tapping on her door. Now she realized that the sound was merely that of tree branches striking the window.

She lay back and stared at the ceiling, its smooth green surface starkly shadowed with light. She could feel the color drain from her face, the strength drain from her body. Who killed Carmel Ritchie? And why?

There was a pattern, wasn't there? Not necessarily to do with Carmel's death, but with Triesius itself. The girls. Alan Randelar's research . . . it was all there.

Beth closed her eyes. Sleep. If only she could catch just a few hours.

Yes, sleep.

And then she saw it. A blade as sharp as the edge of a guillotine. Still dripping blood. The knife was held chest high with the cutting edge toward her.

Frantically, she opened her eyes and sat up. The room was quiet and still. "Oh, God," she whispered. "Oh, God."

In the next instant a look of confusion swept her face, deepened into terror. Almost. Yes, she could almost see . . . Abruptly, her mouth dropped open, her eyebrows knotted, and she began to cry.

SIX

Karl Immer had begun to use drugs again. At first it was only a few drags of a joint in order to relax. Then in a pleasant haze, he had stirred a minute grain of LSD into a glass of water and swallowed it without thinking what he was doing. He sat on the edge of his bed and waited for some time.

Finally he felt it. The familiar weakness in his body, the letting go and, paradoxically, an increased awareness of himself that led him into the bathroom, where he stared at himself in a mirror. He felt both outside and inside his body and very protective of himself. He leaned closer to the glass, his breath making fog and he found himself fascinated with every small line in his face, even the pores of his skin.

In time those lines would deepen, the skin would lose its elasticity. Tears sprang to Karl's eyes and he stared at them too, thinking how beautiful they were. He willed himself to cry for the pleasure of watching those tears flow down his cheeks. Youth, he thought, was so goddamned beautiful. What a pity anyone had to get old. Suddenly there was a dull ache in back of his eyes and he withdrew from the bathroom into the warmth of the kitchen.

The one thing he dreaded was that he would start to think about what had happened to Beth. He promised himself, like his own best friend, that he would not think about her. It was not good for him to think about her. Still, restlessness drove him outside the cabin where he walked for some time beside the lake, tripping out on the brilliance of moonlight glistening on patches of unmelted ice. Cold and remote. He was cold, but believed that in the sharp, biting wind there was also warmth; that the extremes of any pole go hand-in-hand. If there was hate, there was also love. If there was death, there was also rebirth.

"Bullshit," he said very softly. Suddenly his teeth were chattering and he was too cold to even imagine warmth.

Inside the cabin again, his mind was moving a hundred miles an hour, just as his heart was thumping rapidly in his chest. His teeth were completely numb; parts of his body were cold, others sweating. He could feel the stored-up tension letting itself loose, flooding him. Suddenly he was scared, really scared to stay in the cabin any longer.

It took a while to find his car keys; finally he realized they were in his jacket pocket. The jacket had been lying on the bed and it occurred to him that he couldn't remember if he had been wearing it when he'd gone out before. Surely he could not have been walking around in freezing weather without a coat.

The ringing he heard inside his skull grew louder. He cupped his hands over his head, squeezing until he felt pain, and was afraid he'd done harm to himself by squeezing too hard.

There was now a whole passage of time that he couldn't relate to; he felt vague although he was moving better, seemed to have better control. He had flung the last of his suitcases into the Volks. He had driven very slowly and mechanically, making sure his lights were on. It occurred to him once he had reached Rosemont, once he had entered the bar, that the remoteness he felt had been a defense mechanism without which he wouldn't have been able to drive.

The liquor felt wonderful and he ordered two sandwiches, one ham and cheese and one hamburger, and devoured them both ravenously. His mood had changed completely. He was up now, feeling very horny, hardly able to keep his hands off the waitress.

God, what an ass, he thought exultantly and felt himself getting hard. He wondered if he should try to take the waitress home after the bar closed and had a hot picture of making love to her, his hands fondling her, his penis buried inside of her, his tongue rammed down her throat. In his mind, her hair turned from dark brown to blond, her skin lightened. Slowly, his hand in his jacket pocket moved down and at just the least pressure, he exploded. He stiffened, feeling the orgasm, but did not moan or cry out.

Christ, what a relief, he thought for an instant and then the good feeling was gone, replaced by humiliation and hatred. He sat perfectly still at the bar, his coat hiding the wetness of his pants. He imagined that people around him knew what had just happened. He heard two men laughing and thought they were laughing at him.

It was not his fault. It was women. Women confused him, screwed up his head.

"You want another one of these?" the bartender asked. A cigarette hung out of one side of his mouth, the other side was quirked up in a lopsided grin. Grey skin, saggy chin. Big pores on both sides of his long hooked nose. "Another drink?" He was staring at Karl intently, maybe to check how far gone he was, or maybe because he wondered why the young boy refused to answer him.

"Sure." Karl sat straighter. "You got another cigarette?"

"Sure do." The bartender got the cigarette from his pack further down on the bar and held the match for Karl to light up. "You cold or something?" he asked, flicking the match into the ashtray.

"No. Why?"

"Man, you're shaking. Here, I'll get you that drink."

It's women, Karl wanted to scream after him as he moved down the bar and began pouring bourbon into a glass. He had genuinely cared about Beth. For the first time in his life, he had gotten very pure about a girl. Instead of just thinking about her breasts and her ass, he had cared about her. But then his mind had gotten crazy, what with the way Triesius had used his head as a punching bag. And she had found the money, his payoff money, and the magazines, and he thought, shit, who am I kidding, our whole relationship is a lie.

Tears filled his eyes again. Desperately, he tried to blink them back.

Right now, thinking about it, he felt almost certain it wasn't all a lie. Some of that time spent at the cabin was valid good time. Not all, of course, but some. And the hopes. The plans. Never in his life had he been so filled with hopes and dreams, all kinds of crazy dreams.

Suddenly he felt frightened, removed from civilization,

from any kind of human contact.

Those bastards.

No. Forgive them. Forgive one another. Even yourself.

He couldn't. He would have to understand the word first.

Forgive me, Lord, for I have sinned.

Beth gone. All gone.

He could not understand it, had no way of comprehending the charred remnants of his life. Wasted, all wasted. Gone. He knew what he had to do, the only thing left for him to do. He must not hesitate any longer.

Unconsciously he had taken a ballpoint pen from his shirt pocket and began to write on his cocktail napkin. He didn't even notice when the bartender set the drink down in front of him. He scribbled some more, reached over the ledge of the bar and got two more napkins, both of which he covered with cramped writing, then looked up.

He could feel someone watching him. A man several seats down. Average height, average weight, sandy-colored hair. He was staring at Karl intently, a strange smile possessing his lips.

Karl returned the look steadily. He smiled too.

So they're keeping an eye on me just to make sure. What the hell. I have nothing to hide, he winked, his shirt collar damp around his neck. Nothing to hide at all. His smile broadened.

Not anymore.

SEVEN

Sometimes the Angel of Death would drop by to look over her. That was the way Georgia Urie regarded the woman—as the Angel of Death—although her uniform proclaimed her a nurse.

Now as the woman leaned forward, Georgia looked at her through finely slit eyes, pretending to be asleep. She knew the Angel hoped to find her dead, that death, one of life's great mysteries, fascinated her.

The nurse regarded her closely for a moment, probably wondering why the girl's temperature was normal or only slightly above normal, and Georgia tried to make her breathing shallow. She concentrated on the darkness of her room; she listened hard to the wind blowing softly outside her window, anything to put herself in a state of lethargy while the nurse hovered beside her bed.

The nurse leaned still closer. Georgia could detect that under her talcum powder, the woman was sweating. The two scents mixed together, the powder's sweetness somehow making the odor of perspiration more sickening. At the base of her throat, Georgia felt a fullness. She let her eyes close completely as she tried to relax, tried to fight the inclination to gag.

Above her, the nurse released her breath in a low hiss, the warm air blowing full on Georgia's face.

"Dear?" she whispered.

Georgia willed herself to relax deeper into the mattress and felt an incredible weakness flooding her body.

"Dear, are you awake?"

Georgia remained still.

The woman's bones creaked as she slowly straightened herself. She continued to talk aloud as she moved about the room, but Georgia paid no attention to her words as she was obviously talking to herself.

Instead, she watched the woman as she tidied her grey-brown hair in the mirror, then turned on the lamp.

She then spent some moments opening the two top dresser drawers and peering inside. Just when Georgia was getting really tense, wondering what she was so busy staring at, she glanced at her wrist watch and clucked impatiently.

"Too much for one person," she murmured to herself emphatically and nodded as though to agree with her own statement. She switched off the lamp and came to stand over Georgia for just an instant, her eyes shifting in a nervous circle around the room, then back to Georgia. Georgia let her eyes close completely, seeing only blackness. A wave of dizziness threatened to take her under. Another moment and she would be . . .

She counted off the seconds in rushes of pain. Sickness. Still she could feel the woman there, staring, staring, until she thought she'd go completely mad.

She had the sensation of falling. Her eyes flew open and she gasped.

It was a man's face. The Angel was gone and now it was Randelar who stood there. It was the anxiety in his eyes that terrified her. Why was Randelar so afraid for her? Randelar who had always seemed some kin to God. But not now. He was afraid and he had no right to be afraid.

Frantically, she reached for his sleeve, but he was made of shadows. Dissolved before her eyes.

Now she was positive she'd been dreaming. Fallen asleep and dreamed a dream of a god fallen to earth. The unbroken silence shattered the last of her strength.

All at once she felt a wash of despair.

In that moment, they had her. She was theirs. She took a short breath. Then another. Droplets of perspiration began to roll down her face, her chest, beneath her arms. They seemed to spout and spill out of her skin everywhere.

She could feel herself letting go, and in the very peace of surrendering, of letting fate happen to her instead of her always happening to fate, she was able to summon up one final goal.

Vala. She simply had to find Vala.

She began to lower her feet to the floor, but stopped. Suddenly the room had begun to turn upside down and she knew the time to act had not yet come. "But soon," she breathed. "It must be soon."

Courage hesitated then. She waited.

The corridor was empty. It smelled of ammonia and something else—sickness. The kind of smell that could not be washed away, only disinfected.

She wondered what time it was—the Angel of Death had come and gone once again—but what time was it—what time . . . because ghosts have no clear idea of time and she now fashioned herself in the image of a ghost, one who goes through walls and sees what has been denied her to see.

Hesitantly, she opened the door further. Halfway up the hall a man in dingy doctor's green pushed his way toward the nurses' station and disappeared.

Now there were no sounds and no one in sight.

Where in the hell were the nurses? Was it a simple matter of being short-staffed? Or was there death around the corner? Some emergency situation where doctors and nurses gathered around some critically ill girl? Someone she herself knew. Vala?

The thought pushed Georgia through the half-opened door into the corridor. She walked crookedly, feeling the vulnerability of her long white legs and arms protruding from the flimsy hospital gown, too scant for her tall frame. Shapeless foam slippers flapped under her heels as she walked . . . where had they taken Vala . . . flap, swish . . . which door should she try . . . they all looked alike. Systematically, she began to open doors, at least a half dozen. Dull rays of corridor light shone on faces she knew. Most eyes were closed.

As she moved farther down the hallway, a door on the side of the entryway opened and Dr. Hamilton appeared. She quickly opened the nearest door and stepped into the room.

Dr. Hamilton's footsteps came slowly down the hallway, hesitated, then by degrees diminished, until the hallway was once again quiet.

"Hi!" said a tiny voice.

Georgia turned with a start. She waited in silence for her eyes to adjust to the darkness. Almost imperceptibly at first, the figure in the bed took form. Willa Bishé sat up, her body propped on her elbows. A strange expression crept across her face as she continued to stare.

Georgia held a warning finger to her lips and backed out, not even knowing who she was afraid would discover her exploring, not sure why she was afraid. But she was afraid.

She opened another door. And another.

And in the simple way a search is sometimes over, so was hers.

As she stared across the room, she had no idea she was crying until she felt the dampness on her fingers, which she had automatically lifted to her cheeks.

"Vala . . . ?" she whispered, but she expected no answer.

Vala lay nude under a plastic tent, needles in her wrists, her arms, her ankles, even her scalp; tubes were in her nose; a clamp kept her tongue in position. Machines breathed for her, recorded her body's functions.

Georgia could not remove her eyes from the green line that beeped its way across the heart monitor screen. She edged closer to Vala's bedside thinking only that she had never before felt so conscious of life versus death. Conscious of life, yes. Conscious of death, even that. But never so conscious of the straight line of death interrupted by the sudden heartbeat, the pulse, of life. Opposite and yet the same. "In the midst of life, we are in death." For the first time, Georgia fully understood the truth in those words.

Vala's face, grey-white under the dim light, filtered still a shade darker by the plastic, was frightening to see. Georgia had been prepared for the weakness characteristic of the very ill or for etchings of pain around the mouth and eyes or for almost anything except what she was seeing. She blinked, distrusting her own blurred perception. Surely this blankness must be within her. Surely she was imagining that Vala's face was devoid of any trace of personality, feeling, *anything*.

There was no strength in Georgia's legs. She slid backwards against the wall, still staring at Vala's face. There had to be something, she thought. Some trace of Vala. But there was nothing. No involuntary flickering behind the closed eyelids. Vala's throat, wrapped in gauze through which ran long slender tubes, seemed slack. Georgia could detect no instinctive swallowing impulse. No troubled dream caused her to sigh.

She's dead. And yet the machines said she lived.

Didn't they?

"Vala? Vala, it's Georgia."

She's dead. She must be dead.

"Vala, wake up. I said wake up, goddamn it!"

Steadily, air was pushed in and out of Vala's body. Machines beeped, flashed lights of different colors.

Vala's body lay indifferent to machines and needles. Nude grey skin, light brown hair, darker pubic hair. The body's nudity was a different kind of nudity than Georgia had ever seen. In a way, it embarrassed her with its vulnerable sexuality. The legs were opened wide; the arms hooked upward to expose fluffs of unshaven hair from their pits; the breasts were sunken into the emaciated chest so that their large brown nipples seemed swollen out of proportion. Such dead-looking skin except where the boils remained. And the scales Vala had shown her. More of them. Hundreds of them. But, it was oddly at the boils that Georgia found herself staring. In their human ugliness they seemed proof of life.

Which machine, she wondered, was the brain scan? Was it giving a normal reading? Was it giving any reading at all?

Lights flashed, the heart machine beeped. Vala's chest rose and fell as oxygen was pushed in and out of her lungs.

Georgia had never felt so weak in her life. It was not the same narcotic weakness, because she was keener of senses tonight. Less drugged. No, this was an emotional weakness. A weakness for what she felt for Vala Hayes.

Georgia was suddenly desperate to escape from that room. She had her hand on the metal door handle when she heard the voices and paused sharply. A man and a woman were arguing in the hallway. Dr. Hamilton and a woman whose voice she could not recognize. One of the night nurses, probably.

"Just follow orders and don't worry about it, why don't you?" Hamilton said curtly.

"Am I supposed to be a complete fool then? Is that what you think they'll believe?"

"Nurses do what doctors tell them, Miss Anton."

"Only insofar as it doesn't conflict with their own medical ethics, Doctor!" the woman retorted shrilly. "Don't you think that any medical examining board—"

"You're nervous, Miss Anton. You've been reading too many newspapers."

"I'm handing in my written notice, nevertheless."

"Do what you have to do," stated the doctor indifferently. "And now, frankly I have my own problems."

He moved down the hall, the nurse hurrying after him. "Do you know Hollister didn't show up and neither did the practical?" she whined. "There's only two of us on duty. Can't you—"

Georgia hung by the door until the voice faded. Something, she sensed, was happening. An inexplicable, impossible shifting of fear. "You've been reading too many newspapers," Hamilton had said. She had no idea what could have been in the papers; nevertheless, she was convinced this was why they had administered fewer drugs this evening. They had been afraid to drug her.

Cautiously, she cracked the door. The hallway was empty and quiet. She hesitated, casting one last look behind her, unable to keep herself from hoping. Perhaps even now at the last moment, Vala would stir, cry out in her sleep, make some small movement of life.

The body lay passive, legs spread, arms open, uncaring of its vulnerability. Immodest.

"Oh, dear God, Vala," she wept and leaned forward.

Dr. Hamilton's voice spun her around, brought her arms to a protective cross about her chest.

"Jesus Christ," he muttered angrily, "there's supposed to be a guard at this door. Around the clock. You tell him—"

"Why didn't you tell him?" returned LeSabre's frigid voice. "I have my own duties. Am I supposed to run your little clinic at the same time?"

Georgia flinched as they came closer. There was no doubt. They were heading directly for Vala's room. Her eyes jerked nervously toward the window. She took a step.

Hamilton interrupted his own progress by a long soft string of profanity. The coarser his words, the lower his voice.

LeSabre's high heels clicked again. Faster.

Strangely, it was the idea of coming face to face with LeSabre that scared Georgia the most. Trembling uncontrollably, she turned and moved quickly toward the small door beside Vala's bed.

Once inside the bathroom, she waited.

Then she heard a voice. Muffled by the door, the voice sounded muted, toneless. The soft spoken phrase barely audible. "Let me take a look." Then came a stirring in the room, a sound made up of many small movements.

A moment later she heard the shuffling of feet and then the door closing.

Georgia was shaking so violently she could scarcely stand. Both hands on the sink, head down, she stood weeping, the tears stinging angrily against her skin, her knees knocking together. She listened pitiably to the choked sounds of despair that caught in her throat and fought to vent themselves. Her throat hurt from the effort of choking off the cries. But wait—she was trying to remember . . . her throat had been hurting for most of the night, since they had weakened her dosage of medication. Oh, God, she was not going to be able to keep going. She was not at all well and, at last, she must think of Georgia Urie. It was time. She could feel her sobs lessening, but the despair remained, too deep to explore. And the fear. Was there ever going to be a time when she wasn't afraid? If anything, the fear was worsening. She could actually taste it—a bitter, coated taste that lay thick on her tongue.

Slowly she raised her head and stared at her outline in the glass for a moment without turning on the light. Her dim face looked familiar, comforting. She stood there, her hand on the light switch, and wondered why she was avoiding turning on the light. Exactly what was she dreading to see?

She leaned forward over the sink so that she could no longer see into the glass. One step at a time, that was how she'd take it.

But she was unprepared for the depth of her panic when she turned on the light. The brightness stunned her, bewildered her. And then when she finally forced herself to straighten, to look up, to meet her own eyes in the glass, she understood why she was so scared.

To Georgia, it was as though all the sins of Triesius had taken visible form, materializing themselves upon her face as swollen ugly craters. And the scales. Her neck was covered with scales. Her neck, her face, her arms . . . Almost wonderingly, she touched them.

And then she began to scream.

EIGHT

Now it was Sunday, December fourteenth. Ten-fifty a.m.

Across the cluttered desk top, the man and the girl faced each other, their faces in pleasant but neutral lines.

The office was faintly scented with lemon furniture polish and some other indefinable odor which mingled with the lemon; something of old cigarette ashes and hidden dust which his haphazard cleaning had left undisturbed. The carpeting was pale and worn, the furniture of chipped dark wood, the chairs leather and comfortable, but ripped here and there. Several plants in basket stands were placed in different areas, their bedraggled appearance suggesting that the need of proper sunlight and water was often forgotten.

In the midst of this less than impressive setting, Beth Allen found herself marveling at what a good show James DeWitt was managing. The image was steady, guileless, even if there was undeniable panic buried beneath his facade. The lines under his eyes told her he had to be going under minimal sleep and the broken-in-two cigarette that lay in the ashtray by his elbow told her he was operating under an intense degree of pressure. She understood. His whole political career was, in fact, on the line. Beth had in her soft leather bag a copy of yesterday's *Post*. The way the story read, it looked as though the Triesius project had been hung around DeWitt's neck much in the manner of an Army dog tag. His whole identity had become Triesius.

"I was afraid," Beth said, her hands tightly folded in her lap, "that you wouldn't be in your office today."

"Things are difficult now," Jimmy said, not dodging the

issue, and managed a smile. "Or haven't you heard?"

Beth merely inclined her head, wanting him to keep talking, to take the lead. Shane had once said, "When you're not sure, let the other fellow do the talking. Silence is power, baby. It makes you look like you know more than you do."

DeWitt hesitated and then said in an offhand way, "I suppose you had to wade through a mob scene to come here."

"Reporters, you mean. Yes."

"How was it that you—what I mean to say is that it must have been very hard for you to get to my office."

She almost smiled at that. The source of his hidden worry had become quite clear to her. He was afraid she'd told the press who she was. Yes, he was deathly afraid of that. Now the question was what was he afraid she knew.

"I sent a sealed message up," she said gently. "Through the guard, you know. And then your secretary came right down to get me. Didn't she tell you?"

Unconsciously, DeWitt had drawn a revealingly deep breath. "I was on a long distance conference call. Faith is new—just hired because of the, ah . . ." He paused. Then: "I didn't know if she . . ."

"Could act quickly in emergencies," Beth filled in softly.

DeWitt's face flushed deeply, but his voice remained calm and light, if just slightly breathless. "I thought you were in California. What in the name of God are you doing back in Rosemont?"

"I am presenting myself to you," she said, suddenly very sure of what she was saying, "as a self-hostage."

"As a what?"

"As a self-hostage," she repeated boldly. "Either you cooperate—or I'll turn myself over to the press. I ought to make quite a scoop, wouldn't you say? 'Shane Allen's daughter the only survivor of the tragedy at Triesius.' That sort of thing. I could tell them a lot more too."

"What could you tell them?" DeWitt asked in smiling disbelief.

"Oh, well, I could tell them about what the girls used to talk about back in the dorm. You know the way girls talk. And there was plenty to talk about. Starting with the admission physicals—quite a thorough physical, let me tell you. Quite painful and on the last day anesthetic was actually used."

"Anesthetic," he repeated, staring blankly down at the desk

where his forefinger was beating a light tattoo.

"Skin patches were taken from us," she continued inexorably. "And hair follicles. Wouldn't you say that was a strange procedure? A lot of the girls were very frightened because it didn't seem right. It just didn't make any sense and, like I said, everyone was talking about it. In fact, there would have been some problems, I feel sure of that."

"So then why—" DeWitt began.

"Because they stopped. The physicals stopped right after orientation week. So, of course, things cooled off and the girls quit worrying."

"I see."

"But there started to be other things," Beth stated coldly, not returning DeWitt's pleading smile. "There was the matter of a friend of mine. Her health deteriorated right before my eyes. I'm almost sure she was receiving some sort of medication from the infirmary."

"You're not certain?"

"I think Vala was deliberately hiding it from me."

"Vala Hayes, you mean?"

"Yes. She was afraid I'd leave Triesius. But when I see her again," Beth said in a firmer voice, "I'm quite certain she will tell me what they've been doing to her."

He nodded, a strange spark kindling in his eyes.

"No doubt, you are right," he hastened to say. "The truth, that is. She'll tell you what's true."

"There's also the matter of a girl who should have been scalded in a shower."

"But surely—"

She interrupted him. "I haven't finished. There's also the matter of a—a patient I saw in the infirmary. Very little about this creature looked human. And yet one of the nurses called it a 'she' and said that 'she' was in a Control Group. Five girls were in that group, she said, and this creature was one of them. Another one of the five girls, according to the nurse—" She faltered, but finished the sentence. "—was Carmel Ritchie."

As she said the name, both girl and man flinched and for a moment there was absolute silence.

Beth noted that DeWitt looked almost ill. Actually, she had nothing personal against James DeWitt. He seemed like a very personable man caught in someone else's trap. She stilled the slight pity she was beginning to feel by reminding herself that innocent men didn't get caught in these sorts of traps.

"It was you . . ." DeWitt said very slowly, "who called me last night. Wasn't it?"

She nodded. "I wanted to get a reaction from you. Maybe I even had the crazy idea you weren't involved in the cover-up. Maybe I thought you'd pick up the phone and call the police. But I don't guess you did that, did you?"

"Police?" he said. "Ah, yes—your obsession with the Ritchie girl. Surely you didn't expect me—"

"I think you should know," Beth interrupted, "that I saw who killed her." She looked directly into his eyes. "I know what I saw."

"Oh?" The man made an attempt to remain calm, but he was unable to keep from flinching or to control the muscle that had begun to spasm in his jaw. The unnatural silence which followed seemed charged with his unspoken thoughts. After a time, he said only, "Can you identify him?"

She looked at him dubiously. She thought she saw a slight smile appear on his lips. "His face," she stammered, "was in shadows. Just a vague image. That's all I remember."

DeWitt shook his head sympathetically.

"Beth, I saw Dr. Hamilton's report. Your problem was discussed at great length. Believe me, Carmel Ritchie's death was an accident." He reached his hand across the desk. "Now why don't you let me . . ."

Beth drew back. "No! No more talk!" Her voice started to tremble but she held it firm, gripping her long fingers around the edge of the chair. "How much cruelty do you think people will endure before they react to it? Well, I can tell you, Councilman. Even if I have imagined it, even if there is no experimenting going on at Triesius, even if I am completely crazy. No more. If you don't do as I ask, I'm going downstairs and tell those reporters everything; everything I believe to be true, everything I've seen and heard."

His was only a split-second hesitation, but it angered her.

She rose quickly, drew on her jacket and picked up her bag from off the desk. "It'll be very sad when you and the others are hurt by all this. Yes, truly. It will be a pity because—"

"Just a minute." DeWitt rose awkwardly behind his desk. He stood anchored for some time, his shoulders drooping with fatigue, arms hanging loosely. Then he turned and squared off to the window. "What do you want me to do?"

"I want you to drive me back to Triesius."

"Haven't you got a car?"

"I want protection," she said and wondered why in hell she thought she'd be safe with him. Murderers came in all sorts of disguises, even mild nice-guy masks. Then she thought stoutly: He wouldn't dare. Not with all the people who'll see us leave together. It was a strange sensation fearing constantly for one's safety. Aware that danger could be anywhere. Anywhere at all.

DeWitt turned, frowning and nodding.

"But first," she continued, "there's a boy. He lives in a cabin next to Triesius. He's a friend of mine. He doesn't have anything to do with all this. He's not a genius or anything. He's nobody, not to Triesius. He's just a nice boy. And the thing is—even though I got the vaccine—I may have been a carrier. Don't you see? Karl may have—"

She broke off, surprised to find tears stinging her eyes, as if she had just remembered who Karl was. A jeep for a brain, he had said, sitting right there on the cabin steps. "It wouldn't be fair if Karl got the virus," she went on, feeling the choke in her throat.

Through a mist, she watched DeWitt reach for an expensive fur-lined trenchcoat which hung haphazardly on the coat rack along with a disreputable rain hat and corduroy shirt. She noted his silence and couldn't tell if he were angry or merely tired beyond words.

"It's simple enough, isn't it?" she asked uncertainly. "He needs the vaccine. The shot they gave me. Well, doesn't he need it? Doesn't he? Oh, dammit. Goddammit," she finished weakly and DeWitt glanced sideways at her and offered her a lopsided grin.

"Suppose we go find that young boy," he said gently, "and then when we see he's quite all right, let's make sure you're all right. Have you eaten?" At the slight shake of her head, he said, "I thought not." Then, casually: "Does your father know where you are?"

"No. Not yet."

Kindly, he said, "Well, time enough for that later."

And then he held out his hand.

NINE

The black limo was waiting at the side entrance of the building when they came down from DeWitt's office. The Chauffeur saw them coming and moved swiftly to open the rear door.

"Move," DeWitt said tersely. "They've seen us."

Already the group of reporters at the front entrance was swarming toward them. Beth could hear the familiar calls: "Councilman? Could we have a few moments of your time?" "Just a quick question, Councilman. Is it true that—" Dimly, she felt the door slam closed and knew they were still pushing forward. Faces were at the window now, insisting; fingers pointed at steno pads, demanding words to fill empty pages.

The limo pulled away, a plush-cushioned buffer between them and the outside world.

"Sorry about that," DeWitt murmured, indicating with a quick jerk of his head those left curbside to complain.

"I'm used to reporters."

"Ah."

Beth sank deeper into the lush upholstery. "Nice car," she said, her mind already racing forward.

"A new addition, along with the secretary. It's amazing what benefits can be derived from a crisis."

Beth nodded. "I see."

They had just cleared the town of Rosemont when rain began to fall; a sporadic drizzle at first and then a steady downpour that grew in violence until Beth thought surely hail must be mixed with the rain. She could feel herself sinking into depression, even fear, as if every bolt of lightning were a personal danger and as though the weather were going to strand her in a situation she hated. Whereas, ironically, things were absolutely as usual. The outside world was cold, wet, furious and she was sealed away from the storm, riding in the back seat of a chauffeur-driven Cadillac limousine and listening to classical music on the tape deck. The music seemed to orchestrate her inner feelings. Deep somber bass strings. Weeping on a very deep level.

Jimmy DeWitt, who was at work behind a portable desk in the right corner, glanced up. "Would you like something? Perhaps a glass of brandy? I think brandy's good for these rainy days."

"No, no liquor. Do you have anything hot?"

"Oh, yes, of course. There's a thermos of coffee." DeWitt pushed aside the desk and leaned forward to work at the bar. He was curiously relaxed in the plush surroundings. He poured coffee into two immense weighted cups and opened the small refrigerator for cream. "I can offer you a sandwich."

"No. Nothing. Just the coffee. Two sugars, please." She took the cup he passed her and as he went back to work, she turned to stare out the window. If only, she thought, the day were at least a bit brighter, instead of that terrible depressing grey-black that had lowered itself on them.

She drank coffee in small sips, listening to the rain and the music, all part of the same symphony. Half of her wished she was now relaxing in the faint winter glow of the California sun, that she had not come. It was the same sort of longing that an adult sometimes feels for vanished childhood and innocence. The other half of her hung on with grim determination.

The limousine exited the freeway and continued on a well-paved side road some three miles up the mountain northwest of the entrance to Triesius.

"Where are we?" Beth demanded sharply, suddenly rousing from her revery.

"Don't worry. It's only another entrance to the school grounds." DeWitt set a weight on a stack of typewritten papers and drew a lid over the portable desk. The desk was then pushed forward where it clicked into a groove under the bar.

"I never knew about this road."

"Really?" DeWitt's voice was wry. "I'm glad to be able to show you something you don't know. Apparently," he added, smiling slightly, "there isn't much. If you'll notice, this road connects to the highway and is actually a better access to the school than the local road that leads through Rosemont."

"Why isn't it used then?" Beth asked distrustfully.

"Oh, it is." He shrugged slightly. "But you see, it's higher than the other road and a bit of a pull for the school bus. This is probably the road your friend uses to drive to his cabin."

Of course, Beth realized suddenly as the driver turned the car smoothly onto a narrow road that wound into wilderness. A public access road. There was no guard at this entrance. Probably soon, however, there would be.

Now there was no turning back. There could be no other way for her now, just this. Only this winding road through the back entrance to Triesius that was leading her to a new maturity. A maturity that she was not at all sure she wanted.

"We're in back of the lake now. We can wait it out when we—" DeWitt paused, squinting out the window. "Surely," he murmured to Beth in mild disbelief, "that deserted shack isn't the cottage you were referring to?"

For some reason, Beth was reluctant to answer him. Something about the intent look in his eyes, the slight smile playing around his thin mouth. She was convinced that he was leading her in a direction he knew and was in some way calculating to confuse her.

"Is that the cottage?" DeWitt persisted.

"Does Triesius own the property?" she countered, leaning forward somewhat as she strained to see from the front window of the car.

"Oh, no," he said easily, "there's at least two hundred acres around here that are privately owned and a few cottages, but nobody stays in them in the winter. They're fairly primitive. That particular cabin," he added, "was most definitely vacant in September."

"Well, it was most definitely inhabited in October!" Beth flared.

"I'm sure you're right," DeWitt said soothingly, meticulously adjusting the cuffs of his shirt so that they might show beneath the arms of his jacket. It was a reassurance off the top of his consciousness from an older man to a slightly hysterical adolescent. Under it, he obviously had more important worries of his own.

Beth frowned. Or perhaps that was the impression she was

supposed to be receiving. Why was she thinking that DeWitt was playing her like an unknowing fish? That he already knew something about Karl.

The car slowed to a crawl and she glanced from the window. The lower road was flooded, just barely passable. She felt claustrophobic as the car inched through the water. Now she was totally hemmed in and could not leave the car if she wished to. She could feel her body heat rising under her sweater. She knew DeWitt was watching her and closed her eyes, feeling a wave of nausea washing over her. Car sick. She should have eaten something, she thought, and felt a sickening vibration in her throat.

The car had now stopped and DeWitt had cracked a window, because air blew on her face. She breathed in gratefully, feeling cool water droplets against her skin. In a moment she was able to open her eyes and immediately noticed that they had stopped in the cabin's driveway at the base of a thick-trunked oak. The front yard had turned to swamp water which covered even the walking stones.

"It's letting up now," DeWitt said. He was watching her with a knowing smile. "Sure you won't have something? Maybe a glass of Coke would settle you a bit."

"Thanks. I'm fine."

She was thinking that the rain seemed to have completely washed away the picture in her mind of Karl and her. If only she could see him, touch him, she thought vaguely, then perhaps she could recapture the feeling that had somehow disappeared the day Shane had taken her from Triesius. She found herself twisting her hands nervously.

"What's the matter?" DeWitt asked alertly and she marveled at the quickness of his perception. He was a lot sharper than he appeared.

"His car isn't in the driveway," Beth said. "Maybe he went for a drive."

"More likely, he went home," said DeWitt. "Then, you see, you'd have nothing to worry about. Probably he's home and the cabin has been closed for the winter."

"No. He wouldn't do that."

"It would seem the logical thing to me," DeWitt said, "but then I'm wrong a lot of the time. It makes me mad at myself how often I'm wrong," he said, gently smiling.

Beth turned to face him squarely and found herself softening toward this man who was sitting in a riverbed of mud in his new Cadillac, a political crisis foremost on his mind, and who through it all had remained courteous and kind.

"I don't mean to be a bitch," she said sincerely.

He laughed at that, throwing back his head, and murmuring, "A bitch, are you? No. No, not that. Just confused."

"The virus," she said. "It scares me. I never asked you—"

"Ask me," he said. "What is it?"

"Does it—can people die from it?"

"It's more uncomfortable than anything else, I believe." He cleared his throat. "Stay here," he said, stepping from the car. "The driveway is not so bad, but I'll have to wade through the yard."

He glanced down ruefully at his shoes and began to make his way through the front yard, ignoring the slight moisture that was still in the air, wetting his hair and his face. Beth watched him and could not rid herself of the idea that she was watching a scene in a play, staged just for her.

Now he was at the door, knocking repeatedly and loudly. He continued this for some time and then turned, bending to see her face through the car's window, which she hastened to open, leaning from the car. Questioningly, he lifted both hands to her as if asking for further instructions.

"Look in the window," she screamed. "The kitchen is right next to the porch. You can see his things."

He nodded reassuringly and spent some time peering carefully through first one window and then the next. When finally he turned back to her, there was a curious expression on his intense face.

"What is it?" she yelled, cupping both hands around her mouth. "What do you see?" *Oh, my God, it's Karl. He's seen Karl.* Lying on the cot. Sick, probably, very sick, or perhaps . . .

She pulled in the handle of the door and let herself from the car, her heels sinking into mud.

"Stay there," DeWitt called and began to make his way rapidly back to her.

"Where is he?" she gasped, shaking, terribly cold from the sudden blast of wind.

He was by her side now, holding her.

"You don't understand," he said gently.

"What? What is it?"

"There's no one living there," he said. "There's no fire, no luggage, no sign that anyone has been here for some time."

She stood very still, staring into his eyes, which refused to lock with hers. A flash. Leaving his office. "I'll have to make a quick phone call. Wait here in the reception room. I'll be right with you." His eyes. Why wouldn't they meet hers? She ran her hand through the top of her hair, dragging it back from her forehead. What kind of a phone call had he made?

Suddenly she pulled free of his hands and began running through the yard, her suede boots sinking in mud and water.

He made no effort to stop her, but came silently after her to stand on the edge of the porch.

"Karl!" she screamed. She beat with the flat of her hand against the side of the house.

"Look through the window," he said quietly. "Just look, why don't you?"

"Karl! Karl, are you there? It's Beth! Karl!" She was weeping, great gulping sobs.

"Look through the window. You'll see for yourself. There's no one there. There's no one there at all."

Furiously, she picked up a loose brick that sat upended holding a tin can filled with nails and hurled it through the kitchen window. Then she reached through the jagged edges of shattered glass to open the door.

"Why," DeWitt reproved behind her, "did you do that?"

"To show you," she said defiantly, her finger raised to point to a hundred evidences of Karl. His guitar, his books, his suitcase, his food supplies. His robe that hung on the nail.

The air felt sucked out of her. The floor was clean, the cot rolled in a corner, sheetless. Blankets were stacked on top, obviously stored. On top of them were pillows without pillow cases. She ran to put her hand on the stove. Cold. No suitcase, no books, no clothes. Not the faintest trace that a human being had been spending the winter here.

"Now I don't know what to do," she whispered, still staring around in the dimness of the room. "I just . . . I don't know what to do."

"But I do," DeWitt said very gently. His fingers closed around her arm.

Reluctantly, Beth allowed herself to be led from the cabin. She glanced back one last time. The empty room told her one thing plainly: They had been ready for her. They had known she was coming. It was a disquietening thought.

TEN

"Jesus Christ!" said Shane and glanced at her overnight bag beside the door.

Beth sat on the bed. She realized that Shane was more upset than she had anticipated. She watched him pace for a moment in front of the grey curtain that covered the standard-sized window. The curtain was torn around the hem. The room here at the Rockland Inn was less than imposing. Shane at the moment was less than imposing. His histrionics left her somewhat cold. And angry; yes, angrier than she had ever felt at Shane. But it was important now to be calm, to play the game of letting him take charge.

"Look at me when I talk to you!" Shane ordered suddenly and obediently, she lifted her eyes. Little Miss Meek.

"I'm sorry."

"I sure as hell hope you mean that."

She swallowed her quick retort along with her pride and nodded as she had been doing ever since DeWitt had taken on the role of protector and dictator. Yes, she had nodded when DeWitt had insisted on collecting her luggage from the trunk of her rented car. Nodded when he had delivered her to Shane like a parcel post package. Thank you. Thank you. Screw you. Screw you all.

She'd smiled. "Thanks very much, Councilman. You've been very kind." She was surprised to find the words came out warmer than she'd intended. It was difficult to dislike DeWitt. Even at the last minute he seemed curiously reluctant to go, as if even now he was thinking of ways he might be helpful.

Shane had closed the door and let hell break loose over her head. And she kept silent because she didn't find it prudent to say things that couldn't be unsaid, like: "Did you sell me out, Shane? Did you know about Triesius all along? Tell me. Was it a sell-out? Was it?"

In the sudden silence she was aware she'd missed a cue. "I'm—I'm just so tired, you know," she stammered nervously. "It's hard to concentrate."

His eyes narrowed as he gazed down at her. "You'd better concentrate. That—that drivel you told DeWitt about recognizing some man the night you found that girl's body . . ."

"Miss Carmella's body," she said, unable to hold back the sarcasm.

His face burned red, but he did not flinch. "In any event. There was no one to recognize. No man there the night of the—"

"Fifth," she finished and thought: The night of the fifth. And you flew from Kennedy to L.A. International on the sixth.

"There was no one there," he repeated, "and that's the end of it."

"Right."

"No, I want to hear you say it."

"There was no one there and anyhow, I never said I recognized anyone. His face was in shadows."

"You imagined it. There was no man, shadows or not."

"All right," she agreed and studied Shane's face closely for the first time.

He had aged years in a matter of two days. Would those tiny lines around his lips ever again iron out? Where was that Shane Allen vitality she'd thought he would never lose?

"What made you do this?" he was saying. His head shook side to side in perpetual denial.

"Oh, I felt guilty," she said. "I couldn't sit back there all safe and cozy while—"

"Do you think being a pain in the ass is going to help anything? You keep telling me you want to grow up. All right, take a grow-up pill right now. Stop playing 'Mission Impossible,' Beth. It makes you look a little goddamned stupid." There it was again. She had seen him check his watch. The third time in ten minutes.

She forced herself to sit back on the bed feigning exhaustion. In fact, she felt like flying out of there. Like attacking Triesius single-handedly. "I can't seem to keep my eyes open," she murmured. "I haven't slept since I left L.A."

He relaxed by the merest fraction. "Well . . ."

"Is it okay if I take a hot bath? Maybe it'll get the chill out of me."

"Sure. Sure, you should do that." He was quieter now; he had quit pacing and stood facing her, his back to the grey curtain. He gave a short chuckle that sagged somewhat in the middle, and then glanced toward the door and then back at her. "Hey, I guess I sounded more theatrical than my acting. What do you think?"

"I guess so," she said and was dismayed to find tears welling up in her eyes, threatening to overflow. She dropped her head, but felt his finger under her chin forcing it up.

"Hey, look at me."

"Okay," she choked out and felt the first hot traitor of a tear escape down her left cheek.

"You going to be all right?"

"I hurt inside, Shane. I hurt so goddamn bad. All those girls—what's happening?"

"I don't know." Tenderly his finger traced the curve of her cheek and pushed back a flyaway strand of long brown hair.

"You really don't know?" she whispered, wanting desperately to believe that.

He hesitated and when he answered, the words were flat. "No. No, I don't. Hey, listen. You really look tired."

She said, "I guess I've pushed too hard."

"We ought to put you to bed and turn on some TV."

"Oh, I don't—"

"No kidding. That's what we'll do. Now, here's the plan." He was moving to the closet now; tearing a black sports coat from a hanger. "I'm going to grab a quick drink at the bar. Just while you get your bath and get settled. And, listen, call room service. Order up some food. I won't be more than a few minutes. Order me a roast beef on a roll. How's that?"

In a daze, she watched him move toward the door, shrugging on the sports jacket. Her peripheral vision picked up the keys on the dresser. Car keys. What had he been driving—a Pinto? No, these keys were gold.

He turned back. Suddenly his arms were out and she ran right into them as she'd been doing her whole life.

His voice was shaken, sodden, as she'd never heard it sober. "I swear to God," he said, "I never meant to hurt you. You know that, right? You know that?"

"Yes," she whispered uncertainly. "But what—"

"Shh. Listen to me," he said in that new voice, holding her so tight she felt she'd break. "Everything's happening so fast, it's all spinning out of my control. I'm used to being in control, but I—I can't just now—can't get it together." He sounded more than anything else puzzled. A man in a new life situation. "No matter what happens," he said, "I want you to know I love you. More than anything in my life. Without you, there is nothing. No future, no past."

"Shane, please don't—"

"Nothing," he said firmly. "Let me tell you something, my baby. When you get really, really lucky in life, you sometimes forget the word love. That word turns into money, fame, awards, a hundred other words. But I have you, see, and I love the hell out of you. Without you, I wouldn't even remember who I am." Curiously, the last words were almost monotonal, spoken like a man in a dream.

"I love you too, Shane," she said urgently, trying to jolt him out of it. "I really do."

"How can you?" he said as if to himself and put her gently aside.

Mutely she watched him head for the door, thinking only that something terrible was happening and it seemed to have something to do with Shane. Her trembling lips shaped out the words: *Don't leave me, Shane. Because if you go . . .*

The briefest of hesitations occurred and then he closed the door behind him.

Numbly, she continued the thought: *Because if you go, I'm afraid of what I might do.*

Ten minutes later, Beth had reached for the phone and called information for the number of Jack Immer in the Bronx. That there was such a listing gave her another one of those jolts she had been having lately. One moment she would be sure of her footing, knowing what was real, and then as quick as a magician snaps his fingers, everything would have changed and she would be no longer certain.

The closest thing to it was when she was five years old and seeing her first Shane Allen movie. She hadn't been able to make up her mind which Shane was real, the Shane on screen or the Shane who was her father. And when she cried and told him she didn't know who he was, he had joked her out of it by laughing and saying that sometimes he wasn't sure either.

Now, in this instant, she had the same double image of Karl. There was the solitary Karl who lived in a primitive cottage and read Herman Hesse and Emerson. Then there was the Karl who lived in the Bronx with his mother and dad; a more social Karl who perhaps watched television and cared that the Jets were having another rotten season. Which Karl, she wondered, a clutch of anxiety in her chest, was the real Karl Immer?

For a moment she let her hand rest on top of the telephone. Perhaps if she dialed that number in the Bronx, she would have her answer.

Quickly, she picked up the receiver and rang the switchboard.

"This is the Allen suite. Ten-eleven and twelve. I want to make a call to the Bronx."

As the call went through, Beth was unconsciously straightening her hair. She caught herself wrapping a curl around her finger and smiled. Her heart was beating very fast.

"Hello," said a woman's voice, at once urgent and fearful. She had answered on the first ring. Her tone faded to flatness when Beth spoke into the phone. No, Karl was not there, she said. She did not expect him.

Beth hesitated. "I understood he was living at home now."

"No," the woman said briefly.

"Are you sure?" Beth blurted.

"What do you mean am I sure? Of course, I'm sure."

"Of course," Beth stammered, her face burning. "Is this—would you be Karl's mother?"

"Yes, that's right . . ."

"Mrs. Immer, my name is Beth Allen. We haven't met, but I'm a very good friend of Karl's. I was quite sure that Karl was supposed to be coming home."

"No. No, he hasn't." The woman paused nervously. "I'm sorry, but I'm not supposed to talk about this."

A warning signal went off in Beth's subconscious. "You're not supposed to talk about what? Is Karl all right?"

"I have to go now," Mrs. Immer said. "I took a pill and I'm supposed to be lying down."

"But, Mrs. Immer, this is important. I'm worried about Karl. I'm really worried."

"Do you think I'm not?" The woman broke off. "I'll have to say goodnight."

"Mrs. Immer, please," Beth said desperately. "Just tell me that Karl's all right. That you know for sure that he's all right. If you tell me that, I'll believe you. I swear I will. I'll hang up and I won't bother you again."

There was a strangled sound as if Mrs. Immer's breath had caught in her throat, making it impossible for her to speak.

"Mrs. Immer?"

"Do you want me to lie to you? Is that what you want?" The woman's voice broke. "Karl's not—he's not all right. I can't say that he is if he's not, can I? I just can't say that." There was a brief pause and then a sharp click as though she had suddenly slammed the receiver down.

For an instant Beth stared disbelievingly at the telephone and then hurriedly replaced the call. The line rang busy and she knew at once that Mrs. Immer had taken the receiver off the hook.

She forced herself to wait precisely five minutes before putting the call through again and found the line still busy, and then another five minutes, still busy, and one more untimed interval as though to break the pattern. Still busy. She decided that the loud, rhythmic, impersonal signal was the most maddening sound she had ever heard in her life. She sat back on the bed, her shoulders against the wall, still eyeing the phone. Her mind raced with the possibilities.

The easiest explanation was an old-fashioned family quarrel. Karl had gone home, fought with his parents and moved to an apartment of his own. (Why then wasn't Mrs. Immer supposed to talk about it?) Maybe Karl had had an accident and was in the hospital. (And Mrs. Immer hadn't *wanted* to talk about it.) Or maybe he had had some mental break—a lapse. (That image of Karl at the window, his body lean and naked, a hunting knife in his hand.)

Or maybe, she thought unwillingly, and this was what she

really believed, the problem was Triesius. She paused at the edge of completing the thought of what Triesius might do to Karl. She had actually lifted her hand to her forehead as though to block the image of what Triesius might be capable of doing. She was helpless, however, to resist thinking it.

The people at Triesius were entirely without normal scruples. They would start epidemics, conceal murder in order to avoid publicity, use gifted young students as genetic white rats. As far as Karl Immer was concerned, he would mean nothing to them. If he had found out something or posed any kind of threat to them at all . . .

It was her fault. She was the one who had gotten Karl involved in this. If anything happened to him, it was her fault.

She was moving about the room restlessly. It took her some moments before she reached for Shane's car keys.

A tentative solution had entered her mind. The question was did she, or did she not, have the guts to take Shane's car? She knew she had seen a white Mercedes in the parking lot. She glanced at the gold keys. They felt cold and heavy in the palm of her hand. Yes, that had been Shane's car.

Some sort of keen sensitivity had come over her. She felt suddenly convinced that there was something she had to do. She took a deep breath and decided. She would take the car. As if there had ever really been any doubt that she would.

She thought, Shane may not forgive me for this.

But she had to get back to that cabin alone. It was the only way she could think of to begin. Because she did not believe that Karl had left the cabin of his own volition. Perhaps there was something left unpacked. Something they had not known to pack. Something. Some sign that only she would know.

She zipped herself into her suede boots, which were still slightly damp and a mess. No matter. She slipped her lamb's wool jacket over her shoulders and began to leave, hesitating at the last minute. It was not that she had any idea of changing her mind. It was only that it was somehow very difficult to leave. She was so exhausted. Silently she stood gathering her determination.

She was going tonight, alone, back to that cabin. And if she found any sign, any proof that all was not right with Karl, then she would force their hand. She would use all of her influence as Shane's daughter, all of her knowledge as an ex-student of Triesius and they would simply have to take her seriously. If they didn't, then this time she would go to the newspapers, the police and anyone else she could think of who might listen to her.

Suddenly she felt in a hurry as though she were now a link in a chain of events already in motion.

His usual pilot had at first refused the offer.

Shane sat back in the phone booth and let his head rest against the glass behind him. He had just the beginnings of a blinding headache. Rock music blared from the silver-and-black jukebox next to the bar as customers slapped their hands and stomped their feet with the beat.

The pounding in his chest accelerated and became louder as he leaned forward. "All right," he said. "Five thousand, each way. Plus expenses. How's that?"

"You can't charter a plane from New York?" the man said bluntly.

Shane flinched, the music nearly shattering his ear drum. "What?" he said, adjusting the phone.

"I said, they don't have chartered planes in New York?"

"I'm partial to the way you do things, Art. That's the way I am—partial to my friends."

"Why does it have to be on the Q.T.? You can get clearance . . . I can take care of that tomorrow."

"You asshole," Shane said furiously. "Why should I pay you ten thousand dollars to do it by the book? I can get any dumb son-of-a-bitch to do it that way. I'm telling you what I need and what I'm willing to pay for it. And I give you my personal word, Art, that I'm backing you up on this one hundred percent. Anything goes wrong on that trip, it goes wrong for me, not you. That's the way it is. Now if you're my friend, you'll do me this favor and put ten thou in your pocket. If you're not my friend, just say goodnight and hang up. I'll know what you mean."

There was a short pause and a sigh and then Art Hawkins said, "I'll fuel up and get out of L.A. in the next two hours. How's the weather in New York?"

"Hot as hell from where I'm standing."

"And where would that be?"

"I'm staying at the Rockland Inn. Right outside of Rosemont, New York."

"Whoopee," Art said expressionlessly.

A sharp knocking sound brought Shane around with a start. He stared at the anxious face of a long-haired youth on the other side of the glass. He nodded. "Listen, Art, got to run. If you run into a snag, call me."

Shane replaced the receiver without giving Art Hawkins a chance to say anything further. That completed phase one, the preliminaries in dealing with those "six containers," whatever they were. He shuddered. He didn't want to know what they were. He just hoped that the Chairman was right. That Shane Allen, the star, would be able to have a chartered plane land without much question. What's going on? Oh, well, you see those six containers, well—they contain . . . It's all right, Mr. Allen. Oh, by the way. How about an autograph for my wife? Why, certainly.

Shit. It was never going to work.

The knock on the door came again; louder this time. Shane slipped awkwardly from the booth, shaking visibly. The only help for that, he knew, was a shot of booze. A good old Jack Daniels how-do-you-do, followed by a large swallow.

The first double went down easily enough. The second stuck in his throat, then burned its way into the pit of his stomach. The third helped put out the fire and left him feeling kind of numb. He had been gone exactly forty minutes. When he got back to the suite, he found that all the lights were off.

"Beth?" he called softly, thinking that she might already be asleep. He hesitated before turning on the light. The bed was empty.

"Beth, I'm back," he said.

He knocked first and then opened the door to the connecting room. Also empty. He turned quickly to stare at the bathroom door which stood ajar. He paused, wiping the sweat from his face, feeling the sudden rolling of liquor turning over in his stomach.

But he did not shout, nor did he panic. Above all else, he had to maintain control, for what he was thinking was so unthinkable.

It wasn't until he had discovered his keys missing from the dresser, had gone downstairs and found his car gone, it wasn't until then that he was consumed by his own rage.

His own hysterical madness.

ELEVEN

She took the high road up the side of the mountain, slowing as she came closer to the wooded acres that marked the back entrance to Triesius. Her antennae told her that there was something to be afraid of. It was a very strong sensation as though she had made contact with an unseen enemy. She shook it off impatiently and made the turn off the main road to the private road, unmarked save for two stone pillars, cracked and dark with age. Immediately she felt the trap tighten around her. The road was narrow, barely the width of a large car. On these acres there were no houses and thus no driveways. The banks beside the road were soft from the afternoon's rain. To make a U-turn was to take the risk of getting stuck in the mud. No, she must go forward and yet she was afraid to go forward.

Beth hunched over the wheel and wondered why in the name of God she had come here when she should have taken a hot shower, washed her hair, ordered a hot meal from room service and gone to bed.

Smoothly, silently, the Mercedes moved along, as confident as she was afraid. Even when she hit a deep puddle of water, the sleek car did not hesitate although her own stomach turned over. It's a piece of cake, the engine purred. The car pulled easily from the tire-high water and began to make its way up the long curving hill toward the cabin, she the unwilling passenger.

Beth was almost sure that the area had been staked out. She could feel herself being watched. She shifted her shoulders to shake out the tension. The trees, empty of leaves, were bony apparitions of her imagination. They seemed to live. She reminded herself that she was alone. That there was no one—no one at all—watching her. That it was her own fear that surrounded her and no human form lurked in the shadows waiting.

And yet she switched off the car lights to be less visible.

The moon was a pale sliver, affording zero visibility. The road curved unexpectedly, sending the right tire off the side of the small drive. It spun briefly as it sank into mud. She swung the wheel sharply and turned the lights back on. Only when she had at last come to a stop in the cabin's driveway did she again dare to switch off the lights, only to find the pitch blackness alarming. It seemed to be closing in on her, getting even blacker.

Slowly she stepped from the car. The wind stilled around her, leaving her in a center of silence.

For a moment she could not move and desperately stared around looking for something to focus on. She stared upwards at the sky. Only a few stars too distant to be of comfort. How quiet, she thought. How quiet the night was.

Beth drew a long breath and turned her back on the lake, which lay perhaps a hundred yards from where she stood and which was like the rest of the landscape—invisible, secretive.

Hesitantly, she began to make her way to the cabin.

As she walked, her thoughts bounced from her mind haphazardly, out of control. Carmel. Triesius. Shane. Slowly, she walked through mud. Her heart was a fist beating against her chest.

In front of the cabin, she hesitated. Everything inside of her felt jumpy. She longed to leap into the car and drive away. And yet some force held her, sucked her forward. She tried to focus on the fact that Karl had lived here alone and that he had not been afraid.

But where was he now? Maybe he should have been afraid.

She edged forward, began to climb the three steps that led to the porch. On the last step, her boot, caked with wet mud, slipped and she fell forward onto the porch on all fours. A splinter drove through her jeans and imbedded itself in the flesh of her right knee.

Beth cursed softly through gritted teeth and struggled up. But the pain from the splinter was somehow comforting. It brought things back to the everyday. Splinters she knew about. And creaking wood from an old porch.

The door handle, wet and cold in her hand, turned easily. Councilman DeWitt had had no key to relock the door, nevertheless Beth felt vaguely that she should not have left Karl's cabin so insecure.

Inside it was even blacker. Beth took several awkward steps and paused helplessly. She should have remembered that she'd need a flashlight. Hands in front of her, she blundered forward and stubbed her toe on something heavy and sharp. The swift pain angered her and the anger was a strong clean emotion. Suddenly she was functioning again. Her hands were against the wall. She was beginning to put names to various objects in the dark. She had stubbed her toe on the anchor, now her thigh was pressed against a kitchen chair. She leaned forward over the chair, placed both palms on the kitchen table. She was seeing through her memory.

Her hand had now connected with the kerosene lamp on the table, but she could not find the matches that always lay beside it.

"Shit," she said softly, stranded, and then she remembered that sometimes Karl put the glass base of the lamp over several packs of matches so as to have an extra supply close at hand. Carefully she lifted the lamp and set it to one side. Groping, she made contact with a small pile of match packages. It took several matches before she managed to light the kerosene lamp.

In the weak light, the first thing she saw was the knife. Karl's hunting knife. The blade had been plunged into the center of the wooden table. Thoughtfully she placed her fingers on the handle. The knife most probably was part and parcel of the cabin and didn't even belong to Karl. Still she was surprised that he had left it behind. Doubtfully she shook her head. Her eyes moved about the room. It looked very clean, as if even the floor had been scrubbed, except for the glass where she had broken the window this afternoon and some scattered areas of dampness.

Methodically she began to search. In the bureau drawers, on the shelves, even opening the cot and lifting the mattress from its base. Useless. Every trace of Karl had been eliminated. Once again she paced the room, trying to see with fresh eyes. Maybe there was something right before her eyes and she was not able to see it. His books were definitely not on the shelf.

His guitar case no longer stood in the corner. She checked the bathroom, went through the medicine cabinet. The cabinet was empty except for a rusted box of Band-Aids and a bottle of iodine. There was no towel on the rack, not even a cake of soap in the soapdish. It was too clean. She didn't trust it.

She was frowning as she blew out the light and made her way slowly across the room. On the porch, she stood still for a moment. She was saying her own goodbye to a place she never expected to see again. Out of the corner of her eye, she caught a sparkle. She turned to stare, realizing that the dim moonlight had picked up a glint from the lake. Lake Serenity, she and Karl had named it. Ironic that on this lake, frozen into ice, she had found Carmel. It seemed already like a very long time ago.

By now her feet were leading her forward across the swampy earth and she was holding on to trees, pulling herself along. Dampness dripped from branches and her feet sank into cold wetness.

Her first glimpse of the lake drew her breath out of her, stunned her mind. How perfect it was. How beautiful and innocent. The rain had melted most of the ice and the lake lay calm. Not a wave, only wide smooth ripples. Nature's perfect brutal peace.

What a place, she marveled, to die. And she had no idea that not twenty yards from her, hidden in the darkness, a man stood thinking almost the same thing. She had the thought: Something's going to happen. Something.

The man stood silently, staring. The adrenaline was beginning to pump through his body now.

The dead weight of depression reminded her why she had come back. It wasn't the cabin; no, not the cabin at all. She hadn't really expected to find a shred of Karl there. That would have been believing in magic. As if, presto, she would look up and Karl would somehow be standing there. Like a genie, perhaps; made out of smoke. More memory than flesh. No, her plan had more substance than that.

Cold seeped into her body. Liquid chill. She was standing in it, her bare hands were dripping with it. Her hair hung heavy and limp from dampness.

She had come to give herself up to Triesius. A clear choice. The only thing she could do.

A vision of Shane coming back to the suite, discovering that she had gone. In her mind, he was more angry than she had ever seen him. She could feel him yelling to her. "Goddamn it. Goddamn it, Beth, why? Why would you do this?" She faced the doll-sized Shane in her mind. She had come back because it was where she belonged. Nonexempt. One of the girls. And this time they wouldn't send her away. Not after she explained. What she knew, what she believed to be true. What she was prepared to tell the newspapers.

And now Triesius would have gained a powerful enemy. Shane. Again she saw Shane's eyes. Surprised, hurt. You used me, baby. She bit down hard on her lip to keep it from trembling. I had to, Shane. I had to. She had been walking faster; now she paused, her fist in the center of her forehead. Some kind of anguish hissed through her lips.

That's when she heard it. The soft crackling of half-melted ice directly behind her. As though under a heavy shoe. She turned quickly.

"Karl? Karl, is that you?"

She imagined that she saw the figure of a man slip behind the large maple tree to her right.

"Karl, it's Beth."

She moved forward. A sudden wind blew off the lake and she pulled her short jacket closer around her. She was now bitterly cold in her wet boots with a bare head, bare hands.

Near the cabin, something flashed for a split second and then sparked away like the brilliance of a Roman candle. Fascinated, she drew nearer and then when she was just a few feet from the front steps of the cabin, the door shot forward, slamming hard off the face of the cabin. Beth came to a lurching halt. She was quite certain that she had closed the door when she left the cabin. The wind? No, not from the inside out like that.

Awkward and lumbering, she took a step backward. She could see something move again below the brush thicket where the rocks began. Pale moonlight flickered over clumps of bushes. Nothing now. Just silence. Time passed unmeasured.

Perhaps it was the silence that warned her, because she was suddenly aware that someone was with her now. Someone who was playing a waiting game. It wasn't just a warning. It was an urgent push into awareness.

"Who's there?" she cried, but the words came from her lips in a whisper.

In front of her, someone stood blocking the path.

She turned and slushed at full staggering speed back to the car. Slamming the door, she reached for the ignition key, her hand shaking violently. Oh, Jesus. The key was gone. She could hear herself breathing now in sharp gasps and was amazed at how deep fear could go. Reaching forward, she punched on the headlights and switched them to high-beam. The bright lights fractured the darkness directly ahead of her, where the man had been standing.

There was no one there.

Quickly she jumped from the car. The cabin door was banging violently against the side of the building. To her ears, sensitized by fear, the sound was explosive. She began to run, only to stagger into an ankle-deep puddle. She had decided to try for the main road. Straining to see in the half-light, she was confused in her directions. An inner voice seemed to mockingly chant, "You're going the wrong way."

At that moment, someone switched off the car lights.

Trying to run, she fell and, struggling up, found she had lost all bearings, even the ability to tell left from right. For an instant she leaned against a tree, weak, trying to stop her frantic gulping of cold wet air.

She heard a tiny, piercingly high laugh, then a soft whisper that seemed to be coaxing her, luring her to step forward into the brush that lay just ahead of her. Something flickered before her—glistened.

She was running now, through the underbrush, across the creek—and up onto the path that led to Triesius. When she turned she could see him there, standing on a rock, watching her. There was something vaguely familiar about him, but she couldn't connect with that, only that she was frightened by the fact that she knew him. No recognizable features; she couldn't see him that clearly, just a subconscious impression that she seemed to be blocking. She lost sight of him as she rounded the bend in the path. She could hear him now stumbling down the path after her.

Exhausted, she couldn't go any farther. She ducked off the path, moved farther into the underbrush, and lay down; curled herself into a tiny, glass-brittle ball. She waited there in her clammy, wet clothes, and watched as he moved slowly toward her. Her face, her body tightened as she tried to reduce her physical presence to nothingness.

She watched as he moved to within inches of her. He paused for a moment, then lurched forward into a full run, in the opposite direction.

Slowly she pushed until she had managed to get back up on her feet. And suddenly she was sobbing, wrenching against the trunk of the tree. She had no words, she would not beg God to save her. A picture of Mrs. Fazio's face. "Help me, help me." Scratching herself, infectious blood under her nails. Begging. She would never beg. Her sobs lessened but the tears were still flowing down her cheeks, icy cold and stinging against her skin. And then, through the clearing just ahead, she could see the wide expanse of lawn that belonged to Triesius. There were pale slivers of light that shone from the lightposts along the drive leading to the front entrance of the school.

She pushed herself away from the tree. And felt some strength inside her explode itself on the effort. She was running again.

And then from behind a boulder, he had jumped forward, reaching for her. For a moment, her arm was caught fast in his hand. She jerked forward hard and he stumbled, went crashing to the ground. She was shaking and sobbing and running.

When she reached the clearing, she looked back over her shoulder. He was still with her. She broke for the open lawn, heading for the lightposts. It was too late. He was almost on top of her now. "Oh, my God," she gasped and felt herself fall.

At that moment, he dug his fingers into her hair, jerked her head backwards with a sharp snap. The knife stung now against the soft skin of her throat—whether she was cut or not was impossible to tell. Was the pain the coldness of the steel blade or a scalpel slice of skin? Even now, had the bleeding begun?

Oh, God. Am I dying? Am I dying and I don't know it?

The man's face, slick with sweat, wild-eyed, fanatical, was inches from her own as he leaned forward over her shoulder; the knife held steady at her throat.

For an instant his face was elusive, shadowed, as she had remembered it. His eyes, glinting in a pale wash of milky light, met hers. As he smiled, she heard herself cry out.

Overhead clouds had begun to shift, allowing sharp rays of moonlight to cut diagonals across his face. His mouth drew back, baring short white teeth. Even now there was a certain sophistication that clung to his face like a distorted mask.

I should struggle, she thought, trying to find strength. I should at least make a fight for my life. His grip tightened.

"So . . . you saw me?" he sneered, wrenching her head back by the roots of her hair. Yanking, pinching. And then lifting as he might have lifted a test animal from a cage. A cat or a white rat.

The killing, she knew, would be quick. One expert thrust. She watched the tip of the knife dip up sharply.

"RANDELAR!" screamed a voice. "Let the girl go!"

Alan Randelar turned with a start.

TWELVE

In the next instant the lawn suddenly lit up with great floods of light. A voice yelled, screamed actually, and Randelar tore his eyes from Beth's face, from the soft white skin of her throat.

Confused, he put his hand to his eyes, the light nearly blinding him. He stared at men, a lot of men, a field of men. One man, the one who was screaming, was being held back. A more official voice gave instructions over a loud speaker. He couldn't make any sense out of it.

Triesius. His Triesius.

He was suddenly crippled; it was as simple as that.

A trick! A trick in the darkness! He spun, terrified at the games being played on his mind. But it wasn't a game! There were floodlights everywhere. And men.

Light? *Light*? Where was it coming from?

Almost at once he dropped to a crouched position. There was confusion, demands shouted futilely. A cry came from his right. Another from his left.

A trick! he thought.

"A TRICK!" he howled.

"Shoot the bastard!" screamed Sergeant Carrolton.

"Come on!" yelled Randelar off in the distance. He put his arm around Beth's waist and dragged her up against his own body. "Come on, you ineffectual sons-of-bitches! Come get me!" He began to pull Beth back with him toward the edge of the woods.

The Chairman lurched forward, breathing heavily, his black raincoat billowing behind him.

"Randelar!" he screamed.

Randelar seemed to hesitate, then he was moving again, pulling the girl along with him effortlessly, despite the fact that she was fighting him.

"Alan, be reasonable," the Chairman coaxed. "Let the girl go."

Once again Randelar paused. "Reasonable? Is that an order? More orders?" His laugh echoed across the empty space, held, as if locked between the walls of an ancient amphitheater.

In the next moment he brought the knife to Beth's throat.

Shane's sudden yell was silenced by a massive hand over his mouth and nose. "Steady there. Steady."

Then silence, intense. It was apparent that Randelar was contemplating his next move.

Beside Sergeant Carrolton, an officer tensed, focused the sight of his telescopic rifle dead on Randelar's face. The face moved—Beth's face appeared. Randelar's face appeared again. "I've got him," grunted the officer.

"Take him," Carrolton said.

"No! You might hit the girl!" St. John's voice was crisply authoritative.

"Oh, Christ—don't kill my baby!" Shane screamed. "Please, don't kill my little girl." He lunged forward. The arms around him pulled tighter.

"Easy. You're not helping us this way."

"Kill him," Shane cried. "Kill him . . ."

Near the edge of the woods, Beth heard the sound of an approaching helicopter over the edge of the lake, and she looked up. Randelar paid no attention. His gaze remained locked on the men who inched forward as he inched back. "Just a few more steps, little girl, and then . . ."

"Why?" Beth wept. "Why are you doing this to me?"

Absently, he patted her shoulder, his eyes riveted straight ahead. "You're terribly frightened, aren't you?" he murmured, but his tone was indifferent. "I can always recognize fear. Laboratory animals are always afraid. Especially just before they die. They always know . . ."

"But there's no reason now!" Beth pleaded, but he seemed hardly to know she was there.

His eyes were vacant, staring. Now he dragged her forward,

his body lurching, swaying, his feet sinking into the mud, sending up splashes of filth and water around him.

His confidential flow of words seemed aimed not at her but to an invisible third person directly in front of him.

"I was a freshman. My biology instructor—"

"Please don't hurt me—"

". . . pinned a frog to a dissection block and he"—Randelar panted as he staggered through the mud—"he let me cut that frog. I cut it evenly down the center. And the line . . . you could have, you could have drawn it with a ruler, it was so straight." He had reached the tree line. A final tug and he let Beth's body drop to his feet. "The frog," he continued, frowning, "it was still alive, you know. The eyes were bugging out of its head. The heart was beating—I could actually see it beating . . ." He glanced sideways at Beth as though seeing her clearly for the first time.

Their eyes locked for an instant and he laughed. Then groaned as the sweat rolled from his pores. Now he began to lose control of his fluids all together. His bladder emptied itself, and liquid gushed down his legs in a hot flood. Tears from his eyes. Spittle from his mouth. Fluid from his nose. The colorless fluid rapidly turned red and thick and as the blood gushed from his nose, he raised the knife up, and in one final thrust started the blade downward. An explosion; Randelar arched backward, the bullet shattering and splintering the bone of his right shoulder.

Beth turned, and with the last ounce of her strength, started to crawl toward the light. The helicopter skimmed the tree tops overhead, throwing a hot beam of light over Randelar, who was now staggering back toward the cabin. Somehow he had managed to reach the Mercedes.

Beth saw the headlights flicker on, off, then on again. The engine started up. The car was now racing toward her.

Pushing down hard on the accelerator, Randelar thought: *The common man. If only I could have stopped their nagging, their tongues from clicking—the perennial question: What are the moral implications?*

Beth's body loomed ahead of him and he laughed.

Strange how taking life came so naturally to him. It was a gift of sorts, like other talents.

He laughed, louder this time as with a sudden explosion, the windshield shattered. Tiny particles of glass blew forward; he felt glass rip into his cheeks, his neck. He turned the car sharply, slammed on the brakes, but it was too late. Metal crunched as the car smashed off the tree, skidded forward toward the edge of the rocks.

The car seemed to be motionless for a moment, suspended on an overhang of rock thirty feet above the water. It hung there in space, incongruous in this frozen wasteland of petrified time.

He saw a face. And the expression on the face. And was puzzled at the contempt he saw.

Another explosion of gunfire, a blinding flash of light, and he saw his own blood splatter against the dashboard and sensed his own scream echoing through the car as it glided silently through the air, crashing headlong into the lake.

And he thought:

Very few people understand the beauty of perfection. I would not have confessed the tears that were often on my face when I contemplated the seeds of perfection that were within my grasp. I was not cold then. I was a man in love. I could say like Hitler: I will create the perfect race. Only Hitler was a fool. I could have actually done it.

For a moment he could see once again the face of Carmel Ritchie. The first woman he had ever made love to. Before that he was cold—had no interest in women. But the way it had happened with her—knowing that she was to be sacrificed for the ultimate goal of his life—God, it was beautiful . . . beautiful . . .

And for one last precious moment, an unborn species rose to pay him homage—these creatures whom he had hoped to summon into being—yes, he could see them clearly, could almost reach out his hand and touch their perfect bodies, could feel their heads rotate on their flexible necks, their thick membranes roll back from their keen eyes as they focused this one time on their creator. Beautiful . . . so beautiful . . .

Like ice suddenly placed on a burn, he felt the pain of his flesh vanish, felt himself drawn under, deeper into a dreaded void where his mind stopped, frozen in mid-thought.

EPILOGUE

The woman's face was still white three days after the shock had occurred. It had bleached her skin as effectively as a sunbath would have tanned her.

She stood now in the hospital corridor outside her daughter's room and talked to Shane Allen as an ordinary mother talks to an ordinary father. He would never know that she had grown up on Shane Allen movies and even imagined herself a little in love with him in a pleasant harmless way. None of that mattered. They were just two parents who still had their children. When other people did not. That was the point. Other people did not.

"Doris Encoda died this morning," the woman said, whispering the words so that her daughter on the other side of the door would not hear.

Shane passed a hand across his forehead. "Just between the two of us," he said, "I have an idea that way down deep, I must be a coldhearted man." The woman raised a questioning brow and he grinned lopsidedly. "Just now, when you told me about that young girl," he said, "the only thing—the only damn thing I could think of—was . . ."

He broke off, but the woman finished softly, "Thank God. Thank God it wasn't *my* child." Her eyes filled with sudden tears and she could not go on.

"You too, huh?" Shane laid a companionable hand on her shoulder.

She pressed a handkerchief under her eyes and managed a small laugh. "Do you know," she murmured, "that I haven't had a handkerchief out of my hand in three days? I never know when I'm just going to—" She gulped. "Just going to cry, you know. Oh, my God, the *children.* Our *children.* There can't be anything—anything worse than losing a child. I've had my share of grief. I lost my only brother last year. My father's in a nursing home. But to lose your child! That woman's child died. Just the thought of it . . ." She was shivering now and Shane gently squeezed her shoulder.

"We're the lucky ones," he said, looking at her firmly. "It's all right to remember that. To be glad about that. It's all right to be lucky. You don't have to be guilty about that. You don't choose to be lucky. You get chosen. That cost me," he grinned, "close to a hundred thousand dollars in analysis to find that out. I'm giving it to you. A freebie."

"They just told me today," she said. "Three days, and they told me today, 'She's going to be all right.' My daughter's going to make it. I stood there with my damn handkerchief under my eyes and the only thing I could think about was how close it was . . ." Her face seemed even whiter. "My husband cried. I never saw my husband cry," she said. "Not even when his mother and father died."

Shane nodded, thinking how well he understood this woman. For her name was Helen Urie, and whether by luck or the grace of God, her daughter Georgia was still alive.

"Do you know what she said?" Helen Urie asked, her smile dazzling Shane with its undiluted happiness. "She said, 'I love you, Mom.' It was the first thing she said. She never said that. She never said that since she was five years old."

At that moment Beth slipped quietly from Georgia's room and went straight into Shane's arms. "Thanks for letting me see her, Mrs. Urie," she said after a long struggle to speak. "I couldn't go until I did."

"She isn't so bad as she looks." Helen Urie's voice was in control now. Her eyes met Shane's matter-of-factly. "It's a little frightening when you first see her," she explained. "But she'll be just fine. I have to go back inside now. She can't be alone."

"She's coming to California to see me when she's better," Beth said, her face brighter. "We decided we have to at least salvage a friendship out of this. Then it won't all have been for nothing."

Half inside the door, Helen Urie turned back smiling. "Happy holidays."

"Same to you," Shane smiled. He gave Beth a hard hug as the door closed. "You and I have a plane to meet," he said. "And some talking to do. Let's begin on the way to the airport."

Beth involuntarily shook her head, her lips clamped together.

A child, he thought with so much tenderness he felt it might tear him apart. On the brink of being a woman, but at this moment, a child.

He had decided to open the conversation by talking about Janie, and imagined saying: "You have a half-sister, Beth. She's special. She's very special and to tell you the truth, I don't know why I never . . ." It was here that his imagination invariably ran out. He could not think what to say beyond that frightening point.

He was on the freeway before he had to face it and then he just flew by the seat of his pants, hardly knowing what he was saying, what haphazard order he put to his thoughts. He heard himself say "love" a lot and "mistakes," and thought: Is this what you're teaching her . . . that love breeds mistakes, that the one must follow the other as surely as night follows day? He kept on talking until finally it was all said.

In the sudden ring of silence, he felt the kind of panic a gambler might feel with everything on the table riding on one big roll of the dice. When she didn't answer immediately, he felt himself start to dissolve, saw black without a glimmer of white, saw the meaning of his life turn to mockery, and then, a beat later, felt her hand steal across the seat and settle on his arm.

At that instant, looking around, Shane saw Beth smiling. It was only a glimpse, but he was sure of what he saw in her eyes.

"Hey," she said softly, "you and I have some celebrating to do."

"It won't be easy," he said.

"You and I do celebrating very well," she said. And for an instant, her lips pressed against his cheek.

It was a different kind of celebration. Christmas for the first time in Beth's life was not a lavish affair. She could not leave

New York until she had completed an in-depth police questioning and a preliminary interview with the D.A.

Instead, Grandmother Allen had flown in from Florida and Sara had come from Los Angeles and Shane was smiling, not as easily as before, but smiling. A few presents, nothing expensive, and Christmas dinner in a back room of the motel dining room. Learning to laugh again, being a family, and Sara being one of them as easily as though she had been with them always.

Beth liked the way Sara looked at Shane and the way she looked at Grandmother Allen and the way she looked at her. Nice and easy, no effort at all. And she liked the way Sara didn't need to hold on to Shane like his other women had always done.

That evening, it seemed to her that it would somehow be possible to forget. Although, of course, there was one hell of a lot of forgetting to do.

Watching Shane, she thought: He'll never really get over this. He'll be struggling with it the rest of his life.

"How . . . how deep are you into it, Shane?" They had found themselves alone for a moment.

"I'll survive. You know I always survive," he said. The smile he gave her was a present. Not easy.

She covered his hand with hers. "I want you to know, Shane . . . I love you. That's all. Just an unconditional I love you."

He tried to say "I love you too" and ended up clearing his throat.

"What about Triesius?" she said carefully, changing the subject. "What did they find when they—"

"Nothing," Shane said. "They found nothing."

"What about the research notes? Charts. Lab experiments . . . There must have been . . ." She turned to him anxiously, her eyes glued to his face.

He shook his head. "Don't think about it. Just like I have to put it behind me . . . You do the same."

But life is always a welding process, she wanted to cry. Joining the past with the present with the future . . . and the chain breaks when you can't make peace with this trinity.

Karl, she thought unwillingly. Karl who had taken one single step toward redemption and become frozen there. That he had been the one who finally broke the rules by calling the police—well, at present that was not enough for Karl. She knew that by their one meeting at the detainment center. Shane on her right, the two of them facing a blank dull-eyed Karl, who sat slumped beside his father. His father talked for them both.

"I blame myself," Jack Immer said. His face was grey, prematurely old. "I should have seen it. I should have seen his confusion. They used him. It wasn't his fault." He placed his hand on his son's shoulder. "He's young. He's so young. He'll come out of this. I know he will."

Of all the endings she had ever imagined for Karl and herself, she had never pictured anything like this. The limpness of his hands when she gathered them in hers. The slackness of his facial muscles, the absence of any real expression at all. The terrifying emptiness in her own innards when she stood at the door staring back at him.

At first she thought she'd imagined it, that subtle shifting of his eyes that brought his gaze into focus.

"Karl?" she said sharply.

A flickering of his lashes. That slight toss of his head that she knew so well. He did that when, as now, hair had fallen over his forehead. His gaze moistened, intensified.

Just for that one instant they were back in the cabin holding each other, looking at each other, and none of the rest of it had ever happened. She felt herself take the first and last step toward him. And then his gaze dulled and the connection was broken as though the call had come from very far away and had perhaps been sabotaged by the natives. But it had happened. It was something to take away with her. *Thanks, Karl. Thanks for showing up to say goodbye.*

So many people, so confused, Beth thought. Karl. Vala who was always doomed. Some people were. Doomed. Other people were survivors. Like Georgia. And Shane. Even herself. But even the survivors had quicksand sucking at their heels. The memory of Triesius would be that quicksand for those who had gone through it.

For some like Councilman DeWitt, the Chairman and Yvonne LeSabre, there would be unrelenting publicity as they made their way through the courts. For others, who had escaped this part of it, there would be the dreams—the nightmares.

She thought of this again several months later when the letter from Georgia came. A pleasant letter talking about how soon she would be able to make the trip to L.A., thanking Beth for her letters, sending congratulations to Shane on his marriage. She was feeling better every day. A pleasant letter. A flippant, almost embarrassed note that she had been seeing something of her ex-beau again. A two-sentence paragraph, stating something significant in its very brevity. And then at the end:

"Beth. On a somber note before I close. Sometimes I shut my eyes and it seems to me that I can see Triesius, that we are all back there and once again in 'their' power. I have no idea of the true extent of the genetic research that the newspapers were so full of. But I think of the new strain that now runs in my blood. And I remember those physicals and I remember the cells they scraped from under my nails and the hair follicles they dug from my scalp and sometimes I wonder.

"Where are those parts of me now, for I know such things were not left at Triesius for the investigators to find. No, they were long gone. Removed perhaps to an underground laboratory (if we can permit ourselves a bit of sci-fi thinking) or to a private estate who-knows-where? Somewhere. That's what I think. Somewhere.

"When I get these thoughts, I tend to dream of clones and strangely evolved people who sprang from under my fingernails. At such times, I wake up sweating . . . And praying that all of their research will fail. That human beings will just be human beings left to grow on our own and work out our human defects in human ways.

"Is it superstitious of me to believe that already somewhere they are once again at work? That somewhere, someplace, there will be another Triesius."

Beth laid aside the letter. She was devoid of feeling. She ate lunch without revulsion or appetite. She washed her hair. That afternoon she took a figure-skating lesson at an indoor rink in Hollywood. Her instructor was one of the finest, almost Zen in his approach to ice.

"You have to love the sparks of ice that your skates cut in your figures," he said. "You have to be as cold as ice and hot as poetry on top of that ice." His face was crinkly with smiles, ageless.

"I'm skating too hard today, aren't I?" Beth's face was flushed. "I'm trying too hard."

"Go ahead," the instructor smiled. "I give you permission to try too hard. I never had a student do that. But—" He hesitated. "I once tried too hard myself."

"What happened?" she asked curiously.

"On the other side of trying too hard," he said, "there is ease. Perfect ease and perfect truth."

Furiously she skated, pain in her feet, her legs. She was not graceful. She was swift, cutting wide gashes into the ice. She was tired, angry.

Suddenly after a timeless lonely interval, she had lost herself, lost her instructor somewhere along the way. And then she felt an undercurrent. It came stronger, rushing from her subconscious.

She felt her body gliding through space, felt the crystals of ice flying up against her bare legs, felt cold and hot at once. She was spinning and somewhere someone was clapping and saying, "Faster. Faster!"

She was a whirling creature full of graceful abandon. At the height of it, she began to cry. Life was so fleeting, so beautiful. And she too believed that perhaps life, as she knew it, might soon be bred out of the planet. That there would be another species to people the earth. Creatures bred of the human race and yet not human.

Soulless, emotionless creatures.

Creatures not so sweet as man, not so brutal either. Creatures who would function only through their intelligence and who would never be capable of understanding the ecstasy that was like a pain of being one with the ice.

She spun faster and faster. Tears ran down her face. She tasted them. She had never, never in her life, felt so real . . .